ERIN MALLON

Lovebug

Dedicated to my Joonbug,
the fiercest and most authentic girl I know.
Your big heart and zero-efs attitude inspire me every day.

Chapter One

"*I* will have the min-es-tro-nee soup to start..."

"Minestron..." I hear my boyfriend correct under his breath.

"And for my entrée," I continue as if I didn't hear him say anything, "the lasagna with extra ricotta cheese, please."

"An excellent choice, miss," the waiter responds with a smile.

"Rigot. It's pronounced rigot." Bert coughs this bit into his elbow as the waiter reclaims our menus and steps away from the table with a funny look on his face.

I turn to Bert. "Are you okay, sweetie?" I ask. Maybe I heard him wrong. Perhaps he really is coming down with a cough. I like to give people the benefit of the doubt.

"Mabel baby, how long have we been together?" he asks.

"Six years, eight months, and thirteen days," I say proudly.

"Aw, it's so sweet how you count the days we've been together. Makes me feel loved."

"Well, you are loved, Bert Alert."

"Aw, your nicknames for me are the best. They make me feel appreciated."

"You are appreciated." I laugh and lean closer to him. "You're my Bert Alert honeypie flirt, looking so darn cute tonight in that pink polo shirt."

"Awwwww." He drags this "aw" out an exorbitant amount and cups my cheek.

Something is up with him. Time to investigate.

"You're saying 'aw' a lot tonight." I cock my head. "Are you okay?"

"Awwwwwwwwwwwwww, I love how you notice all the little things about me. Makes me feel seen."

"Sweetie," I press further. "Are you giving a prepared speech?"

"Why would you ask that?" he asks.

"Because... it sounds like you're giving a prepared speech."

"I guess I just feel poetic when I'm around you," he says with a weird smile I'm not used to seeing on his face.

"Since when?" I ask this without an ounce of sarcasm. I just truly can't remember a time he's expressed an interest in poetry. Or a time when he's been this verbally affectionate with me. I like it. My guy is generally not the lovey-dovey sort, but oooh la la, tonight it seems he's put his Romeo pants on.

"Since... I don't know, Mabel!" he snaps.

If Romeo were a sweaty-palmed, perpetually irritated, twenty-four-year-old man who lives with his mother. I'm not judging. I too am a twenty-four-year-old living with *her* mother. Her father too, for that matter.

"I'm sorry I snapped, baby," he says, recovering. "I'm just thinking... if we've been together for..." He smiles and pretends to search for the correct duration.

"Six years, eight months, and thirteen days," I supply and smile back at him.

"Right, *all that time*... shouldn't you be used to the Italian way of pronouncing things by now?"

Oh. I thought he would continue with saying sweet and affectionate things. But it seems I'm being reprimanded for not saying his ancestors' food with the proper inflection and flair. Again.

I decide to be bold. "Bert. Are you sure it's not the Italian *American* way of saying things, though?"

He takes in a sharp breath as though he's prepared to argue his point.

"Hear me out," I say before he can get a word in. "I've been thinking about this. Remember the second semester of senior year when Isabella, the Italian exchange student, came to our school?

"Yeah."

"Well, I'm pretty sure she pronounced *all* her syllables, and she's actually *from* Italy, so..."

"Nah. You must have heard her wrong."

"I don't think so." I do my best to keep a sweet smile on my face. "I remember the way she—"

"Mabes?" he interrupts. "It would mean a lot to me if you tried to say it the right way. Particularly when we're out for a special dinner at an authentic Italian restaurant."

I internally sigh as I look at him.

He's not asking that much really.

"Sure," I acquiesce. "Okay, yes. I can do that. I'm sorry. I feel silly saying the words that way, but I'll get over it. I just... why would something that's spelled prosciutto be pronounced pruh-zhoot? And pasta e fagioli has all these wonderful sounds, so why skip them and say fah-zool? Also, I have a hard time believing that mozzarella really wants us to call it mootz-zuh-rell."

"Mabes?"

"Yes, Bert Alert?"

He sighs. "I don't want to fight." He gives me a genuine, warm smile and reaches across the table to caress my cheek.

"Neither do I." I place my hand over his.

He leans over and kisses me.

"Neither do I," his mother pipes up from where she sits between us.

That's right, Bert's mother is sitting between us. Lately, it seems as though Bert's mother is always sitting between us. Bert tries to deepen the kiss, but—call me crazy—it's hard for me to feel romantic with my boyfriend's mom watching us, so I pull away.

Don't get me wrong, Doreen is a dear, and I love her like my own mother—well, not exactly like my mother because they are incredibly different human beings—but I sometimes wish these weekly dinners could be about the two of us, instead of the three of us. It's our Sunday night dinner out as a family, though, so what can you do? True, we're not *technically* family, but when you've been dating since junior year of high school, things do start to feel... blended.

"Sweetheart, we'd like to talk to you about something," Doreen says, looking very serious all of a sudden.

"Alright good, yes, let's do this!" Bert says. He follows that up by slapping his cheeks a few times and punching the air as though he's psyching himself up for the big game. "You're better at this sort of thing than I am. Take it away, Mom."

"Thank you, Bertie," she says. "Mabel?"

"Yes, Doreen."

"We're concerned you're not pulling your weight in... The Business."

"Oh gosh, really?" I say on a bit of a squeak.

I'm actually trying like crazy to "pull my weight." Can't they see that? Lord knows I need the money. Big time. I'm just not sure I'm cut out for this sort of thing. Also, every time Doreen says "The Business," I feel like I've gotten involved with the mob. But we *are* just talking about a multilevel marketing vitamin business. Right?

"Mom, I thought we were going to do the other thing first!" Bert says on a harsh, throaty whisper.

"Ooh, what other thing?" I ask. I'm hoping "the other thing" is something more fun than where this conversation seems to be heading.

"No," his mother replies, ignoring my question. "We agreed the *other* thing would come *after* the first thing. *This* is the first thing."

"Fine!" Bert continues the whisper-shouting contest with his mother. "Can we get the first thing over with quickly then, so we can move on to the other thing? The longer we wait, the more nervous I get about the other thing."

What in the world are they talking about? Jack Canfield, the *Chicken Soup for the Soul* guy, says "When in Doubt, Check it Out," so I decide to heed his advice.

"Hey, what are you two—"

"Would you give us a minute, baby doll?" Bert cuts off my question with one of his own. Full-voiced this time.

I look at him.

He looks at me.

Oh. Looks like I'm being dismissed.

"Uh, sure. Yeah. While you two decide which 'thing' is happening first, I need to visit the ladies' room anyway. So... be right back."

"Thanks, sweetness." Bert takes my hand and gives my knuckles a quick kiss, then immediately huddles back together with his mother, already deep in private discussion.

I make my way toward the ladies' room. As I turn the corner, I hear...

"Psst. Bella!" Clearly, my name isn't Bella, so I continue along my merry way. Though truth be told, I'm starting to feel a little less merry than when I arrived here tonight. You'd think after all this time together, I'd know Bert on a deep level, and he'd know me. But sometimes, he feels like such a mystery to me. Maybe that's my fault. Maybe I'm not giving as much of myself as I could, and that's why—

"Psst. Bella!" I hear the voice again.

I turn to see our waiter standing right outside the swinging doors of the kitchen with a large tray perched on his shoulder piled with plates of steaming hot food. I take a quick glance behind me, but it seems I am the only one within psst-ing distance. Best to double-check, though. "Hi. Are you psst-ing and bella-ing me?"

He chuckles. "I am, yes."

"Alright, well then 'psst' back atcha, sir!"

He laughs again. This is common in my world. People always seem to laugh when I'm being completely serious.

"Do you always stand outside ladies' rooms, blocking the thoroughfare in busy restaurants?" he asks.

It's then I realize that I am completely frozen against the wall between a painting of a bowl of spaghetti and a portrait of a dog. How long have I been standing here?

"Oh gosh, I'm sorry. I'm in your way. Please, please." I step to the side and start mobilizing toward the bathroom again.

"You were lost in thought," he says, stopping me.

"I guess, yeah." I laugh it off as nothing serious. Because it's not.

He gives me a knowing look, then says, "Well. I'm about to deliver the *min-es-tron-e* soup to your table, and I do hope you will enjoy your lasagna with extra *ri-cot-ta* when it arrives."

"Thank you. You're very nice. Wait! You said all the syllables!"

"I did. As do all true Italians. Those people you are dining with this evening?" He says this with a bit of a sneer.

"My boyfriend and his mother?"

He leans closer to me and says in a low voice, "Yes. Don't let them boss you around like that. They are what we call... how do you say? ... idiotas."

"Oh, no! No, they're not. I think pronouncing Italian foods like the Italians do—or how they *think* the Italians do—makes them feel close to their mother country. I don't mind."

I don't mention the fact that the past five generations of the Bozzelli family have been born and raised in suburban Philadelphia or that Bert has never actually even been to Italy—or even out of the country, for that matter.

"Fair enough. Also..." His voice shifts into horror-movie mode. "Beware of the biscotti."

Without another word, he takes off toward the main dining area.

"What did you say?" I call after him.

As he turns the corner, I hear his voice trailing off. "Beware of the biscotti..."

Huh. What an odd guy. I finally push through the door of the ladies' room and am shocked to see my best friend coming out of a stall.

"Cyndi!" I say with glee.

I make a beeline to hug her.

"DON'T TOUCH ME!" she practically screams back at me with her hands held out in front of her.

"Whoa! Why are you yelling at me? And what are you doing here? I thought you and Stuart were going to the Sixers game tonight!"

"Um. We are. I mean, we were. I mean, we're still going, but he was hungry. He's paying the check and—"

"So Stu is here too?" I say excitedly. "Great! I miss him!"

"No," she blurts. "He's not."

"But you just said—"

"Why are you interrogating me?" she snaps as she rushes to the sink.

Wow. Cyndi is usually the epitome of cool, calm, and collected. Not tonight, apparently.

"I'm not interrogating you, Cyn," I say slowly. "I'm just surprised to see you. This is the restaurant Bert and his mom chose for tonight's 'Sunday Family Dinner' and—

"I yelled at you because you were about to touch me before I washed my hands," she says as she scrubs her hands vigorously. "Did I tell you I read a scene in a romance novel once where the guy goes into the ladies' room, finds the girl right as she's coming out of the stall—*before* she washes her hands—and they proceed to get it on immediately?"

"Yes. You tell me this story often."

"Well, it scarred me! Had to turn the page and skip the sex scene! A total heartbreaker!" Cyndi shouts over the hand dryer, which is now blowing full-blast.

"For the record, I wasn't going to 'get it on with you,'" I say. "I just wanted to hug you."

"Noted." She finishes with the hand dryer. "Okay. Bye. You never saw me," she says on a puff of air, then bolts out the door.

"Wait! Cyndi, what are you…?"

And… she's gone.

Why is everyone acting crazy tonight? Is it me? Maybe it's me.

When I return to the table, Bert and Doreen are finished with their appetizers and deep into their entrees.

"Sit, babe, quick," Bert says. "Your soup is getting cold. Your lasagna with extra rigot is too. I took a bite. It's delizios."

Just then, our waiter breezes past, drops another breadbasket on our table, and whispers, "*Delizioso!*"—emphasizing the "o,"—then continues on his way.

I glance down at my entrée and see that Bert's taken way more than just a bite. Looks like half the meal is gone. I internally coach myself.

It's okay. He can eat my food. After all, I'm not that hungry. Actually… I'm ravenous.

"Are we in a hurry tonight or something?" I ask sweetly as I resume my place at the table next to Doreen.

"No, dear," she says between mouthfuls of her chicken piccata. "Why?"

"You're both eating pretty quickly and seem a little... I dunno, distracted?"

"Distracted? No dear, no one is distracted. What we are is incredibly focused. As you should be. That is exactly the point we want to make tonight."

She finishes her last bite, refolds her napkin, and places it neatly beside her plate.

"Right. The Business. You wanted to talk about The Business. Okay, I know I haven't brought as many people into my downline as I should. I'm just having a hard time finding—"

"Any," Doreen corrects with a frown.

"Hmm?" I ask after one of the few remaining bites of my entrée.

"Mabel, you haven't brought *any* people into your downline."

"Right. You're right. Yes. But I'm working on it, I promise!"

"Sweetheart." Doreen's voice lowers and warms. "Didn't you tell me Abe and Helen needed you to help them financially after... the incident? Aren't your parents worth putting in the extra effort? How is he doing, by the way?"

Oh God. She went there. There has been much talk in our little Philadelphia suburb about my father's recent... incident. And there's always that little... pause... before it. Always... the incident. But this is the first time it's being used to make me feel guilty. Is that what she's trying to do? Make me feel guilty? That's sort of my general state of being, so whether that's her intention or not, it really doesn't take much. Here I am, feeling guilty.

"He's doing much better, thank you, I just—"

"Still can't work, though?" she interrupts me.

"It's not that he can't work. My mom just wants him to take some time off before finding something else." I try to steer the conversation back to my delinquency in The Business. Surprisingly, I'm more comfortable talking about The Business than... the incident. "I have been working on gathering prospects. I've been finding, though, that people seem to get a little nervous when I bring up the subject and—"

"Well, then you're not doing it right," she says matter-of-factly, her stern but smiling business voice back in place. "Bert brought on five new team members this weekend alone."

"Oh, really? Five!" I say, impressed. "Good for you, Bert Alert. I take it the networking event in Trenton was successful, huh?"

He clears his throat. "It was. Yep."

"That's awesome. I missed you this weekend, of course, but I'm proud of you, boo! You'll have to give me some more tips!"

"Um. Yeah. I can do that." He clears his throat again. "Sure."

"Mabel," Doreen continues. She's on a mission, it seems. "You're in a decidedly unfeminine field. Wouldn't you agree?"

"Entomology is unfeminine? Huh. I don't know that I would categorize it as—"

"How many other women do you know who play with bugs all day?" she asks.

"Well, I wouldn't say I *play* with bugs all day." I chuckle. "I study them. Their behavior, their rituals, mating habits... You are correct, though, that there are definitely more men in my field than women. but—"

"Exactly. And, as you know, The Business is launching a new line of products specifically for men, so we'd like you to recruit some of your male colleagues while you're out in the mud together digging for worms."

Wow, she really has no concept of what my job entails.

"Can you do that for us?" She says this with a continual nod as though she's trying to hypnotize me.

I start to blubber. "Well, it's camp season. You know I always take a leave from the museum in the summer to be full-time at the arboretum. And our camp staff is mostly female."

She's staring at me with a blank expression, so I continue.

"But! I'll still be at the museum once a week guest lecturing—did I tell you we're doing a special exhibit on grasshopper larvae?—so I can *try* to approach some of my male colleagues there and see if they—"

"Do or do not. There is no try." She cuts me off and hands me some flyers. "Here is some more information on the new masculine line and ten invitations to our product presentation next week. We'll expect at least five of your... bug-men to attend."

"Roger that. Thank you for these," I say as I place the papers in my purse. "And ha! Yoda! Good one!" I give her a friendly smack on her upper back.

She massages the place on her body where I just made contact, and says, "I don't know what you mean."

"The quote you just said: 'Do or do not. There is no try.'" I'm pretty proud of my Yoda impression, but Doreen just stares at me while Bert continues to shovel food—both his and mine—into his mouth.

"It's from *Star Wars*," I explain. "Master Yoda?"

"Mabel, the only master I quote is myself."

"Gotcha," I say.

I pull my lasagna bowl away from Bert and finally take a few bites.

"Bertie, you're up," Doreen says.

"Up? I'm up?" He panics.

"You're up," she repeats. "It's time for the other thing. We did the first thing, so now we're moving on to the other thing."

"The other thing. Yes. Take two."

He reaches across the table and takes my hand. His feels wet.

"Mabel," he says with intensity.

"Bert," I mimic the same solemn tone he used with me. He doesn't laugh, though.

He launches into a speech. "I love that you count the days we've been together. It makes me feel loved. I love how you give me nicknames. They make me feel appreciated. I love the way you notice all the little things about me. It makes me feel seen."

Am I imagining it? Or did we already cover this territory? Also, is his mother really mouthing along to the words he's saying?

"Oh, wait, wait, wait!" Doreen says suddenly. Then she stands up and starts making hand gestures like she's an air traffic controller at Philadelphia International Airport. And with just a few spastic strokes of her arms, our plates are cleared—wait, I barely got to eat!—and a circle of humans holding champagne flutes assembles around us. Not just any humans. My mom and dad, my childhood best friend Cyndi—who is clearly still not at the Sixers game—Bert's Uncle Fred and Aunt Sybill and... our high school zoology teacher Mrs. Preston?

What the heck is going on here?

Suddenly, a sea of frozen smiles surrounds me from where I'm sitting. But their smiles aren't the only things that are rigid. Bert's entire body seems locked in place. His eyes are wide, his lips are tight, and I don't think I've seen him breathe in at least sixty seconds.

"Bertie?" Doreen says.

Silence.

"Bert?" She tries again to shake him from whatever state this is he's in.

"Uhhhhhhhhhhhhhhhhhhhhhhhhhh" is his only response.

"Fine. It's fine. I'm used to doing things myself," Doreen says with a smile, but she certainly doesn't seem happy.

She takes my hand in hers, much like Bert did a moment ago. In fact, his clammy fingers are still wrapped around my other hand, clinging for dear life. Then she connects her free hand with his, so we now have a triangle of familial hand holding happening. Like we're about to say grace. Or hold a séance.

For the record, none of the events of the past few minutes are characteristic of our typical Sunday night dinners.

"Sweetheart," Doreen says. Out of the corner of my eye, I spot my mother beaming and clapping silently in child-like anticipation.

My hand gets a squeeze, and I snap my full attention back to Bert's mother, who is smiling sweetly.

"Yes, Doreen."

"These past seven years with you in our family have been a beautiful thing. You bring so much joy to my son's life. And to my life too. You are the daughter I absolutely never wanted but am so blessed to now have."

"Thank you?" I say. I mean, I think that was a compliment. Right?

Before I can ponder that too much, Doreen snaps her fingers with a flourish, and our eccentric waiter appears again, this time with a beautiful, thin biscotti set on a tiny porcelain plate, surrounded by some sort of delicious-looking cream. He plops it down right in front of me.

Dessert! Thank goodness, because I am still ravenous. Hm. Gosh. No one else has been served yet, and I know it's rude to eat before the rest of the table gets their food, but maybe I could just take a tiny little...

"Will you make me the happiest mother in the world and marry my son?"

"No, Mabel, don't!"

CRUNCH!

I bite down on the biscotti just as Doreen's question hits my ears, and a half a second too late to process Bert's warning fully.

A sharp, searing pain shoots through my mouth, and I suddenly remember the waiter's words: "Beware of the biscotti..."

I look up at all the people around me, feeling dazed, as some sort of liquid dribbles down my chin.

"Um. I fink I bwoke a toof?" I sputter.

My mother screams.

My father shouts, "She's bleeding! My daughter is bleeding!"

I cradle my jaw with my hand and wince as I say, "Wow. That ith thome hard bithcotti! Yowtha!"

"What?" Bert's Aunt Sybill asks in a panic.

Cyndi translates from where she stands behind me. "She said 'Wow. That is some hard biscotti. Yowza!'"

"Someone dab the blood!" my mother cries from the opposite side of the table. "Dab the blood! Dab the blood!"

Bert pushes his chair back and scurries around the table with a cloth napkin. He kneels beside me, dips the cloth in my ice water, then starts dabbing the blood from my chin.

After such a strange night, it feels comforting being this close to him, looking into the eyes that I know so well.

"I'm sorry, baby," he says as he dips and dabs some more. "The biscotti was a bad idea."

"Ith okay. I love bithcotti. Thith wath jutht thuper hawd."

Bert looks up at Cyndi for help with the translation.

"'It's okay. I love biscotti. This was just super hard,'" she says.

"Ah," Bert responds.

It's nice having a friend who's known you forever and always understands you. Gotta love Cyndi.

Alright, it's time to get a handle on what the heck is happening here.

"Bert? Did your mother juthst pwopothe to me?"

"No," he says with confidence. "I did."

"Are you thure? Becauthe it really thounded like your mother jutht pwopothed to me."

"Well, darling," Doreen pipes in, "you know that when you marry someone, you don't just marry that person. You marry that person's family as well."

"Is that true, though?" Cyndi murmurs. "I don't think that's actually—"

"It is," Doreen says. "It's true. And we couldn't be happier that Mabel is now officially going to be a part of ours." She lifts her glass. "Cheers everyone!"

A resounding chorus of "cheers" echoes around the table and several heads tip back with celebratory sips of champagne.

Cyndi speaks up one more time. "Like Mabel, I too am a little unsure of who proposed—Bert, or Doreen—but regardless... I don't think she actually answered the question yet. Did she?"

Didn't I? Huh. I guess I didn't.

Bert jolts into action, sliding a huge diamond ring off the biscotti and slipping it onto my finger.

I look down and see it's speckled with cream and a tiny bit of blood from my toof. I mean, my tooth.

"Mabel. Baby," he says, looking and sounding more earnest than I've ever seen him before. "Will you marry me?"

Everyone holds their breath, waiting for my answer.

I look into his eyes for a long moment. Probably too long, I'm guessing.

And then, I say the words I've always known I would say, from the time we were seventeen years old, holding hands and totally in sync while circling the roller-skating rink.

"Yeth, Bert. I will mawwy you."

"You will?" he asks with a bright smile.

"Of courthe, I will. Yeth."

Chapter Two

"Whoa! Blingedy bling bling bling! Did a massive iceberg crap on your finger, or did you just become a wifey-to-be?"

I knew I should have taken off the ring before coming to work.

It's our final counselor training day at Bucks County Arboretum and Nature Conservancy. Did I mention I'm chief of staff this year? Wait. That's not right. That sounded presidential. Head of staff? Wrangler of counselors? Head counselor! Yes, that's my title. I am head counselor. Sorry. My brain is still foggy from the laughing gas I was treated to during my impromptu dental procedure this morning to fix my cracked tooth from last night. That and the fact that I was late to work this morning—I'm never late—has me feeling all out of whack.

It certainly has nothing to do with the fact that I got engaged last night, and I'm not quite sure how to feel about that. Nope, nothing to do with that at all.

One of my CITs—aka counselors-in-training—has just spotted my "bling," and it's more than a little embarrassing. I don't do so well with lots of attention on me.

"It's no big deal, April," I say all easy-breezy-like. "I'm just taking the next step in my personal and *private* relationship, a relationship I will not be discussing with minors." There. That should do it.

"There's nothing minor about me, baby!" Dante shouts while

doing some questionable pelvic pumps into the air.

These people are fifteen- and sixteen-year-old children whose confidence and awareness are running circles around mine.

"Alright, alright, everybody! Please put your pelvises away. Let's gather around the picnic table so we can get started."

Four teenagers assemble around me with varying degrees of readiness on their faces. I decide to dive right in.

"First of all, I want to apologize for starting a bit late today. Punctuality is super important, and I should absolutely be modeling that for you. I had a dental emergency I had to take care of, but all is well now."

"Are you sure all is well?" Chloe asks. "Because the left side of your face doesn't seem to be moving when you speak."

"True, Chloe, true. I appreciate your attention to detail! That's going to serve you really well when working with the children this summer. See, my dentist had to administer some Novocain to deal with a cracked tooth, and it hasn't quite worn off yet."

"Redheads are more sensitive to pain," Chloe says. Sidling up next to me, she gently strokes the end of her own red tresses secured into a side braid. "They often need more anesthesia for dental and medical procedures. Maybe your dentist knew that and administered a bit too much ." She holds her braid up to my red ponytail. "We have a really similar shade, don't you think?"

"Is that true?" I wonder out loud.

"I think so!" Chloe smiles and smooshes our strands together. "Look, we could braid our hair together, and no one would know whose hair was which."

Chloe is brand new to camp this summer. She's a bit younger than the other CITs. Fifteen instead of sixteen. But she has a real maturity to her. She was one of the few who applied for the job without her parents present. She's one of those rare teenagers super curious about other people and not hyper-focused on herself. She also rivals me in bug knowledge, which isn't easy to do.

"Ha, yeah, you're right!" I smile at her and gently guide my hair away from hers. "But I meant is it true that redheads feel more pain?"

"Oh, totally true," Chloe says excitedly. "It's because the

gene mutation that causes red hair is on the same gene linked to pain receptors."

"Interesting," I say.

"So basically, the dentist gave Mabel too many drugs, and she's high right now?" April says. "Are you high right now? Dante, I think she's high right now."

"No, April, I am *not* high right now.

"'Say no to drugs, kids!'

"'You use, you lose.'

"'No need for weed!'

"'Crack is whack.'

"'Choose to be jolly, stay away from Molly.'"

Why am I rattling off anti-drug slogans?

"Why are you rattling off anti-drug slogans?" Emily asks.

"That's an excellent question. You know what I think it is, Emily? This is my first summer being head counselor, and it's incredibly important to me that I become the role model you all deserve and impart wisdom that will stand the test of time and stay with you for the rest of your lives. I'm here for you, friends. Please feel free to call me anytime if you have questions. I purposely put my digits at the tippy top of your orientation packets so you'll always have a way to reach me."

"Did she just say 'digits'?" Dante snorts.

"Wow." April chuckles. "You're earnest AF, huh?" she asks with her head cocked to the side as though she's studying me. Sizing me up.

"I suppose?" I'm suddenly self-conscious. "But earnestness is cool, right?"

"I guess?" Emily chimes in now, looking at April for her approval. In our short time together, it's clear that Emily is always seeking April's approval. April just looks down at her nails and studies a chip in her polish.

I feel ya, Emily.

Geez, why do I want these kids to like me so much?

Time to take control.

Be the boss.

"So!" I say, perhaps a bit too boisterously. "You've had a solid week of training alongside your senior counselors. I've been observing you all in the group, but today it's my job to hang out with you—our wonderful CITs—exclusively and gauge your readiness for the kids' arrival tomorrow. I may give you a few tips as you dive into the summer. I'll also be looking to determine who might be a good candidate for working on the senior staff next year. Sound good?"

Silence and shrugging ensue. Except for Chloe, who smiles and nods.

"Great! We have a lot to cover. If we all stay focused, then by the end of the day today, I fully expect that we will be a five-person counseling dream team ready to make magical nature-inspired memories with today's youth! Yay!"

More silence.

CITs are tricky. They're almost always former campers who have aged out of our programs, but don't want to miss out on the summer fun with their camp friends. That, or their parents are forcing them to get their first summer job, and coming back to the arboretum is the easiest way to get their folks off their backs while also making a small—and I do mean small—amount of money. I myself was a camper here back in the day, then a CIT, a counselor, and now here I am... head counselor. In my camper days, though, there were different owners, and there was a performing arts spin to the place. Now it's all nature all the time. I don't miss the musicals. I've always been in it for the bugs.

I clap my hands enthusiastically and hope for some cheers and whistles to accompany my excitement. What I get instead is a slow-motion thumbs-up from Emily, a shy smile from Chloe, and a smirk from April. Dante seems to be practicing some kind of dance move.

Whatever. I'll take it. I forge ahead. Because that's what I do.

"Everybody wearing sturdy shoes? As CITs, this is your summer to learn on your feet, so let's get that particular party started right now. It's hiking time, friends! Let's take this show on the road."

I start marching toward the trail, assuming they'll follow.

Thankfully, they do.

Slowly.

"We'll chat while we take in the sights and sounds of our beautiful arboretum and get to know all the beauty and wonder she has to offer."

Dante raises his hand. "What the hell is an arboretum? I've been wondering that for years."

"First, watch the 'hell,'" I say. "And second, that's the beautiful thing about books, Dante. Or even the great Google! You don't have to wonder about something for years. Knowledge is always at our fingertips. We just need to seek it out!"

"Whatevs," he says as though he's already past caring. But I don't let that deter me. I launch into my prepared speech about this gorgeous establishment. There are few things I love more than singing this place's praises.

"Dante, an arboretum is a botanical garden of sorts devoted to trees. You'll be learning plenty about the many different tree varieties we have here, both evergreen and deciduous, so don't you worry about that! But here at BCA, we are an arboretum *and* a nature reserve. As a nature reserve, it is a huge part of our mission to protect the planet's natural biodiversity. We do this in a few ways. The flora and fauna you'll find here are—"

Suddenly, Dante lets out a scream that sounds an awful lot like my mother's tea kettle when it reaches a boil.

"Get it away from me! Get it away from me!" he screeches.

A gorgeous bluish-purple dragonfly hovers above him, her shimmery iridescent wings beating in the sky.

"Whoa, Dante. Whoa! You're fine. She won't hurt you." I try to comfort him. Dante has been coming to BCA for years, but he's a city kid through and through. Each year, he comes this way to live with his grandparents for the summer and gets a crash course in all things nature. It always takes him a week or two to settle in.

He starts swatting at her. "Shoo, shoo!"

"Dante, no! No swatting or shooing the insects, please."

"But what if it bites me?" he says as he continues to swat and duck and generally freak out.

"Relax! She won't. Dragonflies *can* bite, but they usually don't unless they feel threatened, and even then, they rarely break the skin."

"Ugh. I hate bugs." April scoffs.

"You won't by the time I'm through with you this summer!" I say with glee. "I'm going to show you how magical and endlessly fascinating these little creatures can be. Till then, I don't want to see anyone bullying the bugs. Try to remember, we need them. And we're living in their world, not the other way around. They're just being kind enough to share it with us."

I lift my hand up to the sky, and the beautiful dragonfly perches happily on my index finger.

"Dude, she's like Snow White! Though instead of catching dwarves on her fingers, she catches bugs!" Dante says.

"Snow White caught *birds* on her fingers, dumbass, not dwarves!" April fires back.

"Hey," I scold gently. "Quit it with the dumbass stuff. We have to start modeling the language we want the kids to use when they join us tomorrow." I turn back to my tiny, fluttery-winged visitor and smile at her. "Gosh, doesn't she just... take your breath away?"

"How do you know it's a she?" Emily asks.

Yay, a teaching moment! I live for these.

"Oh, well, see how her belly is smooth? If she were a he, there would be a bump on the belly."

"Yeah, there would! Bow-chicka-wow-wow!" Dante responds like the typical sixteen-year-old boy he is, apparently completely recovered from his near-death experience.

I give the little odonate a boost up to the sky, and she flies away.

April watches her go. "Is it true that female dragonflies fake their deaths to avoid being harassed by male dragonflies for sex?"

"Of course not! That's crazy!" Emily says in a rare moment of challenging April.

"Yet completely true," I say.

"Whaaat?" A chorus of voices echoes around me.

Gosh, I love blowing young minds with bug trivia.

I continue. "What April said is one hundred percent true. When a female dragonfly encounters an unwanted male suitor mid-flight, she will often dive to the ground and crash land, then lay motionless on her back until he gives up and flies away."

"Whoa! Cool!"

"Yup! See? Aren't bugs fascinating? The insect world is full of amazing little details like this. April, I'm impressed you knew this particular tidbit! You've been studying up on entomology to prep for camp this year, huh? Good for you! Not that bug sexual behavior is something we should be sharing with the kids, just for the record."

"Hell no. I don't study!" she says, offended.

"Oh," I say, feeling disappointed.

"Yeah, no. My mom is deep in the throes of divorcing my stepdad right now, and she told me the other day that she knew she needed to pull the plug on the marriage when she played 'dead dragonfly' one too many times during sex. So I started looking into it and—"

"Wow! Okay," I interrupt, fully cognizant of the inappropriateness of this discussion, yet completely curious to hear more. "You, um... You and your mom—you're pretty close, huh?"

"The closest, yeah! We're more like sisters than mother/daughter," April says proudly.

And here I thought my mom and I were close. But talking about our sex lives? No way. In fact... has my mom *ever* talked to me about sex? Did she ever even give me "The Talk?" No, I don't think she ever did. I just remember the vague yet constant lesson of "don't ever do it."

I know April's mom, though, and if I'm honest with myself, the things she's saying aren't actually all that surprising.

Just then, my phone rings. Loudly.

"Oh gosh, I'm sorry, team." I fumble in my fanny pack to find it.

Right before I silence it, I see that it was my friend Calliope trying to video call me from Mexico where she's on a dinosaur dig. I hate to miss her, but...

"Hey, I thought we're not supposed to have phones 'on our person' during camp hours," April accuses, sounding thrilled to catch me mid-work crime .

"That's absolutely right!" I chirp. "You're not. I mean, *we're* not. I'm sorry, it won't happen again."

She cocks her head to one side and puffs her lips out in confusion. "Aren't you my boss?"

"Yes?" I try a statement, but it comes out as a question.

"And aren't you like forty?" she asks with full seriousness.

"Twenty-four, actually," I deadpan.

"Same difference," April exhales. "Well, I'm sixteen. So why are *you* apologizing to *me*?"

"Because... I did something wrong. Saying 'I'm sorry' is the appropriate response."

Isn't it?

"Hm." April ponders this. "I would advise against that approach, or we'll lose respect for your authority."

"Really? I thought you'd appreciate the fact that I'm relating to you as colleagues and equals."

"Nope," April answers, then turns to Dante for his take on the matter. "Dante?"

"Yeah, naw," he drawls. "We need to know you're in charge and have some semblance of power over us, or else we'll walk all over you just like we do our parents."

"Interesting," I say, nodding my head, my jaw dropped open far more than necessary. "Thank you for telling me that."

They give me a look as though I've completely missed their point. I adjust quickly.

"I mean, you... You shut your mouths, imbeciles!"

Oops.

"Too far? Did I take it too far?" I ask.

"Too far, yeah," April says. "No one suggested you should be a raging B."

"Yeah," Emily chimes in. "Don't be a raging B."

"OH HOLY SHIT, LOOK AT THAT THING!"

Dante is losing his mind again. He's frozen and pointing at a huge praying mantis, standing in our path, directly in front of me.

God, he's gorgeous. How did I not see him?

"Oh, cool!" April says. "That's the one that rips off a dude's head after she boinks them, right?"

"Well, yes," I start to explain. "The female mantis is known to cannibalize her partner during the mating ritual, but this here is a male. Mantises, in general, are incredible creatures who…"

I hear my own voice trail off as I feel a strong energy approaching behind us. I turn just as a man whooshes by me on the trail. I startle and lose my footing, rolling over my ankle. I've always had weak ankles.

"Ow!" I bend down to rub the tendons there, then realize how rude I'm being. I shoot back up to stand.

"Excuse me, sir, I didn't see you there!" To my surprise, he keeps walking. "Good morning!" I call after him, slightly annoyed, but of course, I'd never outwardly show it. "How are you today?"

He continues on his way. Doesn't respond. Doesn't acknowledge my presence at all. Hmph. I suppose *he's* the rude one.

"The Wall," April says in a horror whisper.

"The what?" I ask.

Her eyes are wide, and she's pointing at the man's retreating back—his clearly very muscular back, clad in a loose plaid button-up. His longish sandy-colored hair sways with each heavy step he takes away from us.

"The Wall!" she continues to hiss under her breath. "That man! They call him The Wall."

"Who calls him The Wall?" I ask, matching her whisper because I have no clue what the heck she is talking about.

"Just, you know… people."

April's body posture changes, and she huddles us together like she's about to go full spooky storyteller on us. The other three teens give her their full attention. I get the impression she's used to having people's full attention.

"Dude is suuuuuper weird and silent," she hisses. "He's been here for like a month, and he's only ever spoken once."

"Whatdidhesay? Whatdidhesay? Whatdidhesay?" Emily is equal parts glee and terror.

"He said… 'CALL ME THE WALL.'" She adopts a classic spooky storyteller voice.

"No, he did not," I say. "Why on earth would he want to be called The Wall?"

"No one knows," April says with seriousness. "They say he's

like the new groundskeeper or something? But I think we all know what that means."

"Whatdoesitmean? Whatdoesitmean? Whatdoesitmean?" Emily is on the verge of hyperventilating now.

"He kills people and buries them in the woods. Obviously."

"April, please," I admonish. "That can't possibly be—"

"I'm serious!" she asserts.

"Hey, April." Chloe gets her voice in there. "How do you know about The Wall and Mabel doesn't?" Chloe asks.

"Naomi is on the board of the arboretum," April shrugs with faux nonchalance. "We know things."

"Naomi?" Chloe questions.

"Yeah, my mom. She lets me call her Naomi."

April's mother is what my father calls "a piece of work." Sure, that's a bit dismissive of him and not an entirely feminist assessment, but it's also not entirely inaccurate.

"Well," I offer, "if he got a job as the new groundskeeper, then clearly he had to have a meaningful interaction with someone. Carol must have hired him, and she's an excellent judge of character. I'm sure... The Wall... is a lovely man. He's probably just—"

"And get this!" April ignores me, fully focused on weaving her tale. The other three are eating it up like chocolate. "He lives down by the lake!"

"Ew! The lake!" Emily says with her nose scrunched up.

"I know." April continues. "In a tool shed."

"Ew! A tool shed!" Emily is eating this up.

"I *know*, right? The dude lives in a tool shed! Probably pretty convenient, though. You know, since he has all those tools available for all the *killing*!"

I have officially lost complete control of the group.

"Alright, April, I'm going to need you to stop this. Rumors aren't nice. Just because someone is eccentric doesn't mean they're dangerous. I'm certain if we just engage him—"

I look up to do that very thing... and lose my words when I spot him at the end of the trail. He's quite far away from us at this point, but he may as well be standing five feet in front of me with all the energy I feel pulsating off him.

He's standing there.

Still as stone.

Staring.

Directly at me.

I won't lie. It's freaky as hell, and I feel a chill rush through me. Just as I take a breath in to call out to him, he turns and disappears through a cluster of evergreens.

What the heck just happened?

I suddenly remember the mantis, but when I look down, he's gone too.

Weird.

Just then, a bell clangs loudly.

"Ahh!"

Shrieks abound as we're all shaken out of our collective spooky story stupor.

"It's okay, everyone," I soothe. "It's okay. That's just the bell from the canteen announcing midmorning snack."

"SNACK!!!" they all exclaim in monosyllabic joy.

My four counselors-in-training instantly sprint in the direction of the canteen without a second thought. Certainly without asking for any permission from me.

"Hey! Guys! We're not finished with our—!" I cut myself off as I watch their speedy retreat.

"And... no one is listening to me," I say out loud.

Why does that feel like a recurring theme in my life?

Chapter Three

I have a little time while the CITs snack up at the canteen, so I start walking with no particular destination in mind. After years of being a counselor here, I know these trails better than my own backyard, and I always find a brisk walk through nature clears my head.

It's probably pretty obvious at this point, but I'm not so sure I'm cut out for this head counselor position.

I was much more comfortable the past six summers managing my own little group of campers. And managing bugs, of course. I can always manage bugs. Yup, gimme bugs any day of the week, and I'm in bliss. But teenagers? Apparently, teenagers and I aren't the best fit. Gosh, you know what, though? If I'm being honest with myself, I'm not all that effective with adults either. Isn't that what Doreen was not so subtly implying last night? That I'm letting everyone down in The Business because of my inability to connect with other adults?

My eyes dart down to the sparkly ring on my finger.

Oh shoot, that reminds me. We have a team meeting later this afternoon. Is it terrible that I want to come up with an excuse not to go? Could I be sick? Sunburned?

My phone's ringtone blares again. I pull it from my fanny pack and see it's another video call from Calliope. I do a quick three-sixty scan to confirm that I am truly alone. All I see is a deer and her fawn about fifty feet away.

Hopefully, they won't mind.

I accept the call.

"YOU GOT ENGAGED AND DIDN'T TELL ME?" she screeches the second her face appears on the screen.

"You're screaming," I state the obvious.

"Well, I'm shocked! And whatever. I'm out digging in a field by myself," she explains at a normal volume. "I'm not bothering anyone. ALSO YOUR MAN'S NAME IS BERT?" she resumes the high decibels.

"Yes?" I answer. Shouldn't she already know this very basic information?

"His name is Bert," she repeats with her signature snark.

"Yes."

"Bert!!?"

"Is our connection okay? Calliope, yes. His name is Bert. It's short for Robert."

"HIS FULL NAME IS ROBERT, AND HE WENT WITH THE NICKNAME BERT? WHAT IS HE, AN IDIOT??"

The deer and her fawn peacefully nibbling on a blackberry bush startle and scamper away. Sorry, friends.

"Okay, you have to stop," I say. "You're scaring the wildlife." I turn down the volume on my phone a few notches.

"Well I'm just... astonished! Rob. Robby. Bob. Bobby. There were more than several ways to go, but your man? Your man went with Bert." Her voice has dropped to a hush as though she just can't believe this bit of information and needs a moment to process it.

"Nicknames aren't usually chosen. They're given."

"That's deep, Mabel."

"I *am* capable of depth, Calliope," I snap. "Despite what you or other people may think!"

Whoa. Where did that come from?

"Whoa!" Calliope marvels. "Where did that come from?"

"Nowhere. Sorry. Rough day I guess."

"Do you have rough days?" Her head is cocked to the side as though she's studying me.

"Of course I do. I'm human, aren't I?"

"Actually, when I first met you, I wasn't so sure that you were." Calliope has an apologetic look on her face.

"What, *human*?" My voice goes up a few notches.

"Yeah!" She chuckles. "I'd never met someone so relentlessly positive before you pranced into my life. I have to admit, you freaked me out and made me feel a bit like a psycho hose beast."

I look at her blankly.

"*Wayne's World* reference?" Her eyebrows lift. "No?"

"Sorry, no."

"Damn, we gotta get you watching better movies, girlfriend. *Any* movies really. You do realize you're twenty-four, and your parents' restricted movie list no longer holds now that you're an adult, yeah? You can watch anything you want. I suggest you start with some porn."

"Calliope!" I scold. "Can we stay on the subject, please?"

"Of course. Yes. Remind me what the subject was?"

"You said I am 'relentlessly positive,' which freaked you out when we first met. And that I prance. I do not prance."

"Yes, you do. But don't worry. It's endearing."

"Do I still freak you out with my positivity?"

"A bit, yeah. But I know you better now, so I see more of your colors. And I think I've changed a lot since we first met too. I've eased up a bit on my inner bitch, don't you think?"

"You were never a bitch, Calliope. You just know what you want, you go after it with the force of a Fukuiraptor, and for the most part, you don't give a flying duck about what others think of you."

"See? The most positive person on the planet. And props for your use of Fukuiraptor, but... 'duck'? Come on, Mabel."

"Sorry. You know I'm not comfortable with... language."

I'm used to assessments like the one she just made.

The ones that say "Mabel is the nicest girl I've ever met."

Or "Oh that Mabel. She has a kind word for everyone."

"Having a bad day? Talk to Mabel. She'll help you see the bright side of things."

And my personal favorite, "Mabel is such a sweet girl. She'd never hurt a fly."

That one is usually followed by raucous laughter because the person assumes they are the first clever one to ever make that pun. But I've heard it more times than I can count.

I used to take pride in assessments like these. But now—for some reason—I'm suddenly finding them inaccurate. And irritating.

"Mabes? You okay?"

"Why?"

"Well, you got a weird look on your face, you started breathing funny, and then you loosened your grip on the phone so much that I've been gifted with a direct view up your nose for the past fifteen seconds."

"Sorry." I grip the phone and lift it back up in line with my face. "I'm fine. Yeah." I'm just realizing something. "Hey... how did you hear I got engaged?"

"Read about it in the newspaper."

"In the *newspaper*?" I screech.

"Yeah, it's in yesterday's *Intelligencer*. I have an online subscription."

How was it in yesterday's paper? He didn't even propose until last night.

"Weird, I know." Calliope continues, seeming embarrassed. "Sue me. I have a sick fascination with our hometown. I like to see who's graduating, who got arrested, who's getting married, who's selling their house, who died. That sort of thing. Plus, it gives me story ideas."

"But you write dinosaur romances," I say.

"You bet your ass I do, but they're set in modern times, and I always base them on bits of real life. So snooping on people helps! I've learned that dinosaur romances are more relatable to readers if I give the animals people personalities and human hobbies. Anthropomorphize them if you will."

"Oh!" I say, a light bulb coming on. "The dinosaurs fall in love with *each other*?"

"Of course! What did you think?"

My cheeks redden.

"I guess I thought *people* were... um... doing it... with dinosaurs."

"Bestiality!? You assumed I was writing bestiality books!?"

"I think I did, yeah."

"Wow, you think I'm a real dirtball, huh?"

"No! No way!" I say apologetically.

"That's okay. I am a bit of a dirtball. However, I do not condone bestiality. Fictional or otherwise. Even if *you* do, ya kinky skank!" Calliope winks.

"I don't condone it! And I'm not a... Gosh! What are you—" I'm getting more flustered by the minute.

"Mabel. I'm just trying to make you laugh."

"Oh."

Calliope is quiet a moment. A rarity for sure.

"You seem a little wound up today. Are you not happy about this engagement or...?"

"Of course I'm happy!" I say with so much forced enthusiasm I think I feel something in my neck tweak.

"Alright! Then I'm... happy for you. Geez, I just can't believe you never told me his name was Bert. I mean, how long have we been friends now?"

"Two months, three weeks, and six days."

"Whoa."

Is it weird that I know the exact day I connect with someone and then proceed to keep track? Yup, it's weird.

"Well—" I try to save face. "That's only if you don't count the years we knew each other at Applause Theater and Nature Camp, when you basically ignored the fact that I existed. In that case, it would be... twelve years, two weeks, and... I dunno... three-ish days? Sorry, I don't remember the exact day we started rehearsals for *Really Rosie*."

"That's... fine," Calliope says with her eyebrows scrunched. "And I don't count those years, no. Besides, it wasn't personal. Didn't you say I ignored everyone's existence back then?"

"Pretty much. Anyone who wasn't a prehistoric creature, that is."

"Right, so not personal. My point is, that after being friends for two months, three weeks and..."

"Six days..."

"Six days, shouldn't I know *something* about your newly betrothed? Like—I dunno—his name?"

"It's not my fault you've never asked!"

"Not true. I have asked. It's not *my* fault you only ever refer to him as 'my boyfriend,' or that you change the subject every time he comes up in conversation."

"I don't change the subject whenever he... You know what? Can we talk about something else?"

"Aha! See!"

She got me there. Caught.

"Fine." I sigh. "What do you want to know? I... I want to talk about him."

"You sure?"

"Of course!"

"Okay, great! Let's get in there. Tell me what you love about him."

"Tell you what I..."

"Love about him, yes."

There's a disturbingly long silence while I draw a complete and utter blank.

Calliope clears her throat.

I begin to sputter. "Oh. Geez. Um?"

"Mabel?" Calliope asks with an uncharacteristic softness to her tone.

"Yeah?"

"Here's a nutty concept, but I feel like you should be able to answer this question about the man you just agreed to marry."

"I *can* answer it! You're just putting me on the spot, and it's making me feel... Why is everyone putting me on the spot lately?"

"Who's putting you on the spot? I'm not putting you on the spot. I'm just making sure you're —"

"You are, though! So is Doreen! So is Bert!"

"Bleh!" Calliope makes a retching sound. "That name! Bert."

Did she just go full *Sesame Street* on me and say "Bert" in Ernie's voice?

"You know what, missy?" I feel my blood pressure rising.

"You're calling me 'missy?' Uh-oh, Mabel, are we having our first fight?" Calliope chuckles.

She's not taking me seriously. At all.

"Actually, yes. I think we are! Listen, I didn't want to say this before and risk hurting your feelings, but *your* boyfriend doesn't exactly have the sexiest of names either you know."

"Screw you, bug lady!" Calliope bursts. "Ralph is the *sexiest* of names!"

Calliope has definitely become much more even-tempered and relaxed since meeting Ralph, but she still is who she is—fiery, opinionated, and ready to throw down at any perceived slight or provocation. Most days, I want to be her when I grow up. And most days, *I'm* the one soothing *her*. But today, for some reason, she's making me... angry?

Gosh. Is that what I'm feeling right now? Am I angry?

"Mabel?"

"What?" I snap.

"Nothing. Just, your face is... I've never seen your face look like that before."

"Like what?" My free hand starts shuffling around on my cheeks.

"I dunno. Like you're confused? Constipated?"

"It's been nice catching up," I say, "but... I'm gonna go now."

"I'm being serious." She pauses. "Are you okay?"

Apparently, I don't have an answer to that either.

She continues through my silence, just as I spot something—someone—in the distance.

"I rescind my 'screw you' comment. That was unnecessary and uncalled for. You are correct. Traditionally, Ralph is not the sexiest name out there. I confess that when I first met him, I was pretty opposed to the moniker myself. But then, I got to know him, and... damn! I realized that every single thing about that man is sexy. Even his not-so-sexy name. Know what I mean?"

"Well... yeah," I say. "Because I, uh. I... feel... the same way about Bert."

"No, you don't," she says bluntly.

"What do you mean?" I say on a sigh.

"Exactly what I said. You don't feel the same way about Bert."

"Calliope—"

"Uh-uh. No way. Don't 'Calliope' me. Listen. What are you doing this Saturday night? Because I'm—"

I know that Calliope is still speaking, but I no longer hear her.

Every ounce of my awareness has shifted to the man I spot stepping out from a small wooden enclosure connected to his shack. He's wearing only a pair of cargo shorts. His chest is completely bare and glistening with water droplets while he scrubs a towel over his head, ruffling his long, damp hair. Did I just witness this man exiting his outdoor shower? The same man who ignored me on the trail a few minutes ago. The one whose mere presence sent some wild, tingling, foreign feeling shooting through my body that I still haven't processed and certainly don't understand.

Hey, why do people say "mere" presence? Is anyone's presence "mere?" There's certainly nothing "mere" about this man. No, he's not "mere," he's... *more*. He's... gosh, he has this-this-this... largeness to him? And I'm not talking about his body. I'm talking about his energy. The space he takes up with his whole... Well, I mean, clearly, his *body* is large too. He has to have at least six inches on me. And his chest? Woooo-eee. That is one broad, beautiful, bare chest. Oh bummer, he's pulling a T-shirt over his head. Now what's he doing? He's... grabbing a long shovel. Is that why he was in such a rush to get back to his shack? He needed to cool off in his outdoor shower before doing some digging? Why? Is he tilling? Planting? *Burying*? Oh my goodness, what if April is right, and he's burying a body after a morning of murdering?

Anything is possible, I suppose. After all, I know absolutely nothing about this man. What I *do* know is that his muscles are rippling with each jab he makes into the wet earth below him, and I'm—well... I'm having this undeniable urge to run up to him right this second, roll around in the wet earth surrounding him, smear the mud all over my body, smell it on my skin, then spread it all over *his* body, smell *his* skin, and—

"Mabel? Mabel. Maaaaaaabel," a female voice says from what sounds like very far away. "Hey! Mabel! Mable-syrup! Maybe-she's-born-with-it-Mabel-ine!"

I realize then that Calliope's voice is coming from the grass where my phone fell out of my hand without my even noticing it.

"I'm sorry, I'm sorry!" I say too loudly as I squat down to retrieve my phone. I brush a few blades of grass off her face.

"What the hell? You dropped me!"

"I know, I'm sorry," I try to whisper, which is clearly too little, too late. "You know I'm clumsy, I just—"

A throat clears. A decidedly manly throat.

Mystery Man and I rise from the ground at the same time.

Totally in sync.

Total silence as we stare at each other.

I can't stand silence, so after a few seconds, I break it.

"Why do people call you The Wall?" The breathy question slips out of me before I even realize what I'm saying.

"The Wall? What are you talking about The Wall?" Calliope is understandably lost.

He doesn't answer me.

Not with words anyway. But he does take a single heavy step in my direction.

And what do I do when that happens? Well, I do what any rational person in my position would do when confronted with a possible killer.

I freak out.

"I'M TOO YOUNG TO DIE!" I yelp. Then I turn, and I run. That's right, my wobbly ankles and I sprint up the trail as far and as fast as we can, not daring to look back.

"You, um—you were saying something about Saturday night, Calliope?" I continue completely out of breath, trying to act as though my bizarre behavior is totally normal.

"Alright, that's it, weirdo. Saturday night. I'm in town. And I'm staging an intervention."

"An intervention? For who?" I ask as I continue to hobble my way toward the canteen.

"For you. Your usual sunny disposition is all sorts of tweaked."

"What? I'm psyched to see you, but I'm fine. I don't need an intervention. Besides, don't interventions only work if they are a surprise attack?"

"Surprise!" Calliope sings. "You're getting attacked with an intervention." Her voice drops to a more serious tone.

"Something's clearly shifting in you, Mabes, and—I realize this isn't exactly my MO when it comes to our newly formed friendship—but I'm concerned."

I don't say this to her, but after the events of the past two days?

I'm concerned about me too.

Chapter Four

"And that is how I achieved Triple Platinum Double Encrusted Diamond Level after only two years in The Business."

Doreen is finishing her spiel while our three newest team members lightly applaud, just as I rush into the coffee shop and take the open seat next to Bert.

He hands me an iced matcha latte, gives my thigh a squeeze, and whispers, "How's the tooth?"

"Good. Fine," I whisper back like it's no big deal even though it still hurts quite a bit. "Put a temporary cap on it until they can get me a permanent one. Hey, um, do you have a few minutes to talk after this? Something I need to run by you."

Bert fidgets slightly in his seat, but says, "Yeah. Of course, baby. I always have a few minutes for you."

"Everyone," Doreen announces, "I'd like you to meet my daughter-in-law, Mabel."

"Daughter-in-law?" the pretty woman in her early thirties seated to my right says, her head cocked in confusion.

"Soon-to-be, yup!" I chirp, then flash my ring at the table and give Bert an overly enthusiastic kiss.

I love my fiancé. I love my fiancé. I love my fiancé.

When I come up for air, I smile at the three new-to-me faces at the table and give them a waggy two-handed wave. "Hey there! Welcome to the team. We're so happy to have you on board! My apologies for being a tad tardy. Final day of orientation at the summer camp where I'm head counselor this year, and wowza, teenagers are tough! Anyone here have a teen?"

A woman in workout gear raises her hand from where she sits next to Doreen.

"Well, bless your soul, spandex lady. I salute you!" Then I do, in fact, salute her. With both hands. I seem to be overdoing a lot of things today. "What's your name? I didn't catch your name?"

I take a sip of my drink.

"Dawn," she says, "I'm Doreen's yoga teacher and the owner at Splooge."

I spit out my matcha latte, and the spray hits the dark-haired elderly lady to Dawn's left square in her chest. Her eyes widen.

"Mabel!" Doreen scolds and smiles.

"Oh, I'm so sorry, my friend! Let me help you with that!" I reach across the table with a scratchy brown napkin and start pawing at this lady's... um, what's the skin called on a woman's chest? The part that's above the boobs, but below the neck? The part that women in internet ads are constantly smacking sleep stickers on to ward off wrinkles? The decoupage? Skin collage? No, no, the décolletage! That's right.

"Wow, Splooge, huh?" I keep speaking to Dawn while dabbing at this other lady's wet, green-spit-speckled décolletage. "That's an interesting name for a gym!"

"Yes, well, there have been lots of studies that single onomatopoeic words are great for grabbing people's attention when it comes to business names. Particularly gyms."

"Well, good for you. That's fantastic." I finish dabbing the dark-haired lady and look into her still-startled eyes. "And what is your name?"

"Mrs. Kim" is all she says.

"Mrs. Kim. Pleasure to meet you. Apologies for the spitting. And the pawing."

"Mrs. Kim runs the laundromat in Doylestown next to the Wawa," Doreen explains.

"Oh, wonderful, great! Let me guess, your company name is... Stain!" I say and then laugh my head off.

The sweet older lady looks confused. "No. It is called Mrs. Kim's."

"Oh. Yes," I say, sobering. "Absolutely. That's a much better name for a laundromat than Stain. You're right." I turn to the woman sitting next to me, the pretty one who looked at me funny when I said I'm Bert's fiancée. "Hi. I'm Mabel again. Well, Mabel. Not Mabel Again. I'm trying to stop doing that. My actual last name is McGonigle. Mabel McGonigle. And you are?"

I extend my hand to her.

She doesn't take it.

She pushes her chair back, rises to stand, and says, "He sure does love *Law & Order*, huh?"

Then she leaves the coffee shop without another word.

My head whips to Bert and Doreen.

"What was that all about?" I ask.

"Bert, go," Doreen says, a distressed look on her face.

"I'll be right back, everyone," Bert blurts, then hustles out the door after the odd woman whose name I never got.

Huh.

I crane my neck and watch him practically sprint down the street after this lady.

"Moving right along!" Doreen says, commanding my attention again, her bright smile and vibrant voice back in place. "So Dawn? Mrs. Kim? I know I speak for everyone when I say that we are thrilled to have powerful business owners like yourselves bringing your knowledge, expertise, and community to our team."

"Oh, is it official? Are Dawn and Mrs. Kim officially part of the team?" I ask. In truth, I'm never quite sure what's going on in this business. I mostly take orders from Doreen and Bert and do my best to keep up.

"Well, I'm sure they *will* be," Doreen says after a quick sharp intake of breath, the kind that lets me know she's not altogether pleased with my question. Right. I forgot. Always assume they're in. They'd be crazy to pass up "the opportunity."

Just then, a young man comes into the shop and taps Doreen on the shoulder. I've seen what's about to happen at least a dozen times.

"Trevor, hello, dear."

"Your mail, Doreen," he responds, presenting several envelopes bundled together with a rubber band.

"Thank you so much, Trevor," Doreen says. Her words are full of gratitude and dismissal. He nods and leaves.

Trevor is Doreen's personal assistant. He always brings Doreen's mail to her when she's meeting with prospective team members. By mail, I mean her weekly paycheck. He did the same thing the first time I sat down to talk about "the opportunity" a few years ago.

"Oh, if you'll excuse me, ladies. I just need to do a little busywork for a moment," Doreen says on a breathy chuckle. "Get all my financial ducks in a row, you know."

She proceeds to open one of the envelopes with an old-fashioned golden letter opener she fishes out of her purse.

"Ah, there we are." She exhales and smiles, then smooths out a piece of paper on the table directly in Dawn's and Mrs. Lee's line of vision. They both lean forward to take a closer look. I see the moment both sets of eyes widen.

Doreen sips her tea, and continues, "It's such a relief to know that my financial future is secure. That I can sit here with new friends late on a Monday afternoon, sipping tea and talking about possibilities without rushing back to a J-O-B."

She spells out "job" like it's a dirty, unmentionable word.

Dawn starts to look uncomfortable and rises to her feet. "Speaking of J-O-Bs, I do have to get back to mine, so—"

"This is your monthly paycheck?" Mrs. Lee asks with interest.

"No, no, no." Doreen laughs lightly.

Mrs. Lee exhales. "Oh, thank goodness. I didn't think so!"

"Weekly." Doreen smiles.

"WEEKLY? YOU MAKE THAT MUCH MONEY WEEKLY!?" Dawn's relaxed yogic personality is officially a thing of the past. She slams herself back in her seat.

"I do," Doreen says. "And so can you."

A part of me wants to say, "When, though?" or "How??" Because I've been involved in this for over a year now, and I've spent way more money than I've made.

I must not be trying hard enough.

Doreen and Bert were right last night. I need to be more proactive in welcoming people to our team. I can do it.

That's it. The next person I have a meaningful interaction with is going to be my new business partner. Yessiree bob.

Doreen launches into the inspiring speech she always gives to get new prospects excited.

"Ladies, this is the moment when you can get in on the ground floor of an exciting new adventure. One where you can build relationships with like-minded entrepreneurs looking to build multiple streams of residual income for years to come. Where you can join forces with a team offering cutting edge products and—"

I see Bert slip back inside the coffee shop. I grab my bag and rush to meet him by the door.

"Hey," I say.

"Hey. Sorry for the interruption," he says, his eyes focused on the table where the meeting continues.

"It's okay, but.. what was that all about?" I ask quietly.

"Oh, nothing. She's fine. Shall we?" He gestures to the table.

"Just a minute." I pull on his arm to keep him from walking away. "She didn't seem fine. But remind me who *she* is? How do we know her?"

"I met her this weekend at the networking event. She's really excited about the opportunity. She's just not feeling well tonight, so she went home to get some rest." He finally looks me directly in the eyes, then cups my face with one hand and rubs my cheek with his thumb. "Okay?"

"Okay." I smile. "Ready to head out?"

"Oh baby, I can't do tonight, remember?"

"No, I don't remember."

"I have to do follow-up meetings with some of the prospects I met this weekend."

"But it's Monday," I say, completely confused. "Monday night is our night."

"I know, baby."

"And we *just* got engaged."

"Hey, listen, baby—"

Geez, he's calling me baby *so* much right now.

He continues, "I'm trying to build a future for us. You know that, right?"

"Yeah, I do. It just feels like you're—"

He cuts me off. "I'll make it up to you next Monday night. Promise."

"Okay then." I look at the time on my phone. "I... guess I'll head to the station and catch the next train back home then."

"Atta girl. Love you," he says, sounding relieved there won't be a fight tonight.

But that's the thing. There's never a fight.

Mabel McGonigle doesn't fight. She never has.

"Love you too," I say, then move to the table where Doreen is still talking strategy with Dawn and Mrs. Kim. I silently grab my backpack and sling it over one shoulder. Bert takes a seat.

"Good night, ladies," I say with as much cheer as I can muster.

"Leaving so soon, sweetheart?" Doreen asks.

"Yeah, I'm going to try to catch the 7:07 back home. You know, spend some quality time with my parents."

"Lovely. Tell them I say hello." She stands and hugs me. "I was so happy they could be there with us last night to celebrate."

"Me too. They're really excited." Before she pulls away from the hug completely, I say, "Hey, um. Could I ask you something?"

"Of course, dear."

We pull off to the side, and I make sure to speak quietly so only she can hear. "My, um. My friend told me about the posting in the *Intelligencer* yesterday?" I tread lightly.

"Did you see it?" Her entire face lights up with excitement.

"Not yet, no."

"Oh, it's lovely! Don't worry, I bought twenty-five copies. So I'll give you one the next time I see you."

"Sounds... great, thank you."

Do I push this any further? I think I have to.

"I guess, um. I guess I was just a little surprised to hear about it, since—well, since you'd have to have submitted it to the newspaper before I even said yes. Hahaha." I follow this up with a good-natured chuckle to put her at ease.

"Well, what were you going to say… no? Hahaha!" Doreen laughs like that outcome would be utterly preposterous. She's right, though. It would. There was no way I was going to say no.

"Of course not," I say.

"Right, so I thought it would be really special if the good news was announced on the same day that the good news happened. I'm sorry, sweetheart. I am just so excited for you to officially join our family. It's not a problem, is it?"

"No…?" I pause and look at her eager face. "No. Of course not."

"Wonderful. Have a great night, dear." She gives me one of those hovery side kisses where lips and cheeks never actually make contact.

"You too."

Feeling like Bert and I have already said everything we need to say to each other for now, I attempt to scoot past him and out the door without any further discussion.

"Hey." He remains seated but manages to grab my hand at the last minute. I turn to face him. "Next Monday," he says. "I'll make it up to you, okay?"

"Okay," I exhale.

"Trust me?"

He traces small circles on my hand with his thumb.

I give him a faint smile and lean down to kiss him gently on the lips.

"Trust you."

Chapter Five

”*B*UG LADY!!!” a tiny voice screeches out in delight.

"Buddy!!" I screech out in similar delight.

I crouch down to the ground, and six-year-old Holden runs into my arms, squeezing me as hard as he can.

”I'm so happy to see you!" I coo. "I was starting to worry you wouldn't make it today."

"I'm sorry we're late." His mom exhales. "His little brother was up all night, one of our pipes sprang a leak this morning, and then, of course, there had to be crazy traffic built up on the—"

"Oh, it's totally fine!" I interrupt her and try to put her mind at ease. "Everyone's just getting to know their groups," I reassure her. "How's my guy doing?" I ask as I pull back and fluff Holden's sandy-colored hair.

"Good! I'm... buggin' out to see you." Holden explodes into a shy smile, then he turns a bright shade of pink before he runs and hides his face in his mom's belly.

"Aw, that was funny, honey bunny!" I say. "I've missed the Holden humor!"

"He's been wanting to deliver that joke to you all morning," his mom says with a sweet shake of her head. "He sure does love you."

"Well, I love him too. I'm psyched he's back this summer. How are you doing, Reneé?"

"Eh," she says.

How do I respond to "eh?"

"Is everything... okay?" I lower my voice a bit, but I'm sure Holden can still hear me.

"It will be, yeah," she says with a curt nod. Then she squats down to hug her son. "I'll see you at three, okay, baby? Have an awesome time, and be a good listener."

"I'm always a good listener, Mommy."

"You are. Aren't you?" she says, a warble creeping into her voice. "You're my sweet, wonderful boy."

Is it me, or are her eyes filling with tears?

What's going on here?

"I love you, bubba."

"Love you too, Mommy!" he says in a rush and starts reaching into the pockets of his shorts. "Mabel, I put a whole bunch of roly-polys in my pockets! Wanna see?"

Oh man, those poor roly-polys.

"Yes, yes! Let's get those guys out of there!" I put my arm around his tiny shoulders and start guiding him toward the pavilion where all the groups of kids and counselors are assembling.

I get Holden settled with his counselor before turning back to check on his mom. I spot her leaning against her minivan, her face in her hands, and she's shaking. I take a step in her direction, but when she sees me, she quickly wipes her eyes, gets in her car, and slowly drives away.

None of my business, I suppose? I'm head counselor to the counselors and kids, right? Not the parents? Gosh, I don't know what my role in a situation like this should be.

Just then, the bell clangs for the morning meeting, so I do my best to put Holden's mom out of my mind and focus on making our first day fantastic for the kids.

A few hours later, the camp is in full swing. I'm in the middle of teaching my Critters Corner class to the turtle tots and am feeling totally in my element. "Is everybody ready to make a critter craft?" I ask the picnic tables full of four-year-olds.

"Yes!" they answer in a tiny-voiced chorus of cuteness.

"Okay, CITs, come on up and gather some construction paper, safety scissors, and glue sticks for your group, and we'll get started on our web-spinning spiders!"

April and Dante approach the supply station. After some careful consideration with Carol, the head of the camp, we decided to place these two with our youngest campers, figuring they could benefit from playing with preschoolers. Maybe it will give them a chance to return to some basic childhood magic? Slow down their rush to grow up? It's worth a shot.

"Hey! Mabel!" April whisper-shouts from where she's gathering googly eyes for her group's spider creations. Not exactly anatomically accurate—I know—but who can resist googly eyes?

"What's up, April?"

"The Waaaaaaall. Six o'clock!" she hisses.

I turn to look directly behind me, and a few yards away, the mystery man from yesterday is busy repairing a water fountain.

I turn back to April.

"Alright, my friend. You have to stop this. Starting rumors and making assumptions about a person is never the way to go. I think you'll find that most people are perfectly lovely if you just give them a chance to show it. Let me tell you a little story."

That's what I'm supposed to be doing as an authority figure to these teens, right? Telling them helpful anecdotes and inspirational stories? Sure, why not.

"So. I work part-time at The Museum of Natural Sciences in the city as a guest bug lecturer and teacher. That's how I know Holden actually! He was in my Critters Corner class and did a spring break camp there with us a few months ago. Anyway. There's an amazing woman who works there as the head of paleontology. Her name is –"

"Dr. Knowles?" April asks.

"Ooooooooooooh." I shudder.

She and Dante look at me as if I'm insane.

"Sorry about that. Ahem. Yes, April," I say, surprised. "That is her name. How do you know, um..." I hesitate to say it out loud.

"Dr. Knowles?" she supplies.

"Ooooooooooooh." I shudder again.

"My mom is on the board of the Museum of Natural History, so we know Dr. Knowles very well."

"Ooooooooooooh." Geez, I thought I was over this. "April, just curious… about how many places is your mother on the board?"

"Oh, a lot. We're very well connected."

I'm learning that this is very true. Her mom is also head of the board for our neighborhood association. She has lots of opinions on, well, everything, such as the proper way to put out your recycling bins, what paint color is "appropriate" for window shutters, oh and whether or not someone can have a beehive in their backyard. But I'm not going to think about that right now because I'd like to preserve my good mood.

"Are you cold or something?" Dante asks me in confusion. "It's like eighty degrees out here."

"Nope! Not cold. Thanks, though. Nice of you to express your concern. Anyway. The point I'm trying to make is that this…. doctor I'm speaking of… she used to terrify me. I used to shudder anytime someone said her name."

"Used to?" April says with a smile.

I ignore her quip.

"I thought she must be horrible because she didn't smile that much and was kind of curt in her responses to people. But in actuality, she's wonderful! She even connected my friend Calliope with an incredible opportunity working on a dinosaur dig in Mexico this summer with the love of her life!"

"Why are you telling us this?"

"Because I was judging her without taking the time to get to know her. I thought I had her figured out based on shallow observations: the way she smiled—or didn't—the way she spoke, the way her eyebrows never moved…"

"My mom's eyebrows and forehead never move," April offers. "But that's just because of all the Botox. I'd be pretty bummed if someone judged her based on that."

"Exactly, April! Yes! We should judge your mother on her gossiping and inappropriate parenting, not on her Botox-ing!"

"Dayum!" Dante laughs.

Bit of a social fumble there, Mabel, but it's okay. Keep talking.

"Has anyone actually ever tried to say hello to this man?" I ask.

"Besides you yesterday when he iced you out like a snow cone?"

"He what? I wouldn't say that he... Nonsense, Dante. He just didn't hear me."

"If you say so, gurl." He shrugs.

"Okay. Here's what we're gonna do. You two, get your groups set up with their materials. The counselors have you covered for a few minutes. We're going to march right over there to Mister..."

"The Wall," they say in unison.

"We're going to march over to that... nice gentleman, find out his *real* name so we can all stop calling him The Wall"—I say this with my index finger pointed at them like a harsh schoolmarm —"then we're going to learn a bit about him and welcome him properly to the arboretum like we should have done yesterday."

"I'm all about protecting ladies from imminent danger and conducting constant acts of chivalry," Dante says with a surprising explosion of heightened vocabulary. "But gurl? You're cray if you think if I'm gonna dialogue with that dude."

"April?" I ask.

"Hell to the no," she answers emphatically.

As I expected.

"Not a problem. I'll go myself. Kindness in action. Watch and learn, friends. Watch and learn." I pause a moment. "Actually? I don't really want an audience for this. Go focus on your kids, and I'll report back on my inevitable success."

"Go on, gurl!" Dante is nothing if not encouraging.

I check to make sure all kids and counselors are settled safely and the craft is underway, then start a slow walk to where the man is crouched down and working with a wrench.

I have absolutely no idea why I choose this approach, but I whip around the water fountain in a sort of sneak attack, and shout, "HI!"

His body jerks as though I've startled him. Because clearly, I have.

I smile and wave. Even though he's right in front of me.

He turns and looks behind us as if he's unsure I'm actually speaking to him. I'm noticing this happens a lot when I greet people. Calliope told me once that I approach strangers with "unearned familiarity," and it freaks them out. Friendliness freaks people out? I'm not sure what to do with that information.

"Yes you, silly!" I say.

His full attention is trained on me, but he doesn't say a word. I'm starting to think the kids were right, and this guy actually doesn't speak.

"Hey you," I breathe.

Was that my voice I just heard? I don't say "hey you" in that shouty way people do when they're trying to get your attention outside the grocery store for leaving your cart abandoned in the lot instead of in the assigned cart area—not that I would ever shout at someone or leave a cart abandoned in a lot. No, the "hey you" I give him is that breathy sort. That shy, smiley sort. The kind of "hey you" people say when they know you so deeply and truly that they almost never say your actual name because they don't need to. Who else could they possibly be speaking to at that moment except... you. You. You. Wonderful, precious, irreplaceable *you*.

Not that I've ever been the recipient of such a "you."

"Did you need something?" he asks.

He speaks! Oh wow, he speaks!

His voice is... gruff. That's the only way to describe it. Is he annoyed? Nah, it's probably just his voice. I've heard of perpetual bitch face. Maybe he has a perpetual bitch *voice*? But he's a guy, so I guess to be accurate, it would be called a perpetual *bastard* voice?

"Before we begin, let it be known that I don't think you're a bastard. Or a bitch."

"Excuse me?"

"I was just thinking that you *sound* like a bastard, but I bet that's just the way your vocal cords operate. They're probably just prone to a gruff, bastardy tone."

"No. You had it right the first time. I *am* a bastard."

"Gotcha! So. How are you? Your name is 'The Wall'? I mean, they *call* you 'The Wall'? What is that short for? Walter? Walton? Wallmeranian?" I rattle off some suggestions.

"Wallace," he huffs.

"Gotcha. Big fan of Wallace and Grommit?" I ask.

"No."

"Gotcha. Can I call you Wally?"

"No."

"Gotcha. Hey, do you think I say gotcha too much?"

"Yes," he says definitively.

"Gotcha. Thanks for the feedback. I'll work on that. Hey, wanna hear something silly?"

"No."

"Cool, here I go. My kids... not my biological kids—though I do hope to have some of those one day, how about you? Sorry, don't answer that. That's an invasive question. See those teenagers over there who are completely unrelated to me?" I point in April and Dante's direction where they are decidedly *not* focused on their kids and are instead "hiding" behind a pavilion post watching my flailing interaction. I wave to them. "Hey, guys!" They ignore me and look off in random directions as if they're suddenly fascinated by all the glorious nature around them. "I'm training them as CITs this summer. That's right, I'm chief of staff this year! I mean head counselor. And well, the thing is, they're... well... they're afraid of you."

Silence.

He goes back to working on the fountain as if he's giving up on his conversation with me.

"Isn't that ridiculous?" I start giggling uncontrollably.

"Fine by me," he says.

"What's fine by you?"

"That they're afraid of me."

"Oh." I feel my head jerk back. "Really? But if they're afraid of you, they'll keep avoiding you and making up stories about you instead of taking the time to really get to know you."

"Perfect. Love that plan," he says and swipes some sweat off his brow.

"Oh."

I'm not sure how to respond to this man.

"Besides," he continues, "you're afraid of me too."

I scoff. "What? No! Why, uh, why, uh, why would you say that?"

"Weren't you the one I caught spying on me down by the

water yesterday, who then hauled ass up the hill the second I looked at you?"

"Nope. Not me. You must be mistaken."

Suddenly I'm a liar? Geez, maybe Calliope is right. Maybe I do need an intervention.

"Will that be all?" he asks on an exhale.

"Huh?"

"Are. We. Done. Here? Because…" He gestures to the fountain. "I'm finished with this and have work to do elsewhere."

He closes his toolbox and rises to stand at his full height.

I look up.

He towers over me now.

"Of course," I chirp. "You're busy. Sure. I just wanted to introduce myself—my name is Mabel, hi—and properly welcome you to Bucks County Arboretum and Nature Reserve."

"*You're* welcoming *me*?"

"Yes. Is that, um. Is that okay?"

"It is what it is, I suppose." He shakes his head.

What does that mean? I wonder.

Without another word, he turns his back—his very broad, muscular back—and walks away from me.

"Actually!"

He stops and turns his head only slightly.

I study his profile but have no idea what I'm going to say. I only know that I don't want him to walk away from me just yet.

"Do you, um… What are you…? Would you be interested in…?"

He huffs out a frustrated breath and starts walking again, and at that moment, I suddenly remember the commitment I made to myself and to my team last night.

"NOTHING TASTES AS GOOD AS FINANCIAL FREEDOM FEELS!"

That stops him in his tracks.

Gosh, isn't being a human being a fascinating experiment? I had no idea I was going to say that, yet… I did.

He turns to face me completely this time, a look on his face that keeps morphing. In the span of a few seconds, I see frustration, confusion, and maybe the hint of a smile?

Time to follow through. I am a girl who follows through. I wouldn't be standing here a fully-fledged, certified entomologist at only twenty-four years old if I weren't, right? I can apply that same diligence to this path I'm on with Bert and Doreen.

I reach into my fanny pack and pull out a flyer, which was folded neatly in thirds, prepared for an occasion just like this one right here.

"Wally—"

"Don't call me Wally."

"Wally, are you interested in learning about the opportunity of a lifetime?"

"No."

"This is a moment when you can get in on the ground floor of an exciting new adventure. One where you can build relationships with like-minded entrepreneurs looking to build multiple streams of residual income for years to come. Where you can join forces with a team offering cutting-edge products and—"

"I'm going to stop you right there."

"Okay?"

"You're inviting me to be a part of a pyramid scheme."

"No! No way! This is the furthest thing from a—"

"Is that a flyer for 'the business'?"

"Did you just use air quotes around 'the business'? I assure you, no air quotes are necessary, sir.

It is a completely legitimate and wildly successful business."

"Let me see the flyer." He reaches his large hand in my direction.

I look down, and I'm still grasping the tri-fold. I was shaking it like a baton to emphasize my points and didn't even realize it. I hand it over.

While he scans the flyer, I attempt to continue my spiel. "As you'll see, we're having a vitamin cocktail party this Monday night. I'd love it if you wanted to attend."

"Tell me something. The people who brought you into this 'business'—"

"No air quotes necessary," I remind him sweetly.

"What do you call them, your downline?"

"Upline, actually," I say with pride as I point upward.

"Right. Your upline. And when your upline brings new people on board, and the team spreads down, what shape is created?"

He's tracing the shape in the air

"A triangle."

"Right. *Or...* a pyramid."

I try to argue. "A triangle is not the same thing as a—"

"It's a pyramid. Don't fool yourself."

He says this as he shoves the pamphlet back in my direction. Like the conversation is closed. But this conversation is not closed. At least not for me.

"I need a man!" I blurt.

He hesitates for half a second before saying, "I assumed you had one."

"Oh. Really? Why?"

"Well, either an iceberg crapped on your ring finger, or you have yourself a man."

He's staring down at my hand, and I have the strangest impulse to hide it in my fanny pack.

"Just out of curiosity... is this crapping iceberg phrase a common one I should be expecting to hear from more people?" I ask. "And hey, why wouldn't you assume I had a-a-a-a woman?"

"Because women tend to have more taste than whoever bought you that monstrosity," he says. "No, that there on your finger is definitely the work of some man-shmuck attempting to compensate for the areas where he is sorely lacking, which I'm guessing are varied and many."

"You know something?" I say, feeling the pitch in my voice rising.

"What's that?" he asks, all brawn and bluster.

"I'm starting to think you're not a very nice person."

"Then you're starting to think correctly."

"And just so we're clear, I didn't mean I need a man for... *me* and my, um... personal needs. I assure you, those are well met."

"Glad to hear it, though I can't say I believe you."

I choose to ignore that completely unwarranted slight and continue.

"What I meant was that my team needs male members."

"Oh, yeah?" he asks. "You need my male... member?"

"That's right," I respond.

Oh gosh, is he being suggestive? Or is this me being a dirtball like Calliope said? This guy has such a poker face, and I have no idea how to read him.

I decide to forge onward with my pitch.

"We focus mainly on health and wellness supplements, and we are beyond thrilled to announce that our new MANicure line specifically for men is launching this fall and—"

"Hold up," he interrupts. "Your man-specific product line is called MANicure?"

"Yes?"

He shakes his head. "Carry on."

"And we need all hands on deck to blast our customers' testosterone into the next time zone!"

"Oof. That is god-awful ad copy. Who wrote that?" he asks with disdain.

"I don't know what you're talking about. I'm speaking from the heart."

"Sure, you are. You know what? Uh... what was your...?"

Is he searching for my name? I place a hand on my chest as I often do when I'm introducing myself.

"Mabel again."

"Your name is Mabel Again?" He chuckles.

"Mabel McGonigle actually. I was just repeating it for you *again* since—"

"I'll be there, Mabel Again."

"You... wait. You will?"

"Sure. I'll be your... MANicure."

"Wow!" I let out a huge sigh of relief. "Thank you! Ohmygosh! Really, this is huge! Thank you. Seriously! So grateful! So happy! So—"

"Alright, don't burst a blood vessel, lady." He takes another look at the flyer, and an odd look comes over his face when he squints closer at it. He stuffs it in his back pocket and says definitively, "See you there. This has been... how shall I say?" He pauses and considers. "It was... *interesting* meeting you."

"Likewise, Wally."

He breathes in sharply as though he's about to protest my use of Wally but then decides to allow it.

I thrust my hand in his direction for a friendly, albeit belated handshake. The one I should have offered him the moment I approached, but I got distracted from my usual good manners somehow. He stares at my hand without touching it. Just as I'm about to pull my arm back to my side, unshaken and embarrassed, he suprises me by reaching out and taking both of my hands in his. His right thumb starts tracing a line across my knuckles, and let me tell you, I feel it... everywhere. It's like the energy from his body pulses directly into mine, spiraling through my arms, skating up my neck, tingling my hairline, then plunging down my chest, all the way to the tips of my toes.

I stumble on my feet even though neither of us moved. Since he's still holding both of my hands, he steadies me. He bends his knees and tips his head down so he can look me in the eyes.

"You okay, Mabel?"

"Yeah," I say, a bit dazed. "Yes. I'm... you remembered my name."

"Well. You told it to me less than a minute ago. So."

"That doesn't usually matter. People usually find me pretty..."

"Pretty what?" His brow furrows slightly.

"Forgettable," I say on a sigh.

"Mabel, I find that incredibly hard to believe."

Wow, those are some icy blue eyes. Like the color of a robin's egg? No. More like the way the sky looks in the spring right after all the rain stops and that delicious sixty-five-degree breeze starts blowing. Yeah, like that. He shakes a few strands of his sandy-colored hair off his forehead without taking his eyes off mine. I find myself mirroring his action, and with a subtle shake of my own head, I come back to myself. He gives my hands one more squeeze, then releases them and walks down the hill.

I watch him until he's out of sight.

I stumble back to the pavilion a flustered mess, but I try my best to appear unfazed.

"How'd it go?" Dante asks as he grabs a few more pieces of paper for his group.

"Great! Fine! He's lovely. No need to fear him in the future," I say and shoo Dante away.

I realize I'm completely parched, so I reach for my refillable water bottle sitting next to the art supplies and start chugging. After I've had my fill, I splash the remaining water all over my face in hopes that I can cool down.

I need to get it together.

"I'm on to you, girl." April sidles up to me with a smirk.

"What's that, April?" I ask, all faux innocence.

"You like the bad boys!" she says in a hushed voice. "I never would have guessed."

"Um. Why would you...?"

"I may only be sixteen, but I can spot a smurfnurblin when I see one."

"A *what*?"

"The Wall read you one chapter of clitorature, and now you want to flog his epilogue."

"April, I have absolutely no idea what you're saying."

"You're hornified!" she practically cheers. "You've sprouted a herection! Yep, our girl Mabel here has come down with a serious case of claustrobonia—"

"I got it, I got it, I got it," I say under my breath. Seriously, why does this child behave this way? "For the record, you're incorrect and also *way* too young for a... discussion of this nature, April. But..." I sigh. "I got it."

"Yeahhhhh, you do. You got it," April says with a smile, then shoots me with a series of fancy finger guns before heading back to her group.

Welp, nothing like some good old-fashioned social humiliation to get the camp season started off right.

Chapter Six

"So. Week one is under your belt. How would you say it went?" my dad asks Saturday night.

"Good," I say between sips of lemon water.

"Just good?" His eyebrows go up.

Good has never been good enough when it comes to my father, so I course correct.

"Great, actually! Yeah, I feel like I'm really getting the hang of being the head counselor."

"Excellent. Staff showing you the respect you deserve then?" He doesn't take his eyes off the newspaper the whole time he's speaking to me. My dad is one of those guys who loves having a physical newspaper in his hands. Not a fan of getting his new from the "interwebs."

"Ohhhh, yeah. Totally."

If respect means teasing me, running away from me, and commenting provocatively on my perceived state of arousal with the new groundskeeper, then yeah, Dad. Totally.

The three days following my epic failed introduction with The Wall and embarrassing interaction with April got only minimally better. I steered clear of the weird, fascinating fella and did my best to engage on the most professional levels with my staff, but I still can't help feeling out of sorts in my new role at the arboretum.

"Good. As they should. I'm so proud my baby is the big boss lady this year."

"Thanks," I say. "But technically, Carol is the boss lady. I'm more of the... manager lady, I suppose. "

"Well, regardless. Oh, that reminds me... I'm incensed!" His chest puffs up, and his nostrils flare. He actually puts down the newspaper this time, so it must be serious.

"What about, Dad?" I brace myself and exhale. My father is always incensed about something.

"The word is regardless, correct?" he asks.

"Ummmm. I don't know. I'm not sure what you're..."

"It is. The word is regardless. Yet today, I learn that the *Meriam-Webster Dictionary* now recognizes *irregardless* as an official word." He clears his throat, a sure sign he's about to launch into full speech-mode. "Just because people have been bastardizing a word for years, must we adapt to their ignorance? Lower our standards to meet the masses? Give credence to carelessness?" He shoves a forkful of Salisbury steak into his mouth. "I mean, what is this world I find myself living in? In my sixty-eight years of life, I've never seen such *dis*regard for common sense and decency as I do today. Irregardless." He scoffs. "Ridiculous."

Rarely does a dinner go by that Mom and I aren't treated to a Dad diatribe. It's easiest for us to just smile and nod. See, he's one of those guys whose opinions are treated as facts. In his own mind, that is. And in our home.

That's right. I'm twenty-four-years old, and I still live at home.

I can't pinpoint exactly why that is. I'm not rich by any means, but with my work at the museum and arboretum, I could definitely afford the rent on a small one-bedroom nearby. Maybe not in Philadelphia proper but certainly "right outside of the city" in the suburbs.

But something keeps me here.

"Wait. Dad. Did you say you are sixty-eight?"

He pauses a moment and flashes an odd look at my mother.

"No," he huffs. "I said I was fifty-eight."

"I'm pretty sure you said you were sixty-eight."

"Will you pass the limas, lovebug?" Mom asks, her arms outstretched.

"Sure." I pass Mom the old-school orange Pyrex bowl full of

my favorite legumes. "Hey, Mom. Why do you always call me lovebug?"

"What kind of a question is that? I call you lovebug because you're such a love, and you've always been bananas for bugs."

"Sure, I get that," I say. "But just in case you weren't aware, lovebugs aren't actually the most beloved insect out there."

"Are any insects beloved?" Dad scoffs.

"Sure!" I pipe up. "Ladybugs, butterflies, fireflies... People go crazy for them. Lovebugs, though? Not so much. They are arguably more hated than the mosquito and considered menaces to society. Most people find them so annoying they think their name should be changed from lovebugs to hatebugs."

"Well, that's silly," Mom says.

"I'm serious, though. There's an actual petition going around on social media right now about that very thing."

Dad snorts. "People need to get a life."

"Well, obviously, *I* don't hate them. I find them fascinating. Get this. Lovebugs mate for hours—"

Another snort from Dad. "Then lovebugs also need to get a life!"

"Oh, that's hogwash, Mabel. No one can mate for hours!" Mom adds with full confidence.

I don't want to embarrass her or my dad by correcting her on that point. I mean, I can't truthfully say I have firsthand experience with that kind of extended... romantic athleticism. But if Calliope is to be believed about the antics she and Ralph have been up to in Mexico? Then it's totally possible.

"Well, *regardless*..." I sneak a peek at my dad.

"Thank you for that." He nods his approval.

"The male dies immediately after inseminating the female, at which point she stays connected to his carcass and drags his body along with her until she's ready to lay her eggs. Wow, huh?"

"Mabel, do you mind?" Dad exhales. "We're trying to eat."

"Don't worry, I'm almost done. *Then* the female lays her eggs on decomposing material found on the ground and dies immediately afterward as well!"

"Sweetheart, are you alright?" Mom asks. "I've never heard

you speak so negatively about a bug before."

"But that's just it! Nothing about what I'm saying is negative. Bugs operate from this fascinating world of instinct. Sure, it looks different than how we operate, but they have their own power. Their own beauty. We're so dismissive of them when we automatically label them as gross or pests. We just haven't taken the time to understand them."

Mom smiles. "This is one of the reasons you're so special, baby. You always see the beautiful. Even in the ugly."

"That's kind of the point I'm trying to make, though. I don't think it is ugly. I don't think anyone is ugly. No person. No bug. No... being."

It's quiet for a moment as we finish our meal.

It feels good to talk about my work in this way, so I continue. "I also find it amazing that the female of the species is almost always the dominant one. The one who takes charge. She's the one who makes things happen."

"Well, I'd venture to say in that regard they're not all that different from human females, no?"

The look on Dad's face says he's not sure how to take Mom's comment, but rather than arguing the point, he stabs his last scalloped potato and stays surprisingly silent.

"Right," I respond. "I think the big difference, though, is that they don't feel guilty about it. They do what they need to do and don't think twice about it. I say or do things and then regret them almost immediately afterward. I'd love to have that kind of confidence. To unabashedly operate from my instincts. Sometimes I feel like my life is one big apology."

"Now what the hell kind of thing is that to say, Mabel?" My dad has a little outburst and slams his fork down.

"Abe, let her talk," my mom says in a soothing tone. "She's expressing something important to her, so we should listen."

"Her life is 'one big apology'? What kind of bullshit statement is that? Where is this coming from?" He gets to his feet. "From the very beginning, we've given her everything we can to make her a confident kid and—"

"Abe, please." Mom tries to reason with him. "Sit down,

sweetheart. There's no reason to be defensive—"

"Hey!" I cut through the argument rising between them with a solid amount of cheer in my tone. "Remember that time we visited Aunt Tina in Tampa? When I was around nine?"

Silence.

"And when we came out of Lettuce Lake Park, there were lovebugs all over the windshield of our rental car?"

"No. I, uh, I don't remember that." Mom immediately starts clearing the table and fiddling with dishes in the sink.

"Sure you do! Dad. Remember, you and Aunt Tina had some kind of intense talk on the walk back, and when we got into the car, we saw that—"

"I'm going to go read the paper."

He pushes his chair in so hard the table shifts a few inches across the linoleum. Then he shuffles out of the room, leaving Mom and me to the cleanup duties. We have one of those "traditional" families—if you can call it that—where Dad has always been the one to go out and make the money, while my mom stayed home with me and took care of all the domestic activities of running the house and family. I don't judge it. Clearly, the arrangement works for them. I do know, though, that I want something different for my own life.

My mom washes. I dry. It's been our nightly routine for as long as I can remember. We both know our roles. No discussion necessary.

"You looking forward to your trip?" I ask quietly after a few moments of swirling squeaky circles on a floral plate.

She sighs. "It should be nice. I just really wish you were coming with us, sweetheart. You love the mountains. And I'm worried about leaving you home alone for a whole month."

"A girl's gotta work. And Mom, I'm twenty-four years old. I'll be fine. I'm always fine."

"I know that. I just... we'll miss you."

"Well, I'm glad you're following the doctor's orders to make him rest," I say. "I think it'll be good for both of you to get away and get some fresh air. I was thinking I should write his boss a thank-you note. Yeah, I'll do that and send it out in the morning.

It's really generous of him to offer you his mountain house."

"It's the least he can do after working the man like a dog," Mom says in a rare show of almost-anger. "He's the reason things happened the way they did."

I want to say, "No, Mom, he's not the reason 'things happened the way they did.' Dad is the reason 'things happened the way they did.'" The man has been wound tighter than a drum for well over a decade. It was only a matter of time before something burst in him.

But what I want to say to people and what actually comes out of my mouth are often worlds apart.

"Is he okay?" is all that comes out.

"Of course. Your father is always okay," she says, her eyes glued to the dishes. "He's just a bit of a curmudgeon. You know that."

"I know, but he just seems especially rattled tonight. And what was that slip saying he's sixty-eight instead of fifty-eight? That's not the first time he's done that, you know. Maybe there's some cognitive type thing going on he should get checked out?"

"Nonsense. He's fine. Fifty-eight and fit as a fiddle."

"Mom." I try to get her to look me directly in the eyes. No luck. She seems so squirrely tonight. "Mom," I say a bit louder this time but not a yell. McGonigles don't yell.

"What, Mabel, what?" She sounds exasperated as she finally turns to face me.

"You don't have a heart attack in the middle of the Willow Grove Mall if you are 'fit as a fiddle.'"

"It wasn't an attack," she says. It was—"

"An incident," I correct. "Right. A heart... 'incident.'"

"That's right." She exhales, then immediately returns her focus to the sink.

I listen to the sounds of the warm water and the squeaky plates for a few moments, considering what I could possibly say next. Then my phone rings from the charger on the counter, startling us both, my "Walking on Sunshine" ringtone blaring through the kitchen. "Oh, I'm sorry. I should keep this thing on silent." I rush to it, check the number, and immediately decline the call.

"You can take the call, sweetheart. Don't mind me."

"No, it's okay." I wave her off. "I'll call them back later." What I don't tell her is that it was an unknown caller, the same one that has already tried to contact me several times this week. A call I've ignored each time. I have a sneaking suspicion it's my student loans company. I missed my last two payments—not like me at all. But since my dad's been off work, I've been helping out more with the bills, and my bank account is starting to feel it. I can't wait until this business with Doreen and Bert starts to pay off. I could really use that extra money.

I get back into the dishwashing flow with Mom. After a few quiet moments, she says, "He doesn't like speaking about your aunt Tina. So when she comes up in conversation, he gets... Well. You know how he gets."

"Why doesn't he just call her? Say he's sorry?" I ask.

"Why do you assume he's the one who needs to apologize?"

"I don't know. She just always seemed so cool. I imagined whatever went down between them that day had to do with his hot temper and inability to admit when he's wrong."

"Mabel, the issues between them went far beyond just that day."

"Okay...?"

I wait for an explanation. It doesn't come, so I continue.

"Is anyone ever going to explain to me what those issues were?"

More silence.

I push a little further.

"When I was nine, the story was 'you're too young to understand adult problems.' Well, I'm not sure if you've noticed, but I'm twenty-four now, so I'm pretty sure I'm at a point where I can comprehend whatever went down between them."

"What does it matter, Mabel?"

"I dunno. I loved her. She seemed to love me. That was the last time we ever saw her. We're not exactly overflowing in extended family and friends. So if you ask me—though clearly *no one* is asking me—we're really not in a place to be cutting people out of our lives."

I guess she has no response to that.

"Don't you think it would be nice to widen our circle a bit beyond just the three of us?" I ask, not altogether certain she's even listening to me anymore.

"Your father is a wonderful man," she finally says.

"Agreed." I shrug. "Never said he wasn't."

"He does what he feels is best for his family. Let's leave it at that."

And thus concludes yet another illuminating conversation with my parents.

"Didn't you say you were going out tonight?" She changes the subject. Mom's a champ at that.

"Yup, heading out for some drinks."

"With Bert?" She brightens.

"With Calliope actually. She's in town for her niece and nephew's first birthday party. Cyndi's coming too. And Calliope's new boyfriend's sister."

"That's nice! Bert joining you there then?"

"No. Bert has a networking event in Paoli tonight." I try not to sound disappointed.

"He has an event most Saturday nights, it seems."

"Yeah, he's super committed to The Business with Doreen, so..."

"Well, that's wonderful," Mom says with a definitive nod. "You want a hardworking man. That's very important. You know, if I haven't said it enough? Your father and I are really pleased to see you two so happy together and taking the next steps. My girl deserves the very best."

"Thanks, Mom."

Am I happy, though?

"Hey, Mom?"

"Yes, baby."

"Would you say we're close?"

"Of course, I would. Wouldn't you?"

"I guess so?"

"You guess so? What does that mean?"

"Nothing. Just—one of the teens I am working with at the arboretum? Naomi Thornton's daughter actually. Seems that she and her mom talk about, um... intimacy."

"Well, that's incredibly inappropriate." She gasps.

"*Is* it?"

"Absolutely!" My mother chortles.

"I dunno, for a minute I thought the same thing, but then I found myself wondering... Aren't mothers supposed to discuss these sorts of things with their teenage daughters? So they know what to expect and how to manage... certain situations? We never did that. You always seemed super uncomfortable around that topic."

"Which topic?" She seems to hold her breath as she asks.

"Sex," I say.

"Oh, dear god!" My mother's body jolts as if she's been tasered... "Oh ho ho ho, hahahahaha." Then she proceeds to giggle like a schoolgirl.

"Mom. I'm serious. I think if I'd had someone to talk to about it when I was younger, I might be less ... closed off now with guys."

"Are you...closed off with guys?"

"Kind of, yeah."

"So I've failed you. That's what you're saying." Here come her defenses. Here comes the guilt.

"No, Mom, you haven't failed me. I just—"

"No, I've failed you! I took away your beloved aunt, and I've offered you no maternal guidance whatsoever in the world of sexuality and womanhood. So let's remedy at least one of those situations right now. Let's talk about sex." She puts down the plate and rubs her palms together in anticipation. "Alright! Mother and daughter sex time. How is Bert's penis?"

"Excuse me?" I choke.

What on earth have I unleashed?

"Come on!" Mom rallies. "Let's share! I'm very open to sharing with you."

"Okay, well maybe we can ease our way in, or—"

"Nope! No easing," she says. "Seems we've already wasted too much time not bonding as deeply as we could have been. So tell me, do you enjoy what Bert does to you with his penis?"

"I am not telling you about that!" I sputter.

"Alright then, shall we talk about your father's penis? Because we can talk about your father's penis."

"What?! No! Mom! Geez, what are you—?"

"Well, I'm sorry, Mabel, but I'm just not sure what you were hoping for by bringing all of this up tonight."

"Me neither, but I certainly wasn't anticipating a dissertation about Dad's penis, for chrissakes!"

"Alright, now," Mom admonishes as if *I* am the one crossing a line. "Don't take the Lord's name in vain."

"The Lord? Since when do we speak about the Lord in our house?"

"We don't!" She's starting to get a bit shrill, not my mom's style at all. "I'm just... You're making me feel very put on the spot and turned around right now with all of this."

I sigh and place my head in my hands. I take a moment to regroup, then place my hand gently on her upper back.

"I'm sorry, Mom. I don't mean to upset you. A sixteen-year-old-kid called me a smurfnurblin today, and I guess... I dunno, I guess it's thrown me."

"What in the world is a smurfnurblin?"

"I have no idea!" I nearly shout. I think of all the times I've felt left out of conversations with my peers regarding sex and dating and general romantic goings-on between consenting adults. Too many to count. "It seems there are a lot of things I don't know. Sometimes... I guess... I dunno, occasionally I feel really... sheltered."

Mom looks at me then. Like really looks at me. She opens her mouth and closes it several times, but nothing comes out. After a few moments of this, she seems to give up on whatever she wanted to say and switches gears.

"Go on, get out of here. I can take it from here." She smiles weakly.

"Yeah?" I ask.

"Mm-hmm," she says.

"You're sure?"

She's already taking the dish towel and plate from my hand.

"Absolutely. Have fun, baby. Tell the girls I say hi. And I'll, uh... I'll see you in the morning. Your father and I are leaving around ten. You'll see us off?"

"Of course. Thanks, Mom."

I give her a quick kiss on the cheek and start gathering my things. When I turn back to her, she's already elbow deep in soapy water again.

Is it possible I hear her sniffle?

"Hey, Mom?"

"What is it, lovebug? Or, um... what's that, sweetheart?" She doesn't turn to face me.

"You know how much I love you, right?" I say slowly and with no small amount of guilt. "And that I think you're the best?"

"Of course baby. I love you too." She still won't look at me. "Go on now. Have fun."

"Okay."

I head through the living room toward the front door. As soon as I enter, I hear the telltale snoring sounds of my sleeping father. He's reclining in his scratchy plaid chair, feet kicked up on his leather ottoman, jaw wide open. He looks almost... innocent when he sleeps. Gentle. Nonjudgmental. Easy to understand.

I wish it could be that way when he was awake.

You know how you have some moments in life you can mark as "before" and "after"? That day in Lettuce Lake Park is one of those for me. Before that day, I had a fun dad. A dad who was playful and free and full of life. After that day? He got... tight. Hard. Afraid? He turned into one of those strict dads who didn't let me go to sleepovers or school dances or... anything really. It was like something shut down in him.

When I got back in the car that afternoon, nine-year-old me was the one who spotted the lovebugs all over our windshield first. They were everywhere. Connected in pairs. I had just started seriously studying bugs, so I didn't know too much about the species yet, but I did know that they were mating. That the heat, vibrations, and exhaust from car engines increased their... attraction. I also knew they weren't doing anything wrong.

"Oh, what the hell is this?" Dad groused. "Disgusting little pieces of—"

"Daddy, I can get them off the car for us. Just gimme a second, and I'll pluck them off safely. It'll just take a minute." I made a move to open my back seat door.

My father spoke harshly to me for the first time that day.

"Mabel? Sit down, shut your mouth, and put on your seat belt! We're going home."

Then he flicked on the windshield wipers.

It was a lovebug bloodbath.

Chapter Seven

"A few days ago, when Ralph and I were having sex inside a laundromat, I thought to myself—"

"Excuse me for interrupting, Calliope, but what?" I gasp and almost spit out my whiskey sour. "You were... doing it... inside a laundromat?"

"Yeah," Calliope says as if this should be an everyday occurrence in a woman's life.

I'm sitting with Cyndi, Calliope, and Louise at Adventure Bar, this great place in Doylestown where you can get specialty cocktails like the Skydiver or the Spelunker. We had our butts in the seats no longer than five minutes before Calliope launched into the epic tales of her sexcapades with her new boyfriend.

"A laundromat," I repeat. "How were you...? Why were you...? But didn't you...?" I sputter.

"Excellent questions, young Mabel."

"Um. I'm actually older than you," I challenge.

"In years, yeah," Calliope says. "But not in experience."

"Okaaaaay..." I respond, feeling a tiny bit offended.

She's not wrong, though.

Calliope continues. "I suppose when your first time together involves a psychedelic-mushroom-inspired reverse cowgirl inside a museum while prehistoric skeletal beasts look on, you're sorrrrrt of opening the door for further sexual adventures. Hence, the laundromat. But let's be real: what else are you supposed to do while you wait for the spin cycle to stop?"

"What, um, what kind of adventures?" I ask. I'm leaning forward on my barstool and sipping my sour like an eager elementary student. Not that elementary students hang out on barstools sipping whiskey sours, but you know what I mean.

"Well, we've become..." Calliope continues. "I guess you would say... a bit exhibitionistic? Sorry, Lou, is this an uncomfortable topic for you?" She turns to the girl sitting next to me, who is starting to look a little nauseous.

"Nooooo," Louise says with a light laugh. "Course not. I love hearing about the many and highly specific details of my brother's sexual prowess."

"Okay, cool. But I do want to be respectful of the potential weirdness this may cause for you. So this is me giving you an out. You should probably take it," Calliope warns her.

"Please don't take the out?" I beg Louise. "I'm really eager to—I just have so much to learn about—"

I stop myself midthought.

The whiskey must be getting to me.

Dial down the need, Mabel. Be cool.

I clear my throat. "I would, uh, I would just really like for Calliope to continue what she's saying. And by the way, my apologies for not being the designated driver tonight. Jiminy is in the shop, or else I would have been happy to."

"Nonsense," Calliope says. "You need to let loose tonight. Besides, that's what ride-share services are for."

"Sorry, who's Jiminy?" Louise asks.

Cyndi perks up. "Mabel's car. It's an old-school green VW bug. Fitting for our entomologist friend, huh?"

"Yeah, yeah." I try to move the conversation along. "Jiminy is amazing, and I love him dearly. Back to what Calliope was saying about screwing Louise's brother."

"Ooh lala," Calliope sings. "If this is you after one sour, I'm excited to see you at the end of the night!"

She turns to Louise for permission to continue.

"Fine," Lou sighs. "I'll just... exit my body for the next few minutes and pretend you're talking about somebody else."

Cyndi claps and squeals. "Yay! I love sex stories!"

"You do?" I ask her. "How come *we* never share sex stories?"

"Oh," Cyndi says, sounding surprised. "I didn't think you *had* any sex stories."

"Hey!" I object.

"No, I mean, I'm sure you do," Cyndi backpedals. "I just meant I didn't realize sex was something you were comfortable talking about."

"I'M TOTALLY COMFORTABLE TALKING ABOUT IT! I'M THE MOST COMFORTABLE PERSON I KNOW WHEN I'M TALKING ABOUT IT!"

And... apparently, I'm screaming. And making very little sense.

All three of my friends stare at me in stunned silence.

BANG BANG!

"Enough about me, this meeting is now called to order!" Calliope exclaims after pummeling a gavel on the tabletop.

"Whoa, you brought props?" Louise marvels.

"Intervention props, yeah. Only the best for my Mabel-Shmaybel-She-Can-Drink-You-Under-The-Table."

"Um. She's not really much of a drinker, actually," Cyndi says. As my oldest friend, I get the impression Cyndi feels a little put off by how close Calliope and I are becoming. "And I don't think a gavel is necessary for an intervention."

"I know," Calliope admits. "But I saw it at The Ninety-Nine Cent Store, and I couldn't resist. And, while I'm not usually one to condone drinking in excess, I think in this case, Mabel could use a little encouragement to loosen up. Hey, James?" She flags down our bartender. "Can we have another round, please?"

He gives her a small salute and starts pouring us more drinks. If I'm not mistaken, his eyes linger a bit longer on Louise than on the rest of us. Her eyes flutter up to his, then immediately back to her drink. No one else seems to notice this, so I stay on topic.

"Why do I even need an intervention?" I whine. "I'm fine."

"You are not fine," Calliope asserts.

"But I am, I—"

"Let me begin by listing all the reasons I know you are not fine." Calliope raises her voice to an uncomfortable level.

"Oh my gosh," I say, looking around at the crowded bar. "Is that really necess—"

"Reason one! You just got engaged to a guy none of us have met, and you never talk about."

Cyndi interjects. "I've met him. Many times. Many, *many* times."

"And?" Calliope asks. "Verdict?"

"Eh" is Cyndi's succinct response.

"Eh?!" I parrot back at her. "You're summing up your feelings on the love of my life with... 'eh'?"

"The love of your life, Mabel?" Cyndi practically snorts. "Just because he's the only person you've loved in your life so far—and I use the word love here with a hefty amount of reservation—doesn't mean he's the love *of* your life." Her voice softens. "You can do better. I've always thought that. I always will."

"Objection!" Louise gets her voice into the mix.

Geez, they're really embracing the courtroom premise, huh?

"Yes, Ms. Anderson," Calliope calls on her.

"Thank you, Ms. FitzGerald. I realize I'm new to this particular group, but isn't it important—in a girl code sort of way—that we support our friend's choice of a mate?"

"That depends," Cyndi jumps in.

"On what?" Lou asks.

"On whether or not you're mating with a douche."

"Cyndi!" I scold. "Don't refer to a human being as a vaginal cleansing spray."

"Sometimes it's the only fitting descriptor." Cyndi shrugs.

"I *know* we're not denigrating the vagina and using it as an insult, right?" Louise says in a warning tone.

"Course not, Lou," Calliope assures her, then continues the conversation between sips of her drink. "'Douche,' I can handle. Can we not say 'mate,' though? 'Mate' sounds all sorts of Animal Planet. Also, doesn't it imply procreation? Correct me if I'm wrong, but I don't think any of us is ready for procreation."

"*Does* it imply that, though?" Cyndi questions.

"Yeah," Calliope says. "When an animal is mating, it's for the sole purpose of making animal babies."

"Hm. Yeah. I guess there is some truth to that," Cyndi agrees.

"Dolphins do both, though," Louise offers. "They fornicate for procreation *and* pleasure."

"Fornicate, wow!" Calliope chuckles. "I didn't expect such a biblical term from you, Lou."

"Bleh, fornicate." Cyndi faux retches. "What a disgusting word for such a delicious activity."

"Well, I'm sorry." Louise throws her hands up. "You guys took 'mate' off the table, so I had to get creative with my words."

"Louise is a marine biologist," I explain to Cyndi. "Hence the dolphin knowledge."

"*Almost* a marine biologist," Louise corrects as she sips her 7 and 7. "I'm finishing up a final internship for my bachelor's now, then onto grad school at UPenn, which I'll start while simultaneously working a job as an animal specialist at Philly Aquarium this fall. Two solid years of that, some more work in the field, and *then* I can call myself a marine biologist."

"Ef that," Calliope scoffs. "You can call yourself a marine biologist right now! I call myself a paleontologist, and I still have a ways to go too."

"So I'm the only nonscientist at this table, huh?" Cyndi says.

"Yup!" I say proudly. It feels good to finally have a solid group of girlfriends, especially ones who understand why I do what I do. These are girls who aren't afraid to get messy, to literally "play in the dirt" digging for dinosaur bones or dive into murky waters to study a blobfish. These women are passionate about science. They would never give me that scrunched-up "ew" face so many people give me when they learn that an entomologist studies bugs, not words. For the record, an etymologist studies words. An *ento*mologist studies bugs. It's shocking how many people get that wrong.

"Hey, Lou—curious—how do you know they fornicate for pleasure?" Calliope asks.

"Dolphins?"

"Yeah."

Louise launches into her explanation with gusto. I totally get it. I'm the same way when I talk about bugs.

"Well, there was this really amazing study done recently on dolphin clitorises. See, up until this point, the majority of dolphin sexuality studies have been done on dolphin *penises*, mostly because—

"Because the world of science revolves around the penis," Calliope says with no small amount of snark.

"True," Louise says. "But... we're working on changing that, right ladies?" She looks at Calliope and me.

"Totally," I say after a moment's hesitation, a bit nervous about chiming in for fear the topic will return to me and my issues. I'm enjoying the dolphin diversion at the moment.

"Anyway," Louise continues, "much like in human female anatomy, dolphin clitorises have erectile tissue, blood vessels, and nerve bundles that all point toward the fact that sex serves more purposes for dolphins than just the procreative ones."

"How about sex purposes for porpoises?" I joke. "Try saying that three times fast! Purposes for porpoises, purposes for porpoises, purposes for porpoises."

"Actually, Mabel," Louise says, "it's a common misconception, but dolphins and porpoises aren't the same thing. They're completely different animals."

Clearly, Louise is not fully acclimated to my sense of humor yet. This is no surprise to me. I've been told I'm an acquired taste. Mostly by Bert. Which now that I think of it, is not the nicest thing to say, is it?

"When the male..." Lou searches for the word. "Lover? Is 'lover' a better term than 'mate'?"

"Ugh! Lover?" Cyndi makes a face.

"Yeah, no." Calliope agrees. "I've always hated the word lover. Whenever someone says 'Oh, let me introduce you to my lover—'"

"Who the hell says that?" Cyndi asks.

"You know... people." Calliope shrugs. "Anyway, whenever someone says 'let me introduce you to my lover,' I always want to be like 'why don't we just call him what he really is: your sexer.'"

"Your SEXER?!" I ask.

"Yeah. Think about it. That's what they mean. They're not commenting on the deep respect and affection between them.

They're merely saying that that's the person they go to when it's time to do the sex-ing. Okay, we've gotten off topic." She takes a deep sip from her margarita. "Back to fixing Mabel."

"I don't need to be fixed. I am perfectly—"

"Reason two I know you are not fine! The other day you snapped at me on the phone."

"Whoa. Mabel's not a snapper!" Cyndi seems shocked.

"Believe me, I know! But she snapped like a sonofabitch. She was all like, 'I have depth Calliope, despite what you or others may think!' What was that all about? Mabes, we know you have depth."

"Do you, though?" I ask.

"Sure, but it's not our fault that you hide it from us."

"Hide it from you? How do I hide it from you?"

"You don't go below the surface with us," Calliope explains. "Which leads me to believe you don't go below the surface with anyone."

"It's true. She doesn't."

"Cyndi!" I scold.

"I'm sorry, but you don't." She shrugs. "I'm your oldest friend, and I can count on one hand the number of times you've confided in me about your feelings. Other than your general state of happiness, which you constantly spread like sunshine."

"And what is wrong with that?" I ask. "Isn't that what we're all supposed to aspire to? Happiness? I'm already there. I'm happy! Sue me!"

"No one is happy all the time," Lou says.

"I know that. Of course I know that. I just... choose to focus on the positive. If that makes me fake or-or-or a bad friend or something, then whatever!"

"You're not a bad friend, Mabes," Cyndi says. "You're an amazing friend. Always there for everyone else. As your friends, though, it would be nice if you'd allow us to be there for you sometimes."

It's silent for a moment as all three of them stare at me.

I'm not comfortable with this kind of attention.

"You know what? I'm not really enjoying this... intervention. I think I'm gonna go."

I start packing up my things.

"Mabel, no!" Calliope cries. "I'm only here for tonight. All day tomorrow, I'll be celebrating the niece and nephew. I'm not sure when I'll be able to visit next."

"So why are we wasting our time doing this?" I say, Calliope completely proving my point. "Why can't we just have fun? I mean, I have to say, I'm finding it a little upsetting that instead of my friends celebrating my engagement with me tonight, they're grilling me and judging me instead."

"No one's grilling you, Mabel. We just want to make sure you're happy and—"

"Well, I *was* until all this started!" I exclaim.

"Guys, can I offer some perspective?" Louise interjects. "Oh wait, we're supposed to make an effort not to address groups of women as 'guys' anymore, right? Gosh, hard habit to break. Because what's the alternative? Ladies? Friends? Humans?"

"We can wrestle with the repercussions of engaging in gendered greetings later," Calliope says. "For now, let's keep Mabel from fleeing, yeah? What perspective were you offering, Lou?"

"Oh. Yes. Okay. From my own experience with interventions, particularly those where you want someone to see the light about a less-than-ideal relationship they are in?"

"Yeah?"

"The harder you push, the harder they hold on. Mabel's a big girl. She can make her own decisions."

"Thank you, Lou," I say.

"You're welcome."

"Now, can we relax on the third degree and just have fun? Please?"

Calliope looks at me with intensity as she considers. "Yes, Mabel. Yes, we can."

I exhale. "Thank you. James? Another round, please!"

Chapter Eight

"That's actually a misconception," I explain. "She doesn't always decapitate him after they mate."

"Oh, good." Calliope exhales, relieved.

"Yeah, sometimes she decapitates him *before* they mate."

We're a few hours into our girls' night, and true to their word, my friends have ditched the intervention, and we're just having fun. We've shifted into the portion of the evening where they fire bug-related questions at me, allowing me to both delight and horrify them.

I find myself in this position more often than I can count, and it's pretty much my favorite thing. Let it be known: people *say* they hate bugs, but they love learning about them and their wild ways.

"Hahahaha, ohmygosh! Oh, you kill me!" Calliope clearly thinks I've said something preposterous.

"I'm serious, though."

"Whaaaaat?" three voices say in chorus.

"Yeah. Sometimes, it's the very first thing she does when they come in contact."

"Then how do they...? I mean, why would she...? But how can he still...?" Calliope is sputtering.

"Oh, his body can still copulate even after decapitation," I explain.

"SHE SCREWS A HEADLESS BUG!?" Calliope screeches.

"Volume, Calliope. Volume," Lou says, looking around to see

75

if we're garnering attention.

"Yup, she does!" I say with cheer. "Well, I guess if you want to get specific, the headless bug screws *her*. She really just stands there while he does his thing. Really fascinating stuff."

"But he's... dead. Right?" Cyndi asks with her eyes wide.

"Sort of? See, at this point, his body is still capable of movement and activity. He's stimulated by nerves in his abdomen, which allow him to still... how should I say... 'get the job done' so to speak. The beheading actually sparks more spasms *and* more sperm. So he may be headless and on his way to imminent death, but as far as virility goes? He's the winner winner chicken dinner."

Three slack jaws hang open.

"Incredible, huh?" I beam.

"Incredible," Calliope mumbles. "Yeahhhhh."

Her eyes are glazed over, and she looks like she's about to barf. Lou hands her a glass of water. "Take a sip, Callie. You're looking a little green. Hey, Mabel, I heard something about the praying mantis the other day that you might not know."

"Oh, really," I say with a hint of cockiness. Cockiness is certainly not my natural state by any means, but the one thing I am supremely confident about is my bug knowledge.

"Yes. I heard that you see a praying mantis when you're most in need of guidance."

"What?" I say and scrunch up my forehead.

"The praying mantis appears when we've lost the ability to hear the small, quiet voice within. He encourages us to reclaim our truth and reminds us that we can adjust to any situation, no matter how painful."

"Oh," I say, lost for words, remembering how I just saw one the other day. "Wow, they didn't teach me *that* in any of my biology or zoology classes! Hahaha! Thanks for sharing, Louise!"

Why am I laughing? And why do I suddenly feel like my face is ten shades of pink?

"So I have a question," Cyndi announces after a quick gulp of her beer. "What's the deal with that?"

"What's the deal with what?" I ask.

"I'm stuck on the beheading thing. Does the dude mantis just not know that this is going to happen?" Cyndi wonders aloud. "Aren't animals supposed to have instincts for this sort of thing?"

Calliope jumps in before I can. "Let's say for argument's sake that the mantis *does* know. In fairness, what's he going to do? Go through his whole life never having sex?"

"Good point. Duh. You're right," Cyndi agrees.

I feel myself instantly getting flustered.

"To address your initial point, though, Cyndi, I'm with you! It's a puzzling part of nature, to be sure," I say. "I mean, if I knew the choice was between no sex or to have sex followed by my beheading, obviously I'd choose the no sex."

Silence.

I look around the table, and all three of them are staring at me with blank looks on their faces.

"Riiiight?" I ask slowly.

Then like they've been choreographed, all three of their heads shake slowly side to side.

"No, Mabel. You choose the beheading," Calliope says with complete seriousness.

"Oh, come on, that's ridiculous!" I laugh.

I fully expect Lou or Cyndi to tell Calliope she's being a nut as well, but they don't. They just sit there, staring at me with wide eyes as though *I'm* the one off track here.

"Cyndi, even you?" Surely, my best childhood friend will back me up on this one.

"Mabes," Cyndi says, "if it were a choice between riding Stuart like the stallion he is just one more time or never getting to experience that thigh-quaking thrill ride again? I would..." She pauses and reconsiders a moment. "Well, okay, I'm not sure I would accept *death* by beheading, but I would definitely be up for a permanent maiming of some sort as a tradesies for that treat."

"But we're just talking about *sex* here! What's so great about it?"

A collective gasp echoes around the table.

"No! I mean, it's great," I backtrack. "Obviously, it's... awesome! Bert's awesome. I just—"

They all seem to be waiting for me to explain myself.

I reeeeeally dislike explaining myself.

"Rest assured, friends. Because my relationship is... off the hook." I try out a phrase that really doesn't suit me. "Wait. Is it off the hook or off the chain?"

"Neither," Calliope challenges. "Because I'm 99.9 percent certain you're lying."

"This is Mabel McGonigle we're talking about here," Cyndi says. "Mabel McGonigle doesn't lie."

"Fair. She doesn't lie *outright*, but she does make the best of things to the point that you can no longer tell how she actually feels about the thing."

It's strange when people discuss you in the third person as if you're not sitting right there in front of them.

"Alright," I say, feeling a little bit bold and a whole lotta bit tipsy. "That's it. I'm ready to share."

"You are?" Cyndi is doubtful.

"Yes! You said before that I don't share with you. That I hide myself. Well, that's awful. I don't want to be that way! You are my friends, and I want to share myself with you. From now on, I'm an open book."

"Great! Bring it, baby!" Calliope rubs her palms together, and they all lean in a bit closer.

"Okay." I start. "Great. So. Let's talk about Bert. He's, uh... he's... hardworking, and he's, uh... you know, he's a dreamer is what he is. He's always cooking up a new scheme for making money and—"

"A scheme?" Louise asks.

"No. My bad. No, 'scheme' was the wrong word. A plan. He's always *planning* for our future."

"Bert got Mabel involved in a pyramid scheme," Cyndi whispers to Louise.

"Nope! Nope, that is incorrect, Cynthia."

"Don't call me Cynthia," she scoffs. "Who are you, my mom?"

"Well, it is not a pyramid scheme," I continue. "You just got that word stuck in my head. It's a... a, uh... a... triangular plan. We sell health and wellness products. Who doesn't want to be healthy and well?"

"We all do," Louise encourages. "We all want to be healthy and well."

"Exactly! Oh, Louise, I can't believe I haven't asked you this before. Would you like to get in on the ground floor of an exciting new adventure? One where you can build relationships with like-minded entrepreneurs looking to build multiple streams of residual income for years to come? Where you can join forces with a team offering cutting edge products and—"

"Um. No, thank you."

"Cool, yeah, no. You're not interested. That's totally fine. Anyway, so yeah, Bert's working really hard on that business for us. The plan is for us to make enough money so we can both get out of our parents' houses and find a place together soon."

"Nice. So when do you two spend quality time together?" Calliope questions.

"Quality time?"

"Yeah, when are you... alone together? Seems like you both work a lot."

"And it must be tricky with you both still living at home," Louise offers. "God, I can't even imagine what life would be like if I still lived with my mother."

"Monday nights," I answer.

"Monday nights?" Calliope asks.

"Yeah. Monday night is our weekly date night after our team meeting. We get a room at the Quality Inn off the turnpike and have—you know—an... adult sleepover."

"Sexy," Cyndi says with no small amount of sarcasm.

"It is, Cyndi." I can't help feeling a bit defensive. "It *is* sexy. Everybody, please excuse Cyndi. She's known Bert since he was a kid. We all went to high school together. So I think she has a hard time shaking the kid he used to be and recognizing him as the manly-as-hell man he is now."

"Okay... so walk us through a night with your manly-as-hell man," Calliope says with a smile.

"Sure. Gladly. Okay. Sooooo... Monday nights after our team meeting, we grab some takeout. Italian usually. Bert's Italian."

"You don't like Italian, though, right?" Cyndi asks.

"Oh, it's fine. I can find something I like from just about any restaurant." I continue, "So we get Italian and have a little bed picnic while we watch a few episodes of *Law & Order*..."

"But you hate violence, and cop shows give you nightmares."

Geez, what is up with Cyndi tonight?

"True," I say, starting to get frustrated with her at this point. "But Bert loves them, and I think Ice-T is a national treasure, so I don't mind at all. *Then*"—my voice shifts to sort of flirty, sort of shy because I'm not used to sharing these sorts of sordid details—"after we've watched two or three episodes and we hear the final 'dunh-dunh' after the ruling and we see 'Dick Wolf' flash on the screen, Bert says... hahaha, oh gosh, this cracks me up. He totally cracks me up..."

I get lost in a fit of nervous giggles.

"What does Bert say?" Louise asks in an attempt to get me back on track.

"He says..." I let out one more bout of giggles. "'Are you ready to see *my* Dick Wolf?'"

There's a moment of silence and then...

"Whaaaat!?" Calliope screeches.

Hm. I guess I need to repeat myself.

"He says, 'Are you ready to see *my*—'"

"Oh, I heard you the first time," Calliope huffs. "I just... I didn't want to believe it, I suppose."

"Oh, believe it! He's hilarious."

"*Is* he, though?" Cyndi sasses.

"Cyndi, seriously," I snap. "What's your problem?"

"No problem," she says. "If you're happy, I'm happy."

"Thank you."

"I just don't see how you *could* be with—"

"Continue, Mabel," Louise encourages me while cutting off Cyndi. "What happens next?"

"Oh, you know... stuff," I mumble.

"Describe the stuff please?" Calliope is back in investigative mode.

"You know what? I think I'm actually ready to move on from this discussion. I'm feeling pretty awkward at this point and—"

"He pulls out his 'Dick Wolf'…" Calliope presses.

"Fine. Yes, he pulls out his Dick Wolf…" I say with hesitation.

"And then…?"

I take a deep breath and go for it.

"He tugs on it, I tug on it. He jerks it, I jerk it. I blow it. He blows it—"

"Whoa whoa, wait a damn second. How does *he* blow it?" Louise asks.

"Sorry. I meant to say he blows *on* it. That's part of his process."

"His *process*?" Cyndi balks.

"Yes, Cyndi, there is a process," I snap again. "May I continue?"

Calliope opens her palm and gestures to me. "By all means, yes."

"Thank you." I pick up where I left off. "I cup it. He cups it. I pump it, he pumps it. Then I gaze at it, he gazes at it. I whisper to it, he whispers to it. I compliment it, he compliments it. Then I turn around, brace myself, and—you know—he *uses* it. The end."

I guzzle down the rest of my whiskey sour with my eyes squeezed shut. When I open them, three pairs of eyes are practically bugging out of their respective heads.

Calliope breaks the silence. "Um. Excuse my language, but… What. In. The. Actual. Fuck."

"It's official!" Cyndi announces. "Bert sucks! Bert's a shellfish shmuck! Damn, it's hard to say those two words back-to-back. Selfish. Schmuck. Selfish. Schmuck. Nailed it. Oh sweetness, for the love of all that's good, get out of that relationship stat!"

"Don't tell me what to do. No one should be telling me what to do right now," I assert myself.

Go me. You know what? I've decided I'm going to start drinking more. I like drunk me.

"Mabel?" a gentle voice pipes up.

"Yes, Louise."

"I may have missed it, but is the entire focus always on… 'Dick Wolf'? I mean, at a certain point does Bert focus on… Olivia?"

"Olivia? Who the hell is Olivia?" Calliope asks.

Louise considers a moment and scrunches her brows. "Olivia… Pope?"

"Olivia Pope is the Kerry Washington character on *Scandal*," Cyndi says, confused.

"Oh, right!" Louise says. "You're right. I meant, um... Olivia... Bennet? No, Benson! Olivia Benson! Mariska Hargitay's character on *SVU* is Olivia Benson."

"I'm completely lost," Cyndi says.

"The heroine of Dick Wolf's series is Olivia Benson, so I'm just suggesting that if there is going to be any balance in the bedroom, then... Olivia deserves some attention too."

"Oh, snap!" Calliope laughs. "Mabel, Louise just named your vagina Olivia Benson!"

"Why!? Why did Louise just name my vagina Olivia Benson?"

"I think it's important to meet people where they are!" Louise defends. "Clearly, you're uncomfortable discussing these things directly, Mabel, so I was trying to help you out by continuing the *Law & Order* metaphor you so expertly established."

"Oh. Well. Thank you." Louise really is proving to be a solid new friend in my world.

"You're welcome. Guys, what do you say we give Mabel a break from the inquisition? She's a big girl. She'll figure out her own relationship. You okay, girl?"

Yeah, it's official. I really like Louise.

"Fine, yeah. I'm always fine."

"I dunno." Calliope frowns. "She still looks all flushed and sweaty and panicky."

"Quick, someone get her talking about bugs so she feels better," Lou suggests.

"So, Mabes... what other female bugs murder their mates?" Cyndi asks sweetly, and I remember again why I love her.

"A bunch actually!"

Louise was right. I feel better already. It's kind of cool how she understands me so well after knowing me for such a short time.

"The black widow, of course, the biting midge, jumping spiders, scorpions..."

"Damn!" Calliope suddenly says. "I wouldn't mind biting *that* guy's head off!"

"What guy? Should I be reporting this to my brother?" Lou

asks, her eyebrows raised.

"Simmer down, sister. You know I only have eyes for Ralph. He's the only guy whose 'head' I'll be biting now and forevermore. Though now that you mention it, your brother actually doesn't mind a *bit* of teeth."

"'Now that I mention' what?" Louise nearly squawks. "I 'mentioned' absolutely nothing."

Calliope is clearly caught up in a Ralph-inspired soliloquy, though, and keeps going. "God, I love that about him. For a guy who's so clean-cut and adorable, you'd never know he's so edgy when you get him behind closed doors. Or perched between a pair of Whirlpool front loader washing machines. Whew!" Her eyes roll back a bit like she's getting lost in a recent memory. "He is just the most delicious—"

"Alright, alright. That's enough," Louise stops her before she can continue.

"But hey," Calliope says. "I'm not dead. I can still admire the hottie at twelve o'clock. See him talking to James at the bar? He's giving me Hemsworthy Thor vibes with the hair and that butt."

Cyndi whips around to get a look.

"Hmm. You know what vibes he's giving *me* with the hair and the butt? Remember that scene in that awful Troy movie with Brad Pitt? He plays Achilles, and he bares his bodacious butt on the beach?"

"Wait," I say. "Didn't that come out when we were in elementary school?

"Yeah, but you know my mom has a Brad Pitt thing." She turns to Calliope and Louise. "Her 'special collection' was packed full of Pitt DVDs."

"Totally get that," Louise says. "My mom was crazy for Swayze."

"Mine was loony for Clooney." Calliope giggles.

Seems the drinks are getting to us all.

They all look at me. My turn, I guess.

"Oh. Um. My mom and I were... high? for Bill Nye?"

"The Science Guy?" Calliope squeals.

"Is there any other?"

"No disrespect meant to the great Professor Nye," Calliope

says. "But he's not exactly known for his sex appeal."

"WHY DOES EVERYTHING HAVE TO BE ABOUT SEX?!??" I burst.

It's at that moment that everything in the bar comes to a screeching halt.

Everything that is, except for the man in question at the bar. He turns at the sound of my voice—my way-too-loud voice—and looks right into me with those icy blue eyes.

And no, he's not a "Hemsworthy" Thor. He's not a bare-butted Brad on the beach in Troy.

He's a Wally. I mean a Wallace.

And he's making a beeline for our table.

Chapter Nine

"**M**abel." He nods in greeting.

"Wallace," I respond.

He scans our table.

"Pyramid pals?" he asks, gesturing to my company.

"No. Just... friends," I respond. "Calliope, Cyndi, Louise? This is my, um, this is... Wallace."

"Hello, Wallace," Calliope, Cyndi, and Louise say in unison and wave in wonder.

He salutes back to them.

"Nice to meet you, ladies. I'm Mabel's manicure."

"Sorry, Mabel's *what*?" Calliope asks. "I mean 'fuck you,' Mabel's what?"

"Calliope!" I scold. "You haven't solved this problem yet?"

"Forgive me for the 'fuck you,'" Calliope addresses him. "I just think women use 'sorry' as an unnecessary filler way too much, so—"

"So you're trying to find a suitable replacement for it," Wallace finishes the thought for her. "No worries. 'Fuck you' is fine with me. I mean, let's be real. Plenty of us men have a whole lot of fucking off to do before we can be deemed worthy of being with a wonderful woman."

I can't be certain, but I swear they collectively sigh.

"Mabel," Cyndi says, sounding breathy and bewildered, "this man does your nails?"

"No! We work at the arboretum together. Besides, when have you ever known me to get my nails done?"

"Oh. He just said he was your manicure, so I thought…" Cyndi searches to make sense of this.

"I'm one of Mabel's prospects." He says this with a smirk. And let me tell you something. His smile? It's beautiful. But his smirk? Completely maddening.

"Oooooh, a prospect?" Calliope chirps. "Clearly, I've missed something! Do tell!"

"A *business* prospect," I quickly correct.

"Mabel's pyramid scheme needs men, so I volunteered to attend her next recruitment event," Wally explains. "She's going to boost my testosterone for me."

He follows this up with a wink.

"For the last time," I protest, "it's not a scheme, and the MANicure line is really amazing, everyone! I'm happy to do a demonstration for any of you at any time…"

"Call me crazy," Calliope croons, "but something tells me Wallace here has no trouble with his testosterone levels."

"I thank you, milady," he says with a slight bow. "But one can never be too sure. Besides, I'm happy to support Mabel's burgeoning business."

I get lost in his B's. That's weird, I know, but there's something about the way his lips bounced on all those B's just now. Besides. Burgeoning. Business. Buh-buh-buh-buh-buh.

I'm drunk.

And… I'm staring at his mouth.

"Big night ahead of you, Wallace?" Louise asks.

"How do you mean?"

She gestures to the boxes of growlers he has stacked on a hand truck. He looks down at them.

"Ah. No. Just transporting these over to the arboretum for my buddy James. His brews are being poured at the festival next Sunday."

"Oh! The Local Artisan Festival? I'll be there too! So will Mabel," Louise says excitedly.

"Oh yeah? What will you be doing, Louise?" Wallace asks.

I'm impressed with how he picks up people's names so quickly. How he looks people in the eyes with such sincerity.

"I'm manning the touch tank."

"The what tank?" he asks.

"Touch tank. Portable aquarium," Louise explains. "Gives kids the chance to touch a turtle, cuddle a crab, stroke a starfish... I've been volunteering at The Philadelphia Aquarium while I'm in town for an internship. So I'm helping them out today."

"Ah. Sounds fun. And what will you be doing, Mabel?"

"Doing what? Who? How dare you! I'm not doing anything, mister! I'm just sitting here. You're the one doing all the doing!"

Why am I suddenly so fired up?

"What is going on with you?" Cyndi murmurs loud enough so only I can hear.

Wallace chuckles.

"You're right. Let it be known that you are 'just sitting there,' and I am the one 'doing all the doing.' Now that you mention it, Mabel"—he drops his voice lower and leans in closer to me— "that scenario sounds delightful. You just sitting there while I... '*do all the doing*.' Count me in."

"What?" I sputter.

"Hmm?" He smiles.

"Oh, wow," Cyndi breathes as she looks back and forth between us.

Wallace continues, "I was talking about the artisan festival, though. What do they have you doing at the artisan festival?"

"Oh. Um. I'm a volunteer for the Save the Bees Foundation, so I offered to man their booth."

"Mabel makes her own honey!" Calliope boasts. "Did you know that?"

"Does she now?" Wally's eyebrows go up.

"Sort of," I say. "I took a beekeeping workshop last Spring, and I got a nice first batch going. I'm going to offer some honeycomb nibbles at the booth to anyone who signs the Save the Bees pledge."

"Nice. Well, I'll be sure to visit your booth for a nibble. I'm sure your honey is delicious."

He winks and takes hold of the hand truck.

"Oh snap," Calliope says under her breath.

"Lovely to meet you ladies. You have a good night." He glances one more time at me and salutes. "Mabel."

I salute back.

"Wallace."

Why in the world we are saluting each other is beyond me.

Then he saunters out of the bar, the door swinging shut behind him.

We all stare at the closed door in silence.

After a few moments, Cyndi starts drumming her fingers on the tabletop.

"So.... That was... um..." She searches for the words.

Calliope raises her hand as though she's in school. "Hey, I have a question."

"Yeah?" I ask, still in a bit of a fog.

"What the hell was *that*?"

"What was what?"

"That... interaction! That was the weirdest, most sexually-tension-filled absurdist exchange I've ever witnessed between two humans."

"Was it?" I ask. And suddenly I don't recognize the sound of my own voice. It's sort of chokey and squeaky.

"It was," all three of them say in unison.

Louise continues. "Mabel. The guy said he wants to 'do all the doing' to you!"

"No," I quickly refute. "That is not what he said."

"He wants to 'taste your honey!'" Cyndi purrs.

"Again," I stress, "*No*. He's just—"

"And the way he looked at you?" Calliope whistles. "I'm surprised he didn't get you pregnant from eye penetration alone!"

"CAN WE PLEASE NOT TALK ABOUT PENETRATION RIGHT NOW!?" I wail.

Silence.

My second outburst of the evening. My three friends stare at me. As does the majority of the bar.

I feel my eyes start to water.

"Whoa, Mabes," Cyndi whispers as she rubs my back. "Are you *crying*? What's going on?"

"Eye penetration, Calliope?" Lou scolds. "Really?"

Calliope frowns. "Oh my gosh. I didn't mean to upset you."

"It's fine. You didn't upset me." I cut her off. "And no"—I shoot daggers at Cyndi—"I'm not crying. I never cry."

"What do you mean you never cry?" Lou asks in obvious disbelief.

"She doesn't!" Cyndi says. "I've known the girl over eighteen years... "

"Eighteen years, two months. and fifteen days," I interject.

"And I've never once seen her cry. Not when her grandma died, not when she got kicked off the Mathletes team, not even when her hamster ate her babies."

"Holy shit," Calliope gasps. "Your hamster ate her babies?"

It's true. My hamster did eat her babies. Her name was Sonya. I was thirteen years old and had just read Chekov's *Uncle Vanya* for the first time—hence the name Sonya. I couldn't believe what I was seeing. It was horrifying, but I didn't cry. Don't get me wrong, I *wanted* to cry. The tears built up inside me, but they lodged in my throat. They always lodge in my throat and don't come up any higher. No matter what is happening in my life, no matter how sad I am... the tears just won't spill. They surface, but they don't spill. The smile always springs up instead.

"I apologize for yelling," I say. "I'm not a yeller. I think I'm still getting used to you, Calliope..."

"Understandable. I'm a lot," she says proudly.

"...and I wasn't expecting you to say the word... penetrate..." I hiccup. "I guess it just made me feel uncomfortable."

"I'm sorry?" Calliope apologizes as if she's asking a question. I can't blame her. Why on earth should she have to say sorry to a grown woman for talking about grown-woman topics?

"Don't be," I say. "I'm twenty-four years old. I should be fine with hearing the word penetrate."

"You really should," Cyndi agrees.

"You think I don't know that, Cyndi?!" I say a little more harshly than I intend. "I shouldn't want to run and hide during discussions like this with my friends! And I should be confident with men, with my body, with sex! Geez... at the very least, I should be confident with my *thoughts* and feelings and opinions! But I'm not. I'm confused and embarrassed *all* the time! I doubt myself *all* the time!"

It's official. I am airing my dirty emotional laundry in a local, suburban bar.

"This is not surprising to me that you feel this way, Mabes," Cyndi says. "You've been groomed to be such a 'good girl' over the years. And your level of good-girl-ness is pretty unsustainable after the age of eight if you ask me."

"Uggggggggghhhhhhhhhhhh." An extended sound of disgust tumbles out of me and extends for way too long. It's met with a moment of silence.

"Whoa," Calliope murmurs.

"What the hell was *that*?" Cyndi marvels. "Did Mabel McGonigle just 'ugggghhh' me?"

"She did, yes." I say. "I mean, I did, yes. I'm sorry, I'm just... getting a bit... tired of that description of me."

"Which description?" Louise asks. "A good girl?"

"Uggggggggggggh. Yes. I also don't really appreciate being compared to an eight-year-old, Cyndi. No offense to eight-year-olds. Eight-year-olds are lovely."

"No, they're not. And I wasn't *comparing* you to an eight-year-old. I was suggesting that perhaps your parents still *treat* you like one," Cyndi says, then turns to Calliope and Louise and explains, "See, Mabel's parents are super overprotective. They have always sheltered the shit out of her. So it makes sense to me that you feel this way, Mabes. You've been in a little Mabel-bubble your whole life. Gosh, you know what you're like? You're like that little baby elephant in captivity whose owners tied her foot to a pole so she wouldn't wander away. Then, years later, when she's a big badass three ton colossus of an elephant who could pull that stake out of the ground with the tiniest of tugs, it doesn't even cross her mind to try. Why? Because she's been conditioned to be docile."

"Now we're comparing me to an elephant?"

"We are," Cyndi says, no remorse at all.

"Elephants symbolize patience, wisdom and strength." Louise soothes. "Also strong familial bonds and commitment. Cyndi's saying you're way more powerful than you realize."

"What's up with you and the spirit animal stuff all of a sudden?" Calliope cocks her head.

Louise shrugs. "I dunno. I find it interesting."

"Hmm." I take this in for a moment. "Well, Mom and Dad are heading out of town tomorrow for a whole month. So maybe this is the time I 'pull the stake out of the ground.'" I laugh.

"Ohmygod, yessssssssss." Calliope's face lights up with mischief and she steeples her fingers like a cartoon villain.

"Calliope," I warn. "I was kidding. Besides, I don't know what 'pull the stake out of the ground' would even mean."

"I have some ideas," Cyndi offers with glee, then turns to Calliope and Lou. "I'm telling you, this is huge. Her parents never go away. Ever."

"Well then this is our moment!" Calliope announces like a warrior going into battle. She closes her eyes and places her fingertips on her temples like she's downloading an idea. "Aaaaaaaand, I've got it. Mabel? We're putting you on a program. A... 'Bad Girl Program.' Effective immediately."

"Oh my gosh," I protest. "What the heck are you even –"

"Cyndi and Louise," she completely steamrolls me and continues with her impromptu mission. She's having way too much fun with this. "Help me out. What are some first steps to get our girl on track to relinquishing her 'good girl' status while the overprotective parents are away?"

Louise pipes up first. "Watch all the movies you were never allowed to watch as a kid. You are an adult and it is absurd that you're still adhering to parental controls over your viewing pleasure. Consult with your peers, aka, us, at any point for some raunchy recommendations."

"Beautiful!" Calliope applauds. "Love it. Cyndi, what do you got?"

"Snoop," Cyndi says with no further explanation.

"Could you please elaborate on 'snoop,' good lady?" Calliope prompts. She's slipping into some weird accent now, and I have officially lost all control over her. Not that I had any to begin with.

"Our girl's gotta snoop!" Cyndi says definitively. "Please don't take this the wrong way, Mabes. I love them, but Helen and Abe are some closed-mouth, shady cats. Investigate their closets. Root through their underwear drawers…"

"I am not rooting through my parents' underwear drawers!" I exclaim. "And they're not 'shady.' They're just… private."

"All I'm saying is… this is your chance to find out more about why they are the way they are. You never know what you might find. Snoopity-snoop, girl! Snoopity-snoop!"

Snoopity-snoop?

Calliope takes control of the conversation again. "The esteemed Cyndi offers some excellent advice. Allow me to wrap up our proceedings. In an effort not to overwhelm you, Mabel, I'll add just one more step toward achieving your long-overdue Bad Girl status for now. A crucial step in the growing-up process that I am nearly positive you skipped. Are you ready?"

"Probably not," I say, but what I don't admit is that I'm feeling surprisingly energized by the turn this intervention has taken. I'd be lying if I said I wasn't all ears at this point.

"You must get freaky in your childhood twin bed while the parents are away."

"Whaaaat?!" I say.

At the same time, Cyndi and Lou say, "Hellllllll yeah, you do."

I start sputtering, "But that is—That is just –"

"Awesome, Mabel. It's just awesome," Calliope concludes, a confident smile on her face.

"Oh shit, he's back!" I squeal and put my head down on the table as though I can disappear. But god help me, I peek under my elbow and watch Wallace re-enter the bar with the empty hand truck. He wheels it behind the bar and slaps a hand on James's back. Before I know it, I've lifted my head, and all four of us are full-on staring at the two men having a conversation.

"Can I say what we're all thinking?" Calliope says on the sly.

"That's pretty presumptuous, Calliope," Louise responds. "What makes you think you know what we're all thinking?"

"Mabes, you're hot for this guy."

"Okay, yeah," Louise admits. "That actually is what we were all thinking."

I go on the defensive and start whisper-spluttering, "I'm not—I don't—I can't—I'm engaged. And I'm happy. That man just..." I look at the bar. "He makes me—I'm not sure what I'm supposed to—"

Louise raises her hand.

"Yes. Louise?" Apparently, I call on people now to chime in on the state of my life.

"I say this with absolutely no judgment, Mabel, but... if you're engaged and happy, why do you think this guy is affecting you so much?"

Her forehead scrunches, and her head tilts. Louise suddenly looks and sounds very therapist-y.

Cyndi chimes in, "Because that guy is the anti-Bert! He is hella hot, and he's... gosh, what word would you use to describe him?" She taps her chin in thought.

"Burly!" Calliope says.

"Burly, yes!" Cyndi agrees. "He's super burly. And hirsute!"

Calliope cackles. "How very SAT prep of you, Cyndi! Throw me a bone here though, I'm forgetting what hirsute means."

"It means hairy," I fill in. "But Wally's hairy in a good way!"

"I didn't say he wasn't, girlfriend," Cyndi says with a knowing look.

"Wait. *Wally*, did you say?" Calliope smiles. "Have you given this man a nickname?"

"Wallace," I backpedal. "Whatever."

God, I'm dying for a subject change.

"Mabel," Louise says. "This is just an observation, not a criticism. I find it... *interesting* that you have knowledge of *Wally's*... hirsute-itude." Again she has this counselor-like vibe about her.

"First of all," I say, "'hirsute-itude' is not a word, and second of all, you're a marine biologist, aren't you? Not a psychologist? Why do you sound so...?"

"Sorry." Louise snaps out of whatever mode she was in. "I've, uh... I've finally started seeing a therapist for the first time in—well, ever—and I think... well, I guess he's sort of rubbing off on me."

"You should never let your therapist rub one off on you, Louise! Never!" Calliope scolds as she takes another gulp of her margarita, then licks the salt rim.

"Not like that, you dork. Gosh!" Louise retorts.

Calliope knocks back the rest of her margarita and takes this opportunity to get on her soapbox. "Hey, while we're on the topic of hirsute-itude... I know society tells us we're supposed to want these smooth Ken doll look-alikes for men, but ef that shit, yeah? Give this girl a little chest and back hair any day! Know what I mean? Ralph is hirsute-as-hell, and I love it. Gives him a primal edge, ya know? Rawr."

"Did you just growl?" I ask.

"Sure did, and I'll do it again. Rawr. Plus, on a practical note, the bit of hair gives me a little somethin'-somethin' to tug on while we're—"

"Enough with the... brotherfucker stuff, Callie!" Louise pleads.

"Oooh, '*brotherfucker*.' I like that, Lou!" Calliope squeals. "From here on in, consider me a proud brotherfucker!" She backpedals for a second. "*Your* brother, obviously. Not mine."

Lou looks queasy.

"For the record!" I proclaim and stand from my stool. "I do not have knowledge of anyone's body except for Bert's. I was only commenting on the fact that Wallace has long... *head* hair and well-trimmed... *beard* hair. Any other kind of hair he may possess is unbeknownst to me and has nothing to do with me."

"I'm not opposed to you finding out," a male voice says from directly behind me.

And... my stomach feels like it falls right out of my butt.

It drops, I mean. My stomach drops.

It's Wally. Clearly, I took my eyes off him long enough for him to perform a sneak attack.

"Nice use of 'unbeknownst,'" he rumbles. "That's not a word that comes up often in casual conversation."

I am tempted to turn around and give him a piece of my mind. But my mind suddenly feels completely empty of pieces to give. I stare straight ahead at my friends, my face surely fire engine red. I feel him lean super close to me. Then he whispers, "Till Monday, Mabel," and leaves the bar for good.

In the ensuing silence, Calliope mutters, "Damn... look at her. He's got her all sorts of smurfnurblined."

"What did you say?" I breathe out in a fog.

"Smurfnurblined. He's got you smurfnurblined," Calliope repeats.

"Yes! What is that-that-that... word? What does that mean? You all know what that means?" I shoot the questions off rapid-fire, suddenly full of energy.

"Of course," they say in unison.

"Enlighten me, please?" I ask.

"Smurfnurblin," Cyndi says like a fourth-grader announcing her word at the National Spelling Bee Competition.

"To be depressingly aroused," Lou offers.

Calliope continues, "An extreme desire for sexual satisfaction that results in a bout of anxiety."

"Smurfnurblin." Cyndi wraps things up. "Want me to use it in a sentence?"

"No, that won't, um, that won't be necessary," I say before dropping my head in my hands.

Depressingly aroused.

I hate to admit it, but now that I know the definition? April was one hundred percent right.

When that man is present...

I am the epitome of a smurfnurblin.

Chapter Ten

The next day, I'm making the rounds at the arboretum, and I am surprised and delighted by what I see. Everywhere I look, I see groups of kids laughing and hiking and singing. I see counselors engaging and nurturing. Even my CITs—who, let's face it, I had my doubts about—are totally in the flow with their groups and are doing great work.

I smile when I spot April with a circle of our youngest campers. They are all sitting cross-legged outside the canteen, chomping on their afternoon snack. She's in the middle of some kind of story, and every one of those precious little faces looks riveted.

I get a little closer to listen.

"So these two American girls decide to take this road trip through Europe. Everything's going okay until they get to Germany, and boom! Their car breaks down in the middle of the night. Uh-oh! So they find this little cottage—wait, a cabin—I dunno... a villa? Yeah, let's call it a villa. And they decide to stay at this villa for the night. But then! Oh ho ho, *then*, when they wake up in the morning? They find that they're actually in this weird tiny hospital, and this psychotic German doctor dude is about to use them for his dream experiment."

"What is his dream experiment?" little Isabel asks with wide, enchanted eyes.

"To surgically connect them in a glorious, horrific line. That's right. One after the other." She starts doing creative gestures.

"Mouth to anus, mouth to anus, mouth to—"

"OKAY, THAT'S ENOUGH. WHAT A TRULY GRAPHIC AND INAPPROPRIATE STORY THAT WAS! LET'S NEVER THINK OF IT AGAIN! YAY, APRIL, YAY!!" I start clapping and squealing like a lunatic.

The kids join me in clapping, though they look understandably confused.

April proudly curtseys.

"Everybody finished with their snack?" I ask. "Great! On your feet! You are all due at Tony's tent next to pick up your binoculars for birding, so chop-chop, everybody!"

The kids seem unfazed—thank goodness—as they gather their little backpacks and assemble in a line. Just then, Laurel, their main counselor, returns from the latrine.

"Thanks for holding down the fort, April," she says as she jogs up to us.

"Not a problem!" April beams. "We had fun."

Yeah, a little too much fun.

"Laurel," I say in a measured tone, "why don't you go on ahead with the group. April and I are going to hang back and have a quick chat, then I'll send her down to join you at ornithology."

"Heh. *Horn*ithology." April chuckles.

"*Orn*ithology, April," I scold under my breath. "The study of birds."

Laurel's eyes dart uncertainly between the two of us for a split second, then she says, "Sure thing!" and launches into a jaunty rendition of "The Ants Go Marching." Seven little voices shout back, "Hurrah! Hurrah!" as the group moves steadily down the hill.

I'm left alone with April.

"So. What's up, boss?" she asks.

Man, is she really this oblivious?

"April. Um. Were you really about to tell a group of four-year-olds the plot synopsis of *The Human Centipede*?"

"Well, yeah. It was relevant to today's nature walk."

"How in the world was a horror movie relevant to today's nature walk?"

"We saw a centipede." She says this with the unmistakable flavor of "duh" peppering her tone. "Also, aren't camp counselors supposed to tell their campers spooky stories by firelight and crap?"

Who hired this person? It certainly wasn't me.

"Maybe older kids at sleepaway camp. But even then, *some* kind of judgment has to be exercised and..." I stop myself when I see her staring at me blankly. I'm clearly not getting through. "Alright." I close my eyes and breathe for a moment. "If you don't realize how unacceptable this is, then I'm sorry, April, but I really don't know what else to do except—"

"THEY'RE DROWNING MY BUNNY!" a tiny, hysterical voice cries out.

I turn and see Holden sprinting up the hill to me, tears streaming down his face. Chloe, his CIT, is running as fast as she can to catch up with him.

Holden hurls himself into my arms.

"Whoa, buddy, whoa!" I say.

"My bunny... he-he-he—"

"Slow down, kiddo. What's going on?" I pull back from him slightly so I can see his face. I brush a few of his tears away.

"My bunny—he's drowning, and no one will help him!" he wails.

I look at Chloe.

Chloe explains, "We were making biodegradable balloon animals with Marcus down by the water. Holden's bunny fell into the lake and—"

"And now, he-he-he-he's drowning in the water, and no one will help him!" Holden finishes the explanation.

"Oh, sweetie, I'm so sorry. I'm sure Marcus will make you another bunny!" I try to console him.

"Tried that," Chloe says.

"But I want *my* bunny!" Holden cries. "He's scared, and he's alone, and I'm his daddy, and—"

"Did I hear that someone's bunny is in trouble?" a gruff male voice says from behind me.

I turn around, and The Wall stands with a really sweet smile on his face. I wasn't sure his face could actually do that. His eyes are trained on Holden.

"Yes," Holden says gravely. "My bunny."

"I'm sorry to hear that, pal. But hey, listen. I may have some good news for ya," this big beautiful man says as he crouches down to the little kid's level. "I happen to live right down by the lake. I have quite a few boats. And I actually have some bunny rescuing experience. What do you say I row out to the middle of the lake and see if I can get your bunny back to shore?"

"Yes, please!" Holden says with hope blooming on his face. For the first time since he ran up the hill, his breath evens out, and he stops crying.

"Great. Then that's what we're gonna do. Your friend Mabel and I will head out there right away and see what we can do."

"We will?" I ask.

"Course," he says. Unless you have more pressing matters to attend to?"

His eyes lock with mine.

"No, I... what could be more pressing?"

"My thoughts exactly," he says.

"Bow-chicka-wow-wow," April sings.

"APRIL!" I scold, then pull my volume back and smile when I realize I've startled everyone. "April... please return to your group down at the *ornithology* tent. And be sure to meet me at the canteen after dismissal. We need to discuss a few things before you leave today."

"Sure thing, boss!" April says happily, and without a care in the world, it seems, as she takes her time sauntering off to rejoin her group.

"So, uh—" I stumble as I look at Wally. I'm going to stop calling him The Wall. His name is Wally—well, Wallace—but I can't help it. He just feels like Wally somehow.

It's silent for a moment. They're all waiting for me to continue. I snap out of it.

"Yeah, so Holden buddy, does that sound like a good plan?"

"Yes!!" he practically squeals.

Geez, I hope we can find this thing. Because something tells me Holden won't accept a replacement biodegradable balloon bunny.

"Great, so, Chloe, why don't you and Holden head back to your group and Mister, uh, Mister..."

"Bieber." Wally fills in my blank in a most unexpected way.

"Bieber?!" we say in unison. That's right, Chloe, myself, and even Holden find this a bit funny.

"Yes," Wally sighs.

"Sorry," I say while stifling my smile. "Something tells me you don't want to discuss it."

"Not my favorite topic, no."

"Okay, I'll drop it," I say magnanimously. "So—"

"For the record, though?" He raises his voice. "Biebers existed long before that man-child musician came on the scene, and they will continue to exist long after he and his little heart handshape pulsing-at-the-camera thingy is over."

"Oh, he doesn't do that anymore," Chloe explains, "except when doing it ironically as a throwback to his early work. Yeah, the 'heart handshape pulsing-at-the-camera thingy' harkens from his debut hit song, 'Baby,' featuring Ludacris, which released in 2009 and eventually went on to oust Elton John's 'Candle in the Wind' from the highest multiplatinum single spot." She pauses for a moment, then says, "I was a devout Belieber in kindergarten. How about you, Mabel?" Chloe continues.

"How about me, what?"

"Were you a Belieber too? Probably, right? I wouldn't be surprised since we already have so much in common."

My eyes dart between Chloe and Holden, whose big, wet saucer eyes are staring up at me while he tries his six-year-old best to be patient.

"Do we?" I ask, really confused as to why she's choosing this moment to force more bonding with me. But since I'm me, I can't just shut the poor girl down. She's new in town. Clearly, she's trying to make friends.

"Of course!" she says wih confidence. "The red hair, our general genial disposition, our love of bugs, and now our love of Biebers!" She looks at me with such hope.

"Uh... can't really say I'm too familiar with Mr. Bieber's musical work really. Justin, not Wallace," I clarify with a quick glance at the Bieber who is currently present. "Though Wallace Bieber may also be a musical prodigy for all I know. Are you, Wallace? Are you a musical prodigy?" I ramble in his direction. Why can't I help wanting to learn more about this guy?

"I am not," he responds and then gestures meaningfully to Holden, who is now fidgeting like crazy.

I pick up my pace. "Right. Off topic." I turn to Chloe. "No, I'm not a Belieber. I've never really listened to much popular stuff. My parents are big into classical music, so that's what we've always played at home." I turn to Holden. "Okay, buddy, let's—"

"Your parents, huh?" Chloe interrupts and takes a step closer to me. "What are your parents' names? Mine are Christina and John." What is up with this girl?

"Um. Helen and Abe?" I answer hesitantly, feeling my eyebrows scrunch up in confusion.

"Cool, cool," Chloe says. "Out of curiosity, did Helen and Abe have you the adoption way or the procreation way?"

"The... procreation way." I stretch out my response like taffy. "Chloe, what is with the strange questions? Why would you ask me that?"

"Just getting to know you better! I'm a generally curious person. Scientists-in-training have to be, yeah? Hey, can we sit together at lunch today and—"

"GET ME MY BUNNY NOW, OR IMMA FLIP MY SHIT!!!!" a tiny but fierce voice explodes.

Whoa.

I take one look at Holden, and the poor guy looks frantic.

"Okay. Holden?" I decide to get things back on track. "Everything is going to be okay. Mr. Bieber—Wally, not Justin—and I will see about rescuing your bunny and report back to you ASAP. You just go have fun with your group and try not to worry, alright?"

"Deep breaths, dude, okay?" Wally encourages him.

"Deep breaths," Holden parrots back and peers up at the man in front of him. Then he makes a valiant attempt at some lengthened inhales and exhales, matching his rhythm to Wally's.

"Good man," Wally praises him. I can't help but smile as I watch the two of them breathing together.

"Chloe," I prompt. "You got this?"

"I got this," she says, dropping her earlier weirdness and picking up Holden's hand. Then she and Holden head toward the reptile house for their lizard lesson.

And suddenly, it's just Wally and me.

He gestures toward the lake. "Shall we?"

"Um. Yeah. Yes. We shall."

Chapter Eleven

We start walking down the hill side by side, which is an odd feeling. Up until this point, I've either been chasing him or running away from him. Now I find myself keeping up with his long strides, hearing his breath, peeking up to see the scruff on his jaw.

"Intense kid, huh?" he says after a few moments.

"I know, right? I'm not sure what Chloe's situation is. She's new to us this year and—"

"I was actually talking about the little guy."

"Holden? Oh. Yeah, Holden isn't usually so emotional. He and his family are going through something this summer, I think. Seems to be a lot going on in his little head and heart right now. I really appreciate you taking the time to make this better for him, though I'm a little concerned the balloon bunny may be a lost cause."

"Nah, he's out there. We'll get him," he says with supreme confidence.

"Okay." If he's confident, who am I to doubt him?

"Not that I mind, but why do you need my help? I'm sure a capable guy like you could pull off a rescue mission of this nature solo, no?"

"Who said I needed help?" he asks.

"Oh."

"Maybe I just wanted some company."

"Oh."

From me, though? Why would he want company from me?

When we arrive at the lakefront, he goes to a weathered wooden trunk next to the boats and pulls out a single bright orange life vest.

"Here, let's get you strapped into this bad boy," he says.

"Where is yours?" I ask. "Aren't you going to wear one?"

"A life vest? Nah. Don't have one."

"But—" I start to protest.

"Never found one that fits me." He shrugs.

"Why, because you're so big?" I chuckle.

We're standing face-to-face now, just a few inches apart.

"Yes. That's it exactly."

"What? Come on. I mean, you're... big." Did my eyes just scan his body? Oh god, I think my eyes just scanned his body. "But not *that* big."

"Lady, I wouldn't presume you understand my size."

He's silent a moment, then his lips spread into a brilliant grin. Before I can even consider a response to that, he reaches the vest over my head and behind me, so I'm gently caged between his arms.

"Arms out," he says.

I immediately plunk both hands up on his shoulders as though we're about to slow dance.

He laughs. "Aw, thanks for the hug, girl. But I actually meant arms *out*. Like to your sides. So we can put this thing on?"

"Right, yes. Of course."

I feel my face flush as I whip my arms out into a bent T-shape situation. He helps me maneuver the vest over each shoulder. My breathing goes shallow as he starts fastening the buckles up the front. Each time he pulls a belt tighter, he gives it a little shake to make sure it's secure. It makes me feel... cared for somehow. Like making sure I'm safe is important to him.

"Alright, in the boat you go."

He bows and gestures toward a rowboat tied to the dock.

"Great!" I chirp. "Let's do it!"

Not quite sure why, but I break into a jaunty jog.

"Quite a prance you got there," he calls after me.

I stop in my tracks and turn around.

"Would you call it a prance, though?"

"I would. Nothing else would be an accurate descriptor. I've seen it twice now. You panic-pranced away from me the other day when I caught you spying on me after my shower. And you prudence-pranced away from me just now to avoid that intensity you felt between us."

"I didn't... terror-prance, mister."

Do I sound defensive?

"But you did prudence-prance?"

"No way, mister! *Prudence*-pranced? What are you even talking about?"

"Why are you suddenly calling me mister?"

"Because I—unlike some people—have manners. Plus, you're my elder."

"Your elder? I'm your *elder*?" he chortles.

"Yes! I mean, I think so? You seem older than me. You've got this sort of... grizzly thing going on? And you're so confident and sturdy and—"

"Thank you for the compliments, ma'am."

"I don't know if I'd consider them compliments. You're just so—"

"How old are you, Mabel?"

"Twenty-four."

"Really!" He seems genuinely surprised, then offers me his hand so I can lower myself safely into the rowboat. I take it and get myself settled on the side farthest from the oars.

He stands, staring at me from the dock.

"What?" I ask, looking up at him and bracing myself for some snide comment about... about what, I don't know. I can't keep up with the way this guy's mind works, but I'm bracing myself for the worst all the same.

"Just... you've accomplished a lot for being so young."

"Oh." I feel my body relax a smidge. "You think so?"

"Absolutely," he says as he climbs in, unfastens the ropes from the dock, and shoves us out onto the water. "You're twenty-four and already a fully licensed entomologist?"

"I am, yeah," I say, pride sneaking into my voice. "Wait. How do you know that?"

"I have my ways."

"Okay…" I stretch the word out and wait for him to elaborate. From the look on his face, though, that won't be happening anytime soon.

I watch him row, his strong arms propelling us across the water.

"So," he says. "Tell me more."

"About what?"

"About you. About how you became a twenty-four-year-old entomologist."

I always feel a bit shy talking about myself in this way. "It's not a big deal. I doubled up on credits and graduated high school a year and a half early, then headed straight to undergrad, and after that, I dived into my masters. Just finished."

"Impressive," he whistles under his breath.

"Nah. Just eager, I guess." Self-deprecation is my specialty it seems.

"Eager for what?"

"To get my life going on my own terms?"

He pauses and looks me square in the eyes for a moment.

"I can understand that," he says with seriousness.

We row a bit more. Well, he rows. I watch him.

"Aren't you afraid to be in a boat with no life jacket?" I ask after some silence.

"Nah. It's a safe lake. Not deep. No undertow. Plus, I swim the length of it every morning when I wake up."

"You swim the entire *length* of it?"

"Three times, actually. Forward and back." He says this as if it's no big deal.

"Wow! Well, I guess that explains your whole…"

"My whole…?"

"Just the way your upper body is so…"

"So…?"

"Ya know… Dooszh!" I hold my arms out wide as a visual to accompany the *dooszh* sound.

"Dooszh, huh?" He laughs.

"Yeah." I feel my face flush. "Whatever, I don't know how else to describe it."

"Dooszh is fine," he says with faux seriousness. "I'll take dooszh. Yeah, been a swimmer my whole life. Swam competitively throughout high school and college. That'll keep you in pretty dooszh shape, especially in the upper body. You just gotta make sure you hit the gym too and work your body evenly, or else you start to look like a triangle." He pauses a moment, and this may be the first time I've ever seen him look the slightest bit uncomfortable. "Let's, uh, let's change the subject. I'm starting to sound like a real basic bro, and we can't have that."

"What's your favorite stroke, bro?" I laugh.

He scoffs. "Not exactly a subject change, but okay. Butterfly."

"Why are you calling me butterfly?" My voice goes soft.

"No. My favorite stroke. It's the butterfly," he responds.

"Oh! Okay, yes. Butterfly!" I exclaim. "Sorry, people give me a lot of buggy nicknames. Comes with the territory, I guess. Truth be told, though? Despite its obviously awesome name, the butterfly stroke has always made me uncomfortable."

"Why is that?"

"I'd rather not say."

"Alright. Not sure why you brought it up then..."

"Because it looks like the person doing it is humping the water," I blurt, the words just flying out of my mouth without my permission.

Silence.

"Did you just say *humping*?"

"I did."

"*Humping*! Hahaha!" Then he proceeds to lose his mind with laughter. "Oh, you slay me. Lady, you are full of surprises!"

"Happy to amuse you, I guess."

"I'm amused, yeah." His laughter starts to taper off. "But honestly? Now I'm also concerned about you."

"Why?"

"Because who the hell have you been... humping?"

"Just... people. I mean person! *One* person!"

"Right, right. Where's the iceberg?"

"Huh?"

"Your finger." He points at my naked left hand.

"Oh. It was just a little tight, so I took it off until we can—"

"Honeymoon over so soon?"

"Of course not. Everything's fine. I mean... this is none of your business! Gosh, how rude are you?"

"Hey, I'm not the one who broached this particular topic! I was very innocently discussing my swimming regimen. You're the one who brought our discourse to a full... hump."

I stare him down. "You are so..."

"Go on," he taunts. "You have something to say? Say it."

I feel my breaths quickening. My heart rate is skyrocketing.

"Speak your mind," he continues.

"I-I'm not sure what you think you're—"

"You know what, Mabel? You strike me as someone who has much more depth and layers than what she puts out there."

"What are you? You *just* met me, *Wallace*."

"True."

"So maybe you can withhold the psychoanalysis a few more days?"

"I used to be like you."

Geez, he's relentless!

"Used to be like me how?" I huff, though I'm almost certain I don't want to hear the answer.

"I was a people pleaser too."

"A people pleaser? I am not a people pleaser!"

"Sure, you are! Always doing the right thing. The kind thing. The... palatable thing. Mark my words, sweetheart, that shit will wear you down."

"Don't call me sweetheart," I chide. "And don't..."

"I'm listening..." he goads me. "Gimme what you got, girl. Tell me what's on your mind."

I hesitate, but then start to sputter.

"You have no idea what you're... You make me so..."

My words hang in the air for one supercharged moment.

He says nothing, and neither do I.

Then...

I leap on him.

And I fully plant my lips on his.

And for one glorious millisecond, he responds, kissing me back.

SPLASH!

Right as the boat topples and we fall into the water.

I go under for a split second and bob immediately back to the surface, thanks to my trusty life jacket.

I splash left and right, fully prepared to yell at this infuriating man for… for… for what? *I'm* the one who kissed *him*, right? But he made me do it by being so… so…

Wait.

Why is he not surfacing?

Ohmygod ohmygod ohmygod.

"Wally? Wallace?!" I scream and splash.

I internally panic.

He said he was a swimmer! He said he's in this water every day! Did he get a leg cramp? Did he hit his head?

"Wally!!!!!"

"Yes?" a completely calm and… distant voice responds.

I thrash around in the water and spot him—no joke—about a hundred feet away, holding the balloon bunny over his head.

"Got him!" he announces jovially, as if he didn't just scare the bejeezus out of me.

"What is wrong with you?!" I scold.

"Well, that's not a very nice question, Mabel." He says this as he does a sort of one-arm side stroke toward me, holding the bunny high above the water. "Not a thing is wrong with me. It seems those manners of yours could use a bit of work, though."

"My manners? *My* manners? I am overflowing with manners, mister! Manners have been drilled into me since I was an infant. If you looked up 'manners' in the dictionary, you'd find my picture there. Having manners is basically the crux of who I am, so don't talk to me about manners, you-you-you manner-less sonofabitch!"

I slap both hands over my mouth in shock.

My legs continue to tread water.

"I am… so sorry," I say in about an octave lower than my usual voice. "That was—"

"Accurate," he finishes the thought for me as he reaches the side of the rowboat and places the bunny safely inside. "It was accurate. I gave up having manners a long time ago. And believe me, I'm happier for it."

"Well, I shouldn't have said that. You just... you scared me when you didn't come to the surface and—"

"Let me ask you something, Mabel-with-all-the-manners. Was it mannerly to kiss me without my consent?"

He is so close to me now. We're treading water, our faces six inches apart, our bodies hidden behind the boat. If anyone onshore were to look out in our direction, they wouldn't see us.

"You're right. I shouldn't have done that. You were just being so..."

"Irresistible?" he offers with a smile.

"I was going to say irritating."

"Do you always kiss men you find irritating?"

I can feel his breath on my face.

"No, I—" This man has me all sorts of flustered. "Can we just forget this ever happened, please?"

"Hmm. That's going to be a problem for me."

"How so?" I ask in frustration.

"I assure you, I won't be forgetting about this anytime soon."

For a moment, all I hear is the lapping of water against the rowboat.

Is it me, or did he just inch the tiniest bit closer to me?

"Well, I'm sorry, truly. It won't happen again."

"Why not?"

"Because... I'm engaged!" I say as if it should be obvious. It *should* be obvious. To me, especially.

"Yeah, but you're not happy about it."

I'm embarrassed to find that I have no comeback for that.

"Are you." He says this like my unhappiness is a fact.

"I'm... getting back in the boat."

"Fine. Let me give you a boost."

"I need no boost from the likes of you."

"The 'likes of me'? Alright," he says on a laugh. "You suddenly sound like a sopping wet Scarlett O'Hara."

"How can I *sound* sopping wet?" I pause for a split second

when I see his smirk. "Don't answer that."

I then proceed to hurl my body at the rowboat in several attempts to get back on board.

"Easy, champ. Reconsidering that boost?" He smiles after my third unsuccessful attempt, still treading water like it requires exactly zero effort.

"Yessss. Please." I manage to hiss this out through my anger and embarrassment.

"Alright. I'm gonna weave my fingers together like this. You just step that there lady foot into it, and I'll boost you up."

"Fine. Just don't touch any other part of me, you hear me?"

"Excuse me, miss. Have we forgotten that *you're* the one who kissed *me*? I should be warning *you* to keep your grubby little hands off the goods."

"My 'grubby little…'? You're ridiculous!"

"Are we boosting you?" he asks, having the nerve to sound exasperated with *me*. "Or do you want to swim all the way back?"

I glare at him, then take in the considerable distance back to the shore.

"We're boosting me." I exhale.

"Alright then." He weaves his fingers together and creates a little step. "Put 'er here."

I silently place my foot in his hands.

"And one… two… three… alley-oop!" he exclaims as he springs me up and over the rim of the boat.

I land on the bottom. Hard.

"You okay?" he asks.

I sit up on the bench seat and look down at him bobbing in the water, his eyes tipped up to mine in question.

I took a photography class as an elective in college one semester. The portrait lessons were my favorite. I remember my teacher saying if you want to see the inherent innocence in your subject… shoot their portrait from above. When your subject looks upward to meet the camera's gaze, their face naturally softens, their hard expressions pull back, and the youthfulness and hopefulness inside them—inside all of us—are exposed.

Seems my teacher was on to something.

I wish I had a camera right now because looking at his face from above, his bravado melts into the water below, and all I can see is this precious, perfect boy.

"I think it's best that we don't talk anymore," I say more softly than I intend to. "It's just not... appropriate."

"Hm." He pauses and considers this a moment.

"As you wish, Mabel Again."

"Don't call me that."

"Don't call *me* Wally."

"You like it, though," I sass, surprising us both.

"Oooh, she does have some fire in her after all." He looks proud. "I knew she did."

With that, he smiles and hoists himself back in the boat, not letting a drop of water on board with him, looking like he's done this a hundred times. I suppose he has.

He starts rowing us back in silence.

I cling to the bunny to ensure he doesn't take another aquatic adventure anytime soon. I'm finding it difficult to look directly at Wally—I mean, Wallace—but I can feel his eyes burning into me.

I know steering clear of this guy is the right thing to do. So why do I feel so undeniably sad about it?

"Hey, Mabel?"

I don't respond.

"Aw, are we having our first fight?" he coos.

I still stay silent.

"Alright, fair enough," he says, adopting a serious tone for what feels like the first time during this whole boating expedition. "You are engaged. I respect that, and I respect your wishes. Though in my defense, I do think kissing me was a biiiiiit of a mixed message, but hey, it's certainly a lady's prerogative to change her mind." He pauses and considers something before continuing. "Before we officially cut off all communication, can I just offer you some quick food for thought? You know, since I'm your elder and all?"

I give in the tiniest bit and meet his eyes.

"If the fiancé is going full butterfly hump on you? Well then, my man is doing it *all* wrong."

He gives me a wink, then rows us silently to shore.

And I have to suppress the smile that wants to spread on my face the whole way back.

Chapter Twelve

The rest of my afternoon was a combination of highs and lows. High? Getting Harvey the Hoppinator – apparently that was the balloon bunny's name – back into Holden's arms. Low? Walking back to the main office soaking wet and having to borrow unwashed clothes from the camp's lost and found. Lowest low? Firing April. Well, that's not entirely accurate. I didn't exactly fire April. I suspended her for the week. I had to. I mean, let's put aside for a moment the fact that she's been completely disrespectful and inappropriate with me. I simply can't have her responsible—even marginally—for little kids when her judgment is so spotty. I'm bracing myself for the inevitable parent phone calls tomorrow morning telling me their children couldn't sleep due to nightmares of the human centipede variety.

And April did not go easy, I'll tell you that. There was much talk of "Wait till my mother hears about this!" and "You'll regret this decision!" and "You have made a big mistake. Big!" That last one made me think she was quoting Julia Roberts in *Pretty Woman.* I watched that movie for the first time the night my parents left, I guess as a way to dip my toes into Calliope's "Bad Mabel" challenge. Did you know Julia Roberts plays a sex worker? Everyone knows that, right? No wonder my parents never let me watch that one. Despite a few obviously delightful moments, though, I have to say that I found it to be pretty problematic overall. I mean, is a guy like Edward slash Richard

Gere really the goal? Vivian slash Julia Roberts seemed pretty darn savvy throughout the whole movie, but she still wanted him to rescue her at the end with a Rapunzel fantasy? Also, why was every woman in the movie who had blond hair super-duper mean? And here was my biggest issue—after George Costanza from Seinfeld tries to sexually assault Vivian slash Julia Roberts, why doesn't Edward slash Richard Gere call the cops?"

"Boo?" a male voice floats in the periphery of my awareness.

Seriously. He punches him, sure—which I suppose was a step in the right direction—but I think calling the cops on the bastard was definitely in order... Oh snap, I called him a bastard.

"Boo-oo?" that same voice sing-songs in my direction, louder now.

"Bert Alert!" I startle out of my daze. "Hey boo, hey! I was just... thinking."

"Mom's ready for the bug juice," he says.

"Oh good, I'll go get it set up."

We're at Doreen's place in Rittenhouse Square, one of the more affluent areas of Philadelphia. Bert grew up in the suburbs like I did, but a few years back, when "The Business" started taking off for Doreen, she decided to get a place "in the city proper," saying that it was a more impressive place to hold events with prospective partners and generally "less depressing than the suburbs."

Bert of course moved with her. I don't think there was even a question that Bert would move with her.

Tonight is our big monthly event where we share product demonstrations with our new and prospective partners. I offered to make some vitamin "bug juice" infused with the very best supplements available on the market today.

I'm pouring the juice into tiny crystal cups when the doorbell rings. I look toward the spacious living room with floor-to-ceiling windows showcasing a glorious view of the Philadelphia skyline and see that Bert and Doreen are both in full-schmooze mode.

The doorbell rings again. I look around, and no one is making a move toward the door. Looks like tonight I am the greeter.

I open the door and look up almost a full foot into ice blue eyes.

"Hi, 'Mabel Again.'"

I slam the door in his face.

Then immediately open it again.

"Oh my goodness," I say. "I am so sorry! I have no idea why I did that. What are you... Um, why are you...? How did you...? Are you stalking me?"

"Do you *want* me to stalk you?" he asks.

I consider this for a moment... then slam the door in his face for a second time.

And... immediately open it.

"I'm sorry. I did it again, didn't I?"

"You did."

"Rude. So rude. I was not raised to be rude. Come in. No, stay out. Make yourself at home. I mean, leave please."

"Are you okay?" he says with a little laugh.

"Why are you here?" I whisper harshly as I look around for signs of Bert. "And how did you know where I would be tonight?"

"I was invited, remember?" He pulls out the flyer I gave him the other day.

"Oh. Right. Yes. I guess I just thought..."

"You thought..." He leans toward me slightly from where he's standing in the doorframe, and it's the first time I'm taking in the sight and smell of him. I'm learning that this guy is a walking, talking sensory experience. His hair is damp as though he just got out of the shower. His outdoor shower. I wonder what it would be like to shower under the stars like that? Gosh and he smells like... what is that... lemongrass soap? Man, that's delicious.

"Did you just smell me?"

"No? No... no! Why would you think that?"

"You leaned toward me, your adorable little nostrils flared—twice—and... your eyes are still closed as though you're caught up in olfactory enjoyment."

Olfactory? What kind of a guy uses a word like olfactory? Oh shoot, he's right. My eyes are still closed. I shoot them open and realize how close we've gotten. So close I can see the specks of silver in his clear blue eyes.

"How do I smell?" he rumbles.

I hesitate. I stare at his specks. His sparkly, sparkly specks.

"Mabel?"

"Terrible," I blurt.

"I smell terrible?"

"Yep. Just awful." I take an exaggerated inhale when a woman walks past us toward the restroom. "Bleh. Ugh. This guy stinks to hell. Who invited this guy?" I point at him and wave my hand around my nose, all for this lady's benefit. She gives me a confused look and continues on her way.

I'm lying, of course. This man smells delicious.

He sniffs his armpit, an action that should be gross, but somehow it's not. It's... hot?

"Damn. And I put in an effort too. Showered, combed my hair. Wore my big boy pants and everything."

I take in his clothes. His "big boy pants" are dark blue jeans that look like they were made for him. He has his regular work boots on, but if I'm not mistaken, he cleaned them up a bit, and the button-up light blue denim shirt he's wearing has the sleeves rolled to his elbows. Apparently, this is a thing, this exposed forearm thing on men. I was feeling like a bad friend, so I've finally started reading Calliope's dino romances. After the third novella in a row where the male dinosaur rolled his sleeves up, inevitably leading the lady dino to go crazy with lust—yes, Calliope's dinosaur characters wear clothes—I asked her about it. "Oh, Mabes," she said. "Forearms may as well be called fuck-arms. They are the gateways to all things sexy on a man."

I had no idea.

Until now.

Looking at Wally, I am in complete agreement with Calliope. Forearms *should* be called fuck-arms.

I'm snapped out of my fuck-arm trance by my phone vibrating in my pocket. "Oooh!" I squeak to attention and realize I was unabashedly staring at him. My pocket continues to buzz.

"You need to get that?" He gestures toward my hip.

I pluck out my phone, take a quick look, and hit decline. "No. No, I do not." What I need is to get things de-escalated with this guy, stat. "Wallace," I say, putting my head counselor voice on.

"Aw, what happened to Wally? I was starting to like that."

"*Wallace.*" I repeat. "I'm starting to think you misunderstood my message earlier."

"When you shoved your tongue down my throat? Nah, I got that message loud and clear, darlin'."

"Shh! Shh! Shhhhhhhh!" I put my hand to his mouth to silence him, and we both freeze.

When I feel those pillowy lips beneath my fingertips, I'm taken right back to the way they felt against my own. I drop my hand and whip around to see if anyone is watching. We're alone. For the moment.

When I turn back to him, he's smiling. His eyes are twinkling. It's beautiful and infuriating.

"I, uh... I already apologized for the lapse in judgment this afternoon. You did not consent to that, um... to that... "

"Kiss, Mabel." He finishes the sentence for me. "It's called a kiss."

"Shhhhhh! SHHH!" I spin around again to scope out our surroundings, then lower my voice to a whisper. "Right. A kiss. You did not consent to that kiss."

"No, I did not."

"I took advantage of you at that moment."

"Yes, you sure did."

He grins. He is enjoying this way too much.

"Like I already said," I grit my teeth, "I am sorry, and it will not happen again. But, um, I'm confused about why you're here. I thought it was understood that the invitation for tonight was no longer operational."

"No longer operational, huh?"

"That's right."

"And why would that be the case?"

"Because!" I say it like he's a bit dense. "I said that we shouldn't talk anymore."

"Who's here to talk?" He chuckles. "I'm here for a product party! I'm here to boost my T!"

Suddenly, I feel a surprise hand on my lower back, accompanied by a concerned voice.

"Mabes? You okay?"

I startle.

"Ahh! Bert! It's Bert! The man I kiss on a regular basis! Bert! Hi, Bert!"

Bert is standing beside me, shooting glances at Wally and looking confused.

"Hello," he says, though I'm not certain if it's to me or the burly man in front of me.

"Hey there!" Wally says with enthusiasm as he extends a hand to Bert. "You must be the butterflying fiancé!"

"I... am the fiancé, yes." Bert reluctantly shakes his hand and sneaks a quick glance at me before saying, "And you are?"

"Wallace Bieber. Prospective team member. Mabel here tells me you have a fantastic new line of products designed to boost male stamina and testosterone, and let me tell you, pal, I gotsta get me summa that!"

Bert looks him up and down from where he stands, considerably shorter and smaller than our unexpected visitor.

"Alright. Uh. By all means, then. Uhhhhhh. Come on in," he says. It's really interesting seeing Bert rattled.

"Fantastic." Wally barges past us and rubs his hands together in anticipation. "I heard there would be vitamin bug juice in this joint. Lead me to it, team! Papa's parched!"

Papa's parched?

"You'll, uh, you'll find the refreshments around the corner to your left," Bert calls after him.

"'Preciate it, pal!" Wally shoots him a finger gun, then disappears from sight.

"Interesting guy..." Bert starts.

"Sort of. I guess. Not really."

"Where did you meet him?" His head cocks to the side. "The museum?"

"No, the arboretum actually. He's the groundskeeper. Or the handyman. I actually don't know what his title is. But you and Doreen wanted me to bring some of my work colleagues tonight, so."

He's looking at me like he might be regretting that request.

I continue, "Right?"

"Yeah." He shakes his head a few times. "Yes! Absolutely. I guess I just thought they'd be more…"

"More what?"

"Nothing." He takes a deep breath and smiles. "Nice work, baby."

"Thank you." I beam at him, despite feeling insanely guilty on the inside.

At what point should I be telling him that I kissed that odd man who just entered the living room? Now? Never?

Never sounds ideal of course, but I can't do that. That's not who I am. Mabel McGonigle does not keep secrets, and she does not tell lies. Even lies by omission. She does not usually reference herself in the third person either, but clearly, she's going through a strange time right now.

"You okay?" Bert asks, searching out my eyes. "Where'd you go just now?"

"Nowhere. I am right here with you, Bert Alert." I shake off the guilt and flutter my eyelashes up at him.

"You have something in your eye?" he asks.

"No. Why?"

"They just went all spastic."

"I'm fine." Guess I'm not a natural eyelash flutterer. "I, uh… I packed a bag. Are we still on for tonight?" I ask, changing the subject.

"Of course. It's Monday, isn't it?" he says with a smile.

It was also Monday last week, but that didn't seem to make a difference to him. I don't say that, though.

"Great," I chirp. "Can't wait."

He peeks over his shoulder at a few guests making their way into the main room, sipping their vitamin bug juice.

"Mom has me leading the first product demo, so I have to go prep."

"Okay. You'll do great."

"I know," he says, giving me a quick peck on the lips, then returning to the living room around the corner.

I stand alone in their fancy foyer for a moment, close my

eyes, and take a deep breath.

Wow, I have absolutely no idea what I'm doing.

I hear the plinky plunky intro music Doreen uses for product demonstrations start to play, so I slowly make my way toward the spacious living room—which, now that I think about it, is not designed for actual living. It's designed for event-ing. Rows and rows of chairs for prospective members fill the space, the whole perimeter of the room packed with tables full of products.

I scan the room and instantly lock eyes with my one and only prospective team member. He points at the chair next to him.

I make my way over to his row.

"Saved you a seat," he says.

I speak quietly. "Hi. Thank you. But that wasn't necessary. I'll sit with my..." I look toward the front of the room but see no seats available with Bert and Doreen. "Team."

Wally smiles and rubs his palm in a circle on the empty chair next to him. I silently slide into it.

"Splooge!" he says after a moment, jerking his thumb in the direction of the woman sitting on his other side.

"Excuse me?" I ask.

"Dawn. She's the head yoga instructor at Splooge."

"Oh, yes. So I hear!" I lean forward and smile. "Hi, Dawn. Nice to see you again. Glad you could be with us tonight."

"Likewise," she says.

I return my attention to Wallace and whisper, "You, uh... you do yoga?"

"I do," he says. "Big time. Mostly on my own down by the water. But when I lived in the city, I was one of Dawn's regulars."

"He did his teacher training with me too. The way he dove into his practice so fully during his recovery was inspiring."

I turn to Wally. "*You* are a certified yoga instructor?"

"I am." Somehow he says it with a straight face. I, however, burst out laughing.

"He's very good," Dawn says. "Gives excellent adjustments."

"Oh my gosh, you were serious?" I gasp, and instantly feel terrible for laughing. "And you were recovering? Recovering from what?"

He bats the air like he doesn't want to address that topic any further.

Dawn is apparently lost in a yogic reverie. "Oh yes, Wallace is very serious about his practice. When he sat on my pachimottonasana this spring, I almost passed out. You know, in a pleasurable way." She gives me a subtle wink at that, then softly shuts her eyes and breathes out a single word. "Sukha."

"Sorry, what-uh?" I ask.

"Sukha," Dawn says again in that sultry yogic voice she's clearly perfected. "It's Sanskrit for pleasure." She gives him a look that even I, inexperienced, have-only-ever-slept-with-one-guy Mabel, recognize as lust.

Okaaaaay.

"I really should find somewhere else to sit," I say as I try to rise from my chair. Operative word

being "try" because he places his hand on my shoulder, and without so much as an ounce of pressure, I slowly sit back down beside him. Like he has some kind of power over me.

"Thank you, Dawn," he says. "You're a sweetheart."

"Well, I only speak the truth. Satya."

"Sayta." He whispers to me, as if I'd asked for clarification. "It's Sanskrit for truth."

"Ah," I say, leaning back and settling into my seat, acting completely uninterested.

"What's that look on your face?" he asks quietly.

"I don't know. I can't see my face."

"It looks like this." He scrunches his eyebrows together and protrudes his bottom lip.

"My face is not doing that," I protest. I make a point to soften my expression before continuing.

"I think I'm just... kind of surprised you teach yoga."

"Why is that?"

"I guess because..."

"Because...?"

"Because you're kind of a dick."

"Wow." He laughs.

"Ohmygosh, I'm so sorry!" I whisper and cover my mouth

with both hands.

"Don't be. You're not wrong. I *am* a dick. Though, you bring up an interesting point. One I've been pondering more and more lately."

"What's that?" Somehow even as I ask the question, I know it's a mistake.

"Why do we use our private parts to insult one another?"

"What? Who does that? I don't."

"You called me a dick."

"Oh. Right. Sorry, again."

"*Again*, don't be," he says kindly. "But what's so wrong with dicks, I ask you, that they should be used to insult and wound?"

"Nothing, I suppose." I feel my face flush. "I'm not someone who uses language like that. "

"Apparently, you are. You know, while we're at it... pussy."

"Excuse me?" I squeak.

"Tell me. What's so wrong with pussy?"

"I, uh... I didn't... say pussy," I stammer. "Nor did I say there's anything wrong with it."

"No, I know you didn't," he continues. "You're 'not someone who uses language like that.'" He smiles when he parrots my own words back at me. "But have you noticed how uninformed guys everywhere use that beautiful word to tear their fellow men down? Now does that make one bit of sense to you? Because it doesn't make an ounce of sense to me."

"Um." I look at the front and see Doreen taking her place at the podium. "Are we really talking about this right now?"

"Not if you don't want to." He shrugs.

"I *don't* want to," I say emphatically, shifting my gaze to the front of the room.

"Alright then. Pussy case closed."

Pussy case closed? This guy might actually be a lunatic.

"Thank you," I say curtly.

"You're welcome." I sneak a peek out of my right eye, and he's smirking. He always looks pleased with himself as though he's in a constant state of winning conversations.

"Welcome, everyone!" Doreen's voice rings out clear as a

bell from the front of the room. "We're so thrilled to see all of your beautiful faces in the room tonight. A sea of gorgeous, hopeful faces who've come out this evening because they know there's something bigger out there for them. Something better. Something meaningful and thrilling. You are a group of entrepreneurs who are craving an experience made of—"

"Madoff?" Wally interrupts on a shout.

Doreen looks confused for a half-second, then responds with confidence, "What did you say, sir?"

Wally smiles and volleys back over the crowd, "Did you say we'd be having an experience like Madoff?"

"No." Her face slips and turns sour for just a millisecond before it's back in its usually smiling glory. "No, I did not. I was starting to say that we are embarking on an experience made of..."

"Ah! Made of, made of," Wally repeats. "My mistake. I thought for sure you said Madoff.

"Well. I did not, sir." Doreen's lips thin.

"Understood, ma'am. Carry on!"

What the heck was that?

Wally leans back in his seat and crosses his arms over his chest as though he's settling in for a show. He catches me staring at him, and he gives me what I'm now discovering is his trademark wink. I haven't a clue what he's up to, but I'm getting a sinking feeling in my stomach that it's not good.

Somehow, Doreen gets her bearings and continues her welcome speech.

"So, as I was saying to every single one of you gathered here tonight... I am honored that you have joined us. Together, we are about to embark on a journey of wealth and health and wellness, and I couldn't be more excited to get started."

"Me neither!" Wallace shouts. "Wooooooo-hoooo! Let the healing begin."

Chapter Thirteen

An hour later, the presentation is in full swing. There have been product demonstrations galore. Doreen has been the hostess with the most-ess as always, and the people assembled tonight seem genuinely jazzed about the supplements and creams and powders and oils and balms and soaps and serums that the business has to offer. Yeah, there's a lot of products. I've learned over the past few months that health and wellness is apparently not cheap.

Despite his earlier weirdness and disruptiveness, Wally has been surprisingly quiet and respectful since, only bursting out the occasional whoop or cheer from time to time to match the others' enthusiasm. Unlike Mr. Landis, though, the man in front of me who claps after every demonstration and even seems to have happy, hopeful tears in his eyes, Wally's hoots don't quite seem genuine. But what do I know? I barely know the guy. Maybe these past sixty minutes have made him a believer.

The slideshow presentation at the front of the room shifts, and the energy in the room shifts along with it. A big beautiful triangle is blaring from the screen. The Triangle of Trust. Excited whispers flutter throughout the space. It's time to talk about the compensation plan.

I may be imagining it, but it seems like Wally's spine goes ramrod straight at that moment. He clears his throat. His eyes narrow.

Uh-oh.

I missed Doreen's introductory words since I was so focused on the man beside me, who is now fidgeting and mumbling something indecipherable under his breath. All I catch is the tail end of her spiel when she smiles, and says, "Now, who would like to volunteer?"

Wally's hand shoots up like a rocket. My heart rate does the same.

"What are you doing?!" I hiss.

"Volunteering," he hisses right back. "The lady asked for a volunteer, did she not? I'm volunteering."

I spin in my seat and take in the sea of hands, hoping somehow his hand stays unseen.

"She did, yeah," I hedge, "but—"

"But what?" He jerks his hand higher toward the ceiling.

"But does it have to be you?" I hear myself whine.

"Yes, you!" Doreen's voice rings clear as a bell over the heads in front of us. Her eyes zero in on Wally, and she wags her arm toward her body. "Come. Join us up front!"

I have to give it to Doreen. She always welcomes a challenge.

A wave of nerves washes over me. Somehow my body knows this isn't going to go well.

Wally gives me a wink and lowers his hand onto my upper thigh for a moment. It's just a moment. A milli-moment really. A simple pat. A quick little pat-pat before he stands and heads down the aisle, but I feel a zing course through my body at the contact. My *entire* body. And that zing lingers. I can honestly say I have never once felt a zing from physical contact with Bert. Not even in our early days in high school. Up until this point, I haven't minded the lack of zinging. Truth be told, I didn't think zinging was a real thinging. I mean a real *thing*. I thought that was just something made up that people talked about in books and movies. But it must be real because here I am with a body that's zinging like crazy from a simple pat on the thigh. From a man who is not my fiancé. A man who I kissed less than eight hours ago.

It's official.

I'm a jerk.

I'm a cheater and a jerk.

That's right, ladies and gentlemen! Mabel McGonigle is a cheating jerk!

Laughter snaps me out of my self-induced guilt fog. I look up and see Wally has reached the front of the room, and his arm is around Doreen. Her face flushes, and she's laughing too. Seems I'm not the only one affected by this guy.

"So. Tell us, Wallace. What brought you here tonight? "She beams up at him from where she's tucked under his arm and giggling. In the six years, ten months, and seven days since I first met her, I don't know that I've ever heard Doreen giggle.

"Mabel," he responds simply. His deep voice resonates throughout the room.

"Mabel?" Clearly, that wasn't the response she was expecting.

"Yes, ma'am. The enchanting Mabel brought me here tonight." He points at me and gives me his salute. I see Bert swivel in his seat to find me as well. I sink lower into my chair. I'm definitely getting a bad feeling about this. "Well, Mabel and my desire to spend the night being an Ovis Aries."

"I'm sorry, an Ovis... what?" Doreen asks with a smile and a little shake of her head.

"Ovis Aries," he responds with an unspoken "duh" in his tone. "A sheep. The scientific name is Ovis Aries. Doreen. Wouldn't you say the majority of people in this room are a bunch of sheep?"

"I'm not sure I understand what you—"

"Baaaaa!" He bleats like an animal. "Baaaaa."

Oh, my God. The man is baaaa-ing in front of a roomful of fifty people. You know, I got the sense that he's a bit of an eccentric person, the kind of guy who doesn't care much about what others think of him, but I didn't see this particular quirk coming.

Is my dad right? Am I "book smart but not people smart"?

I shake that thought off and take quick stock of what I actually know about this man. Besides the fact that he lives alone in a shack in the woods, he can swim great distances under the water without a blowhole—though, in fairness, I haven't checked for one. He seems to fix anything that's broken, and he incites fear in teenagers and titillation in grown women? I know virtually nothing. Oh dammit to hell, he's still baa-ing.

"Baaa!"

Doreen's body is blown back by the strength of the sound. Or maybe by the sheer weirdness of Wally. She scans the room as if she's about to call out "security!" like they do in the movies. But we don't have security.

"Dora." Wally chuckles. "Dora, chill." He's apparently finished with his barnyard game. For the moment anyway. He slaps his knee and points at her. "Oh, look at your face, girl."

"My name is Doreen." She tries to keep her perpetual smile in place, but I can see she's struggling.

"I know that, girl," he rumbles. "I just gave you a nickname. You're welcome." He winks.

Her mouth opens, but nothing comes out. This may be the first time I've seen Doreen speechless.

"Alright, let's do this!" He rubs his hands together in anticipation. "You asked for a volunteer, I volunteered. What do you need?" He peers at the slideshow. "Someone to help perpetuate the outrageous myth that they can actually make money in your 'business?'"

"There's nothing outrageous about it, Wallace," Doreen answers smoothly. "People make excellent money as distributors in our company."

"Is that right?" He purses his lips and nods.

"It is," she responds with confidence.

"Not what I've heard, Dora. Not what I've heard," he says. And then he gets directly in her face and softly says, "Baaa."

Bert rises from his chair. "Do not denigrate my mother and her sheep! I mean her followers!"

Wow, Bert's getting red in the face.

"Bertie, sit. It's okay," Doreen says in a soothing tone.

"I'm not *denigrating* anyone, Bertholomew," Wally rumbles. "Though I do appreciate the filial chivalry you're showing for Dora here."

"It's Dor*een*." Bert practically spits. "And why the hell are you calling me Bertholomew?"

"Your name's Bert," Wally says matter-of-factly." Short for

Bertholomew, no?"

"Um. No," Bert sneers. "Short for Robert."

"No shit!" He seems genuinely stunned. "And you went for *Bertie* as the nickname? A bold and bizarre choice, my man. Alright, back to business."

"Yes, back to business sounds wonderful," Doreen says with a strained smile. "You seem like a very... *unique* gentleman, and we're so pleased you've joined us tonight, but perhaps you can take your seat now."

"No, thank you, ma'am. I'll stand. But yes, back to business indeed. As I was saying... Baaaa."

I should say something, right? This is my guest, and I should say something. But I don't. I stay frozen to my seat.

Wally addresses the room at large.

"Listen, everybody. Don't get me wrong. I love sheep. They're beautiful, gentle, giving creatures. Without sheep and their fluffy generosity, I wouldn't get to luxuriate in my lambswool socks, as I read Proust by the fireplace, my toesies soaking in the cozies."

This guy has a very odd way with words. Is he giving some weird speech? Also, he reads Proust?

"Without sheep—and I apologize to the vegans out there tonight—I couldn't fill my belly with my mama's mutton stew on lonely winter's nights watching HGTV. Without sheep, I couldn't sit and admire a glorious green field speckled with wondrous white grazing creatures while crisp breezes carry the sweet scent of manure up my nose holes..."

Nostrils. Why doesn't he just say nostrils?

"Without sheep—"

Good lord, he's still going.

"I couldn't visit a precious petting farm with my nephews and marvel at the beauty of delighted children nuzzling their muzzles while inserting the ass ends of carrots into their mouths. So let me be really clear here. I. Love. Sheep."

I have to hand it to him, for better or for worse, he has absolutely everyone's attention.

"But do I want to *be* one? Do I want to *be* a sheep? No. Because you know what else sheep are? They're meek. Docile. They play follow the leader. Their whole damn lives. And as I look around this crowd tonight? It pains me to say it... but everyone in this room is a damn sheep."

Alright, I have to step in now.

"Wallace!" I'm up on my feet, doing my best to maintain a reasonable tone. "Please. Clearly, this isn't the business for you, so why don't we just go?" I gesture toward the exit.

"We?" Bert's on his feet again, and I marvel for a moment on how he turned the one-syllable word "we" into a three-syllable snarly one. "Since when is there a we here? Are you going to leave with this guy?"

"There isn't a we!" I exclaim. "No way! No we! He and me, we are not a we! I just meant I brought him here, so I should politely escort him out, no?"

"The lady doth protest too much, methinks, no?" Wally says, then takes in Bert's beet-red face. "Kidding, buddy. I'm sure she doth protest the exact right amount."

"I think you should go," Bert says through clenched teeth.

"Agreed. On my way out. Gimme just a quick sec to wrap things up, pal."

Bert opens his mouth to respond, but Wally disregards him completely and continues to address the room.

"I've been a bit verbose tonight, friends. So let me get right to the point. This lady here?" He gestures to Doreen, who has sunk back into the shadows a fair amount, something I've never seen her do. "Sweet as she may seem? She's not. No, friends. This lady here is a sheepherder hell-bent on pulverizing all of your piggybanks."

Doreen gasps and steps forward. "That is ridiculous. That is completely and utterly—"

"True." Wally finishes the thought for her. "It's completely and utterly true. And don't ask me how I know. I have sources. So many sources it would make your head spin. You know something, Doreen? Sheep are givers. Wool, milk, cheese... the list goes on." He gazes out at everyone assembled. "The people in this room are givers. They've given you their time, their trust, their enthusiasm. And you have disrespected that gift. You, ma'am, are not a giver. You are a taker."

"I am not a taker! I am a—"

"Friends!" he shouts. "Raise your hoof... forgive me, raise your hand if you've received a paycheck from this woman."

Doreen's mouth shuts in a tight line, and her eyes widen.

Out of fifty attendees, only five people raise their hooves. I mean hands.

Doreen starts to babble. "Well. Most of them are new. Paychecks go out monthly and—"

"Okay, five of you. Out of the five of you, what are we talking? Are we talking the big money you're being promised?"

"Hell no!" sweet Mr. Gaddis, who runs a house cleaning company, shouts, surprising everyone around him who knows him. Up until this point, I've never heard the man speak above a murmur. "I've been at this for six months!" Mr. Gaddis continues, "And I've spent more than I've made!"

"I don't doubt that's true, sir," Wallace says to him. "And I'm sorry to inform you that it's going to continue being that way in the future. Hey, hey! Ho, ho! Stick with this biz, you're gonna be po'!" he begins to chant. That's right. This strange man I invited here tonight starts a full-on *chant*.

I lock eyes with first Doreen and then Bert, and they. Are. Horrified.

Freida Newton, the young woman whose dream of opening an acupuncture practice is on hold until she makes a dent in her student loans, speaks up next. "She keeps showing me these bloated weekly payouts she's getting, but the biggest check I've seen so far is twenty-five bucks!"

"What's your name, lady?" Wally asks, pointing at her as though he's a jolly talk show host instead of the wackadoo currently ruining my life.

"Freida!" she says, seemingly unable to stop yelling once she's begun.

"Well, Freida, get used to it because twenty-five dollars is all you're gonna see if you stay committed to this madness! Hey, hey! Ho, ho! Stick with this biz, you're gonna be po'!" he chants his refrain again.

By this point, the majority of people present have gotten to their feet. Some are yelling, a few are crying, and most of them are grabbing their belongings and joining the chant.

I make my way over to him, and whisper-hiss, "What are you doing?!" I try pulling him to the side by his undeniably beautiful—even though I want desperately to deny them—fuck-arms. He barely budges.

"As human beings, we need to be looking out for each other, yeah?" he responds. "Taking care of each other? You bleat, I bleat, yeah?"

"I believe the saying is you bleed, I bleed," I say with no small amount of snark. "Emphasis on the D."

"Emphasis on the D indeed." He says this just loud enough for me to hear, then winks and continues his cheer, lifting his arms and waving them this time to rouse the room.

"Hey, hey! Ho, ho! Stick with this biz, you're gonna be po'! Hey, hey! Ho, ho! Stick with this biz, you're gonna be po'!"

One by one, the rest of the room rises to its feet and joins in the refrain. Mr. Gaddis, Mrs. Kim from the coffee shop, and even Dawn, the yoga splooge lady.

"Hey, hey! Ho, ho! Stick with this biz, you're gonna be po'! Hey, hey! Ho, ho! Stick with this biz, you're gonna be po'!"

Shoot, that's actually really catchy. I find myself tapping my foot and singing along under my breath as, one by one, they form a line to file down the aisle directly out the door.

Within a matter of minutes, I'm left alone with Bert and Doreen, the room hollow and empty, both sets of their eyes shooting daggers into me.

Chapter Fourteen

*B*ert and I make our way through the halls of Quality Inn in silence.

There was silence the whole cab ride here too.

I can't take it anymore, so I break it as we key our way into our suite.

"So, um. I guess I didn't invite the ideal prospect tonight, huh?"

"Understatement, Mabel. I'm pretty sure The Business is over for us."

"No! No way."

"Mabel? We lost seventy-five percent of our downline," he snaps. "And my mother has been branded a financial pariah."

I'm silent for a moment with absolutely no idea what to say or how to make this okay.

"I'm so sorry," I try. "I'll get better. Promise."

"Better at what?" he asks.

"People-ing? I guess? You're great at people-ing. How do you do it?"

"I don't know, Mabes. I just follow my instincts. My gut."

"And it always leads you to make the best decision?"

An odd look passes across his face. He looks almost... sad? Before I can ask him about it, though, he slaps on a smile.

"Want to watch a little *L & O*?" he asks, surprising me with his willingness to change subjects.

"Of course," I say, but I feel a strange churning in my stomach.

A fogginess in my brain. I suddenly feel like I want to escape my body.

Bert turns on the TV and starts spreading our takeout containers on the thin floral carpet. I settle next to him on the floor and take the lids off the food I don't really like but will eat nonetheless.... for him. I hear the opening song to a show I don't really enjoy—with the exception of the great Ice-T, of course—but I will watch anyway... for him. For a moment, I'm actually grateful for this bit of predictable normalcy. For a moment, I find it comforting.

But then I start thinking of all the aspects of our life together that I tolerate... for him.

And I realize I can't do it for another minute more.

As our second episode wraps up, Bert starts to clean up our containers and places our leftovers in the mini-fridge. And then I hear it: the final dunh-dunh. The famous producer's name we all know—and sort of love—flashes on the screen. And I know exactly what's coming next.

"Are you ready for my Dick Wolf?" Bert says as he stands and moves toward the bed.

This is the part where I say a classic Ice-T line to heighten the mood. Something like "Do Twinkies last forever?" or "Were you planning on getting frisky with the Hamburglar?" or my personal favorite, "It's all fun and games until someone loses a penis." Okay, in fairness, that last one is a Captain Cragen line, but it's too good not to bring out on a Monday from time to time.

But on this particular Monday night... I can't make myself say a thing.

I'm learning that I'm the kind of person who can make the best out of something for a long time. I can tolerate something less-than-ideal for a long time. I can make excuses for someone for a long time. A *really* long time, in fact. Like... six years, eight months, and twenty-one days long. But then, I inevitably reach a point of no return where I shut off to the person or situation. I'm just no longer available to them, and there's nothing I can do about it.

I was like that with Brianna Bentz in second grade when she pulled my braids one too many times. I was like that with

Dominic Vasquez in fifth grade when he wrote "Mabel is a dork" on my desk every day for a month, and I was like that in grad school the twentieth time Professor Nelson told me that I was "an exceptionally smart scientist... for a woman."

People are always shocked when I turn that corner. When I'm finally done dealing with their unsavory behavior. It takes me a while. But I get there.

And now, I too am shocked to discover that I've reached that point with Bert.

But—of course—this is still me we're talking about. I'm still Mabel, "the girl who wouldn't hurt a fly," the girl who would do anything to avoid making someone I care about feel anything less than loved and adored.

"Did you hear me?" Bert asks. "I said..." He drops back into his 'seductive voice'—at least I assume seduction has been his intention all these years—and repeats, "Are you ready for my Dick Wolf?"

"Oh, um. Sort of?"

"Sort of?" He looks more confused than I've ever seen him.

"I'm sorry. I mean, yes. Yes, of course. The, uh—'the smell of pimple cream turns my stomach.'"

"What?" His face continues to twist. "Did Ice-T say that?"

"He did," I say matter-of-factly. "Season three, episode sixteen. But yeah, perhaps not the best line to quote at this moment."

Come on, Mabel, have a grown-up discussion with this man. You can do it.

"Could we, uh—I feel like we should maybe—"

But before I can get the *thought* out, his proverbial Dick Wolf is out. And... our usual series of events starts to unfold in the same way I described it to my friends on Saturday night.

He tugs on it.

I tug on it.

He jerks it.

I jerk it.

I blow it.

He blows *on* it.

And for the first time, as I watch him blow on it, preparing myself for the cupping portion of the proceedings, I realize how truly absurd this is.

There has to be more than this, right? There has to be.

I find that I can't participate another second, and I'm racking my brain for a way out of this without hurting him.

A light bulb goes on, and I do what I have to do.

I take my cue from the female dragonfly.

And I decide to die.

"Cuppy cuppy, my little hush puppy!" he says as he juts his hips up in my direction.

This is clearly my call to action. But instead of scooping my hands together and cradling his, um, his... wolf globes like I always do, I stand on the mattress, go ramrod straight in my spine, my arms, and my legs, and...

... I dive face-first into the mattress.

My body absorbs the fall with a few residual bounces—the mattresses at Quality Inn are surprisingly springy—until I'm silent and still.

"Mabel?" I hear him say after a stunned moment. "What the hell was *that*?"

I don't move a muscle or make a sound. I'm face-down on the mattress, as still and as silent as can be.

"What are you doing?"

Nothing.

"Mabey baby?"

Silence.

"Mabel?"

He pokes me.

Shakes me.

Slaps me on the butt.

I'm completely frozen.

He rolls me over now.

I keep my face soft and expressionless.

"Mabel!"

He pats my cheeks.

"What the hell happened?" He pants. "Are you breathing? Oh

my God, she's not breathing."

Clearly, he's starting to panic.

Suddenly, he suctions his lips to mine, and I realize he's giving me mouth to mouth.

With tongue.

He follows it up with some fumbling pumps to my breasts.

Wow, this is more focused physical attention than I've ever received from him.

I'm fairly certain this is not how CPR is done, of course, but I'm not at liberty to tell him that—not if I want to keep up this ruse. It also takes some intense focus on my part to avoid gagging while this is happening, not because I find Bert heinous—I still love the guy—but housing a swirling, uninvited tongue inside your lifeless mouth is a challenge I hadn't anticipated.

In truth, I hadn't anticipated any of this. I suppose it's noble that he's trying to save my life, but the male dragonfly is just supposed to fly off when he realizes he's chosen the wrong mate, thus allowing the female to go on her merry way—a free woman—without ever having to hurt the male's delicate sensibilities.

He comes up for air, and I hear the tone of three numbers being entered into his phone.

"Mabel, I'm so sorry. Please, just please be okay, and I swear I'll never cheat on you again."

"YOU CHEATED ON ME?"

I spring back to life.

His eyes widen five times their regular size.

"No, I... " he stammers. "Oh, thank God you're alive. I—"

"9-1-1, what is your emergency?" a nasal voice comes through Bert's phone on speaker. It's always on speaker. Even when we're in public. Yup, he's *that* guy.

"You called 9-1-1?!" I squeal.

"Well, yeah! I thought you were dead! Wait. Why are you not dead?"

"Did you *want* me to be dead?"

"No! Of course not, but—"

"9-1-1, what is your emergency?" the voice asks again, more emphatic this time.

I grab the phone from Bert and speak into it.

"Hi, there. I'm so sorry we wasted your time. There is no emergency here. My fiancé thought I was dead, but I'm not."

"Are you sure, ma'am?"

"That I'm not dead?" I look down my body and pat myself a few times. "Yes, I'm sure. Gosh, this is all my fault. See, I was actually *pretending* to be dead to avoid conflict and intimate contact with my fiancé. I guess I did a pretty good job since he called you in a panic. Yay me! Up until this point, I've never been celebrated for my acting skills. Nope, I was stage crew throughout school and summer camp, so this is really surprising and not at all unwelcome, but I am terribly sorry to have disturbed you and concerned you this evening. What is your name?"

"Ethel."

"Nice to meet you, Ethel. I'm Mabel."

"Mabel, give me back my phone," Bert says with impatience.

I continue, undeterred.

"Thing is, I thought Bert and I were relatively happy, but recently I've been feeling less than fulfilled. I thought it was just me, and I needed to adjust my perception of the situation, but I'm coming to realize that there are actually some major flaws in the relationship itself."

"Mabel, you don't need to tell her about our—"

"See, what you need to understand about me, Ethel, is that I'm the kind of person who makes the best of things. You know, that person who looks for the good in people no matter what? And now—"

"Will you stop!" Bert says before snatching the phone from my hand and silencing it.

"Bert!" I scold.

"What?" he snaps.

"You hung up on Ethel! That was incredibly rude!"

"No, you know what is incredibly rude? And *illegal*? Placing a fake 9-1-1 call."

"*I* didn't place the call. *You* did!"

"Again, because I thought you were dead!"

"The male dragonfly is just supposed to fly away after his

would-be mate's descent. You did it wrong! But... thank you—I suppose—for trying to revive me."

"What the hell are you talking about?"

"Wait a second, what were *you* talking about? You cheated on me?"

He is silent a moment.

"Mabey baby, I'm so sorry."

"Cheated on me how, though?"

"What do you mean?"

"Like in Words with Friends? Fortnite? Candy Crush?"

"No..."

"Wait. Are you telling me you cheated on me with... sex?"

"Um. Yeah."

"Well, how in the hell is that possible? Excuse my language, but from what I understand, you're not very good at the sex!"

"Who told you I'm not good at 'the sex?'" he practically squeals.

"Basically everyone I've described your moves to. Calliope, Cyndi, Louise, Wally..."

"Why have you been 'describing my moves' to people?" He freaks. "And who is Wally?"

"Wallace," I say like it should be obvious. "The prospective team member I brought tonight?"

"You discussed our sex life with that cretin?!"

"Don't call him a cretin! *You're* a cretin! A cheatin' cretin!"

I don't know what gets into me at that moment, but I turn violent. I grab one of the way-too-thin Quality Inn pillows and start beating the heck out of him.

"I'm sorry, sweetie," he says between pillow thwacks. "It won't happen again."

"Okay," I breathe.

"Actually, that's not true," he says. "It probably will."

"What?"

"Baby, I'm trying to build The Business."

"With your penis?!"

"Well. Sort of. Yeah."

"That's how you 'network' on the weekends?!"

"If that's what it takes, yeah."

I hit him some more until I'm hit with a sudden flashback of the coffee shop last week.

"Oh my gosh. That is why the woman in the coffee shop ran off when she was introduced to me. That is why she said 'he sure does like *Law & Order*, huh.'"

He at least has the decency to look sheepish.

I look down at my left hand at the way-too-big ring that was never my style. It wasn't being resized like I told Wally the other day. I was just embarrassed to wear it. Too flashy. Too indicative of how wrong we are for each other. How wrong we've always been for each other if I'm being honest with myself. And how I have been holding on to this relationship for years, too scared to do what clearly needed to be done and end things between us.

At that moment, I can't say that I make a decision. It's almost like the decision makes me.

I take the ring off, place it on the bedside table, and walk toward the door, not intending to say another word.

"Wait a second," Bert says, suddenly sounding panicked. "What are you doing?"

"I'm leaving."

"When will you be back?"

He's equal parts hopeful and terrified when he says it, his eyes wide, his body frozen in place.

"I won't, boo," I say softly. "I'm leaving *you*."

"What? No," he says. "I'm sorry. Please, Mabes. I can't lose a good girl like you."

The expression on his face is so telling. He looks like a lost little boy at that moment, and I can't help but feel sorry for him. Can't help but want to take care of him. Never in a million years did he think I would give up on him. I can't blame him for that because neither did I.

Then something hits me.

"Wait. What did you say?"

"I said, I'm sorry. And I am, Mabes. I'm so so sorry."

"No, after that. You said you can't lose..."

"A good girl like you."

He finishes the sentence for me, and at that moment, I know

two things for certain. One, there's nothing left for me here. And two... this is the last time someone uses me being a "good girl" as an excuse to treat me badly.

"Good Girl Mabel" has been running the show my entire life, and look at what she has to show for it. She lives at home with angry, overprotective parents. She has no extended family to speak of. She was duped by a pyramid scheme run by her almost mother-in-law and cheated on repeatedly by a man who thinks a glorified version of "Bop it" is a suitable form of foreplay.

No more.

I may not have actually died tonight, but "Good Girl Mabel" most certainly did.

My friends were right. It's time for "Bad Girl Mabel" to come out and play.

Chapter Fifteen

"Are you serious right now?" Louise's face is full of utter shock and disdain.

"Hundred percent," I say with a nod.

It's Sunday morning, and I'm setting up my Save the Bees stand at the arboretum's Artisan Festival. I pulled some strings and got The Philadelphia Aquarium's Touch Tank booth lined up directly next to mine so I could spend some quality time with my new friend, Louise.

It's been almost a week since my breakup with Bert, and I'm catching her up on all the sordid details.

"How many women do you think he's pulled this with?" she asks.

"Hard to say. But since Monday night, I've spoken with five women who have confirmed their... *involvement* with him. But I have a feeling plenty more just don't want to talk about it. Or at least talk to *me* about it."

"Ohmygod, you poor thing," Louise croons.

"Eh," I say with a shrug.

"Did you just say 'eh' and shrug over your fiancé boning his way through all of his business prospects?" Her voice pitches up in disbelief.

"I think I did, yeah." I surprise even myself when I say this.

Seriously, if you would have told me a few weeks ago that I'd break up with my boyfriend of six years, eight months and twenty-one days after an explosive night of Ponzi scheme revelations and unrepentant confessions of infidelity, and I would barely bat an eyelash at the whole situation? That I wouldn't shed a single tear? I would've told you no way José. But here I am, not caring. Honestly, I wasn't even thinking about him until Louise asked me how we're doing. I wonder how much of that is because my mind was on a completely different man.

"His... promiscuity makes no sense to me, though." Louise's brow scrunches as she continues the conversation. "You told us he was terrible in bed, didn't you?"

"I never said that!" I say, shocked she would say something so crass. Accurate, I suppose, but crass.

Oh my gosh, why am I still defending him? Looks like "Good Mabel" isn't as easy to shake as I'd hoped.

"Mabel," Louise says, her features very serious. "We all heard the Dick Wolf story last week. You didn't need to explicitly say he was terrible in bed. That story was enough for me to *deduce* that his skills are beyond subpar. What do all these women see in him? For that matter, what did *you* see in him?"

It's a fair question. What did I see in him?

"He's a gentleman," I say with confidence, but then I have to pause. "Or I thought he was."

Louise stands there with a blank face, clearly expecting a solid answer. So I search for it.

"He's kind!" I enthuse, though those words no longer feel right in my mouth either. "Or I *thought* he was." I feel my voice getting softer with each attempt as if my vocal cords can't collaborate on such blatant untruths now that I know who he's become. Correction. Who he's been for a while now, it seems. I make one more attempt. "My parents adore him and... Gosh, I don't know Lou, we were a couple for six years, eight months, and twenty-one days. It's hard to end something that's been that much a part of your life, ya know?"

"Why do you do that?" Louise interrupts.

"Do what?"

"Keep track of the exact number of days you've known everyone."

"Well, not *everyone*..." I attempt to defend my weirdness.

"How long have you known me?" Louise challenges.

"Uhhhhh..." I pretend to be stumped, but I just end up sounding like a tea kettle.

"Come on," she goads. "I know you know."

I sigh. "Two months, three days, and..." I look at the time on my phone. "Sixteen hours."

Louise smiles.

"I know, I know. It's an odd thing to do."

"A little bit," she says with a laugh. "But it's sweet too. Shows you're paying attention. Shows the people in your life that they are important to you." She pauses, looks deliberately into my eyes, and says, "Bert should have appreciated that more. He should have appreciated you more."

"Thanks." For the first time since the breakup, I have to fight a lump in my throat, thinking of how much time I spent with him, and how, ultimately, none of it added up to anything of value.

I consider how to explain my counting-the-days quirk.

"I didn't have many friends growing up. A part of it was my parents, I think. They've always been super overprotective. Not entirely sure why. But I was the kid who was never allowed to go to sleepovers or parties or school dances. Tell people you're not allowed enough times, and they stop asking after a while." I feel a brief pang in my heart, remembering that left-behind feeling that was such a big part of my growing-up experience. "Bert was the one person who never stopped asking."

Louise inhales like she's about to say something, but I keep going before she can.

"I mean, Cyndi's been a constant throughout the years too, but she's from a military family, and they moved around a lot. We were pen pals most of our lives until now, and pen pals are great, but at some point, you want more than letters."

Lou's looking at me with a strange glassy-eyed expression. Is it sadness? Pity?

I decide to steamroll right past the potential pity. "When I got a bit older, one thing my parents *did* start allowing was summer camp. You know that's where I met Calliope, yeah?"

"Oh, yeah?" Apparently, she didn't know that.

"Yup! It was a performing arts and nature camp. Calliope starred in the plays, and I was her costumer. The year she was *Really Rosie*, I handmade her a boa out of duck droppings. Feathers, not poop."

"Sure, that's an important distinction," Louise says as she adjusts some seaweed sprays.

"I'm not sure why camp made the cut for my parents as far as extracurricular activities went, but hey, I certainly wasn't going to complain or question it. Oh, Lou, I loved it so much! That's probably why I still 'go to camp' every year for work. It's day camp, but still. Twenty-four years old and I still get that rush when I arrive each morning and see all the kids gathering in their groups. Every summer feels like a new beginning. Each year, I launched myself into the season like a-a-a... friendship-seeking missile, so eager for buddies you would think my parents locked me in my room for the other nine months out of the year." I recognize how bad that sounds. "They didn't, though. My parents are wonderful. They're the best friends I have."

"Yeah, you've mentioned that a time or two." Louise smiles.

"Gotcha. So. Week one of camp, I'd always be surrounded by new friends. It was heaven. But then by week two? I'd, um... well, I'd always find myself alone again. Took me years to understand why, but in hindsight, I think my over-eagerness made the other kids skittish. Even now, as an adult, I find it hard to shake that energy in me. People don't always trust enthusiasm. I've been told that people think I'm 'fake' more times than I can count. Apparently 'no one can actually be that happy.' BUT I AM, OKAY? I'M FREAKING HAPPY!"

My volume has gone up a few decibels, and my breathing is starting to feel choppy.

"Mabel, is that a tear rolling down your cheek?"

"NO WAY, IT'S JUST EYE SWEAT!" I shout.

"Eye sweat." She nods. "Okay."

"Anyway," I continue and swipe at the moisture on my face. "I guess this is my long-winded way of saying that when you're used to being left out, it can be pretty intoxicating when you're finally chosen. Bert... chose me."

I pause as a realization hits me and say, "Aaaand apparently upward of thirty to forty other girls along the way."

Not sure why, but this strikes me as hilarious at that moment. Louise just watches me spiral, not sure what to do.

"Hahahahaha! My one-hundred-forty-five-pound fiancé who collects vintage Beanie Babies for fun and waxes his body hair—and I do mean *all* his body hair—has been lying to me and cheating on me for months, boinking his way through a pyramid scheme, and I had no idea! Hahahahaha! And listen to me just blabbing away about his virtues! 'He's a gentleman, he's kind, my parents love him...' Blabbity blab blab blab! Hahahaha! Ohmygosh!"

"You okay, Mabes?" Louise asks tentatively.

I keep laughing. "Fine, yes! I'm fine. Mabel McGonigle is always fine!"

"You're not fine, lady. And you're not blabbing," Lou says. "You're sharing. That's good."

It takes a minute or so, but when I finally get my laughter under control, I sigh. "I guess. Let's drop it. Can we drop it?"

"Sure, we can drop it."

"Great. Thank you."

I go through the motions and put the finishing touches on my honeycomb display, a little embarrassed I let myself get so emotional. I spread out my pamphlets while listening to the sounds of vendors setting up their stands filled with local artisanal cheeses, woven baskets, and handblown glass art.

Listen," she says as she drops a starfish into the touch tank. "I'm probably the last person who should be doling out advice on self-worth and getting the relationships you deserve, but that's exactly what—"

"So what did you do for the Fourth?" I try abruptly changing the subject. "Bummer that the fireworks got rained out, huh?"

"Mabel, you're avoiding an important discussion that could really help you, and—"

"Heck yes, I'm avoiding it!" I surprise myself with how vehement my voice sounds. "I thought we were going to drop it. And anyway, Lou, you wouldn't understand."

"Why not?"

"You're gorgeous. You're confident. Your social media feed is a constant onslaught of fans and friends. And level with me for a minute, will ya? Are you at 'da clubs' every night? Because I've never seen so many selfies of someone wearing sequined halter tops and tiny black dresses in all my life! It's inspiring!"

She seems a bit defensive when she says, "Not *every* night, no. And please don't call them 'da clubs.'" She mimics the goofy way I said it a moment ago. "Besides, I'm letting go of that lifestyle moving forward."

"Why? The endless adoration and attention from guys getting you down?" I huff.

"Whoa." Louise's head jerks back in surprise.

"I'm sorry. I don't know what I'm..." I take a moment to regroup. "Clearly, I'm super out of sorts today, and I appreciate you letting me vent."

"Not a problem. But I do not get 'endless adoration and attention from guys.'"

I double down on my statement. "Louise. Every guy with a pulse stares at you."

She wags a whelk at me, then plops the fancy snail in the water. "That is plain not true, Mabel."

"Case in point, my friend," I whisper and subtly nod to the booth across from us where James, the bartender from the other night, has been stealing not-so-subtle glances at her since we arrived. He waves shyly when he realizes he's been caught.

I wave back. Louise does not.

He continues setting up his beer-tasting station.

"Pay no attention to that," she says. "That means nothing. I'm off men."

"Okaaaay. Does that mean you are *on* women?" I chuckle.

Lou doesn't laugh with me. Instead, she sort of freezes, then softens.

"Well, I was. Once," she says quietly. "But that was complicated. She was my... I wasn't really in the right space to be..."

Her voice drifts off.

Then she clears her throat.

Oh geez, now I feel like crap. "Louise, I'm sorry. That was a lame joke. I didn't realize you were—"

"We're not talking about me," she says with a strained smile. "We're talking about you."

I'm learning that Louise is quite good at avoiding topics she doesn't want to discuss.

"Okay, but we *can* talk about you," I counter. "If there's something you want to—"

"Nope! You, you, you." She grabs my face with both hands. Grabs sounds harsh. She *smooshes* my face with both hands? "Mabel," she says with full seriousness.

"Louise," I respond, mimicking her tone.

"Haven't you ever looked in the mirror?"

"I don't know what you mean." I shake my head and laugh uncomfortably.

"Girlfriend, you're absolutely stunning."

I fall silent. That's the last thing I thought she was going to say.

"Oh," Louise pipes up, "but let's get one thing straight before we continue. Despite that juicy tidbit of information I just gave you about my dating past, I am not hitting on you. This is just weird timing that I'm taking this particular moment to affirm you, okay?"

"Understood," I say with some finger guns for flourish.

"Good. Back to my point. You have no idea how beautiful you are, do you?"

How in the world do I respond to that question?

"You are, Mabel. Inside and out. But let's start with the 'out,' shall we? With that gorgeous red hair and sweet face? Girl, you look like Ariel after she got legs."

I draw a blank. "Who is Ariel?"

She looks at me like I'm crazy, but I don't mind. I'm used to being the girl in the room who doesn't get the cultural references being bandied about.

"*The Little Mermaid*?" Louise says as she plops a starfish into the tank.

"Oh! Sure! Okay! *Den lille havfrue*, the Danish fairy tale by Hans Christian Andersen!"

I give the pronunciation a little extra pizazz by adding a

Danish accent to the proceedings. Also, for the record? I have no idea how to do a Danish accent.

Louise chuckles. "Um. I was thinking more of the animated Disney movie with music by Alan Menken and lyrics by Howard Ashman? You know, with Sebastian the crab and Ursula, the sea witch?"

"Oh, okay. I never saw that one," I admit.

Suddenly, a male voice vibrates past me.

"Not into Disney movies myself, but I agree. She definitely looks like Ariel after she got legs."

Wally cruises by and gives us a wink. He somehow manages to surreptitiously skim his eyes down past my denim skort—yes, I'm wearing a skort—while hoisting a huge, bulky cooler in his arms. He nods to James and starts unloading at the stand next to him, the muscles in his forearms flexing the whole time.

"That man wants you," Louise croons.

"That man destroyed my mother-in-law's business and ruined my relationship."

"What?" Her voice goes up in pitch. "I'm pretty sure Bert is responsible for ruining the relationship."

"Can we not talk about him, please?"

"Who? Bert or Hot Guy?"

"Hot Guy!" I say with exasperation, then turn to face him as he assembles what looks to be about a hundred tiny jars filled with amber-colored liquid. What is he doing?

"Hey, what are you doing?" I hear myself tossing the question his way before I even realize my mouth is open.

"Setting up," he shouts back with a shrug.

"Setting up what?" I huff.

"My stand."

Ugh. I don't like it when people do that. When they act like something should be obvious when clearly, it's not. It's not obvious. Since when does the groundskeeper get a stand?

I stomp across the grass toward him with Louise hot on my heels. "No way am I missing this interaction," she murmurs excitedly.

"Since when does a groundskeeper get a stand?" Boom. Look at me being all sassy. He deserves it. Business breaker.

Relationship ruiner. Watch out, mister, because Bad Mabel is coming out to play. I put my hands on my hips and try to look intimidating, but let's face it, the guy towers over me, and I don't think I've ever intimidated a living creature in my entire life.

"Sweetheart, I do a lot more than just 'keep the ground' around here. And hey. You've been avoiding me this week. What gives?"

"Don't call me sweetheart. And no, I haven't."

"Don't call me 'The Groundskeeper.' And yes, you have."

"Today, you can call him 'The Sugarmaker,'" James adds as he pokes his amused face between the two of us. "It's one of the many titles my boy Wallace holds."

As soon as James approaches our little group, Louise averts her eyes to the ground and hightails it back to her booth. James opens his mouth like he's going to call after her but seems to think better of it and returns to his own station.

There is definitely a story there. But I can't focus on anything other than the infuriating man in front of me.

"The Sugarmaker," I repeat with a slight frown. "I don't get it. You make sugar?"

"Syrup," Wally says as he returns to his stand filled with tiny jars. My legs follow him without my brain's permission. "Someone who makes syrup is called a sugarmaker. Though I wouldn't say I *make* it really. The tree is the maker. I'm just her partner."

"How do you mean?" I approach and lean my palms on his table. I'm giving him a fair amount of attitude, and I can't seem to help it. But the man did cause the end of my relationship and my business Monday night. Right?

"Tree produces the sap. I collect the sap through plastic tubing, boil it down in a special evaporator, monitor it for viscosity and sugar density, then get it filtered, graded, and hot-packed," Wally mansplains all the apparent steps of syrup making.

Wait, sugarmaking? No. He's a sugarmak*er*, but it's syrup mak*ing*. Whatever.

"That's... interesting," I say slowly. "But I was asking more about your use of the word partner."

"Oh." He casually tosses a lock of sandy hair off his forehead. "Well, we're all looking for a partner, aren't we?"

He gives me a pointed look. I'm getting really tired of this guy being so cryptic.

"Um, sure. I guess? But a tree?"

"Course." He shrugs and gestures to my honeycomb display. "Surely, you know a thing or two about partnering with nature."

What on earth is he...

"Bug Lady!!" a sweet little boy voice calls and shakes me out of... whatever is happening between Wally and me. Are we fighting? Flirting? Philosophizing?

"Holden buddy, hey!" I turn and squat down, and he runs right into my arms. "So happy to see you, pal!"

"Can I finally have a honeycomb?!" Holden pulls back and asks with a huge gap-toothed smile. He's been excited about this festival and tasting his first honeycomb this whole week.

"Of course you can! You know the scoop! All you have to do is have your mommy sign the 'Save the Bees' pledge at my booth and—"

"Will Daddy's signature do?" a handsome guy who looks a heck of a lot like Holden says from a few feet away. He strolls up to us and reaches out to shake my hand. "Holden's father, David," he declares proudly, then points at the tiny baby strapped to his chest. "And Holden's little brother, Carl."

Carl. Hm. An odd choice for a baby. Maybe it's a family name.

"Wow, hi!" I say a bit too enthusiastically. "It's so nice to finally meet you. I'm—"

"Mabel. The bug lady, I know." He cuts me off. "Holden never stops talking about you."

"That's not true, Daddy!" Holden says with pink-tinted cheeks. "Sometimes I talk about arachnids."

"That's true, pal. Sometimes you do talk about arachnids." He faces me and answers the unspoken question on my lips. "Renée is getting some much-needed 'me-time' at home."

"Oh, good," I say. "She has seemed a bit stressed at drop-off lately."

"She has been, yeah. So I'm babysitting the boys today."

I take in the expression of pride on his face, then ask, "Wait, how can you be babysitting if you are the dad? In this case, shouldn't it just be called... dadding?"

His face falls. Oh, shoot. Should I not have said that? I've definitely lost my polite filter today.

"I, uh... Yeah, uh. I guess you're right." He laughs awkwardly, then breaks the tension by addressing someone over my shoulder. "Hi there. Are you Mabel's boyfriend? Husband?"

"I am. Hi." A male voice rumbles from behind me.

I whip my head around to see Wally flashing his megawatt smile and sidling up next to me, just before his heavy arm wraps around my shoulder. I'd completely forgotten he was there. Why was he hovering over me like that? Though I suppose in all fairness, I was the one hovering in front of his booth.

"Which one is it?" Holden's father chuckles as the two men shake hands. "Boyfriend or husband?"

"Yes" is Wally's weird response.

"What?!" I squeak and make a quick escape from underneath his meaty arm. It falls down heavy at his side. "No. No, he is not my husband! Or my boyfriend! He's... he's my..."

Silence.

"I'm your what, babe?" he prompts. Then he immediately turns serious when our gazes lock. "What am I to you, Mabel?"

Time stands still for a moment.

As I stare into his clear blue eyes, I realize something. For the first time since I was seventeen, I'm single. I'm available. I'm... free. The possibilities are wide open again. And if I wanted him to be, he really *could* be something to me. Also, did he call me babe?

"Aw, I remember that look," David says. "Holden's mom and I used to have that look. A piece of advice, lovebirds? Never. Lose. That. Look."

"What look?" I sputter. "I wasn't looking at him with any look!"

"Okay..." Holden's dad says with a knowing smile on his face.

I make the mistake of turning back to Wally. His lips are twitching, and his eyes are sparkling. "I should get back to work," he says and slips behind his booth.

"Yeah, you do that!" I yell. "You-you-you go! And actually get some work done for once!"

Then I start stomping back to my own stand, Holden and his

family following close behind.

If I'm going to be the kind of person who hurls insults, I've really got to up my game. Because that one just now was completely inaccurate. Wally works harder than anyone I've ever met. The cool thing I've noticed, though, is that nothing ever seems to be a slog for him. Whether he's digging holes in the ground, fixing fountains, or selling syrup, he seems to put his whole self into the work and really enjoy himself while he does. It's really admirable.

Dammit, why can't I stop seeing the best in people when I want to be angry with them? It's truly maddening.

"Here you go, bud," I say to Holden as I grab his long-awaited honeycomb and place it in his hand. "Just unwrap it, and you can bite right in."

"Yeah!!" he cheers and starts ripping at the little logo I made, tearing it into tiny pieces.

"Comb and all?" his dad asks skeptically.

"Comb and all, yeah," I say with enthusiasm. "Eating honeycomb has bountiful benefits for the body like..." I pause for a second and repeat that phrasing under my breath this time. "Bountiful benefits for the body... Eh." I shake my head. "I have to rewrite that copy. Not loving that anymore."

"This is fucking delicious!" Holden squeals as he chews happily.

"Holden!" his father and I scold at the same time.

"What? It is," he responds with faux innocence.

"Sorry about that." David pulls me to the side and says softly, "He's been testing us quite a bit since Carl was born. Looking for attention."

"Makes sense." I smile. "That transition to becoming an older sibling can be a tough one. I'll be sure to give him a little extra love at camp this week."

"Thanks for that."

"Sure thing."

My eyes are suddenly drawn to the booths across from us, where a woman I recognize is chatting with Wally. Naomi Thornton. I wouldn't go so far as to call Naomi my nemesis—good girls don't have nemesisses do they? Is that how you pronounce the plural of nemesis? Or is it nemiseez? Let's just say I've always found Naomi to be rather... unpleasant. And for some reason, she's never seemed to like me either.

Wally, however, seems rather fond of her.

I'm so committed to watching their interaction that I barely hear David when he says, "New business?"

"Hm?"

"New business?" he gestures to the honeycomb display.

"Yes? No? Sort of?" I crane my neck to get a better look. "Is she touching him? Why is she touching him?"

"Why is who touching whom?" David is genuinely confused and whips his head around to get a look of his own.

"No one!" I say a bit too emphatically, my eyes glued to the two of them across the way as Naomi laughs, and he flashes her that smile I have come to love and hate in equal measure. "That *whom* can be touched by whatever *who* he likes! Makes no difference to me! I certainly have no say in the matter!"

"What are you ...?" He tries to interject, but I'm apparently on a roll.

"And despite what that cocky *whom* may think, I definitely have no desire to be the *who* who is touching him! So he can shove his... up his..." I stutter. "Shove his ... up his... Starting over. He can shove his... up his..."

"Are you okay?" David asks with concern etched on his brow.

"Fine," I murmur. "I'm always fine. Just not great with insults. Yet. But don't worry, I'm working on it."

"Ya know what?" David says and wraps his arm protectively around his son. "I think Holden, Carl, and I are going to go check out the dunk tank. My buddy is one of the firefighters who could go under, so..."

"Oh, that's great! Sure, yeah! Go, go! Have fun! See you tomorrow, Holden buddy! Nice to finally meet you, David! Send my best to Renée!"

"Will do!" he says over his shoulder, but he's already over twenty feet away and can't seem to get farther from me fast enough.

Great, I've been entrusted to watch over his child thirty hours a week, and now he thinks I'm a lunatic.

I don't dwell on this for too long, though, because that loud, throaty laugh captures my full attention again. I look over and see them standing super close. Her hand is on his chest, rubbing a small circle.

And suddenly, what feels like a tiny scorching ball of fire settles in the pit of my stomach, and I feel like throwing up.

So this is jealousy, huh?

Can't say I'm a fan.

Chapter Sixteen

"We're still on for noon, tiger?" Naomi practically purrs and continues to rub circles on Wally's chest. That's her move, apparently. And again, Wally doesn't seem to mind.

Noon? What the heck are they doing at noon?

"You bet, Naomi," he says back in a tone I can't decipher. Is he responding to her flirtation? It's hard to tell because everything he says and does is somehow sexy.

"Mabes? You okay?" Louise says from her booth beside mine. I can see her shifting her gaze back and forth between me and the scene Naomi is making with Wally.

"Fine. I'm always fine," I murmur, my eyes starting to glaze over.

"Okay, you really have to stop saying that," Louise says as she gently drops a starfish into her tank. She walks the few steps to my booth. "You know you don't always have to be fine, right? A lot of times when people say they are fine, what they really mean is they are suffering below the surface, but they are ashamed to admit it. A lot of times, what they really mean is 'I am the opposite of fine, but if you saw just how *not* fine I am, I'm afraid you would judge me.' A lot of times, people don't want other people to think they're weak and—"

"Lou?" I cut her off as politely as possible. "I'm so glad the therapy is working for you, but seriously, I'm fine. I don't need any well-meaning speeches to—Oh crap on a cracker! Bert Alert!" I exhale on a crazy, loud whispery breath and then drop to the ground like I've been shot.

"What alert?! What?" Louise rushes over and crouches down beside me, presumably to tend to my wounds. "Have you been shot? What's going on?"

"Bert. Alert. Ten o'clock," I eek out through clenched teeth.

"What? I don't understand."

"My boyfriend, I mean, fiancé. I mean, ex. Bert."

"Ohhhhhh." Louise finally catches on to what I'm saying. "Okay, let me look."

"No, no, no, don't look, don't!"

She disregards me and rises to her full height. "That guy? Really? In the turtleneck?"

"Would you call it a full turtleneck, though?" I murmur while trying to stay hidden. "I was under the impression the turtlenecks he wears are mock."

"Mock or not, it's eighty degrees out here, and that man is dressed like a mime." Louise's light laughter cuts off, and she's suddenly serious. And sad? "Oh," she breathes. "Oh, god."

"What?"

"Mabel, I'm so sorry," she coos.

"What? What's happening? Why are we so sorry?!" I peek up from my crouched position and see Louise squinting a bit at what she's studying.

"It looks like he already has a new girlfriend, sweetie. A much older girlfriend. Not that the age should matter! Like Calliope always says, 'hashtag love is love,' right? Not that they're in *love*. I'm sure they are still in the 'like' stage, so soon after losing you. Geez, I am really sticking my foot in my mouth right now."

"It's okay, Lou. He's here with his mother."

"Sorry, Mabes. That is not his mother. They're holding hands and sort of... cuddling while they stroll."

"Yeah. That's them." I say. "They're close."

"Yikes," Louise marvels.

"You know something? I think in hindsight, that was a big part of our problems. We could never really have an adult relationship because the parental chaperoning never stopped. But... I dunno, maybe it was understandable. Bert's dad up and left when he was a teenager, so his poor mom leaned on him and—"

"Oh wow, now they're French kissing!"

"THEY ARE?! WHAT KIND OF FUCKED-UP PEOPLE WAS I ASSOCIATED WITH?"

"Whoa! Kidding, Mabes!" She chuckles. "I was kidding."

"Oh," I exhale. "Oh, gosh, good. Not a very funny joke, in my opinion, Louise, but... good. Phew!" I let out a nervous laugh. "Apologies for my language a moment ago, by the way. Not sure where that came from!"

"Scary part is you actually believed the French kissing was feasible," Louise says. "Hey, I like how you say 'phew' unironically."

"Thanks," I say from my position still on the ground. "Now that I think about it, though, I should have known it wasn't feasible. Bert's never been very active with his tongue."

"*That's* why you should have known?? Damn, Mabel, it sounds like you dodged a major Bert-sized bullet this week. You know what we should be doing? We should be throwing you a divorce party! People have those now, you know."

"We weren't actually married, though. Hadn't even started planning the wedding."

"I realize that. There's just no succinct word for splitting with a fiancé. It's bigger than 'breakup,' but not so epic as 'divorce.' Anyway, someone should come up with something." She gazes back out amongst the festival-goers. "FYI, they're gone. You can get up now."

Louise reaches her hand down to me and pulls me to my feet, where I immediately come face-to-face with Naomi Thornton.

"Hello, Mabel," she sing-songs.

My body jolts back a few inches.

"Oh shit! I mean, oh, snap! I mean... Hi, Mrs. Thornton. Hello."

Naomi Thornton—president of the board, mother of April, my human-centipede-storytelling-CIT, and woman who not five minutes ago was rubbing sensual circles into the muscular chest of the infuriating man I apparently can't stop thinking about—stands with a clipboard and a strained smile, staring at me. For some reason, I start frantically rearranging my honeycomb display.

"May I have a word?" she asks smoothly.

"With me?" I chirp.

"Yes."

"Which one?" I feel my lips quirk up on one side.

"Excuse me?"

"You asked for a word. Which word do you want? Hahaha."

"Oh, you're telling a joke. I see." Her lips flatten into a thin line.

Hm. I guess she's not feeling as friendly as she was a few minutes ago with Wally.

"Sure." I make a conscious effort to sober my tone. "Yes, of course you can have 'a word.' Whichever word you want. Of course."

"Wonderful." She shifts her gaze to Louise, who is still standing beside me. "Alone, please?"

"Oooookay, that sounds like my cue. Don't mind me, I have some purple sea urchins to plop in the water anyway," Louise says and slinks back to her stand.

We stand across from each other in silence for a moment.

Uh-oh. I'll bet I know exactly what this is about.

"Hello, Mrs. Thornton," I say. "It's good to see you."

"We already covered the hellos, didn't we? And sweetheart, you know you can call me Naomi."

"Thank you. I was just raised to call all adults by their last name only, so I don't think I'd be comfortable with that."

"*You* are an adult too, aren't you?"

"Uh. Yes. Yes, I am."

"So should I be calling you Ms. McGonigle?"

"Oh, no." I laugh. "I'm younger than you, so—"

"Oh, please. Barely." She scoffs.

Barely? She's at least twenty years older than me, isn't she? Also, is this woman difficult for everyone to talk to? Or is it just me?

"True," I backpedal. "I meant you're a tiiiiiiiny bit older than me, but by no means *old*. But even if you *were* old… what's wrong with that, ya know? Why are we all so conditioned to think that aging is bad? I hope when I'm old I can embrace my age, let my hair go gracefully gray, rock my wrinkles, celebrate all the things I've learned and—"

"Alright, that's enough. Relax, Mabel."

"I'M TOTALLY RELAXED!"

I'm not, though. I'm never relaxed around Naomi Thornton. She's one of those people who seems to be everywhere. Involved in everything. On the board of the museum. On the board of the arboretum. She's even on the board of the housing development where I live with my parents. Yup, she's the gal who lets you know if your hedges need trimming or if you've painted your mailbox a shade that goes against community color regulations. She's always up on the local gossip. Always in charge. And ever since I was a kid, I've always gotten the impression she doesn't like me. Like she wants to see me fail.

"I hear congratulations are in order," Naomi continues.

"Congratulations on...?" I seriously don't have a clue what I should be celebrating right now.

"Your engagement?" She intones like it's obvious. "I saw the announcement in the *Intelligencer*?"

"Oh," I say, internally cursing that damn newspaper. "Thank you. But it's... Well, we're actually... We're not going to move forward with that. So."

"Oh no, a broken engagement, how humiliating!"

"For whom?"

"For you, sweetie!"

"Nah. It's okay, Mrs. Thornton—I mean, Naomi. I don't feel humiliated."

"Well, you should!"

"Wait. Aren't you divorced?" I ask with full sincerity. "Several times, actually?"

"*Excuse* me?" Her head rears back.

"I'm sorry, that came out ruder than I intended. Not that I intended to be rude! April just mentioned that you and her stepdad were—" I pause when I take in the stoic look on her face. "Well, it's none of my business."

"That's exactly right. It's none of your business," she says with a hint of that ferocity that's always just below the surface.

But *my* business is *hers*? I'm not really sure how her logic works.

An awkward moment passes as we stare at each other in

silence.

"Mrs.—I mean, Naomi... was there something you needed from me? Because I should really focus on my station here. I'm starting a honey harvesting demonstration in just a few minutes."

"Oh, you're so sweet with your honey hobby."

"Well, I'm hoping someday I can make it more than a hobby. You know that."

You know how I know she knows that? Because when I worked my tail off at the museum this past spring and put enough money together to get a starter beekeeping kit: the hive, the protective gear, the smoker, the hive tool... the works! And on the day I was placing my hive in my parents' backyard, feeling giddy with the fact that my was goal so close I could taste it... she promptly informed me it was "against neighborhood regulations" to keep bees. Hive disassembled, dreams dashed. All of my neighbors were fine with it—excited even. I asked every single one of them personally. They started placing orders for jars of The Bee's Elbow honey before I even finished telling them my plans, but the plans never got off the ground because of her. She saw to it that I couldn't move forward. It's okay, though. I'll find a way. Everything is figure out-able, right?

"That's adorable. Good luck with that, sweetie. Listen. I'm going to need you to reinstate April to her position as CIT. Okay? Thanks."

She rushes through her... can you call it a request? It was more of a demand, really. Then she turns and starts to walk away as though she doesn't have a single doubt that I will do exactly as she asked.

What would it be like to be that confident?

Surely "Bad Mabel" would be confident. I call after her.

"I wish I could, Mrs. Thornton, but with all due respect, I don't think she'll learn her lesson if I do that."

She turns around, walks toward me with purpose, and speaks in a harsh whisper.

"With all due respect, Mabel, as her parent, shouldn't *I* be the one doling out the lessons?"

"Well, yes, you *should*... " I stretch out the last word a bit too much and experience instant regret.

Mrs. Thornton gasps. "Was that judgment in your tone?"

"No!" I yelp. "No, of course not. I'm agreeing with you that yes, it is your job to dole out lessons. But as head counselor, it's my job to make sure our campers are in excellent hands, and it seems that April could use a bit more guidance and growth before she's able to handle the responsibility of being a CIT."

"Right. She's a CIT. That stands for counselor-in-training, correct?"

"Correct."

"So counsel her. Train her."

"You have a valid point, and I've tried. I just—"

"Mabel, you do realize I am the president of the board, yes?"

"Yes. April has reminded me," I murmur. "Many times."

"Then you know I hold a great deal of power when it comes to making decisions at the arboretum. Particularly when it comes to hiring and firing."

Is she threatening me?

"Um. Yes, Mrs. Thornton, I do know that. But—"

"Wonderful. Then we understand each other."

We're silent for a moment. It's as if she's daring me to say something. What, though, I don't know.

"*Do* we understand each other?" She starts nodding as though she's trying to hypnotize me.

I nod in response.

She nods more.

I nod even faster.

We're like a pair of really intense nodding bobbleheads who have no business nodding or bobbling together.

"Mabel?" a deep male voice startles me out of my staring and bobbling.

"Wallace," Naomi coos and places a perfectly manicured hand on his arm. "What can I do for you?"

"I need Mabel."

"You need Mabel?" She sort of half laughs, half scoffs.

"That's right," he says, looking directly into my eyes. "I need Mabel."

Gosh, those blue eyes really are something. They draw me

in. Every single time. I wonder if he knows he has this snowflake-like pattern swirling in the blue and—

"So could you give us a moment, please?" he asks with only the tiniest hint of impatience.

"Yes," I say. "Of course, yes." I start removing myself from whatever it is these two have going on between them.

His big hand lands gently on my shoulder to stop me.

"I was talking to Naomi. Naomi, could *you* please give us a moment?"

I see a look pass over her face that is decidedly displeased. But it's gone almost as soon as it appears.

"Of course, Wallace. I need to keep making the rounds anyway," she says tightly and taps her trusty clipboard. Her eyes shift back to me. "By the way, Mabel, how are your grandparents doing? Give them my regards, will you?"

My grandparents? What is she talking about?

"My, uh... my nana and grandpop passed when I was seven," I say, completely confused. "I don't think you ever met them, did you?"

"Oh, I'm sorry, I meant your *parents*. How are Abe and Helen doing?" Her smile is unconvincing.

"They're... fine, thanks. Great, actually."

"I'm glad to hear it. I heard about Abe's... 'incident.' We are calling it an 'incident,' right? Not a breakdown or an episode or a—?"

"Ahem." Wally clears his throat and gives her a look.

She looks at him and switches gears. "Anyway, I was concerned. He's doing better now?"

"Much better, yes."

"Oh good. Wonderful news. I'll see you at noon, Wallace." She gives him a little wink, then turns her back and saunters in the direction of the main pavilion where festival attendees are gathering for a music performance by a local band.

What the heck was that? Was she mocking my parents for being conservative? Old-fashioned? For looking slightly older maybe? Well, *excuuuuuse* them for not embracing Botox like *some* people we know. It disturbs me how often unkind people are put in positions of power. It disturbs me even more how I feel a need to bow down to them and cater to their every demand. I'm tired of feeling like people can just—

I take in Wally standing beside me, watching me.

"A lot goes on in that head of yours, doesn't it? I just watched you go all over the place. Where were you?"

"Eh. Nowhere."

"Was she bothering you? Naomi?"

"Nah."

"That's surprising."

"Surprising? Why?"

"Because she's a bothersome human being."

"You didn't seem to think so when she was fondling your man boobs a few minutes ago."

"My *man boobs*?" He looks offended.

"Yeah. She was fondling your man boobs. What, is the term 'man boobs' offensive?"

"Uh, yeah! Right up there with 'dad bod'! For the record, these..." He points at his chest. "Are called pecs."

"Yeah. Sex pecs," I murmur.

"Excuse me?"

"Nothing! I didn't say anything."

"You did, though." He snickers. "You mumbled 'sex pecs' under your breath."

"You wish," I retort sophomorically.

"Okaaaay. I'm not sure how to respond to that."

"You were certainly responding just fine to Mrs. Thornton's nipple stimulation, now weren't you?"

"She did not stimulate my—"

"Save it, Wallace. I could see your pectoral erection from here."

"My pectoral..." He smiles, then seems to give up on questioning my choice of words and changes gears altogether. He gets close to me and asks very softly, "Mabel. Are you... jealous?"

"JEALOUS OF WHAT?!"

A nearby baby startles and bursts into tears upon my explosive reaction. The young mother pushing her stroller past my booth gives me a dirty look.

"Oops!" I call out meekly. "Can I offer you a free The Bee's Elbow honeycomb in apology?" I scoot out from behind my booth, fully prepared to chase after her.

The young mom just shakes her head and keeps strolling. I'm left standing there looking silly, a honeycomb in my hand, a maddening man by my side. A maddening man who is smiling so widely at the moment he's undoubtedly in danger of straining a facial muscle.

"What?" I snap.

"Nothing," he says, both hands up, that smile still on his face.

"Fine," I huff and turn to head back behind my booth. He stops me with his words.

"To put your mind at ease... I assure you, Mabel, that whether you choose to call them man boobs or sex pecs, Naomi Thornton would be the last person granted the honor of fondling them."

"I don't care."

"I think you do."

"Well, then you'd think wrong."

"Okay." He seems to end the conversation with that, but neither of us moves. "The Bee's Elbow, huh?"

"Hmm?"

He points at the label on the wrapped honeycomb I'm still holding. I look down.

"Oh. Yeah. It's silly. Just some stickers I had made."

"I like the name," he says.

"You do?"

"It's clever, yeah. Bee's *elbows* instead of bee's knees."

"Yes!" I exclaim.

"I've actually considered that saying before. With six appendages on an insect, who's to say which are the bee's knees and which are the elbows?"

"Exactly!" I'm pretty sure my cheeks are getting pinker by the second.

"So this is your business?" He gestures to the stand and my small inventory of honeycombs.

"Uhhhh..." My voice inches up a few too many pitches. "Business is probably too strong a word. More like... a pipe dream not worth piping. I'm just using my last bit of inventory as giveaways today to help spread word and support for the Save the Bees Foundation."

"Why?"

"Because a world without bees would mean a world on the brink of famine. A world without bees would be a world where seventy percent of our food crops would go unpollinated. A world without bees—"

"Sorry to interrupt what I'm sure was going to be a fantastic speech. What I actually meant though was why is it 'a pipe dream not worth piping'? But I couldn't agree more that the bees need to be saved. Shall I sign your petition?"

"Oh, yes. Yes, yes, yes, yes, yes. Please sign the petition."

I reach behind me to the booth, grab the fluffy yellow bumblebee pen, and hand it to him. Our fingers connect a moment longer than necessary, and that zing thing happens to me again.

"Nice touch," he says.

"I'm sorry, I didn't mean to touch you for so long."

"I meant the bumblebee pen. It's a nice touch."

"Oh! Yes. Thanks! It is, yes. I have a thing for fluffy pens. And bees. So a fluffy pen *with* bees felt like a perfect match."

I'm talking too much. It's then I realize that this big beautiful man is standing there with a fluffy bumblebee pen in his hand and nothing to sign.

"Here you go, here's the petition."

He takes it from me, no extra touching this time.

"Thank you."

I watch him skim the petition and start to sign.

"To, uh, to answer your question from before... it's not that I actually think it's a pipe dream unworthy of piping. I think having my own honey-making business would be out-of-this-world amazing. I just... well, what you're looking at here is my full inventory from an amazing, life-changing workshop I took last summer. Tried to get my own up and running this season from my parents' backyard—yes, I know, I still live with my parents—but I got shut down by 'neighborhood regulations' before I even began. Anyway—"

"Set your hive up next to mine."

"Excuse me?"

"Your hive," he says simply. "Set it up next to mine."

"You have a hive?"

"Of course," he scoffs. "Who doesn't?"

"Um. Most people?"

"Most people don't understand the awesomeness of partnering with nature like you and I do, Mabel. You still have your hive?"

"It's in pieces, and I sent the bees back, but, yeah, I have it."

"Great, bring in the pieces tomorrow when you come to work, and I'll get you set up. Reorder your bees, and you'll be all set."

"But it's already July," I protest.

"And the best times to harvest are July, August, and late September. You know that. Soon, we'll harvest my first batch, then I bet we can get you a nice haul by September if we start now. Don't worry, Mabel Again. We still have time."

I can't help but feel giddy over his use of the word "we" here. And the ridiculous nickname he's given me.

"Um. I'm sort of speechless right now. Are you even allowed to—"

"Sweetheart, you'd be amazed at all the things I'm 'allowed' to do here."

"Okaaaaaay." Not sure exactly what that means, but okay.

"And you're here at the arboretum five days a week—sometimes more—anyway, right?"

"Right."

"So you can visit your hive anytime you like," he says like it's a done deal. "It's perfect."

I hesitate for just a half-second before saying, "Perfect."

"Great! Perfect! Did someone order drinks?" another voice says. I tear my eyes away from Wally's to see his buddy James approaching. "Don't mind me," James says as he slinks up beside us, unfolds a cocktail table, sets it to its highest height, then cracks open two cold craft beers he pulls from his pockets and places one in front of each of us. "Summer Ale okay, miss?"

"Fine, yes. Um. What's happening right now?" My head whips

back and forth between Wally and his friend.

"Drinks are on him." James gestures to Wally. "Well technically they're on me, but figuratively, they're on him. Also on him?" James pulls out a small jar filled with amber-colored liquid. The syrup he's selling? "Nectar from the gods! Or from the trees anyway." He unscrews the lid and guides the jar under my nose. "Breathe it in, buttercup. Does that smell like cozy winter morning wrapped in the arms of your beloved, or what?"

"I mean... it smells like syrup."

"James? Wally warns. "This better not be..."

"Tap Dat Asp?" I read the label out loud.

"Get it?" James enthuses. "Kind of like 'Tap dat ass'? But instead of tapping asses, we're tappin' trees?"

"Sure, yeah. I get it!" I smile. I can't help it. In general, I try to be an encouraging person.

"It's good, isn't it? Come on, Mabel, tell him it's good!" James sort of whines.

"It's certainly... catchy. But can you tap Aspen trees for making syrup?" I look at Wally.

"Technically, you *can*," Wally says, "though Aspens aren't typically known for their sugar content. And this syrup is definitely from a Maple tree, so—as I've been trying to tell James here— the product name 'Tap Dat Asp' is inaccurate, and quite frankly, on the verge of being anti-feminist."

James scoffs. "Whatever, trunk man. It's a good name and you know it." He catches the eye of a couple looking to do a beer tasting at his booth. "Gotta run. Enjoy, lovers!" James slaps Wally on the back, then hurries back to his potential customers.

I'm left alone with Wally, standing at this makeshift cocktail table, two, frothy delicious-looking beers at the ready.

He breezes right past the fact that his friend just called us "lovers," gestures to the beers and says, "Shall we?"

"Uh, yeah. Sure. No one seems to be lining up to save the bees at the moment, so I have a few minutes. How about you?"

He peers over at his syrup stand. "Yeah. Looks like I'm in the clear for now too. Cheers?"

He picks up the glass in front of him and lifts it toward me.

I do the same.

"Cheers."

We clink and drink.

It's quiet for a moment. We both steal glances around us and seem to realize simultaneously that we've been set up. Now, here we are on what feels like a quasi-first-date in the middle of a festival for the whole town to see.

Wally breaks the awkwardness.

"James graciously came up with some potential titles for my syrups, created labels, and slapped said labels on the bottles while I wasn't looking," he explains after a sip. He seems almost embarrassed.

"Gotcha." I sip. Perhaps a little too quickly. "You two seem really close. Have you known each other for a long time?

"Since we were in high school, yeah. Same swim team. He's a solid guy. Great friend."

"Nice. Did he, um. Did he call us lovers?"

"He did, yeah."

"Why?"

"Well, I maybe sort of might have told him about how you kissed me last week in the rowboat."

"Wally!" I scold him.

"What? Was it a secret?"

"Heck yes, it was a secret! I was engaged at the time!"

His body immediately goes on alert.

"At the time?"

"Yes!"

"But you're not *currently* engaged... at *this* time?"

Oh. Right. That bit of information might not have reached him while I was actively avoiding him all week.

"I'm not. No. Not at this time."

"I see," he says, then takes another sip—or perhaps it would be considered a gulp—of his beer. Then he continues. "James is a romantic. He's had to put up with listening to me talking about you for a few weeks, so..." He cuts himself off and changes the subject. "Listen, I'm sorry if I was the cause of any tension between you and your fiancé. I do realize what a scene I created on Monday night and how that may have reflected poorly on you. I apologize for that. At some point, I do want to explain why and how I brought Doreen's business down and how I'd like to see to it that—"

"You've been talking about me to James?"

Apparently, I don't care about anything else at the moment other than the fact that he was talking about me.

He clears his throat. "Talking about you, thinking about you... fantasizing about you. Yes. All of the above."

"Interesting."

"Why is that interesting?"

"Because um. I've been." I exhale. "I've been doing the same thing. It started the first moment I saw you and it hasn't stopped since."

He leans closer to me.

"Interesting," he repeats my earlier response.

"Right? That's what I said. Interesting."

"Hm. Well, what are we going to do about this, Mabel?"

He leans even closer to me. So close I can smell his aftershave.

"I'm not sure," I say in a velvety voice I'm not even certain is mine. My reactions to him are so foreign to me, I'm realizing I don't quite recognize myself whenever he's near me.

He slips his large hand over my small one. It feels so warm and safe. I close my eyes on instinct, waiting - hoping - for his lips to finally land on mine again. Only this time, it won't be brash and rushed. It will be slow and sweet and—"

"Get your filthy paws off my fiancé!"

And those are the last words I hear before all hell breaks loose.

Chapter Seventeen

"*I* knew it. This is why you broke up with me, isn't it?! This guy?" Bert is all hyped up and breathing heavy. His eyes are ping ponging between me and Wally.

"Actually, no," I say with supreme confidence. "I broke up with you because you've been sticking your Dick Wolf in every willing Olivia you could find in the tristate area."

"Whaaat?" Wally rumbles.

I go into explanation mode. "Oh, see, Bert refers to his penis as—"

Wally interrupts me. "I could not be less interested in learning more about Bert's penis. When I said 'Whaaaat?' I meant *he* cheated on *you*? This man is wearing a turtleneck in the middle of summer."

"It's a mock!" Bert scoffs.

"Told you!" Louise shouts from her touch tank where she's helping a child handle a horseshoe crab.

Wally's eyes narrow on Bert, and for the first time, I see "The Wall," that scary, mysterious side of him the CITs told me about. "Allow me to repeat myself. This guy cheated on you?"

"Yes. He did." I wince. "But I suppose *technically* I cheated too when I kissed you in the rowboat."

"You kissed him in a rowboat?!" Bert bellows.

"Yes!" I shout back. "But you got multiple blowjobs in a Barnes & Noble, so I think we're even!"

This gives Bert pause. "You've been talking to people."

"I have, Bert. I've been talking to people."

"Mabes, I'm sorry," Bert says as he takes a step toward me. "Let me fix things with us. I just want to—"

"Don't come near me, Bert."

He takes another step.

That's all it takes before Wally has him in a headlock.

"Get off me, you oaf!" Bert struggles in Wally's hold.

"No can do, pal. The lady said not to come near her and you went near her. Is there a problem with your comprehension?" Wally says somewhat jovially into his ear.

Bert kicks the air. He squirms. He squeals. He tries to punch but Wally has his arms pinned.

"What's up with this guy?" Wally chuckles.

"Let me go!" Bert sneers.

"I don't know what's going on," I say with a bit of wonder in my voice. "This isn't like him at all! This is by far the most passion I've ever seen spurt from Bert!"

"Can we not say 'spurt from Bert' again, please?" Bert blurts as he struggles.

"Sure!" I chirp. "I can stop saying 'spurt from Bert.'"

"You just said 'spurt from Bert again'!!" he wails. He's getting incensed now

"Oh shoot. I did say spurt from Bert again. I'm sorry."

"Why are you saying sorry to this guy?" Wally snarls. "No one should be saying sorry to this guy."

"You're right! Bert, the only thing I'm sorry about is that it took me this long to break up with you."

"Get! Off! Of! Me!"

"You got it, bro," Wally says nonchalantly. "I'm tired of cuddling with you. Off you go!"

With that, Wally releases him. Apparently Bert didn't expect to actually be freed at that exact second, because he loses complete control of himself and crashes right into James' makeshift cocktail table, splashing the seasonal brew all over you-know-who.

Me.

I'm suddenly transported back to the summer I was fifteen and worked at a retirement center as a busgirl in the cafeteria. One day while I was walking to the dishwasher with a huge tray on my shoulder, loaded with sauce-covered dishes, half empty water glasses and dirty steak knives, I tripped. Instead of letting everything fall to the ground, my good girl instincts told me to catch as much as I could so they wouldn't break. The only thing I managed to catch was a steak knife in my arm.

I didn't catch a steak knife this time, but I did manage to bathe in seasonal summer ale and catch a bottle of Tap Dat Asp with my tits.

That didn't sound right did it, me saying the word tits? Even in my internal monologue it felt wrong. I guess I just liked the potential alliteration of tap and tits. But in hindsight, boobs would have been the better more "me" choice.

Anyway, I'm currently on the grass, with a bra full of syrup, crumbled honeycomb in my hair and beer... everywhere.

Two male voices say simultaneously "I'm so sorry Mabel" just as two male hands reach toward me to help me up.

I look left at Bert, the guy I thought I'd always be connected to, the boy I met in high school. The man I said I'd marry. Then I look up and to my right and see Wally, a guy who for all intents and purposes I know very little about, but with whom I already feel safer and more understood in the few days since I've met him than I did the entire time I was with the man on my left.

I take a deep breath and reach my hand to the right.

Wally's large hand wraps around my small one and guides me to my feet. I take in our surroundings for the first time since Bert made his appearance and see that a small crowd has gathered. I feel my face turn ten shades of red.

"Louise?" Wally calls over his shoulder as he puts his palm on the small of my back. Can you look after Mabel's booth for a few minutes.?

"Sure! Absolutely." she says.

"Let's get you cleaned up," Wally whispers and turns me toward the path down the hill.

I can feel Bert's eyes burning into my back as we walk away, but I keep my eyes straight ahead this time, far more interested in where I'm going than in where I used to be.

We walk briskly down the hill, away from festival-goers. After a bit of silence, Wally is the first one to speak.

"I'm sorry about that. Had I known he was going to barrel his way into you like a spastic bull, I would have held on to him longer. Are you okay? The cups didn't crack, right? They didn't hurt you?"

"No no, I'm fine. A little embarrassed maybe, but fine."

"Okay good." He exhales.

"Are *you* okay, though?"

I can't help but notice how aggravated he seems, how out of breath and full of angsty energy he is. He's also walking pretty fast all of a sudden and I'm having a hard time keeping up with him. I haven't even thought to ask him where he's taking me.

"That guy," he huffs. "Your ex? Know who he reminds me of?"

"No. Who?"

"That punkass kid in The Giving Tree."

"I'm sorry, but I have no idea what you're talking about."

"You don't know The Giving Tree?" his deep voice goes up in pitch.

"Oh! The Giving Tree! Yes, of course! Such a beautiful book."

He stops in his tracks and gives me a pointed look. "It is *not* a beautiful book. It's a book about an entitled, self-serving, tree-murdering psychopath."

"Are we talking about the same story?" I cock my head to the side. "By Shel Silverstein?"

"That's the one." He starts walking again. "That book is so far up its own ass it can see its esophagus. It shouldn't be called The Giving Tree, it should be called... The Taking Turd."

"Did you come up with that right now?"

"I did."

"And... a *turd*? You're calling a fictional child a turd?"

"I am," He says definitively. "And you should too. Sure, the reader may be tempted to let him off the hook early in the tale when he's a kid, but the guy grows up and his selfish douchery just keeps on douching until the tree is left a literal stump, devoid of her leaves and her branches and her majesty. I'm just glad you escaped your 'taking turd' before you were left stunted and stumped like that gorgeous, giving tree."

I smile and shake my head at him.

"I don't - I don't understand the way you talk sometimes. I mean, I guess I *do* understand it, but It's so...saucy. So unlike anyone I've ever met."

He takes that moment to weave our fingers together, and... suddenly we're walking hand in hand.

I look down at our joined hands.

"This okay?" he asks.

"Totally okay," I say softy. "Yeah."

"So. You think I'm a saucy talker, do ya?" He gets closer to me and rumbles in my ear. "Lady, you ain't seen nothing yet. Stay tuned, will ya?"

"Sure," I say. "Yeah. I'll... I'll 'stay tuned.'"

"Good." With that bit of business taken care of he returns to our previous discussion. "Also, looked at in another way, it's a book about martyrdom. About pillaging our natural resources. It's really up in the air whether Shel meant it as inspiration or a cautionary tale. Whatever his intention though, you better believe that when I have kids I will *not* be reading it to them."

"When?" I sort of choke on my own spit.

"You okay there? Swallow."

He gives me a gentle smack on the back.

"Fine, yeah. Thanks. It's just... you said '*when* I have kids,' not '*if* I have kids.' I would have expected you to say '*if* I have kids.'"

"Why is that?"

"I guess maybe because you don't seem like the kid type?"

"What are you saying, Mabel, you don't want to procreate with me?" he asks with a face like stone.

"Oh. Um. I didn't say—I mean I'm sure you'd be—But we haven't even—"

"Because I'm going to need you to get onboard and provide for me, woman. I'm twelve weeks along and you're the father."

"Whaaat?!"

He breaks into a huge grin then bursts into laughter. "Hahaha.

Your face!" He bends over, points at me and rests his hands on his thighs.

"Oh! Hahaha! I" I laugh right along with him. "I mean obviously I know you can't get—And we certainly haven't –" Stop stammering, Mabel. "Woo! You have a really weird sense of humor."

"I thank you." He bows slightly.

"Sure. Yeah. I guess it was a compliment."

It's then that I realize we've stopped walking and we're standing in front of his shack. More specifically, in front of his outdoor shower.

He gestures to the wooden structure. "Here we are." He opens a rustic cabinet off to the side, pulls out a fluffy gray towel and a square, cream-colored bar of soap and hands them to me.

"Oh," I say, sort of startled. I'm not sure why I hadn't fully considered what "let's get you cleaned up" might entail. "You, um. You want me to use your shower?"

"I don't *want* you to do anything. You're covered in syrup and summer ale though, yeah?" he says as he swings open the wooden door and begins adjusting levers.

"Yep. Uh-huh."

"Right. So, just gimme a second and it's all yours."

"What are you going to be doing while I'm in there?"

He scoots out of the small space, letting the door slap shut behind him.

"Relax, Mabel," he chuckles. "It's not like I'm going to watch."

"You're not?"

He freezes.

"I'm confused. Did... you... want.... me to... watch?"

"No!" I shout. "Not like watch *me*. But could you maybe watch out there?" I point into the vast amount of nature surrounding us. "What if a deer or something barges in here while I'm naked and wet?" Oh geez, that sounded—"Let me rephrase. When I'm unclothed and... moist? Nope, nope that's even worse. Everyone hates the word moist. When I'm nude and –"

"I have no problem with the word moist," he says completely seriously.

"You don't? Everyone does."

"People are so easily embarrassed. They're embarrassed by the word moist because it's one of those experiential words, one of those onomatopoeic words. It sounds the way it feels, and that makes most people uncomfortable. Most people don't want to feel. They want to think. They want to talk. But they will make a lot of noise and ruckus and excuses to avoid having to feel."

"But not you? You're not that way?"

"Used to be. Takes a hell of a lot to make me uncomfortable or embarrassed, Mabel. And I'm not afraid to feel. The old me was. But the new me? The new me knows that's one of the main reasons we're here on the planet. While we're here, we owe it to ourselves to feel everything."

He looks at me and I know this is the point where I am supposed to speak, but I've got nothing to contribute at the moment. All that is swirling inside my mind at this moment is "who in the world is this guy?" The man who I thought was all grunts and dirty looks is actually funny and intelligent and emotional.

And so incredibly handsome, I sometimes find it difficult to look directly at him.

When it's clear I won't be adding to this conversation anytime soon, Wally says, "No, a deer will not barge in on you. And yes, I can keep a lookout for you. I'll keep my back turned, but I'm here if you need me."

"Thanks."

"You got it."

He does exactly that. He turns his back and I shimmy my way into the stall. Once the door is secure, I start slowly peeling off my sticky clothing and drape it piece by piece over the door.

Without turning around, he says, "You're gonna want to turn the knob on your left about ninety degrees to the right, then pump that foot pedal a few times to get the water pressure how you like it."

"Okay..." It feels a little strange being naked in the open air like this, only a flimsy wooden door that starts at my knee and ends just above my shoulders separating me from him. Strange... but exciting.

Wally might not be watching me, but I'm certainly watching him.

I do what he suggested and warm, wonderful water pressure starts pelting my back.

"Ohhhhhhh god," I moan.

He immediately whips around to face me.

"You okay?"

"You're looking at me!" I scream.

"I'm sorry!" he bellows. "You just—You said 'oh god!' I thought you were in trouble and needed something."

"But I didn't say it in an emergency way. I said it in a—a—a —a porny way."

A 'porny' way?"

"Yeah. Didn't you think it sounded porny?"

"Mabel… and I mean this in the most respectful, gentlemanly way possible… I find everything you do to be 'porny.' If by porny you mean sexy. I find every single thing about you to be incredibly sexy."

"Really?"

"Really."

"I don't think anyone's ever thought that about me before, let alone said it to me."

"Well then they haven't been paying an ounce of attention, because Mabel Again?"

"Yeah?" I can't hide my smile every time he calls me that.

"You are adorable, sexy perfection and I haven't been able to stop thinking about you since the moment I laid eyes on you."

Our eyes stay connected over the stall, him on the outside, me on the inside. The warm water pouring down my body softens me somehow, energizes me, emboldens me.

Desire sweeps over me at that moment, and I don't think I could stop it if I tried. I place my hand on the wooden door and slowly creak it wide open, not caring in that second that anyone wandering down the path, human or animal, could see me standing there completely naked. Completely wanting him.

Wally's eyes widen and slowly trace down the length of me. He smiles and breathes out one single word. "Wow."

Then… I reach out, grab the lapel of his shirt and pull him under the spray.

Chapter Eighteen

We kiss like it's our purpose on the planet. Like we've been waiting our whole lives to express ourselves fully and this is the moment when we finally do.

It feels like we've done this a thousand times before, instead of just the one fumbling, yet still earth-shattering kiss we shared—or I stole rather—before we crashed into the lake.

Here we are crashing together in the water again, but now in a completely different way. And somehow I'm completely unselfconscious about the fact that he's fully dressed and I'm completely naked. Unselfconscious, yes, but apparently still apologetic.

"Your clothes are getting soaked," I say when I come up for air.

"Yup." He kisses my neck.

"Sorry about that."

"Don't care one bit, darlin."

Looks like old good-girl habits die hard and we're going to have to reach Bad Mabel status in stages. But a naked outdoor underwater make out with a sort of co-worker in the middle of a family-friendly festival where we're both manning booths has to be considered progress, right?

"I'm so glad this is happening," he murmurs.

"Me too," I breathe.

"But can we uh —" He pulls back slightly so he can look in my eyes. He runs his hands down the length of my wet strands. "I want to..."

"You want to what?"

"Can I take a moment to just... look at you?"

"Oh." That is definitely not what I thought he was going to say. "Sure. Okay."

He steps back from me and proceeds to just... stare.

I'm left standing alone under the spray, water droplets raining down my body while his eyes drink their fill.

Alright, *now* I feel a twinge of self-consciousness creep in. I mean, it's not every day I stand completely naked and wet in front of a sexy-as-hell sugarmaker—that's what James called him, right? I recognize the urge to do a Flashdance reenactment, you know when that whole bucket of water pours on her and she juts her boobs up to meet the spray like "Yeah, take it water!" I checked Flashdance off the do-not-watch list the other night. I enjoyed it, except for the abundance of mullet hairstyles. Anyway I recognize the urge to do this, but I know it would just be me avoiding a serious moment.

I can be serious.

I can let a moment unfold.

Even a naked one with a very attractive almost stranger.

I decide to just stand there and breathe. Is it possible that our breaths have synced? I watch his chest empty and fill, empty and fill.

"You're..." he shakes his head in wonder. "God, you're everything Mabel."

"Everything?" I feel my eyes fill. I don't think anyone has ever said something so tender to me before.

"Who am I kidding," he exhales. "I can't stay away from you for another second."

He steps back into my space and kisses me again. But it's slow this time, intentional.

His soft warm lips land first on my forehead.

Then on my nose.

Then my mouth.

My lips respond and kiss him back, but he moves on pretty quickly. He places a soft kiss on my chin. Has anyone ever kissed my chin before? It's sweet and strange, but not where I want his mouth to be right now. I'm about to settle into disappointment, but then his lips latch onto my neck, and I am whatever is the opposite of disappointed. I tip my head back to give him more room. He licks a cool trail down the bones of my throat and pauses when he reaches the divot between my collar bones.

"Wow. I don't think anyone's ever kissed my suprasternal notch before," I breathe out in unexpected pleasure as the warm water trickles down both our bodies.

"Your what?" He pulls back a few inches and smiles, his hands stroking the strands of my wet hair.

"You're right, you're right," I say smoothly. "I should be more specific. Ahem. 'Wow. I don't think anyone's ever kissed my *fossa jugularis sternalis* before.' There, that was better."

"Somebody's talking fancy today," he chuckles, then gathers me in his arms and places more warm kisses in the same spot. My back bows gently and my pelvis presses forward to accommodate him.

"Can't help it, I guess," I pant. "Apparently I speak science when I'm turned on."

"Oh yeah? That's a thing for you?"

"Not exactly sure. Can't say I've ever been this aroused before. Also I took—oh my gosh, why does that feel so good?—a lot of science classes on the way to becoming an entomologist. Zoology, Biology, Anatomy... That stuff sticks with you. And it's good to be accurate with terminology, don't you think?"

"I do think," he murmurs as his mouth moves to the left. "So let me be accurate too. We'll start with a little detour to your left *clavicle*..." he exhales, and nibbles my left collarbone. "And then your right..." He does the same on the other side, then positions his lips directly over the space between my breasts. "Your *sternum*..."

Geez, this is soooo intimate. You'd think I'd be shy with him, but surprisingly, I'm one hundred percent not. His mouth seems committed to tracing a path down the entire length of my body and all I can focus on is how much I want him to continue his delicious descent.

I let out another little moan.

"You're right, you're right," he says. "I should be more specific," his voice rumbles right over my heart as he uses my words from before. "The manubrium…" He places a soft kiss at the top of my sternum. "The body…" Another kiss a bit lower. "And the xiphoid process." He kisses that tiny place where the rib cage fans out. I feel actual flutters in my belly

"Ooh, listen to you," I say, impressed in more ways than one.

"Yoga teacher training, remember? We studied all the anatomy."

"All the anatomy?" I ask, surprising myself with the amount of sass and innuendo I'm able to send back his way.

He releases me from the tight protective hold he's had me in and steadies me on my feet. Just as I stand to my full height he lowers to his knees and slides his big hands along my sides on his way down.

Ohmygod, this big, burly beautiful man is on his knees.

In front of me.

He peers upward, locks his eyes with mine, and says, "Yes, ma'am. *All* the anatomy."

Then he places his tongue at the apex of my thighs and proceeds to create what only can be described as magic. Utter and complete magic.

So basically, you know, this is turning out to be just another typical day in the life of Mabel McGonigle.

"Wow. Oh my God, wow."

"You like?" He rumbles from below.

"Yessssss. I do. Oh, my God, I dooooooooooo!"

"Good." He chuckles.

"Oh, gosh, I need to be quieter. WHY CAN'T I BE QUIETER!?"

"It's okay, no one can hear us down here," he assures me. "And there's no reason for anyone to wander down this way. All the booths and events are up by the main pavilion."

"Okay, good good good." I take a moment to luxuriate in the exquisite sensations he's creating in me. But then, I can't help but ask, "How do you think this all started?"

"Well… you approached me on the trail and invited me into a pyramid scheme and—"

"No, I mean this. What you're doing to me right now. The funilingous. Who do you think was the first person to figure this out? Do you think the cavemen and cavewomen were busy doing cave things, and then they suddenly thought, 'Hey, you know what might be an interesting experiment'?"

Up until this point, he's been doing a masterful job of alternating between pleasuring and conversing, conversing and pleasuring. But sadly, at this point, he takes a full-on pause from the pleasuring, sits back on his heels, and says, "Sorry—did you just say *fun*ilingus?

"I did," I breathe. "I just really dislike the word cunt. Ooooohhhhhh." I shudder. "Sorry. I can't really say the word cunt—oooooohhhh—without shuddering. I thought I was over the shudder thing, but I guess not. It's a reaction I've always had to words and people I find intimidating. Anyway, back to cunt—ooooooooooh. The word itself is just a bit rude, don't you think? Unless you're British of course, then you can call all your friends and family and coworkers cunts to your heart's content, and no one bats an eyelash. Wow, I made it through that one without a shudder. Progress!" I reach my hand out and high-five him. "But here in America, I just think it carries quite a connotation." I'm pretty sure I'm overexplaining at this point, so I take a deep breath to recalibrate. "Feel free to continue what you were doing. Because holy fuck I was enjoying it."

"Oh, I will, and listen, I appreciate the discourse on how Americans and Brits differ in their use of that potentially inflammatory or celebratory word, depending on how it's used. I guess I'm just confused about what that has to do with—Ohhhhh, okay." I practically see the light bulb go on in his eyes. "The, uh... *activity* we were engaged in a moment ago—one I hope to resume in a matter of seconds—out of curiosity, how do you think that word is pronounced?"

"Cuntiligus," I respond with confidence.

Wow, this guy seems so experienced, but apparently, he doesn't know the basics.

He cracks up laughing. His mouth rests against my belly as he wraps his arms around me, so I feel the vibration of his laughter throughout my entire body. "You crack me the hell up, woman."

"What's so funny?" We're both grown-ups in this adult shower situation, yeah? Why my using a technical term like cuntilingous is inspiring such raucous laughter in him is beyond me.

He pulls back again and looks at me.

"It's actually *cunni*lingus, not *cunti*lingus." He breaks this news to me with a barely concealed grin.

"Wait. Are you serious?"

"Quite."

"Well, consider my mind blown, sir. Because that makes absolutely no sense! *Cunti*lingous would be far more appropriate."

"I actually have to agree with you on that."

"Can we just agree to call it funilingous?" I ask.

"We sure can. May I continue then, milady?"

"You may."

With that, he returns to his heroic ministrations, and I lose all further ability to think or speak coherent thoughts. I give myself over completely to the burst of amazing sensations billowing through me, all because of this brilliant man.

When I woke up this morning, I had absolutely no idea this was the kind of day that lay ahead of me. I guess we never really do, though, do we? Some days you find out your fiancé is boning his way through the entire tristate area—ha, "boning." I guess Calliope's books are starting to rub off on me—and other days, you end up being worshiped from head to toe by a sexy, charismatic man who makes anything feel possible. We just never know.

As I'm coming down from the high, I hear a faint sound off in the distance. Like a voice calling out for something or someone? Now that I think about it, I did have a fuzzy awareness of this sound filtering in over the past minute or so, but my mind was obviously wrapped up in other things.

"Did you hear that?" I ask as Wally rises to his full height and cradles my face.

"I sure did. I told you, don't worry. You can be as loud as you want. You certainly won't hear me complaining about the sound of a woman enjoying herself."

"No, not that. *That.* Is that the loudspeaker?"

We both look upward, like little gophers peeking out of their burrows, straining to hear.

"And now," a voice crackles. "It brings me great pleasure to introduce someone very special."

"Oh shit," Wally says. "What time is it? Is it noon?"

"Turn off the water, turn off the water," I say.

He turns the knob, and the sound of the rushing water instantly shuts off, so we both hear it loud and clear when the voice says, "Please welcome to the stage—the new owner of Bucks County Arboretum and Nature Reserve—the wonderful Wallace Bieber!"

Chapter Nineteen

"**O**h, shit," Wally says. "I'm supposed to give a speech at noon. Let's head on up."

He exits the wooden shower stall and grabs two towels out of a small built-in cabinet.

"Let's head on up? All you have to say right now is 'let's head on up'?" I feel my pitch rising.

"What else should I be saying?" He hands me one towel over the door then starts running the other one roughly over his hair.

"Oh, I don't know, how about 'Hey Mabel, before I go down on you, guess what? I OWN THE ARBORETUM! You know, WHERE YOU WORK'?"

"Well, that wouldn't have been very romantic, now would it?" He has the audacity to chuckle. "But sure, yes, you're right. We should absolutely talk about that later. Oh, I pulled this out for you."

He presents me with an odd, eggplant-colored women's garment—what is that, a power suit?—and drapes it over the side of the enclosure.

I have no idea what my face is doing at the moment, but he's clearly responding to it when he says, "Well, there's no sense in putting your dirty clothes back on that are covered in beer and Tap Dat Asp, right?"

"Right," I say slowly. Dumbly. Suddenly, I feel ten times more naked than I was a moment before.

The speaker crackles again. "Wallace? Are you out there?"

"Alright. Gotta shake a leg," he says so cooly and calmly I'm almost aggravated. Almost.

Then he literally shakes a leg in an attempt to get the excess water off his soaked clothing, leans over the shower door, and looks deeply into my eyes.

"I think you're amazing, you know that?"

"Ummmmmm" is all I can manage.

"I'll see you up there." He kisses me quickly on the lips, then takes off up the hill.

What. In the world. Just. Happened?

I begin the process of toweling off my body, but soon, I hear his voice coming over the loudspeaker—geez, did he beam himself there?—and decide to forgo the towel and just throw these clothes on and head up the hill myself. I need to understand what the heck is going on here.

When I make it to the main area, Wally has just wrapped up his speech. He's soaking wet, seemingly without a care in the world, shaking hands and kissing babies. Well, he's not *really* kissing babies, but you know what I mean. Naomi is standing close by him, smiling and nodding at everything he says to festival-goers.

I'm standing there, mouth open, taking in the scene. How in the world is this jovial people person the same grumpy monosyllabic guy I met a few weeks ago? The curmudgeonly man who the CITS were certain spent his days murdering people and burying them in his backyard? How is he the owner of the arboretum?

But I suppose the real question I should be asking myself is how did I let myself get so weirdly intimate with someone I clearly know nothing about?

I'm so lost in my wondering, I almost don't see her as she saunters by.

"Aunt Tina?" I call out.

A woman in her early forties turns at the sound of her name. Her eyes widen and her mouth falls open when she sees me.

"Mabel?"

"Oh my gosh," we both say at exactly the same time.

She instantly wraps me up in a hug. "How did you? Why are you—? My gosh, you're..."

"Soaked?" I laugh uncomfortably. "Sorry, I just—" Not a clue how to explain my recent water sports to my long-lost aunt, who I haven't seen in fifteen years.

She pulls back and looks at me in what can only be described as wonder. She doesn't say anything. Just continues to stare at me.

"What are you doing here?!" I squeal, suddenly out-of-my-mind excited.

"I thought I'd check out the festival."

"No, I meant here in Pennsylvania. Surely you didn't come all the way up from Tampa for the festival."

She laughs lightly. "No, I didn't. I actually, uh ..." She hesitates. "I live in the area now."

"Seriously? Wow! That's amazing! I can't wait to tell my dad! He'll be so—"

"He knows," she cuts me off gently.

"What?" I cock my head to the side. "No, he doesn't."

"Mabel, sweetie. He knows," she says. "We've been here for three months."

"Oh. Really? Wow, he never said anything." I feel a Mabel monologue of epic proportions brewing, and it won't be stopped. "Not that he ever says much. About anything really. And certainly not about you. Last time I brought you up, boy, did he almost blow a gasket! And you know with his heart thing—do you know he has a heart thing?—we can't risk gasket blowing. But boy, I'd really like to know what went down between you two. I miss you. You were my favorite aunt. My *only* aunt, of course, but don't let that lessen the expression of affection. I'm pretty sure you'd have been my favorite even if I had fifty aunts."

She doesn't respond for a moment. Just smiles. She seems to take in my appearance.

"Are you wearing... an eggplant-colored power suit?"

I look down at myself. "I... think I am, yeah."

"Wow," she says, shaking her head. "You're doing really well for yourself then, huh?" Her eyes go a bit misty at that.

Right on cue, as if to remind me of how well I'm *not* doing, I feel my phone buzzing. I don't even need to look to know it's that unknown number again. I just let it ring this time until the caller gives up. They never leave a voicemail. Shouldn't they leave a voicemail?

I shake it off. This is my opportunity to connect with my aunt, not to worry about money. So I go all in with the questions.

"Who's, um. Who's 'we'?" I ask.

"Huh?" she responds. Am I imagining that she's looking around us every few seconds? Does she not want to be seen with me?

"Who is 'we'?" I repeat. "You said 'We've been here for three months.'"

"Oh. My husband and our daughter."

"You have a daughter?"

She hesitates a half-second.

"I do. She works here, actually. She's around here somewhere, running around with a friend." She takes this opportunity to look around again. "My husband got transferred up this way for work, so... off we went." Suddenly, her energy shifts, and she leans forward as though she's about to let me in on something personal. "I knew it might cause—But I guess I couldn't—" She seems to think better of whatever she was saying and drops the thought completely and just says, "Well."

Man, I always imagined that if I ever saw her again, we'd still have this great bond. An awesome rapport. Just like when I was a little kid. But this is awkward. This is sad and strange.

"You said your daughter works here? *I* work here. Who is your—"

"My god, you're beautiful," she says sort of wistfully. "You've always been beautiful, adorable, but... wow, you're a woman now."

At that, she instantly bursts into tears.

"I'm sorry," she says between quiet sobs. "I shouldn't be—"

"Are you okay? Do you need me to call someone or—"

"I'm fine," she says firmly, composing herself. "I'm always fine."

A strange jolt goes through me at those words. And the way she says them.

"What did you say?" My voice is weird and whispery when I ask it.

"That... I'm okay," she says with a little head shake. She's managed to get a smile back on her face.

"No," I say. "You, um. Just now, the way you said…"

"I heard you were back in town, but I didn't believe it." We're interrupted by a smug voice that has been way too present today for my liking. I look to my right, and it seems Naomi is finished fawning over Wally and is back to make my life difficult.

"Hi, Naomi," I say in what I hope is a kind and welcoming tone. "This is my aunt Tina. We haven't seen each other in—"

"No introductions necessary. Your 'aunt' and I go way back. Don't we, Tina?"

Why does Naomi sound like she's perpetually putting air quotes around things? Your "aunt" Tina. What the heck is that supposed to mean?

Tina looks at Naomi for a moment like a deer in headlights, then responds with a smile. "We, uh… we do, yeah." She turns and explains to me. "Naomi and I went to high school together." Her tone completely changes when she faces Naomi again. "Could we… speak privately for a minute?"

"Of course," Naomi croons. "I'd love to 'catch up.'"

"Great," Tina responds, then turns and places a gentle hand on my cheek. "So good to see you, sweet girl. You have no idea. You keep being amazing, you hear me?"

Before I can respond, Naomi chirps, "So sweet of Wallace to lend you his wife's suit, Mabel. It looks adorable on you."

My stomach bottoms out.

I played soccer for three years during middle school. I played defense. The problem was, I was terrified of the ball. I basically ran away from it whenever it came near me. Not a great defender, right? Understatement. In the rare moments when the ball did reach my foot, I punted it up the field as fast and as far as I could, closing my eyes and crossing my fingers that it reached someone on my team and not the opponents. The worst moments, though, were when the ball sailed across the field and slammed into your belly. In those moments, it absolutely knocked the breath out of you. Left you literally gasping.

But that feeling was nothing compared to what was happening in my belly right now.

His *wife?*

Too shocked to respond, I stand there motionless and breathless for... I don't know how long. Long enough, though, that when I do get my wits about me again, I realize two things.

One: Tina is out of sight, and I have no way of contacting her again. And two: Wally is staring at me across the crowd with a concerned look on his face.

I avert my eyes from his immediately, and I get the hell out of there.

Chapter Twenty

I'm midway through my inaugural viewing of *Dirty Dancing*—holy moly Patrick Swayze!—

and drinking what I'm starting to suspect *may* be a corked bottle of wine. Someone must have given it to my parents as a gift. In like 1987. But isn't wine supposed to get better with time? Maybe it needs to "breathe?" Guess I'll keep sipping.

Despite how truly awesome the movie is, I'm having a hard time focusing, and I press pause right as Baby runs her hand over Johnny's truly spectacular rear end while they're dancing in his shack.

I also know a sexy guy who lives in a shack.

Stop it. Do not think about the sexy guy who lives in a shack. He's a liar. A married liar. Or at the very least a married truth-withholder. I'm not interested in spending time with any truth-withholders. And being married is obviously and absolutely a deal-breaker. You know what I need to do? I need to find out who his wife is and send her the world's most epic apology letter asap. Also a fruit basket. That's appropriate under the circumstances, isn't it?

But my head is filled with more bizarre events from today than just the ones involving Wallace. (Yes, he's been demoted to Wallace. He'll get no more "Wallys" from me). I'm starting to think that he's not the only one who's been withholding the truth from me. My parents, Tina, even Naomi Thornton... what do they know that they're not telling me?

I did do some snooping today. Cyndi would be proud. I started out on the computer, googling around, trying to find more information on Aunt Tina. Searching for a phone number, an address, a place of employment. Anything. Being that I don't know what her married name is, though, I came up with very little. A few mentions of her standings in track meets back in her high school days and a photo of her winning a local science fair were about all the internet had to offer. Sure, I could call my parents in the Poconos and tell them what happened today. But they've never been forthcoming with information on this subject before, so I'm not fooling myself into thinking that will magically change now. So I moved on to some physical spaces in the house I'm never privy to. Maybe Mom and Dad's things will tell me the stories they refuse to. I started in their closet and medicine cabinet. But when I found a bottle of generic drug store lubricant on mom's side and a bottle of "erectile dysfunction support" pills on dad's... well, that was enough feedback for me for one day, and I returned to my corked wine and classic 80s films.

Just as I'm about to un-pause Patrick's booty swirl, a text from a number I don't recognize lights up my phone.

Unknown: I can explain.

Me: Explain what? Also, new phone. Who dis?

FYI, I don't actually have a new phone. I've just always wanted to say, "New phone. Who dis." So I decided to make that particular little dream come true. Boom. Go me.

Unknown: It's Wally.

I'm undeniably angry with this guy right now, but that doesn't stop me from programming him into my contacts quicker than you can say 'can-you-get-fired-for-showering-with-your-boss-if-you-didn't-know-he-was-your-boss-at-the-time'?

Me: Hello, Bieber.

I wonder if he picks up on the classic Seinfeld inflection I use when I type this. My snide "Hello, Bieber" sounds an awful lot like Jerry's "Hello, Newman." At least in my head. As we all know, it's hard to convey tone over text.

> **Wally:** Please don't call me Bieber.

> **Me:** Okay. Boss?

At that point, my phone rings.

It's him.

Nerves hit me in a wave. Well, I can't pretend I'm not available to pick up the phone because clearly, I am. I press the answer button, and my hand shakes a bit as I lift the phone to my ear. Why is the thought of talking to him more intimidating than texting?

"At what point were you going to tell me that you are my boss?! My *married* boss?!"

Wow. I surprise myself by being the conversation opener.

"I wasn't." A delicious male voice comes through the phone.

Delicious? Since when do I think a voice can be 'delicious'?

"You wasn't what? I mean, you *weren't* what?" I stumble and immediately correct myself. I'll be damned if I let this untrustworthy man make me tangle up my verb tenses. My grammar-loving father would be ashamed.

"Let's start with what I think is the most important thing you said. I wasn't going to tell you I'm married—"

"You weren't!?" I screech, completely incensed.

"*Because*," he stresses and essentially silences me. "I'm not."

"You're not married." I test out the words.

"No. I am not."

"Then why would Naomi say you were?"

"Because I *was* married, and Naomi likes to cause trouble? Who knows why that woman does what she does. I also wasn't going to tell you I'm your boss. Because I'm not. Carol is your boss."

"But you own the arboretum!" I protest.

"*Technically*, I suppose that's true," he says. "But can we ever really own nature? No. No we cannot. Nature owns *us*. We just partner with it."

There he goes again with that nebulous partner stuff.

"You're an annoying person," I huff.

"Fair assessment. But you know, for someone who's

supposedly so nice and sweet, you're actually proving to be quite saucy and mean."

"Gosh, I wonder why!" I feel my volume and pace ramping up. "I should be in a fantastic mood! After all, I engaged in oral pleasures with my surprise boss this afternoon who may or may not be married—"

"I assure you, I am not married," he interjects.

"And will now most likely be fired from a job I adore because of it. Oh, and immediately after I learned he was my boss, the boss in question ran up the hill soaking wet to give a speech he knew he had to give but oh, conveniently forgot to mention to me. This was, of course, after offering me his wife's power suit to wear, ensuring that I look like a complete, naïve idiot in front of Naomi Thornton who seems to know absolutely everything about everyone and has an insatiable desire to jump your bones and make my life hell."

"Ex-wife's power suit," he corrects me again. "And oral pleasures, huh? Not that I'm opposed to that description, but what happened to funilingous? I liked that."

"I'm hanging up."

"Come over, Mabel." His voice rushes through the speaker just as my finger is about to press "End Call."

I slowly bring the phone back up to my ear.

"What did you say?"

"To my place," he rumbles. "Come over."

"To your shack?" I ask, a bit in shock. Shock at the mention of his shack. Shack shock, if you will. Because we all know what happens when Baby pays a visit to Johnny Castle's shack. Look at that, my Bad Girl mission is paying off. Suddenly, I can make pop culture references.

He laughs. "I wouldn't call it a *shack*, per se, but... yes. Come over. Bring your hive so I can get it set up for you. I'll cook you dinner, and I'll explain anything and everything you want to know. I'll—"

"See you in an hour!" I shout and promptly hang up on him.

And that's how I end up standing outside Wally's shack wearing high heels and lipstick and holding a potted plant, feeling incredibly awkward at seven o'clock on a Sunday. In hindsight, I probably shouldn't have been so eager to accept his invitation. I probably should have "played it cool." Or played "hard to get." But I'm generally not in the mood to play at all right now. And I couldn't pass up the opportunity to finally get to know what this guy is all about.

A video call springs up on my phone just as I'm about to knock. It's Calliope. I pick up.

"I didn't interrupt the sex, did I?!"

"Shhh, geez! No!" I whisper-shout and turn the volume way down on my speaker. "I am standing on his doorstep as we speak." I look down at the wood slab I'm standing on. "Well, actually, it's not really a doorstep. More of a door*stump*? Huh. I wonder if he crafted this himself."

"You don't really think I called you to talk about the craftsmanship of his doorstump, do you?" Calliope gently scolds. "I'm more interested in his *other* stump. Yikes, ew, forget I said that. We don't want him to have a stump. I know you don't have a ton of experience, Mabel, but for the record? Stump is bad. Stump is very bad."

"Got it. Um. Why *did* you call then?" I continue to whisper and turn my back to the door. "And I am not here for sex, Calliope."

"Mabel. You can't send a text saying 'Wally is cooking for me in his shack tonight' and expect me not to call you. Wait. Whoa." Her face zooms closer to the screen. "What the hell is that on your lips?"

"What?" I panic and race my fingers up to touch my mouth. "Oh. Um. Lipstick?

"Mabel McGonigle is wearing lipstick?!"

"Yes? What? Is that weird? Too much? Should I rub it off?"

"No!" she exclaims emphatically. "I've just never seen you wear lipstick before. Ralphalpha, have you ever seen Mabel wear lipstick before?"

Calliope's boyfriend, Ralph, suddenly pops up on the screen, looking disheveled and happy, startling me.

"Oh no, I guess I haven't," he says. "You look great, though, Mabel. Nice to see ya."

"Thanks, Ralph. Nice to—"

My words cut off when Ralph dives back down where he came from.

"Oh yes baby, that feels amazing," Calliope moans.

"Um, Calliope? If this isn't a good time..." I say, feeling super uncomfortable and very much the third wheel all of a sudden.

"Don't be silly! It's a great time! Besides, *I* called *you*. Anyway," Calliope continues, "we thought you might benefit from a quick pep talk. Oh god, yes please, never stop what you're doing, sir."

How did I get myself into this situation?

"Um, 'we' as in you and Ralph?" I ask in a small voice. "Because Ralph seems a little busy right now, so..."

"Ralph is an incredible multitasker, but no, not him. Cyndi and Lou. They should be joining the call any second. Oh look, here they are!"

Right on cue, Cyndi and Lou's faces pop up on screen.

"Git it, girl!" Cyndi says to me. "I'm so psyched for you!"

"Git what?" I ask. "What am I gitting? We're just having dinner and talking."

Lou looks saucier than usual when she says, "Girl, you know what you're gitting. The way that man looked at you today, you can git whatever you want..."

I slide right past that assessment and say, "Thank you again for manning my booth, Lou. I know I left really abruptly and unprofessionally."

"Oh holy shit," Calliope moans. "Right there. Hell yes."

"Whoa," Cyndi snickers. "Speaking of gitting what you want..."

"What the hell is happening over there?" Louise asks.

"Sis, hey what's up?!" Ralph pops up onscreen again.

"Ew!" Louise shouts. "God, ew! Calliope, was my brother just going down on you?"

"No! Geez! He's giving me a foot rub!"

"Oh, thank God!" Louise and I say simultaneously.

"You too, Mabes?" Calliope marvels. "You thought Ralph was downtown on the ladybus, and you stayed on the call with me?"

"The ladybus?" Cyndi murmurs in disapproval.

Calliope is clearly undeterred by Cyndi's judgment and waiting for an answer from me.

"Yes, I stayed on the call," I say sheepishly.

"Wowza," Louise says, still looking visibly sick.

"What can I say? I'm a good friend, and I generally don't like to be rude."

"Wowza indeed." Calliope has the audacity to agree and then actually tsks me. "Well, listen, Mabel, my plan was for the three of us to quickly ambush you with sexy-time advice for your date, but apparently, you're way sicker than I thought! Fantastic! I guess my work is done here! Go forth and be frisky, friend! Enter the bone zone!"

"There will be no frisking here tonight! I mean frisky-ing! I mean—"

They all start collectively laughing.

"I'm serious! I'm here for answers. For serious discussion. Not to enter the-the-the bone zone."

More laughter.

"And for the record, I'm not sick. I'm supportive!" I yell.

"Am I interrupting something?"

I turn around to see Wally leaning in the open doorway, and all laughter from them and protests from me immediately stop. Holy smokes, he looks dreamy.

"Holy smokes, he looks dreamy," Calliope says from my phone screen.

"Took the words right out of my mouth," I say under my breath.

"What's that?" he asks with a knowing smile on his lips.

"Nothing. Uh. Hi. I brought you a plant. A *spider* plant. Haha, get it? Because I'm into—"

"Can the bug jokes if you know what's good for you!" Cyndi hisses.

"It's, uh. It's just a plant." I plunk it in his hands.

"Thank you very much," he says as he looks it over. It suddenly feels ridiculous handing this man a plant when his home is completely surrounded by, almost swallowed up by... plants.

"I was just wrapping up a call here, as you can see."

"I can. Good evening, ladies." He leans forward and salutes my friends.

"Hi, Wally," they singsong in unison.

"Oh God, Ralph, you are effing magic," Calliope croons.

"Bleh." Lou lets out a faux retching sound.

"Enjoy the foot rub, Calliope," Wally says and laughs.

Geez, how long has he been listening?

"Oh, I will, Wallace," Calliope purrs. "And you two enjoy whatever kind of rubbing you embark on once you're past your 'serious conversation'…"

"Bye! See ya! Bye!" I immediately press End Call and drop the phone in my purse. Wally is staring at me in amusement. "They had to go," I explain.

"Understood." We stand a moment in silence on his doorstump. Oh, man. I was hoping this wouldn't be awkward. But here it is. Super awkward. "You look beautiful," he says.

"Oh. Thank you. You look… fine. I guess." I shouldn't give this guy too much too soon, right? After all, he has a lot of explaining to do.

"High praise. Care to come in?" He steps aside and gestures for me to move into his space.

"Yesyesyes," I rush. "Coming in." As I approach him, I realize I have no idea what the social norms are for a moment like this. How does one comport herself when seeing her boss for the first time after engaging in funnilingous with him? "Do we um. Do we shake hands or…?"

He places his warm hand on my shoulder. "Mabel, this doesn't have to be awkward."

I peek up into his blue eyes, still a few inches above mine, even while I'm wearing heels. "It doesn't?"

He shakes his head. "It doesn't. And no, we will not be shaking hands tonight."

"What will we be doing?" My voice sounds a little husky when I say it.

"That is completely and totally up to you. But…" He gets so close I can feel his breath on my face. "If you're wondering how we should greet one another… "

"Yeah?" I feel my head tilting to the side, instinctually preparing to line our lips up on just the right angle…"

"I was thinking maybe we should start with a little bit of…"

"Yes?"

"WAPOW!" He smacks my butt. I startle.

"Did you just smack me on the butt and say 'WAPOW?'"

"I did, yeah."

"Given the fact that you're my boss now, would you agree that what you just did could be considered harassment?

"I would. Yes," he smiles, but then seems to think better of it. "Are you... okay with that?"

"I am. Yes. Completely okay." I say without a second thought.

We laugh.

"I'm sorry. I won't do that again if it made you uncomfortable," Wally says. "I just had to break the tension somehow, and a wapow ass smack is what came to me at the moment. I suppose I felt it was okay since we've already been... familiar with one another. But in light of recent revelations..."

"Is Wally Bieber rambling?" I tease. "It was funny. You're fine." At that, I lift my hand in the universal prep for a high five. You know, because I'm not awkward at all. Instead of smacking my hand, though, he weaves his fingers with mine and holds on for a moment.

I don't want to let go.

I finally enter the space, fully, and he shuts the door behind me. He really did relax some of the tension I was feeling. My shoulders have dropped at least two inches. I take in a deep breath.

"Wow, it smells amazing in here. What are you cooking?"

"Broiled wild striped bass drizzled with ginger-scallion oil, stir-fried asparagus, and lemon-encrusted potato wedges for sides, and then for dessert, I whipped us up a spiced pear, blueberry and almond shortcake with whiskey chocolate glaze."

I stare at him blankly.

"Sound okay?"

"Yeah. That sounds... amazing."

"You like a crisp Alsatian Pinot Gris?"

"Sure..." I chuckle. "Who doesn't?" Full disclosure? No idea what he just said.

"Great. I think it pairs nicely with the fish."

Who *is* this guy?

One thing is for sure. This date is a far cry from Monday night Italian food at the Quality Inn. Wait. This is a date, right? He hands me a stemless wineglass and pours the chilled white wine inside. Yeah, it's a date.

"My buddy James who you met?" he says as he pours. "He brought a few bottles of this back for me from a snowshoeing trip he took there this past winter."

"James is into snowshoeing?"

"Snowshoeing, racecar driving, scuba diving... he's an adventure-seeking kinda guy."

"Oh wow, and he works at Adventure Bar!"

"He *owns* Adventure Bar," Wally gently corrects.

"Oh, wow. I had no idea. How about you? Are you an 'adventure-seeking guy' too?"

"Not so much anymore. Lately, I'm working on being a happiness-seeking kind of guy. A... simplicity-seeking kind of guy. Cheers." He lifts his own glass in my direction.

"Cheers," I respond with a smile. We clink our glasses together. I keep my eyes on him while we each take a long sip. That's not the first time he's alluded to having made big changes in his life lately. That's the thing with this guy. He alludes to a lot, but he explains very little.

Tonight, that's going to change.

If he keeps his promise to spill all his secrets, that is.

"You bring your hive?" he asks.

"Yup! I leaned the pieces up against your bench outside."

"Perfect. I'll get everything assembled for you in the morning. I placed the bee order with my guy about an hour ago. He says they'll arrive mid-afternoon tomorrow."

"Wow, thank you. Are you sure that this okay, though? It feels a bit early to be 'moving in together.' Hahaha. That was a joke. You could tell it was a joke, right? I know we're not moving in together, but blending bees is sort of intimate, isn't it? And will the arboretum really be okay with my hive taking up residence on-site?"

"Mabel Again?"

There he goes again with that nickname.

"Yeah?"

"I sort of *am* 'the arboretum,' yeah?"

"Ha, yeah. I guess you are."

"And I say it's fine."

I give a quick, silent nod, my lips feeling sort of tight.

"Well, that's as good a transition as any." He chuckles. "Want to head outside with our wine to talk? Food needs to simmer for a few more minutes still, and the air is really nice tonight."

"Sounds great."

As he ushers me toward the back door of his small home, I finally take a moment to observe my surroundings. "Wow. This isn't what I was expecting. Your home, I mean."

"Oh, no? How so?"

"Well, for one thing, this is no shack." I take in the knotty wooden floors, the braided throw rugs, the sleek cabinets, and stone counters.

"What, did you think I was living in squalor? Sleeping on a dirt floor, eating tuna out of a tin can?"

"I didn't consider your sleeping arrangements or eating habits, but sort of, yeah. I thought you were living in a tool shed." I wince.

"A tool shed!" he exclaims. "*Amongst* the tools?"

"Well, I didn't know!" I say a tad defensively. "You've been very strange and mysterious up until this point, and I have to say, my counselors had some convincing theories about you that are somewhat hard to shake."

"Like...?" he prompts.

"Like... you live in a tool shed and bury people in your backyard."

"Clever but untrue. At least the tool shed part," he adds with a wink.

I keep looking around, surprised by how classy the place is. "But this is more like one of those 'tiny house' situations you see on HGTV, huh?"

"It's exactly like that, yeah," he says, "Built it myself this spring with all recyclable materials. It's solar-powered, which I feel really good about. It's a process, but I'm working to make it as self-sustainable as possible. Watch your step."

He takes my elbow and guides me down the drop from his home to the patio area out back. It's adorable. He has a clearly handcrafted table with a simple ivory candle burning in the center, already set with silverware and two cloth napkins. The two chairs, wide, tall tree stumps with cream-colored cushions are positioned so whoever sits there has the perfect view of the lake.

"This is... lovely, Wallace." I breathe as I take it all in.

"Hey!" he lightly admonishes. "What happened to Wally?"

"You like Wally?"

"From you?" he rumbles. "Yeah... I like Wally."

It's getting dark out now, and I wonder if he can see me blush. I can certainly feel the warmth in my cheeks. Who am I kidding? I'm feeling the warmth everywhere. But before I can let anything further happened between us, I need to ask some serious questions.

"Care to swing?" he asks and gestures to a two-seater high-backed tree swing hanging from a sturdy oak.

"Uh. Sure. Yeah."

He holds my wineglass while I position myself on the seat, then places it back in my palm once he settles himself beside me.

"Alright, girl. Hit me." He taps his hand on my thigh again, just like he did the night he brought down the pyramid scheme. And just like that night, I feel the zing.

"Twenty Questions time?" I ask after a long sip of the wine.

"Mabel, you can do *two hundred* questions if you want. Seriously. I'm an open book."

I take a deep breath and say, "Okay. Here I go."

With that, he pushes us forward with a press of his feet, and we start to swing.

Chapter Twenty-One

I start off easy, lobbing some preliminary get-to-know-you questions at him. You know, basic things we just never tackled before diving into passive-aggressive rowboat kissing and ill-advised shower shenaniganing. Can you use the word shenanigan as a present progressive verb like that? Shenaniganing? Well whether you can or you can't, I just did. That's right, people. Bad Mabel does what she wants!

We cover the "where were you borns," the "do you have siblings," and the "what did you want to be when you grow ups," with the obligatory conversational side dish of "what's your favorite color." I'm not sure why the color question is the one humans have repeatedly asked to learn about other humans. The answer is never particularly illuminating, is it? For what it's worth, his is navy blue. Mine? Scarlett Johansson. Seriously I got this box of celebrity color crayons once when I was a tween, and Scarlett Johansson—this gorgeous red shade—was my absolute favorite. Though Jada Pinkett Smith and Forest Green Whitaker were also delightful and were tied for second place.

Anyway, once we're warmed up, I get to the more pressing matters.

"So." I exhale sharply. "Tell me more about the woman whose clothes I wore home this afternoon after our shower shenanigans."

He scoffs. "Is that what we're calling them... shenanigans?"

"I don't know." I feel my cheeks heat. "What would you call it? A shower… conference? A meet and greet? An assemblage?"

"Assemblage," he parrots back. "Nice. You took French in high school, I take it?"

"Oui." I joke. "Et tu?"

"Deutsche," he says.

"Dutch? You speak Dutch?" This man is truly full of surprises.

"No." He chuckles. "Deutsche. Don'tcha know Deutsche? It's German for German."

"Right, right. I know that," I say, sensing the embarrassment rising up in my cheeks. I can't help it; I get defensive. "Just so you know, this is not one of those cases where Mabel is 'book smart but not street smart,' so you can keep that assessment to yourself. My mind is just a bit all over the place right now. I have to say, though, that I may have discovered the one thing you can't do. Accents. That sounded more like Minnesota than Munich."

He stops swinging and stares at me.

I take in his horrified expression and backpedal immediately. "Sorry. That was rude of me. Your dialect work is lovely."

He shakes his head. "My 'dialect work' is shit. Your assessment on that front was accurate. And I spent winters in Minnesota as a kid, so maybe the accent clung on. But what I want to know is… what asshole told you you're 'book smart, but not street smart'?"

My Dad, my teachers, my fiancé… the list goes on.

"Um… who *didn't* tell me that?" I say, rather than naming names. "That's sort of been the refrain throughout my life when people try to explain my… Pollyanna nature? My naivete?"

He looks steamed. "Anyone who calls you a Pollyanna is a punk who wouldn't know how to be positive if a plus sign lodged itself in his ass," he blurts, then quickly recovers. "Sorry. That was crass, but you catch my drift. Negative does not equal realistic. Positive does not equal naïve. From what I've observed, Mabel, you live your life with a hopeful curiosity. And when we recognize that in a person, we should lift it up. What we should not do is try to belittle it or tear it down."

"Wow, you're… really passionate about this," I say a bit bashfully, seeing how worked up he's become on my behalf.

"Well, yeah! That's some small-minded ridiculousness right there."

"Yeah..." I hesitantly agree but can't help playing devil's advocate for the other side. "I get it, though. I think people assume because I'm so 'nice' that I can't possibly understand the magnitude of things. Or the ugly side of things. I know there's an ugly side to things, but I choose to focus on what's good. What feels good. What's so wrong with that?"

"Absolutely nothing's wrong with that." He takes a sip of his wine. "So long as you're not lying to yourself. There's a big difference between being positive and being willfully ignorant. Or pretending things are better than they are. If you do that, you're just going to sell yourself short. And you deserve more than that."

"Do I?"

"Hell yeah, you do. You... you deserve the world, Mabel." He wraps an arm around my shoulder. "And not that you need any affirmation from me, but I'd be remiss if I didn't tell you... I think you're smart as hell. And fascinating. In *all* the ways someone can be smart and fascinating. Book smart, street smart... heart smart. You, Mabel McGonigle, have all the smarts."

I don't say anything. I just turn my head to look up at him. He's so close. He looks deep into my eyes, and I know he means every word he just said. "You warm enough?" he almost whispers as he rubs my upper arm. But the goose bumps he's noticing aren't because I'm cold.

"Yeah. I'm fine," I say. "We've, uh... we've gotten off topic, though, yeah?"

"Yes. Yeah. Sorry. You asked whose suit you were wearing after our assemblage." He smiles and unwinds his arm from my shoulders, which elicits no small amount of regret from me. He pushes his feet off the ground and gets us swinging again. "My ex-wife. Her name was Jamie. *Is* Jamie. We split a little over two years ago. Divorce was finalized in April. I still had one of her suits—not intentionally, mind you. I found it mixed up in my things when I moved here. Meant to give it to Goodwill or..." He cuts himself off. "In hindsight, I should've offered you something of mine when your clothes got messed up. But my things would all be huge on you, and I didn't want you to be embarrassed when you went back up to your booth, nor did I want there to be very clear evidence of our shower shenanigans. Not that it's anyone's business or that we have anything to hide. But there ya have it."

"You separated two years ago." I try the words out.

"Two years ago, yes."

"So you're not *currently* with her." Can't blame a girl for double-checking. After all, I am just out of a relationship filled with lies.

"Mabel. No. I'm currently with *you*." He pauses. "Or at least I'd like to be."

He seems to hold his breath while waiting for my response. It only takes me half a second to say, "I'd like that too."

"Great." He exhales in relief and laces his fingers with mine. His calloused hands brush gently against my skin, and I love it.

"Who would ever let you go?" I ask the question before I consider the fact that I should probably hold it back. But I sort of can't help it. I've been stuck on that question ever since he first said the word "ex-wife."

"That's sweet of you to say, but plenty of people. I mean, when you think about it, everyone you've ever been with ultimately let you go. Otherwise, you'd still be with them. A part of life, yeah? A part of being a grown-up?"

"I suppose that's true. I just... I don't have a lot of experience with breakups. Just the one." I'm not sure why this embarrasses me, but it does. I let my eyes drift out across the water while we continue to swing.

"I see." He nods and looks like he's internally debating on what to say next. "Listen. That guy. What's his name, Ernie?"

"No. Bert."

"Right. Knew it was one of them. I was going to say Mr. Snuffleupagus, but I didn't want to be *too* disrespectful." He winks.

This gets a little laugh out of me.

"He hurt you, yeah? He lied to you. I'm sure those feelings are super fresh right now. But I want to assure you. I might be gruff. I might be a dick—"

"You're not a dick," I protest.

"Uh... less than a week ago, you were shocked I took a yoga

teacher training course because—and I quote—'you're a bit of a dick.'"

"Sorry," I grimace.

"Don't be. The point I'm trying to make is that yes, I *can* be a bit of a dick. I think it comes from me giving up giving a damn what other people think of me anymore. What I am *not*, though, is a liar. You hear me? I will never lie to you, Mabel. Never. You will always get the straight story from me. All you ever have to do is ask."

He squeezes my hand. I nod and smile.

"Next?" he says.

"Hm?"

"You said you have a lot of questions. Hit me. Ask."

"You sure?"

"Hundred percent. Get 'em all out there in the open."

"Okay..." I take a deep breath and unleash my rapid-fire curiosities.

"Why were you so grumpy and okay with people avoiding you and making up stories about you when we first met? You didn't really tell my CITs to call you 'The Wall,' did you? How did you know Doreen's business was a sham? And what made you take it upon yourself to get all those people *out* of that business? And not for nothing, but what was up with all those sheep metaphors? Are you a farmer or something, and you've just never mentioned it? Okay. All this talk of partnering with nature—what's going on there? What made you move from the city and build a tiny home on an arboretum? Also, how can a handyman who occasionally teaches yoga afford to buy an arboretum? For that matter, *why* would you buy an arboretum? That was the third time in a row I said arboretum, and now the word arboretum officially sounds nonsensical. Isn't that funny when that happens? Oh, how do you know Naomi Thornton? Did you two date or something? Clearly, she's hot for you. And how did she know the suit I was wearing was your ex-wife's? Were they friends? And did your ex-wife have a thing for power suits of the eggplant variety? Also, that splooge lady—who also seems to have the hots for you—she mentioned you being in 'recovery.' What was that all about? What were or *are* you recovering from? And lastly—for now—I know we established that you are my elder, but exactly how much elder—excuse me—*older* are you?"

I draw in a huge gulp of air and let it out.

There. That ought to get us heading in the right direction.

"Did you breathe at all during that monologue?" He chuckles.

"No," I pant. "No, I did not."

I turn sideways on the swing and pull my knees up into my chest to settle in for his explanation.

"Alright," he says. "Let's see how concise I can be while chipping away at all of that." He tops off first my wineglass, then his, takes a sip, cracks his knuckles, and says, "I picked up my life and moved it to the arboretum because I was starting over."

"What made you decide to start over?" I ask tentatively.

"It was less of a decision and more of a ... directive. Every single aspect of my life told me I was going the wrong way. Wrong relationship. Wrong career path. Wrong way of viewing the world around me. I wanted to take a break from people and just... be alone and quiet with nature." He smiles. "Which is an excellent plan until you realize that every summer for two months straight the place will be crawling with children and counselors who just won't leave you alone."

"Sorry," I wince.

"Don't be. One counselor, in particular, has made quite the impression. I certainly wouldn't wish her away."

"Ahem. *Head* counselor, thank you very much."

"Oh, excuse me, ma'am. *Head* counselor." He stares out over the water. "And the kids have turned out to be pretty great too. But yes, I did initially try to scare the CITs off. Needed some time to tune out from people and tune in to nature."

"So you did tell them to call you 'The Wall'?" I ask, surprised.

"I did. It's what my work buddies used to call me. *And* my ex-wife."

"Why did they call you that?"

"Well, for one thing, it's short for Wallace."

"Sure..." I stretch out the word, hoping to stretch out more of an explanation from him.

"But also… I wasn't always very…" He considers his words before continuing. "I was kind of a… You've heard that phrase 'like talking to a brick wall,' yeah?"

"Yeah…"

"Well… that. I was pretty immovable in most areas of my life. Business? Definitely. Relationships? Absolutely."

"What changed?"

"What makes you think something changed?" He sort of half laughs.

"Look at you now. You're the total opposite of 'The Wall.' You're kind. You're generous. You care about other people. All other people."

"Ugh. Don't let that get around," he jokes.

"You singlehandedly rescued a room of fifty strangers from imminent bankruptcy—still not clear on how or why you did that—but, it's pretty clear you're not the mysterious curmudgeon you wanted people to think you were. Seems like 'The Wall' tumbled down somewhere along the line, and you've been figuring out how to pick up the pieces."

He's quiet for a moment. For a guy who just proclaimed to be an open book, he certainly seems reticent around this particular topic.

I push just a little bit more.

"Before, um, Dawn, the splooge lady, said you were recovering? What was that all about?"

"You can hold the splooge," he says.

"Excuse me?" My voice rockets to an interesting pitch. I try again in a lower tone. "I mean… excuse me?"

He laughs. "You don't need to call her 'the splooge lady.' I'll know who you're talking about if you just call her Dawn."

"Oh, okay," I breathe. "Good to know."

He continues, "To answer your question, though… yeah. Two years ago, I got the kind of diagnosis no one wants to get. I was working this high-level finance job, making a ton of money, but making absolutely no authentic connections or relationships. I thought what I had with my ex was real. But it turns out… nah. When I got sick, she wasn't too interested in sticking by me. She was even less interested when I quit the job and the paycheck she found so attractive. I made a pact between myself and…" His voice drifts off, and he shakes his head a little bit.

"A pact between you and who? What were you going to say?" I encourage. I wasn't aware this guy needed encouragement. He always seems so completely confident in everything he says and does.

"I don't wanna weird you out with my woo," he says.

"Your 'woo'?" I laugh.

"Yeah, I've been told in recent months I've become a 'spiritual woo-woo.' I don't think that's entirely accurate, though." He pauses for a breath before continuing. " What, um, what word are you comfortable with: The Big G? The Expansive U? Universal E?"

"I… have no idea what you're talking about," I say apologetically.

"God, Universe, Energy," he rattles off. "I'm more of a Universe kind of guy. Or nature really. It's all the same thing, isn't it? No matter what you call it?"

"I guess?"

Wow, who is *this guy?*

"Anyway, when I got better, I knew I was one of the lucky ones. I was getting a second chance. I made a pact between me and nature that I would turn things around and get back to the basics. That's where the real magic in life is, ya know? The basics. I wasn't sure what exactly I should be doing next, but my gut told me the first step needed to be stripping away all pretense. All busy-ness. All ego. All desire to please. Feeling free again was the goal. And when I thought about the last time I truly felt free, it was when I was a kid and spent my winter breaks on my grandparent's tree farm in Minnesota. When I was there, I felt like I was in a constant conversation with nature. I'd spend my days climbing oak trees, feeling their sturdy energy lifting me up. I'd run in and out of the evergreen trees, breathing in that pine needle scent, feeling like it was speaking to me. That's where I first learned to tap too."

"You're a tap dancer?" I squeak.

"Haha, no. My grandpa taught me to tap *trees* for syrup."

"Right, right. Of course."

"So when I saw Naomi Thornton at a fundraiser, and she told me the arboretum was up for sale, it seemed like the perfect next step to take." He takes in the puzzled look on my face and explains, "She and I are on the board of the same charity."

"Geez, is that woman on every board known to man?" I marvel.

"I believe she is, yes." He laughs lightly, then continues. "And no, we have never dated. What else...? You asked how I knew about Doreen's 'business?' Finance people talk. I knew the guy who started it. He brought the plan to me about a year ago and asked me to partner with him on it, but all signs pointed toward it being a disaster. In hindsight, I should have been a better person and steered folks away from it from the get-go. But I guess it took meeting you and seeing you deep in it to really care."

"And now, you really are better? Recovered?" I ask.

"Completely in the clear, yeah."

"Amazing," I breathe. "I'm so, so happy about that."

"Me too, Mabel Again. Me too."

He kisses me softly on the lips, and I feel my heart flutter.

"Now. Did I cover everything?" He squints up at the sky like he's trying to remember the litany of questions I fired at him a few minutes ago. "Ah, one more. I'm thirty-three," he says like it's no big deal.

"Oh, snap!" I blurt, then cover my mouth with both hands.

He laughs. "Did you just 'oh, snap' me?"

"I did. I'm sorry! You're just even *elder*-er than I thought."

"Is that a problem?"

I consider his question a moment.

"Not at all. Just... wow. You're nine years older than me."

"Almost ten actually. My birthday is next Saturday."

"Whoa. Happy... almost Birthday."

"I thank you."

My eyes drift over to the outdoor shower that now holds quite a vivid memory. He follows my gaze and smiles.

"Can I make a confession?" I say in a small voice.

"Of course."

"I'd, uh, I'd actually never done that before. What we did this afternoon."

"You'd never pulled a fully-clothed snarky sugarmaker into an outdoor shower and had your naked way with him?"

"Oh no, I do that constantly," I joke. "But the particular *way* I engaged with the sugarmaker... that was new for me."

"You're kidding me." He suddenly looks pretty displeased.

"I'm not, no."

"Let me get this straight. You're telling me that schmuck I met this afternoon never went down on you? Not that I really want to think about him doing *anything* to you. But listen, I'm a modern man, I can handle knowing you've been with other people before me. What I can't handle is knowing you were with someone for so long who clearly didn't treat you the way you deserved to be treated."

"In fairness, the lack of funilingous wasn't really his fault."

"Oh, no?" he says doubtfully.

"No. See, he was tongue-tied as a baby, and the doctor didn't snip his frenulum fully, so his tongue tires quickly."

"Ridiculous excuse," he huffs. "Pitiful. In case it wasn't completely clear, you can rest assured now, beautiful. Because my frenulum is fine."

"I... can attest to that, yes."

"Now, can I ask *you* something?"

"Of course."

"Why were you with that guy in the first place?"

"You're not the first person to ask me that. You're not even the first person to ask me that *today*." I consider the best way to explain it. "Tonight," I say slowly, "while I was waiting for you to call—"

"You were waiting for me to call?" he asks with a saucy smile.

"Shoot, no. I wasn't *waiting*. Hoping maybe?" We lock eyes for a breath, and I think better of what I just said. "Um. Can we forget I just said that?"

"I can try..." he says. "No promises, though."

"Let's see if I can explain it this way. Tonight while I was absolutely *not* waiting for you to call, I broke open a bottle of

Malbec. Not quite sure why, since I'm mostly a Pinot Noir girl, but for whatever reason, I opened it. I thought it tasted a bit funny. Didn't love it, but I kept sipping it. I figured I was *supposed* to like it, ya know? Like there must be some tannins or 'notes' I just wasn't appreciating. I've heard wine has tannins and notes. And legs! Did you know that wine has legs? Anyway, I drank a whole glass of it and was about to pour another when I finally admitted to myself that it was corked. I think... sometimes I look so hard for the good in things— in people—that I don't realize I'm drinking vinegar until I start to feel sick." I peek over at him to see if he's still listening. "Does that make sense?"

"It does. Well..." He gently clears his throat and lifts his glass, his eyes twinkling over the rim. "How's the wine tasting tonight?"

"Delicious."

"Good. I couldn't agree more."

We clink our glasses.

We kiss.

Chapter Twenty-Two

"Am I interrupting the sex?" Calliope's voice comes through loud and clear on the video call I just picked up.

"Calliope, if you think you're interrupting 'the sex,' why do you keep calling?"

"You know..." She pauses. "I actually don't have an answer for that. Ha! Well? Am I?"

"No," I emphasize. "You're not interrupting 'the sex.' Like I told you an hour ago, we needed to talk. So... we talked."

"And?"

"And it was really good. I feel better."

"You sure? Because you look a little constipated."

"Calliope!" I scold quietly. "I'm not constipated. I'm just...I don't know." I sigh and peek toward Wally's house. "Listen, I don't have long. The only reason I picked up in the first place is because Wally went inside to get our food. He'll be back any minute."

"Then hop to it, biznatch. Tell me everything."

I do a rapid-fire retelling of the events and conversations from tonight.

When I finish, she says, "Oh man, this shit is crazy."

"What's crazy?"

"He's an even better person than you are! I actually didn't think that was possible."

I can't decide if I'm offended by this or not, so I just say, "What do you mean?"

"He builds and lives in a sustainable tiny home, grows and catches his own food, and 'partners' with trees? Geez, what does he do for drinking water? Leave out a bucket and collect rain?" she says sarcastically.

"Well, actually... yeah," I say. "I mean, it's not a bucket exactly. It's more like a big metal barrel that catches the rain, then sends it through a filtration system, but yeah."

She laughs. "So what's the problem?"

"There are several, actually."

"Okay, hit me."

"Well, first of all," I prep her, "He's a lot older than me."

"Define 'a lot.'"

"Nine years. He's thirty-three."

Calliope whistles. "Thirty-three, huh? Wooooo-eeeee."

"I know. It's a pretty big age difference, right?"

She scoffs. "Who cares about an age difference! That kind of thing is irrelevant."

"Oh," I say, somewhat relieved. And confused.

She continues, "Yeah no, I 'wooo-eeed' because it's his Jesus year."

"His what?"

"The year he's supposed to perform all his miracles! You know, like Jesus did."

Calliope grew up in a super religious family. I did not. We were more of the go to church on Easter and Christmas kind of family. And only if we woke up in time.

"I have no idea what you're—"

She cuts me off with full-throttled enthusiasm. "Alright. Check this. Jesus was like this quiet thirty-two-year-old nobody dude living in Nazareth with His mom. Then He turns thirty-three and BOOM! Suddenly, He meets all twelve of his best friends, starts performing miracles like a maniac, begins His own religion, throws one hell of a dinner party, gets arrested, dies, and then rises from the freaking dead. Make no mistake, thirty-three is huge."

"Well, now that you mention it, Wally has had a pretty miraculous few years: beat cancer, left a bad marriage, quit his big, important finance job, bought the arboretum—"

"Met the love of his life…"

"What?" I shriek. "Who?!"

"*You*, you goober." Calliope cackles.

This gives me a definite pause. "Me? No. He doesn't *love* me. We've known each other for less than a month."

"I know that, but give it time. There's no clock on a connection. Sometimes when you know… you know."

Calliope certainly has become quite the romantic since meeting Ralph. An exhibitionistic, freaky romantic, but a romantic all the same.

I look over at the glowing window of Wally's tiny home and see him assembling our meals for us. I consider Calliope's words. "He is pretty incredible," I say softly. "He's like this amazing combination of compassion and caring while not giving a single shit about what anyone thinks of him."

"Oooh, look at that!" Calliope hoots. "Mabel McGonigle curses now?"

"I guess. A lil bit, yeah." I chuckle.

"I like this guy's influence," she says, then cocks her head to the side. "So. If he's so amazing, why do you still seem hesitant?"

"Well"—I lower my voice even though I'm fairly certain he can't hear us from inside the house—"I thought *Bert* was amazing, and look what happened there."

"Did you, though?" Calliope's voice gets pitchy. "Be honest, friend. Did you feel proud to be with Bert? Excited to see him? Was he the person you wanted to tell all your stories to pretty much the moment they happened?"

"No," I breathe out the word with no hesitation. "I didn't feel that way about Bert. But… I do feel that way about Wally."

"Yeah, you do!" she shouts. I think she even does a fist pump in the air. Either that or she was punching someone out of frame. Oh gosh, I probably should have asked her if Ralph was secretly pleasuring her during this call as well—you never know with those two—but she seemed to be behaving herself, so I think we're in the clear.

The door to Wally's house swings open. "He's coming back," I whisper. "Dinner time. Gotta go."

"What are you having?" she whispers back.

"Why are you whispering?"

"Because whispering is fun. Everyone knows that. Quick, what are you having?" she repeats. "You know, besides the sex."

I ignore her unnecessary sex assumption and rattle off the menu he told me before. "Broiled wild striped bass drizzled in ginger-scallion oil with stir-fried asparagus and lemon-encrusted potato wedges for sides, and a spiced pear, blueberry, and almond shortcake with whiskey chocolate glaze for dessert."

"Holy shit. Marry him, Mabel. Marry him today," she says with complete seriousness.

"Shhh!" I hiss. "Goodbye!"

I slip my phone back into my skort pocket right as Wally settles our plates on the long wooden table and looks over at me. "How was Calliope?"

"How did you know it was Calliope?" I ask as I make my way over to join him at the table.

"Because the look on your face is the same as it's been every time I've seen you in her presence."

"And how is that?"

"Equal parts shocked and delighted."

"Ha, that sounds about right."

"Shall we?" He gestures to the truly gorgeous plates of food set side by side, so we can sit next to each other and face the water.

"Wow, this looks... amazing."

"Glad you think so. Sit. Eat," he says while grabbing our bottle of wine from near the tree swing and topping off our glasses.

I take a bite, and before I think better of it, I say, "Fuuuuuuuuck me."

"If you insist, madam." He laughs, a hint of surprise in his voice.

"I'm sorry. I don't know what's come over me and my language, but hole-eeeee shit on a stick, this is delicious!"

"Thank you. And lady, let your language be free. You never have to excuse it with me."

"That there sounded like a little poem, sir."

"What can I say? You inspire me."

We eat for a few minutes in comfortable almost-silence, the

chirps of birds overhead and the rowboat tapping gently against the dock the only sounds we hear.

"You know, this is all pretty Walden Pond of you."

"What, romancing a beautiful woman by a body of water and feeding her striped bass? I wasn't aware Thoreau was stealing my best moves." He snaps on a stalk of asparagus and takes a sip of wine.

I laugh. "I meant the whole living by the water in a tiny home, growing your own food, and attempting to hide yourself away from other humans thing."

"Attempting is the operative word, yeah? Because let's be honest. If I had *truly* wanted to give up on humanity, I could have chosen a more suitable locale than a nature reserve with rigorous educational programming and full-on summer camp operations, don't you think?" He laughs, then gets quiet. "I suppose, on some level, I wasn't actually looking to cut myself off but to connect. With nature *and* people." He looks out over the water. "Fun fact: they call it Walden *Pond*, but it's actually a classic kettle hole. Did you know that?"

"No, I did not."

"I suppose 'Walden Kettle Hole' doesn't sound nearly as romantic, though, does it?"

"No." I chuckle. "It doesn't. What exactly is a kettle hole?"

"Blocks of dead ice left behind by retreating glaciers create a depression. That then gets filled up to create a pond or a lake," he says matter-of-factly.

"Oooh, look at you," I tease. "I'm going to start calling you 'Wally Wikipedia.'"

"Please don't," he jokes.

"I take it you're a Thoreau fan?"

He shrugs. "Ole Henry David did get a few things right, I think. 'Life is frittered away by detail... simplify, simplify.'" Wally performs the quote with a little extra pizazz. "I'm obviously down with that line of thinking," he explains by gesturing to his house and our surroundings. "And the Civil Disobedience thing I *generally* agree with. Truth be told, sometimes I think I'd benefit from being even more disobedient in my life."

"Oh, yeah?" I say between bites of bass.

"Yeah. And from what I've learned about you so far"—he tips his head toward me—"I'd hazard to say you might as well?" He says this gently like it's a question, but we both know what he's getting at: that "Good Girl Mabel" could benefit *a lot* from being more disobedient.

"Have you been talking to my friends?" I ask, giving him no small amount of side-eye.

"How do you mean?"

"They're on this mission to hang up my 'good girl shoes' and get me to embrace being 'bad.'"

"Hm." Wally considers that a moment, then says, "I dunno, I feel like I've already experienced Bad Girl Mabel."

"And?" I feel a sudden spike of nervousness.

"And... she's a hell of a lot of fun." He winks. "But all of your sides are fun. 'We contain multitudes,' yeah? For the record, that's a Walt quote, not a Thoreau."

"Disney?" I ask.

"Nah." He laughs. "The other Walt. Whitman."

"Right, right."

"Here's another Thoreau-ism I like. It makes a solid argument for 'goodness'—whatever that means. 'All good things are wild and free.'"

"I like that," I say sort of wistfully. My eyes catch on the huge, beautiful tree right next to the water's edge. "That's a weeping willow, right?"

"It is," Wally says. "One of my favorites. Though you have to be careful with that one. Many folks will tell ya she's a bad tree to have around."

"Why is that?"

"Well, her roots spread really wide. You always want to build at least fifty feet from a willow, or your pipes and foundation are at risk. But God, what a perfect climbing tree she is." His whole face seems to soften as he looks out at this tree. "Good, solid branches. Lots of shade and coverage. Cozy places to hide."

Our attention is taken for a moment by a flock of birds flying overhead.

"Maybe…" He shifts his gaze back to the weeping willow. "Maybe none of us needs to strive to be 'good' or 'bad.' Maybe being authentic is enough."

"Is that a Thoreau-ism too?"

"Nah," he says. "Just a Wally-ism."

I flash back for a moment to the time when I was nine and got much further in the elementary school-wide spelling bee than I ever imagined I would. I was a science geek from day one and always placed all my attention and passion there. Spelling was always hit or miss for me, so I was shocked to have made it that far. I remember standing on the podium, my knees literally shaking, waiting to receive the next word I needed to spell correctly in order to move onto the finals. The word was "authentic." I panicked. Drew a blank. So I did that thing all kids do during spelling bees when they need to stall for time. I asked for the definition.

The school librarian kindly spoke into the microphone, "Authentic. Of undisputed origin; genuine."

I liked that concept so much, even back then.

I smile at the memory and say to Wally, "Authentic. Authentic I can definitely do."

Wally's energy shifts, both of us suddenly more light-hearted. "A lot of people think Thoreau was kind of a dick, though."

"Really? They do?"

"Oh, hell yeah!" he exclaims.

"Well, being that no one alive today ever met the guy, maybe we should give him the benefit of the doubt."

"That's your MO, isn't it?" He smiles at me.

"What? Giving people the benefit of the doubt?"

"Yeah."

"Sure," I say with confidence. "Most people are inherently good when you give them a chance, don't you think?"

He hesitates for a second, then nods with a little purse of his lips before taking another bite of food.

"Do you disagree with that?" I challenge.

"Not generally, no. But taken to its extreme, that thinking can get us all into trouble. I guess we just need to know when we've given someone enough chances."

I wonder if he's thinking of his ex when he says that. I know my thoughts certainly shift to mine for a millisecond.

"Anyway," Wally continues. "I think Thoreau's gone down in history as a bit of a punk mostly because of the whole not paying his taxes thing. Funny, no one's ever bothered *me* about that."

"DO YOU NOT PAY YOUR TAXES?!" I spit out a mouthful of perfectly good white wine... directly onto the man's chest.

"Relax, lady!" He starts toweling himself off with his cloth napkin. "I pay my taxes! I was kidding!"

"Oh my gosh, I'm so sorry!" I exclaim, both hands shooting up to cover my mouth in embarrassment.

He waves me off. "Eh, no big deal. Probably only fair you douse me in white wine since I was somewhat responsible for getting you covered in craft beer and syrup the other day."

"Well," I say flirtatiously, "You more than made up for it afterward."

"I did, didn't I." He smiles and leans in for a kiss.

The kiss quickly escalates. Before I know it, we're making out like teenagers under the stars, and I'm overwhelmed by how happy and right everything feels with this man.

"I like you," I say as I rest my forehead against his, a bit breathless.

"I like you too."

"No, but like... a lot," I breathe.

"Oh, okay, well that's different." He laughs and rears back, both arms up in defense. "If you like me *a lot*, then I'm out!"

I smack him on the shoulder and laugh along with him. "You know what I mean, you dork!"

"A dork?" He pulls back even further in mock offense. "You're calling me a dork?"

"Yes, any man who quotes Thoreau the amount of times you have this evening definitely qualifies as a dork."

"Fair enough," he acquiesces and slides back closer to me on the bench. "As long as we're in agreement that you *like* dorks."

"I do," I say and cup one hand then the other around his scruffy jaw. "Very much."

"The feeling is beyond mutual, madam." He kisses me oh, so tenderly on the lips.

"Can we just... take things slow?" I look deeply into those gorgeous blue eyes and wait for his answer.

"Yes, of course we can. You're calling all the shots, Mabel. We can absolutely take things slow."

Chapter Twenty-Three

"*O*HMYGOD IS SEX SUPPOSED TO FEEL LIKE THIS?"

So much for taking things slow.

"Is sex supposed to feel like what?" Wally pants.

"Like this!" I exclaim. "Like incredible! Like awesome! Like out of this world!"

"Yeah, I think it is," he says proudly. "And thank you very much. Back atcha, baby!"

Let's backtrack and explain how we got here, shall we?

After dinner—and my request to take things slow—we took a walk around the lake, which led to more conversation, more connection, and fewer and fewer reasons I shouldn't dive into this relationship headfirst and with my whole heart. Cut to him mentioning that he has a tent with a "moon roof" that he camps out in on warmer nights, then me asking if I could *see* it... and well, here we are, sexing it up under an evening's summer sky.

This man's hips are from heaven. His mouth is a miracle, and his abdominals are the bumpity-bump-bump thrill ride I didn't know I'd been dreaming of climbing aboard.

"I wonder if you actually understand the way you're making me feel right now!" I exclaim.

"Possibly not," he says without missing a beat, a thrust, or a touch. "But I can make certain inferences."

"Hey, question for ya," I say, my head thrashing left then right, making space for the kisses he's raining down the column of my throat. "Have you ever thought about the fact that from your perspective, I'm basically having sex inside out right now? And from *my* perspective, *you're* having sex inside out? You know, penetrationally speaking?"

"Uhhh.... No. No, I haven't considered that," he says and lifts his head as though he actually is considering it now. What a guy. He's seriously the best.

I lock eyes with him and smile. "I know! It's mind-blowing stuff, right?"

"Well... " He stretches out the sound. "I don't know if I would call it mind-blowing exactly, but—"

"Sorry to interrupt, but do you know if penetrationally is a word?"

"It is now!" He laughs.

"Not a very sexy word, though, is it?"

"Not really, no," he agrees, then proceeds to bury his head back in my neck.

"But anyway," I continue, "you get my point, that—"

"Hey, Mabel?" He slows his movements, looks up, and gently brushes the hair out of my eyes.

"Yeah?"

"There's suddenly a lot of talking happening."

"True! Yeah." I feel a tiny panic arise. "Is that okay? It appears that I'm a talker."

"Sure. Of course, it's okay," he says. "Talking is... great. Talking with *you* is great. I love it. I'm just... I dunno, I guess I'm kind of wondering why you're choosing now for a philosophical discussion on the mechanics of sexual intercourse."

"Oh, man," I sigh. "I'm sorry, Wally."

"No, no, no, don't be." He strokes my hair and kisses my forehead. "Nothing to be sorry about. You just seemed to be really enjoying yourself a moment ago and then—"

"I was! Ohmy*god* I was!"

"Great! Me too. So... do you want to resume the enjoyment?" he asks softly. "Or..."

"Yes, absolutely. I want to resume," I say.

And then, this man proceeds to rock my world.

I'm not kidding. He does things to me inside that tent that I had no idea were even possible. In fairness, I'm certain in all likelihood that my sexual bar was set a bit low, what with my previous Dick-Wolf-Quality-Inn-Once-a-Week regimen, but even if that wasn't my experience, I have absolutely no doubt that these here, these moves he's busting out with beautiful abandon would still be utterly life-changing.

Honestly. I. Am. Changed.

Afterward, we lie there, catching our breath, both of us lying on our backs and staring at the sky through the mesh roof of the tent. My head rests on his shoulder, his arm around me, his fingers stroking up and down my side.

"That was…" I start.

"I know," he finishes.

"Wow, we're really…" I start.

"I know," he finishes again.

We're all breath and heartbeats and finishing each other's sentences, and I think I could actually lie in his arms forever without moving again and be a completely content and fulfilled human being.

Well, that's not entirely true. It would probably be best if we let me up from time to time to go teach a Critters Corner at the museum, and it would be nice to grab an adult beverage with my friends on occasion, but other than that, yup, this here is where I'm staying for almost-eternity.

"Fireflies are late this year," I murmur while he strokes my hair.

"Are they?"

"A bit, yeah," I say. "They typically show up between late May and early July." I scan the sky, hoping to spot one. No luck. "You know they're not actually flies, right?"

"Aren't they?"

"Nope. They're flying beetles."

"Interesting. Is it true their light patterns are for attracting mates?"

"Mostly," I say, laughing lightly. "Though don't fool yourself, Mr. Bieber. It's not all romance and happily-ever-afters out there in the bug world. There's also a fair amount of thriller and suspense. Horror even."

He chuckles. "Oh, yeah? How so?"

"Well. There's this genus called Photuris?" I put on a spooky voice. Or is it a sexy voice? Spooky sexy?

"Photuris…" he repeats.

"Yes. They're sort of like the femme fatales of fireflies." I climb on top of him, straddling his waist. He places his hands firmly on my hips. "They're experts at mimicry. They copy the light signals of other species so they can attract, kill, and eat their males." I claw my fingernails down his chest, not too hard, but enough to leave a light trail of marks on his skin. But Wally isn't complaining. He arches his back in what looks to be pleasure.

"We contain multitudes, yeah?'" he repeats the quote from earlier on a bit of a groan, and I have to say… it delights me.

"I guess we do." I look directly up, searching the sky one more time. "I miss them. I count on seeing them this time every year. They always feel like a little bit of magic. "

"Well, we still have a few days to go then before they can be officially counted as tardy, yeah?" he asks. "Give them time. I have a strong feeling the magic's still a-comin.'"

"Me too."

He smiles then, and it lights up my whole world.

"Can we, uh… can we talk about what happened earlier?" he asks gently.

"Sure, yeah. Sorry about that. I'll talk less next time."

"Mabel," he says, his tone firm. "You talk as much as you want. I'm here for all of it. All of *you*. I just kind of got the impression that you were trying to… I don't know… resist the moment?"

Ding, ding, ding! He's absolutely right. And that's super annoying. I'm quickly learning that this guy's perceptivity is equal parts awesome and infuriating.

I look at him, and he seems to be patiently waiting for an answer, so I decide to give it a try. "I think I felt like maybe I was enjoying it too much."

"How could you be enjoying yourself too much?" he scoffs.

I just shrug at that.

"Is pleasure scary to you?" he asks.

"What? No!" I laugh a little too loudly. "Pleasure is… awesome."

I lift my arms high and point both my index fingers down at my own head. "Modern woman over here. I'm all about da pleasure."

"You sure?" He chuckles. "Because 'da pleasure' was happening, and then you all but pulled away to have a platonic fireside chat with me."

I sigh. "I guess… I'm not really used to… You were just lavishing so much attention on me and…"

"And that's exactly as it should be," Wally fills in the tail end of my thought, though differently than I would have ended it. "Mabel, you know that, right? You're a strong, incredible woman. You deserve the world." His demeanor shifts, and he says, "I swear to God, if I ever see that Ernie guy again—"

"Bert," I correct.

"Whatever. If I ever see that guy again, I guarantee you he's gonna hear some words from me."

Just then, my phone blares its "Walking on Sunshine" ringtone. Gah, I really have to change that.

Ordinarily, I would ignore it, but I'm suddenly feeling bold. After all, I had relations with an incredible man tonight— outdoors, I might add! I was literally wined and dined. And Wally is right. I deserved it. I am Mabel Frickin McGonigle. I am strong, and I am incredible. I am a twenty-four-year-old licensed entomologist who sailed through multiple degrees with ease. I'm great with children. I'm an excellent friend. Yes, I still live with my overbearing parents, and I don't stand up for myself nearly as often as I should, but all that can be fixed. I can do whatever I set my mind to. I can certainly clear up a little situation involving an overdue student loan payment. Here I go.

"Are you okay?" Wally asks hesitantly. "Your face looks funny."

"*Your* face looks funny!" I lash out before I can stop myself. "Gosh, I'm sorry. No, it doesn't. Your face looks gorgeous. As usual. What I meant to say was 'Shh. I'm fine. I'm always fine. Just gearing up for this call.'" With that, I lift my chin like Val Kilmer in *Top Gun*, say, "Watch and learn, Wallace," pick up the call, and immediately let my verbal freak-flag fly.

"Hello. Hi. Good evening. Let's cut right to the chase, Sir or Madame or whatever your name may be. I surrender! You caught me. Caught me red-handed! But I refuse to be chased like a dog and cower in the corner each time you call. I will get you your money when I'm good and ready—"

"Mabel," Wally whispers, "are you talking to a drug dealer?"

I silently wave him off and continue my tirade, a whole lot nicer this time, as it's not the poor person on the phone's fault they have such an unfortunate job. "Listen, I'm good for it. I am a wildly capable woman who is just starting to realize the extent of her powers, and I will absolutely produce the Benjamins for you ASAP. In the meantime, if you could stop calling me over and over again and giving me heart palpitations each time you do, that would be most desirable and appreciated. Bye-bye now."

"Mabel?" A small voice comes through the phone right before I press the End Call button. I recognize it yet can't place it right away.

"Who is this?" I ask as I pull the phone back up to my ear.

"It's, um… It's Chloe. Hi, Mabel! Sorry, am I interrupting something?"

"No! Well, actually yes, you are, big time." My gaze shoots to a practically naked Wally. "But that's okay. What's going on? What can I do for you? Chloe, is it you that's been calling me this whole time? What is this number?" I rattle off a whole list of questions at her, probably because I'm naked. Apparently, I'm a bit high energy when I'm naked.

"It's my house phone," she says, "and yeah, I've called a few times. I'm sorry. But you said we could call you if we ever needed you, right?" Her voice sounds like it's on the verge of breaking.

"Of course, yeah," I say in what I hope is a soothing manner, then preemptively reach for my clothes. Something tells me I'm leaving this tent sooner than later.

"Could you come over?" she asks.

"To your house? Why? Are you okay?"

"Sort of? I don't know." She stumbles over her words. "I just… I don't think I can talk about this over the phone. Please?" She's practically begging now.

"Of course. Yes, yes, yes. Text me your address, and I'll be right there."

"Thank you so much." She sounds equal parts relieved and scared. "I'll see you soon."

What in the world is going on?

I end the call and her text with the address comes right through. I enter it into my phone's GPS and see it's only about five miles from here.

I turn to Wally, looking so sweet and vulnerable, lying there where I left him, all shirtless and sexy.

"It's Chloe, one of my CITs," I explain. "She's kind of an odd duck, seems to like me *a lot*—"

"Chloe and I have that in common then."

"Ha. I'm sorry to leave like this." I pull on my skort and toss my shirt back on over my head.

"Go," he encourages. "It's fine. You coming back, though?"

I hesitate. "Do you want me to come back?"

"Always, Mabel Again." He sits up at that and brings me in for a long, warm kiss, his hand gently tipping my chin up so my lips meet his. "I'll be waiting."

"Okay," I say, feeling light-headed and happy as I grab the rest of my things and slip out of the tent. I hop into Jimeny and drive toward Chloe's house, having absolutely zero idea of what I will find once I get there.

Chapter Twenty-Four

I pull up to a nice two-story colonial. That's not actually true. Or it could be true. I actually have no idea. I've never been one of those people who know architectural house types. I marvel at those people, though, the ones that are like, "Oh, what a lovely split level ranch!" or "She has the most darling Tudor-style home." Not a clue what they're talking about.

I pull up to a... house. A pale yellow house with flower pots on the steps and a wind chime hanging from the porch. Two sensible station wagon type vehicles are in the driveway, and I spot a cat sleeping on one of the windowsills. It all looks so... nice.

Seems like her parents are home. Do they realize Chloe's having a panic attack of some kind right now? Are they the cause of it? I'm starting to think that maybe my whole "here's my phone number, call me anytime" offer to the CITs was ill-advised. I know bugs. I don't know people. I mean, I'm doing my best with my head counselor position this summer, but I ultimately don't know how much of a difference I'm making.

I take the few steps up to the porch and am about to ring the doorbell when the door flings open.

"Hi, Mabel! Hi, hi, hi! Thank you so much for coming!" Chloe throws her arms around my body and squeezes the bejeezus out of me. And she seems fine. Absolutely, totally and completely fine.

"Want to come in?" she chirps. "Want something to eat? Or drink? My mom's just finishing up cooking dinner. We eat late. My grandma—my dad's mom, not my mom's mom—is always saying 'why do you people eat so late? Eating that late at night leads to weight gain and nightmares!' but I don't think that's true, do you? I'm reasonably thin, I think, and I never have nightmares. Or maybe I do and I just don't remember them? That happens, right? Do you believe that we're dreaming all night every night and we just don't remember?"

Chloe finally stops to take a breath and just stares at me in anticipation.

"Oh," I say. "Do you want me to actually answer that?"

"Sure!" she shrugs and smiles, like she wasn't close to tears on the phone just a few minutes ago.

"Chloe, what's going on? You sounded really upset on the phone. Why am I here?"

"I think I was more nervous than upset, but now that you're here, I'm feeling so hopeful and—"

A voice comes from the other room.

"Chloe, who are you...?" My Aunt Tina is suddenly standing in the doorway. "Talking to?" she says the last part of her question under her breath when she sees me.

Have you ever seen a puppy trying to figure something out? The way they just tilt their head to the side and wait? That's what I find myself doing at this moment.

What. The heck. Is going on?

"Mabel," Tina says, looking as confused as I feel. "What are you doing here? I mean, I'm thrilled you're here. Come in, come in, please. But *how* are you—?"

"I called her," Chloe interrupts. I fully enter the house in a daze and Chloe shuts the door behind me. "Mabel? This is my mom. I thought it was time you two reconnected. For real this time."

"Your daughter works at the arboretum," I say on a breath, recalling Tina's words from the other day at the festival, words that I stupidly didn't investigate further, I guess because I was so caught up in Wally and figuring out what was happening there. I direct my attention to Chloe. "You're my... cousin?" I'm not exactly sure why, but this makes me angry. "How long have you known?" I say this a bit more harshly than I intend.

She doesn't answer me directly. Instead, she reaches into a nearby backpack propped against the wall, pulls out a stack of photographs and hands them to Tina. "I found these in your sock drawer." Tina closes her eyes. I walk around to her side and see that the photo on top is one of me. A fairly recent picture of me.

"May I?" I ask, and Tina reluctantly hands me the stack.

I flip through. Me winning the science fair in fifth grade. Me blowing out the candles on a birthday cake. Me opening presents on Christmas. Me roller skating. Me riding my bike. Me baking cookies. Me. Me. Me. Me. Me.

"Did... my mom send you these?" I ask.

"Your mom." She nods and sort of chokes. "Yes."

"All these years?" I marvel, continuing to flip through the pictures. "But she never said anything. I thought they'd lost touch with you completely."

"I can't know for sure," Tina says hesitantly, "But I always got the impression Helen sent these on her own. I don't think Abe knew."

Alright. That's it. I've had enough.

"What happened between you guys?" I demand more than ask. "I'm tired of being in the dark about this."

"Sweetheart, I'm sorry," she says, "But you need to ask them."

"I have! Repeatedly! For years! They tell me nothing!"

I look back at her and am met with what can only be described as guilty silence.

And it pisses. Me. Off.

"You know what would be nice?" I say with sarcasm for what I think may be the first time ever. "It would be nice if I had people in my life who told me the truth. People who didn't see me as some naïve little Pollyanna who doesn't deserve the real deal on things. Just because I'm sweet doesn't mean I'm stupid. Just because I look on the bright side doesn't mean I can't handle the darker things of life!"

"I understand that, sweetheart," she tries to soothe me. "But I promised your parents that—"

"Fine!" I almost shout at her. "Clearly, you're not going to fill in any blanks for me. Chloe? How long have you known this?"

"I, um..." The girl who's always had this maturity about her suddenly looks and sounds very much like the young fifteen-year-old girl she is. "I've suspected since we moved here a few months ago and I found the photos. We look alike, don't you think?" she asks with a hopeful look on her face.

I can't answer her, even though she's right. We do look a lot alike, now that I really consider it. The red hair, the freckles, our builds.

"I did a reverse image search online of the most recent one and found the arboretum website. Your picture and bio is there on the staff page," she admits.

"And then you applied for a job?"

"Yes."

"Without telling me who you were."

"Yes."

"Why not?" I ask. "Why not just tell me about the connection so we could actually do something about it? I would have been so happy, I would have—" I cut myself off when I notice the strange look passing between them. "What am I missing here?" I say as I scan back and forth from Chloe to Tina and back again.

Neither one of them says a thing.

"We're done here," I say, surprising even myself with how harshly it comes out. I shove the stack of photos back into Chloe's hands. "Thanks for lying to me and thanks for wasting my time. I'm glad you're okay."

With that, I push out the screen door and let it slam behind me.

I don't look back.

Chapter Twenty-Five

I call out of work sick the next day.

That is not something Mabel would normally do. But you know what Mabel also wouldn't normally do? Mabel wouldn't normally find out one of her counselors-in-training has effectively been stalking her. She wouldn't discover that said girl is actually her cousin, the daughter of her long lost beloved aunt.

Mabel also doesn't normally refer to herself in the third person.

That is an absurd thing to do—I know this—but it seems appropriate at the moment, and right in line with how I'm feeling: like I'm standing outside my body watching someone else's life. Someone named Mabel who used to know who she was, but now doesn't have a clue.

Last night's visit with Chloe and Tina rocked me.

Angered me.

Confused me.

And I needed a day to get myself together.

If I've learned anything during this crazy month, it's this: being the good girl sucks. It doesn't get you anywhere, except for on people's gullible list. It gets you cheated on by your fiancé and lied to by family members. Being a good girl makes it so everyone withholds information from you.

And there's more. More information they aren't telling me. I can feel it. My parents. My aunt. Chloe.

I'm realizing that maybe Calliope's crazy idea for a Bad Mabel Experiment wasn't so crazy after all. Clearly I didn't give the concept enough of a chance. I mean what did I actually do? Watched a movie or two then took one look into my parents' medicine cabinet before giving up? Lame. In my education and career I've always gone all in. I do all the reading, all the studying all the applying of myself all the time. But when it comes to my own emotional growth? Then I act like someone's going to sweep into my life and magically make me into a fully functioning adult. But no one can do that for me. Not even Wally, the guy who is more of a grown-up than anyone I know.

He called and texted a bunch last night when I didn't return to his place like I said I would. I told him enough of what happened that he wouldn't worry, but was emphatic that I needed to be alone. Today he's left several messages checking to see if I was okay and asking if there is anything he can do to help. I told him that there was in fact something he could do—eventually—and with no questions asked, he said he'd head over as soon as I gave him the green light that I was ready for his company.

So. Let's review those steps my friends so graciously spelled out for me as starting points in the Bad Mabel Experiment.

Number One: Watch all the movies that were off-limits when I was a kid.

I'm all over number one. And as it turns out my mother has quite a stash hidden under her bed. Mostly from the 70s and 80s. And still on VHS. I'm learning that old-school doesn't even begin to describe my parents. Today alone, I've watched *Sex, Lies & Videotape*, *Top Gun* – for a second time – and *Grease*. Quick wrap up on those: That monologue about the trash was amazing, Val Kilmer does way too much chin acting and—excuse my language—the end of *Grease* is a total shitshow. Right? I mean, John Travolta doesn't take Sandy seriously until she starts smoking cigarettes and dressing like a super slender black sea lion? Who uses a ton of hairspray? Seems like bad messaging to me, but clearly Sandy was in the same disgruntled good girl boat I am, and she certainly seemed much happier once she jumped ship, so who am I to judge? On to...

Number Two: Snoop.

Cyndi will be so proud of me. I snooped like it was my job. I was in the attic, the basement, even the crawl space next to the laundry room. I explored sock drawers, underwear drawers, dusty boxes tucked at the tippy top of closets. I snooped like my life depended on it. And I did find some very puzzling items. The first was a stack of photos in my mom's sock drawer, tucked way in the back in a soft envelope and hidden under one of the rose-scented cedar chip sachets she makes so her clothes smell nice. The photos were all of Aunt Tina. Some of her as a kid, but most as an adult, and many of them included pictures of Chloe growing up over the past fifteen years. Weird that she kept their correspondence a secret from me all these years. Really really weird. But before I could take that all in too much I found something even more alarming. In my Dad's drawer there was a cigar box. Inside I found two passports, my mom's and his. At first I didn't see anything out of the ordinary, but then his birthyear caught my eye. 1953. I checked Mom's. Also 1953. That would make them... *sixty*-eight years old, not fifty-eight like they've clearly been pretending. So those "slips" Dad had last month suddenly make much more sense. He was caught in a lie. But why? Why would they want me to think they're ten years younger than they actually are?

Ding dong.

I'm interrupted from my thoughts by the doorbell. Perfect timing for...

Number Three: Get freaky in my childhood twin bed while the parents are away.

I fling open the door. Wally's eyes widen as he takes me in.

"Wow. You're wearing... spandex. And your hair is... really poofy."

"Tell me about it, stud." I say, surprising myself with the impressive huskiness I add to my voice. I give my puffy-haired-head a shake, then pull the fabric back from my pants with my thumb and forefinger and let it snap back against my thigh. "Ow."

I recover quickly and raise my opposite hand to my mouth.

"And oh my God, are you smoking a cigarette?" he marvels

"Yes." I hesitate. "Well. Sort of." I puff some "smoke" in his face. "It's the candy kind."

He starts to laugh.

"Shut up!" I say, then wince. "I mean... please be quiet. I'm doing something here."

"I can see that." His lips get tight like he's trying to hold back his amusement.

"Let's fuck. Let's screw. Let's do the nasty things that nasty people do."

Yes, I know Olivia Newtown John doesn't say that in the movie, but who can actually say what happened after they got off those rickety amusement park rides? From here on in, I'm improvising.

With that, I grab his face with both hands and kiss the hell out of him. He responds in kind. After a minute or so, he comes up for air.

"Not that I'm complaining," he pants, "but what's happening right now? What *are* you doing?"

"*You*, you sonofabitch, I'm doing *you*." I take a step away from him and start doing some light calisthenics.

"Oh wow, you're stretching. And a moment ago you were rhyming."

"Well, we don't want a muscle getting torn. And *am* I rhyming? I didn't notice. All I noticed is your throbbing horn." I dive for his belt buckle.

"My throbbing—There's a lot of mixed metaphors happening here. Was there source material for this particular performance? I mean, the abominable final scene in Grease, clearly, but you've lost me on the horn talk."

"I've been reading Calliope's dino porn," I admit. "She's all about the horn." I give him a little shove in the center of his chest and fire off my demand, "Upstairs. Now."

I have to say, it feels awesome to be this confident. This forceful.

"Yes ma'am," he salutes, then turns and takes the stairs two at a time, with me trailing close behind him.

He hesitates at the top of the steps, not knowing which way to turn. I place my palm in the center of his back and shove him in the right direction. He responds with an "Oof. Geez, Mabel, what are you—"

"Welcome to my room, stud." I whip around him and prop myself in the doorway of my bedroom. Gosh, I really am proud of how well I'm mimicking Miss Newton John's breathy voice from the end of the movie right now.

"Holy. Shit." Wally dips under my arm and marvels aloud as he enters the room, pink not-so-plush-anymore wall-to-wall carpeting squishing under his feet. The place is pretty much frozen in time. Trophies from science fairs line my child-size dresser. Animal and insect books are stacked on the shelves, and late nineties wallpaper wraps the room in floral splendor, speckled with framed posters of bug anatomy that I put up as a preteen. Nothing like diagrams of compound eyes, hindwings and Malpighian tubes to get a grown ass man in the mood, right? Right.

"You like what you see, stud?"

"I'm not... sure," he says hesitantly. "Question though. Are you going to keep addressing me as 'stud?'"

"Why? Do you not like being called stud, *stud*?"

"I don't *mind*, per se. You just—Are you okay?"

"Better than okay, yeah," I say as I push him toward my twin bed with the shiny pink comforter. It hits him in the back of the knees, causing him to land in a seated position on the mattress. The squeaks that reverberate through the room would be comical if this wasn't such a serious and sexy situation.

A serious and sexy situation. The Mabel McGonigle Story.

I stand in front of him, my legs caging his, as I start slowly and meticulously unbuttoning his shirt. He tips his face up so his chin is basically resting in my cleavage—side note: I have cleavage today! Hooray for push-up bras!—and he says, "Are you sure? Because you've apparently never missed a day of work in your life according to the rest of the summer camp staff, and your CIT Chloe said –"

"Not interested in what Chloe has to say," I scold and place my finger over his lips. "Not right now. Please don't bring her up again."

"You got it," he says.

I release my touch from his perfect lips and I instantly miss the connection. I dive in for a kiss. His fingers shoot into my hair... and get stuck in the nearly full bottle of aqua net I unloaded into my strands to create the poof effect. "Ow!" I shout as he gently pries his fingers out.

"Sorry, sorry," Wally murmurs. "Hey, can I clarify something you said a minute or so ago?" he says between kisses.

"Sure. Yeah. What." Oh man, I'm losing my Newton John voice. I decide to give it another go with more breath this time. "I mean 'Sure. Yeah. What.'" Nailed it.

"Your friend Calliope writes dino porn?" He asks as he slips my shirt off over my head.

"She does! Well, dino *romance*." I've had enough of fumbling with his buttons and bust through the last few like the boss bitch I am. Boss bitch. That's a phrase people use, right?

"Whoa!" he exclaims as the buttons fly free. I slide the shirt down his shoulders. "You don't say."

"I *do* say. *Teasing Triceratops*, *Seducing Stegosaurus* and *Boning Brachiosaurus* are all USA Today Best Sellers."

"Impressive." He kisses down my neck.

"It is. I'm really happy for her."

"Maybe you should write insect romance," he says as he peels me out of my spandex pants.

That gives me pause.

He laughed when he said it, so I assume he's not serious. But just in case I say, "No Wally. No one wants to read about insect romance. Believe me. Insect romance is dragging your lover upside down. It's marathon lovemaking sessions lasting upward of seventy-nine days. Insect romance is high speed chases, mid-air mating dances, spiky stunt penises designed to break off in case of emergency, cannibalism, decapitation..."

"Jesus," he says.

"I know." I marvel right along with him.

Then... a sudden stillness comes over my body.

An idea has landed.

"What?" Wally cocks his head as he takes in my stillness. "What is happening right now?"

I take a deep breath and rattle off my desire. "A woman dressed like Olivia Newton John dressed like Bad Sandy in Grease wants to role-play a praying mantis mating ritual with you in her childhood bedroom. Any objections to that?"

He takes that moment to rest back on his elbows and then he gives me this look. *The* look. That's right, this incredibly sexy, shirtless man is lying in my tiny bed giving me the look I feel like I've been waiting for my whole life. The look that says *I know you. I know you and I want you.*

You. You. Wonderful, precious, irreplaceable you.

"Mabel," he rumbles, "I'm game for whatever you've got in mind. You're a grown ass gorgeous woman and I think you're fucking incredible, so..."

"So...?" I realize I'm holding my breath until he speaks.

"So... game on." He flashes me a gorgeous grin.

"Excellent," I purr. "Time for me to rip your head off."

"What?!"

With that, I dive on top of him and latch onto his neck with my teeth, never feeling so understood and seen and wanted in my life. I had no idea how much I'd been needing that, missing that. It's been so long since I felt truly connected to someone. It's a feeling I want to hold onto for as long as I—

"Mabel Geraldine, what on earth are you doing?!"

I feel Wally's body still beneath me. We hold our collective breath, like if we don't breathe, maybe we can make it so that what's happening isn't actually happening. Then a masculine voice clears a throat. I've heard that throat clearing my entire life, and it's never failed to snap me into awareness and action. As soon as I hear that sound, I unlatch my mouth from Wally's neck.

We turn our heads toward the door in unison.

Abraham and Helen McGonigle stand frozen at the entrance to my room, mouths agape, my mother's hand over her heart.

Chapter Twenty-Six

"Mabel, why are you dressed like a whore?!" my father seethes. "And who is that man?"

"Why am I dressed like a—" I can't even bring myself to repeat that ugly word. "Dad, I'll have you know that I am dressed like the remarkable, wholesome Olivia Newton John in the final scene of Grease!"

"Sweetheart, you watched Grease?" Mom gasps.

"I sure did, Mom! And *Pretty Woman* and *Dirty Dancing* and *Top Gun*, and the list goes on!"

"Abraham, I told you we shouldn't leave her alone," my mother slurs a bit.

"Mom, are you drunk?" I marvel.

"Noooo honey, nooooo. Tipsy maybe, but not drunk." She stumbles the tiniest bit on the old pink rug.

"Your mother had a glass of wine at dinner," Dad says as though that's not a monumental occasion. But it is.

"She did?" I turn to my mom. "You did? You never drink. Are you okay?"

"I'm fine, baby. But who is this man? What would Bert say about this situation? I don't think Bert would appreciate this kind of behavior."

"Mom, Bert is a mock turtleneck-wearing cheater with mommy issues who named his penis after a crime show producer."

"Oh, I don't like crime shows," my mother winces.

"Did you hear me, Mom? I said he cheated on me."

"And he named his penis," Wally mumbles under his breath.

"I'm sorry, sweetheart," Mom says, "I'm sure that was painful for you, but I'm certain you can work things out. Would you like me to call his mother?"

"No, Mom!"

"Because I'm sure if we all just sit down and—"

"So the engagement is off?" my dad interrupts, cutting through all the chaos.

"Yes Dad, the engagement is off," I say, but when I look at him I realize his eyes aren't on me. They're boring into Wally.

Wally takes this as his opportunity to introduce himself. He places me gently to the side and unleashes quite the mattress squeak as his stands and reaches his full height, towering over my dad. He offers his hand. "Abe, was it? Wallace Bieber. Pleasure to meet you, sir."

"Get out of my house," is my father's only response. No hand shake. No pleasantries. Nothing.

"Very well, sir." Wally moves to gather his things.

"And don't you dare come near my daughter ever again," he barks.

"With all due respect sir," Wally says as he buttons up his shirt—the few buttons still remaining—"your daughter is a grown woman, so I think she should be the one making decisions about who she sees and how."

"You don't know my daughter. She needs someone to look after her."

"No, I do not!" I shout as I finish up—mostly—dressing myself.

"I'm sorry, Abe," Wally interjects, "but I won't be engaging in this with you any further."

"Engaging in what with me?"

"I will not continue to speak about Mabel with you as if she's not here. Like it or not, Abe. I'm in love with your daughter. And there's something you should know about me from the get-go."

He's in love with me?

"And what's that?" Dad huffs.

"I'm FAF, sir," Wally says with seriousness.

"FAF? What does that mean?"

"F-A-F," he spells it out. "Feminist as fuck, sir."

Dad finally turns to face me. "This is the kind of man you want to be with, Mabel?"

I look directly into my father's eyes, take a deep breath, and say, "It is, yeah." Then I look at up Wally and gather his hand in mine. "*He* is."

Wally smiles that glorious smile.

Am I imagining that my mom smiles too?

My dad, however, immediately starts sputtering. I know I shouldn't be getting him riled up. I know I should be thinking about his heart and his blood pressure. But how many times will I be afraid to speak my truth with him, for fear that he'll be upset? How many times will I let him determine the course for my life?

"Mabel?" he starts getting red in the face. "No! History will not repeat itself. I will not see you go down the same road as your—"

He cuts himself off and gets a really strange look on his face.

The room gets eerily quiet.

A strange energy moves in.

"The same road as my... who, Dad?" I say slowly. "Or my... what? What are you talking about?" I feel my voice go breathy, and my heart starts to pound.

His eyes flit up to my mother then back at me. "Nothing. No one. Just—get out of my house," he repeats.

"Happily," I say and start gathering a few of my things so I can spend the night elsewhere. There's clearly no reasoning with this man.

"No, not you, Mabel. *Him*," he says in anger and exasperation.

"Him. Him,'" I imitate the way he says it. "His name is Wally, Dad. And you don't even know '*him*.' You know what? Why are you two even home? You're not supposed to come back from the Poconos until next weekend."

Mom says, "Naomi Thornton let us know that an unknown Ford Focus was sitting outside of our house this afternoon, so we came back to check on the situation."

"And it's a very good thing that we did!" Dad glares at Wally.

I look at Wally for an explanation. "You were sitting outside my house all afternoon?"

He says without hesitation, "You were upset by what happened last night. I wanted to be close by if you changed your mind and decided you needed me."

"That's…" My hand goes to my heart. "Thank you, that's really…." I turn my attention on my parents. "Wait. You could have just called. And what the hell is up with Naomi Thornton butting her nose into our lives at every turn?"

"Naomi is just a bit of a busybody," Mom says. "Plus she always had a competitive thing with your mother, so after she left it carried over to us." Her face immediately turns ghostly white. "I meant Tina. Naomi had a competitive thing with your Aunt Tina and…"

Her voice trails off.

She closes her eyes.

The silence that falls around us at that moment is deafening.

"What did you say?" I say in a near whisper.

"Sweetheart…" Mom pleads. For what though, I don't know.

I repeat, more forcefully this time, "What did you say?"

"Nothing baby. I've had too much wine. See, this is why I don't drink," she tries to laugh it off, but there is no chance on earth that I'm letting this go.

"You said she had a competitive thing with my mother." I pause. "You're my mother, mom."

More silence.

"Aren't you?"

I hear my voice crack before I feel it.

"Mom, are you telling me Aunt Tina is actually my mother?"

"No. No she is not." My father starts. "She is not. She is—"

"I am asking mom right now!"

I turn to Mom in time to see a tear slide down her cheek. "I'm sorry baby," she says. "We had our reasons. Good reasons…"

"To lie to me? To—" At that moment I think my head might explode. Suddenly so much makes sense. "I found your passports," I say shakily. "You've been lying to me—to everyone— about how old you are?"

"Honey—"

I cut her right off. "You pretended that I was your –? Oh

my God, are you telling me you're actually my *grandparents*? And *she's* your daughter? Why would you –? How could you –?"

"She was a teenager," Dad bellows. "A pregnant teenager. It was shameful and it was going to ruin both of your lives if we didn't step in. So we helped. We helped where we were needed."

I gape at him. "By taking me from her and cutting her out of your life? Out of *my* life? By lying to me for twenty-four years? Did you know I have a cousin? Wait, no." My thoughts are going a mile a minute and a realization hits me.

Something inside me cracks.

And I start laughing.

Hysterically.

"Hahahahaha! Chloe isn't my cousin. She's my *sister*. Hahahahaha! Ohmygosh! She said we look so much alike! Hahahaha! She said—oh man you have to hear this—she said redheads feel pain more acutely! Hahahahahaha! And… she wants to go to a redhead convention together someday! Hahahahaha! Hahahahahaha!"

They just stand there, staring at me. All three of them. Mom, Dad and Wally.

I gather my sanity—sort of—and move toward the door without a word.

I hear them take a collective breath like they're each about to try to stop me in their own way.

"No one speak to me," I warn. "And no one follow me."

To their credit, no one does.

Against my better judgment, just before I leave the room, I turn my head to take it in one last time. I know instinctively that I won't be back any time soon. Wally and I catch eyes. He slowly reaches out his strong arm and offers me his hand, but I don't take it. I *want* to, but I don't.

My brain knows he has absolutely nothing to do with this deception, but right now, my heart feels like it can't trust anyone. Not a single person. They all lie. And apparently, it's only a matter of time before you figure it out.

I feel sick to my stomach, but I do it.

I tear my eyes away from him, and I leave.

Chapter Twenty-Seven

Duhn duhn. The telltale sound of *Law & Order* vibrates through my skull. I'm sitting on the only chair in a stark white room at a raw wooden table, a single overhead light hanging directly above me. Ice-T approaches and leans his hands on the table, getting in my face. "Alright now Mabel, in just a moment you're gonna see a lineup of characters, cats, punks and skunks. They've all played a crucial role in your life. Not literal cats and skunks, but you know what I'm sayin,' yeah?"

"I do, Ice-T, I do," I answer, somewhat in awe being in his presence. "Ice-T, sir, may I take this opportunity to tell you how much I love your work?"

"You may." He stands up straight and purses his lips together in anticipation as though this happens to him all the time. I'm sure it does.

"Awesome. Well, I dislike the show intensely but admire your work immensely. I always say, 'That Ice-T, he's a national treasure.'"

"You're not alone in that," a warm female voice washes over me as a gentle hand touches my shoulder.

"Mariska Hargitay slash Olivia Benson?" I look up and breathe out in reverence.

"Hello, sweetheart," she says. "I heard you named your vagina after me."

"I did! Well, my friend did. And we named it Olivia, not Mariska. Are you mad?" I rattle off at warp speed.

"Mad? Honey, I'm honored." Her hand is on her heart now, and there's a sweet smile on her face. Then her voice goes loud and harsh. "Bring 'em in!"

With that, a string of people walk out in single file behind the glass and turn to face me. My mom, my dad, Tina, Chloe, Bert, Doreen, Cyndi, Calliope, Louise, Wally... they're all there. As are Patrick Swayze, Val Kilmer, John Travolta and Bill Nye the Science Guy.

"Look at that lineup of humans, Mabel. Really look at them. Every single one of these people has contributed to who you are. Even—perhaps especially—the ones who didn't say or do the right things. Even—perhaps especially—the ones who hurt you. You have to find a way to be steady in who you are, despite what the people around you are saying and doing. Despite who *they* decide you are. It doesn't mean you have to rush to forgive them. It doesn't mean you need to dismiss the things that they've done. But you do need to find a place for them that allows you to keep growing and changing in the ways you want to grow and change."

Damn, Mariska slash Olivia is so insightful.

"Want to hear one thing I know for sure?" she asks as I continue to scan the lineup of—in the words of Ice-T—characters, cats, punks and skunks from my life.

"Yes, of course," I respond quietly as I watch Swayze doing those sexy hip circles he's known to do. Can you blame me? They're mesmerizing.

"You are loved," she says.

"I am loved," I repeat.

"You are not a victim."

"I am not a victim."

Just then, the room is bombarded with green smoke and purple strobe lights! The sounds of a bass guitar playing a funky jazz rhythm bounces through the air!

"Speaking of victims..." a creepy, crackly voice fills the space as a massive, human-sized praying mantis stomps her way through the lineup, tearing off head after head after head.

I scream, but no sound comes out. The mantis hears me,

though. She whips around to look at me, and says, "Oh Mabel! Would you like to be next?"

Again, I try to speak—to answer her—but nothing comes out.

"Mabel?"

"Mabel?"

"Mabel." The voice morphs to a more tender, familiar one.

"Mabel sweetie, wake up."

I startle awake, the dream I just had fading away as all my awareness snaps to attention in the here and now.

Mildred, the elderly camp nurse is standing over me, concern in her eyes and an apology on her lips. "Sorry to startle you dear. Are you alright?"

"Fine, yes. I'm always fine." For the first time I really hear myself say those words. The words I have said throughout my life as a mantra.

"Did you... sleep here last night? Also, why are you dressed like a slender black sea lion with extremely puffy hair?"

I shoot up to sit on the little cot I passed out on last night and pat my hands along my body, landing on my still buoyant curly coif. Wow, Aqua Net is not messing around.

After I left my parents' house, I realized too late that I didn't actually have a place to go. Calliope is in Mexico, Cyndi was staying at Stuart's, and as much as I've come to love Louise in the short time I've known her, it didn't feel right springing a surprise sleepover on her. Of course I could have gone to Wally's, but... I don't know. I just felt like I needed some space to really hear my own thoughts. Plus, I didn't want to subject him to any more drama. He'd likely witnessed enough in those few short minutes with my parents to last him a lifetime. So, that left the arboretum's health center as my crash pad for the night. I didn't realize until I arrived that in my haste to get the heck out of there last night, I neglected to grab my overnight bag. Hence, the reason I'm still fully costumed.

"I did sleep here, yes," I say in a still sleep-crunchy voice. "And the outfit is because..." I consider lying to her for a moment, but if the past month has taught me anything, it's that lies only lead to heartache. So, I look this sweet lady directly in the face, and say,

"Mildred, sometimes you just gotta snap on some spandex for a little role play and shake things up in the ole sex life, you know?"

"Girlfriend, say no more," Mildred says with seriousness. "Last night, my Harold and I played a few rounds of cocky pilot and the sassy stewardess, and I'll just say that I woke up this morning with peppity pep in my steppity step."

Mildred, my goodness. Who knew?

"Is he hiding in here somewhere?" She whips her head left and right, bends down to peek under the cot, then says quietly out of the corner of her mouth, "Because I will happily create a diversion to get him out of here without any of the higher-uppers seeing his exit."

"That's amazing and much appreciated, Mildred." I stifle my laugh. "But it's not necessary. I stayed here solo."

"Alright, then. Well, if you ever need a wing-woman in the future, I'm your girl." She pats me hard on the back. "For now, though, you better get yourself together and head out. They've been calling your name over the loudspeaker for the past twenty minutes."

"They have?" Panic arises in my chest. "What time is it? What's happening?" I don't deal well with being late, being in trouble, being anything less than responsible.

I peer out the window of the health center and see that daily camp operations are in full swing. Various groups of tiny campers march between checkpoints.

Shoot, it's already second period. I'm beyond late.

I spot a stack of Bucks County Arboretum T-shirts peeking out of the closet, grab one and pull it over my head, hoping to limit the fallout of my spandex situation as much as possible. I slip on my heels—these should be interesting on the trails today—say a quick goodbye to Mildred and head outside.

I'm out of the health center no more than five minutes before Chloe is approaching me, her eyes watery and her voice wavery. "Mabel?" she cries, but I keep walking, trying my best to ignore her and reach my destination. "Mabel! I need to talk to you!"

"Oh, it's my stalker," I say, sarcasm still seeming to cling to me. "Don't worry, I found out the full scoop yesterday from my parents—or my... whatever I'm supposed to call them now." I say this as I hightail it toward the main office where I'm *supposed* to start my day. "Your secret's fully out. So nothing more to talk about."

"That's not actually why I'm—" She stumbles while trying to keep up with me. "Man, how are you doing this in heels? Listen, I know you might not believe me, but I didn't know for sure that we were sisters. Not until after you left last night, and my mom finally leveled with me."

I give her a quick you're-right-I-don't-believe-you look, then keep my eyes focused forward.

Chloe prattles on as she chases after me. "I'd be lying if I said I wasn't hoping that was the case, though! And for the record, I didn't tell my mom that I'd met you. And I didn't mean to stalk you as you said. It was just—geez! Ow!" She trips over a rock and recovers instantly. "She started acting sadder and weirder than usual once we moved up here. Then the day I found those pictures of you, I knew she was definitely hiding something. So I started looking into you, but I never imagined you were—"

"Chloe, I don't have time for this right now—"

"And I called you last night because she was an absolute mess after seeing you at the festival – I spotted you two talking – the same kind of mess she is every year in early October, which has always been mysterious to me. That's when she sort of retreats and cuts herself off from the world for a few days. When I did some digging and realized that October 3rd is—"

"My birthday..." I finish the thought for her and finally stop walking for a breath to look at her.

She takes a breath too and slows down.

"Exactly. Your birthday. When I figured that out, that was the push I needed to go full Carmen Sandiego on the situation. Oh." She reaches into her fanny pack, pulls out an envelope, and hands it to me. "She asked me to give you this."

"Carmen Sandiego?" I'm so confused.

"No. My mom. Or I guess I should say... *our*—" She must see from the look on my face that I'm not ready for that, so she course corrects, "Tina. It's a letter from Tina." I slowly take it from her, Not wanting it and wanting it in equal measure. Chloe continues with a hint of "duh" in her tone, "Carmen Sandiego is an animated bombshell detective who solves cases all over the world, Mabel."

I stare at the letter in my hand, feeling a bit dazed. "My, uh— my pop culture references aren't really up to snuff, but you know what, Chloe?" I shake my head.

"What?"

Her eyes look so hopeful at that moment.

I think back to the crazy dream I just had, and although I don't think I've fully processed or understood it yet, I do know that I don't want any harm coming to Chloe, ever. By way of a huge, human-sized insect, or by her new half sister saying something harsh and hurting her feelings. I know that I don't want to close the door on a relationship with her. I mean, God, I have a sister! How potentially amazing is that? But I also know it's going to take me some time to wrap my head around everything that's happened so I can be fully present with her.

"We're not going to solve the weird feelings between us in one conversation," I say gently.

"I know that," she responds with a nod.

"But we'll get it figured out eventually. I promise. No more crying over this, though, okay?"

"Oh, I wasn't crying over you," she says, surprising the heck out of me.

"You weren't? Then... why were you crying?"

She cringes.

"I lost Holden."

Chapter Twenty-Eight

"You lost Holden?!" I screech.

"Yes! I'm sorry!" Chloe says. "He got upset when one of the other kids said something to him, and he ran off. Man, that kid is fast! That's why they've been paging you over the loudspeaker. Apparently, your walkie is off."

"My walkie is in the main office in my—" I cut myself off. "Ohmygod, why wasn't this the *first* thing you said to me?"

"You looked so mad! And you were running away from me! I panicked! But don't worry." She places her hand on my shoulder. "We know he's alive and on the premises."

"Oh, good!" I say with some of that sarcasm still clinging to me because "alive and on the premises" is a pretty low bar for not worrying about a six-year-old. "And how do we know this?"

"He swiped my walkie before hauling ass away from me. He communicated with Laurel."

"What did he say?" I ask, getting more exasperated by the minute.

"This is Holden. I'm alive and on the premises." She does a somewhat accurate impersonation of my little buddy.

I start racking my brain on where he might be.

Chloe continues, "He also said something about wanting to see some Jerries die? I thought that was creepy and strange and totally unlike sweet little Holden to want to see *anything* die, but—"

"Gerridae!" I shout. "Water striders! He's by the lake!"

I immediately toss off my heels and tear down the hill barefoot toward the lake since I can't think of many things more frightening than a child who can barely swim being unattended near a body of water. "Ow. Ow! Ow, geez, YOW!" Stones and roots and pebbles stab into my feet as I go, but I don't let them slow me down.

I reach the lake in record time and don't see Holden anywhere.

"Holden! Holden, where are you?"

No answer.

"Holden?!"

Nothing.

I turn in a full circle, scanning every which way I can when my eyes land on Wally's shack. I have to stop calling it a shack. I run up to Wally's *home* and immediately start pounding on the door.

"Wally!" The door rattles under my fist. "Wally, are you here? I'm sorry I ran out on you last night. I thought I needed to be alone, that I needed space, but I actually don't need that. Not from you. Never from you!" I pound some more.

"That's great to hear, baby," that deep warm voice I've come to love so much says from just a few feet away. I turn, and Wally is standing by the edge of the house, his arms opening up for me.

I run straight to him and start talking a mile a minute as he wraps me up in a hug. "Wally, I'm freaking out. Holden is lost. He apparently got really upset by something and took off. I thought he was by the lake looking for water strider bugs, but I don't see him anywhere and—"

"Mabes?" he cuts me off.

"Yeah?" I quiet and look directly up at him.

Without a word, he points at the huge weeping willow tree, which I know from our discussion the other night is exactly fifty feet from his house.

My eyes trace up the trunk to a thick, low branch where a small boy sits, partially obscured by willow sprays, reading a book.

"Holden!" I say, relief spilling out of my lungs. My body jolts, and I'm about to sprint right over to him when Wally touches my arm to halt me.

"He's fine. I'm sorry we didn't answer right away when you

were calling his name. I'd just gotten him settled and didn't want to shout and get him all riled up again." We both turn to look at him. "Found him down here by the lake crying a few minutes ago. Gave him a sip of water, a quick climbing lesson and a book, and he's good as new. Was just about to call up to the main office."

"Oh my God, thank you," I say.

"Of course," he says and threads his fingers through mine.

We start walking toward the tree, hand in hand.

"Did he say what was upsetting him?" I ask.

"Couldn't get that outta him, no."

I squint a bit. "What's he reading?"

"A little present I picked up for you actually," Wally says. "Sorry. Didn't think you'd mind if a fellow bug lover took it for a spin first. Somehow, I knew it would make him smile."

"Oh my gosh, of course."

He gives my hand a squeeze and turns me to face him right before we reach the tree.

"Are *you* okay? Last night was..."

"A lot, I know. But yeah. I'll be okay. Especially with you by my side." I scrunch my eyes shut for a moment, worried what I just said may have been super presumptuous. "Unless I've completely scared you away?"

"Mabel Again?" He tips my chin up with his fingertips, and I open my eyes. "You'll have to try a hell of a lot harder than that to scare me away. I'm in it to win it with you, baby."

He runs his hands down the length of my hair.

"During that awful conversation with my parents..." I hesitate. "You, um. Well, you said you love me."

He looks so vulnerable at that moment I want to kiss him. "I'll admit, it was a bit of a strange time to declare it, and we haven't known each other that long, but—"

"I love you too," I blurt and dive in to kiss him, my hands cupping his stubbly cheeks, his big arms wrapped around my back and lifting me off my feet.

"Brown-chicken-brown-cow," a sassy, melodic voice sounds from behind us.

I look over, and April is standing there with Chloe, walkie-talkies in hand and smiles on their faces.

I feel my face get warm, and I instinctively take a tiny step away from Wally after he places me back on my feet. "Welcome back, April," I say.

"Thanks, lady," she says and gives me a little punch to the upper arm. "Happy to *be* back, and from here on out, I promise to be on my best behavior. Case in point, did you notice how just now, before commenting on your burgeoning sensual affair with the man formerly known as 'The Wall'"—she takes that opportunity to wink at Wally—"I saw an impressionable young child present. Therefore I opted to say 'brown-chicken-brown-cow' instead of 'bow-chicka-wow-wow?'"

"I, uh... I did, yeah," I say.

"Who's got two thumbs and is evolving?" She points both thumbs at herself. "This girl. But you know who's *not* evolving? My mother. Heard she cockblocked you last night by calling your parents, huh? Shit, I said cock," she whispers as she peeks up at Holden. "Cock, I said shit! Ugh. Sorry about that. I *am* trying. Anyway," April prattles on, "I love my mom, but clearly, she has some major jealousy issues. With me, with Chloe's mom, with women in general, I think!" April leans closer to me at that point and looks left and right before speaking in an excited hush. "Hey Mabel, did you know that my mom and Chloe's mom went to high school together, and they were both hot for the same guy, and that guy got Chloe's mom *pregnant* back in the day?"

My eyes dart to Chloe, whose eyes are scrunched shut.

"No... I did not know that, April," I say softly. "But that, uh, that actually makes a lot of things make sense."

And it does. If Naomi knew all this time that Tina was my mom and she had issues with her, I can see why she's been taking it out on my family and me all these years. I don't agree with it, but I suppose I can understand how a grudge-holding person like Naomi might go that route. I have to say, though, that I'm surprised she never spilled that secret. To me. Or to her daughter. Maybe she's kinder than I think?

There I go again, assuming the best in people. I guess that's not a character trait I'm going to shake any time soon. But...

maybe that's exactly as it should be.

I get the impression April doesn't even hear my response. She's so lost in the excitement of gossiping. "I know, right?" she enthuses. "My mom was talking smack about Chloe's mom the other day after she ran into her at the festival, and she was all like 'Don't trust McGonigle women, April. Don't trust McGonigle women.' And I was like 'McGonigle women? Chloe's mom's last name is Thomas. *Mabel*'s last name is McGonigle.' Whatever. Anyway"—she switches out of gossip mode—"glad to be back, glad Holden's okay, and I'm hella glad to see our girl Mama Mabel is finally gettin' some. What-what!" She does a raise-the-roof gesture in Wally's direction, turns to go, then whips back to me once more. "Oh, almost forgot! Here's your walkie. I'll report back to the higher-ups that Holden is golden." She slaps the walkie-talkie in my palm and starts making her way up the hill, throwing up a peace sign in the air as she goes. "Peace out, cub scout!"

Wally, Chloe, and I stare after her a moment. That girl is a whirlwind.

I look at Chloe. "So you didn't tell April, huh?"

"Nah." She shrugs. "I figure she'll find out eventually. Besides, it feels sort of nice to have such a special secret with you. Guess I kinda want to hold onto that for a little bit." Chloe catches Wally's eye and says hesitantly, "You know, though. Right?"

"I do." He nods. "I know."

A massive smile sprouts on Chloe's face as she extends her hand to Wally. "Well then hi! Hi, hi, hi, hi, hi. I'm Chloe, your new sister-in-law!"

Wally coughs out a laugh and shakes her hand.

"Too much?" She peeks at me and giggles. "Or is it just too soon?"

"Too much *and* too soon," I say, but I can't help laughing right along with them. I turn to the tree and call to Holden. "Hey, buddy! Can we join you up there?"

He looks down, shrugs, then goes back to the book.

"Maybe just you should go," Wally says quietly and takes a step back. "Perhaps my new 'sister-in-law' will skim a few rocks with me while we wait for you."

"Sure! Sure, sure, sure! Hell, yeah! I mean heck, yeah—let's skim!" Chloe says.

I watch them walk to the water's edge and start chatting and throwing rocks. It fills me with something I don't think I have a name for yet.

I tentatively make my way up to Holden and settle next to him on the sturdy tree bough.

"Hey, buddy." I tap him on the brim of his baseball cap.

He doesn't take his eyes off his book, just says, "Your hair looks weird."

"I know, right?" I say with faux seriousness. "Tried something different last night. What do you think?"

"Too puffy. And your clothes are weird too," he responds in that direct, sort of rude way only small kids can pull off.

"Eh, sometimes you gotta try new things," I say real breezy-like. "So. An exciting day so far, huh?"

He shrugs again.

"Whatcha reading?"

"A book Wallace let me borrow about bugs," he says, and despite his best efforts, I hear the excitement creep into his voice. My heart feels like it flip flops in my chest. Wally bought me a bug book? You'd think after all these years I'd have seen them all, but somehow, I've missed this particular one.

"Cool, cool," I say as I scoot closer and peek over Holden's tiny shoulder. "Ooh, the peanut bug, huh?"

"Its real name is Fulgora laternaria," he snaps. "People only call it a peanut bug because of its weird, hollow peanut head."

"I know, buddy," I try to be soothing. "It's just kind of fun to call it a peanut bug. But you're right, its real name is—"

"Did you know it's one of the most bullied bugs in the world?"

I let that sink in for a moment.

"Is that true?"

"Totally true, yeah. That's why he has like seventy-five million defenses. Well, five actually, but five is a lot. He has the hollow peanut head, the two weirdo eyeball patterns on his wings, the stinky skunk spray he squirts from his butt when he's scared and—and—and—"

As Holden's been talking, he's become more and more upset, his breath getting choppy and eyes turning watery.

"Buddy, buddy, buddy. Slow down. Breathe." He breathes and gets a bit calmer. "Is that why you got upset today?" I ask.

"YesnosortofIdon'tknow." He says it all as one word.

"Hm. You feel like telling me a bit more?"

That's apparently all it takes, and he starts spilling his little heart out. "Jonah said he heard my mommy doesn't live with us anymore and that she doesn't want to be my mom anymore, but that's not true! She has 'partum problems'—that's what my dad said—and she just has to stay someplace else for a few days to get some rest and start to feel better, and she'll be right back."

Suddenly his mom's behavior at drop-off is making more sense. I wish his dad had told me this. It's so much easier to care for the kids when we know what's going on in their home lives.

"Oh, okay," I say. "So she's been kind of sad since she had the baby?"

"Yeah," he murmurs and sharply turns a page.

"Hmm. That happens sometimes. But you know it has nothing to do with you and your little brother or your daddy and how much she loves you all, right?"

He just looks up at me with those big eyes of his but doesn't say anything in return, so I take a deep breath and continue.

"Did you know that my mommy had to go away for a while too?" I say.

"She did?"

"Yeah. A long while actually. She needed some time to take care of herself and figure some things out so she could be a good mommy again."

I glance over at Chloe and Wally skimming rocks and laughing together.

"Did she come back?" Holden asks.

It's then that I remember the letter tucked in my pocket.

"She did, yeah."

The little guy seems to start breathing easier at that.

"Hey, buddy," I offer. "What do you say we just chill out in this tree a little longer and read quietly together before heading back up to our groups. That sound good?" I wrap my arm around him. He lets me.

"Sounds good." He nods and leans his head against my shoulder as he returns to his book.

I reach into my pocket, pull out the letter, and silently read.

Dear Mabel—

I've started and restarted this letter about a dozen times. Each time, I come up with the words "I'm sorry" as a way to begin, and each time, those two words feel inefficient. Insufficient? Both, I suppose. People use the word "sorry" so often and for the tiniest offenses: their grocery cart takes up too much room in the aisle, their dog barks while out on a walk. And as women, we often say sorry when we have absolutely nothing to be sorry for.

When I was growing up, nearly every time I had a question, Abe said, "Look it up." We had this huge bulky set of Encyclopedia Britannicas lining the shelf next to our dinner table, so that's where I went day after day "looking up" whatever it was I was curious about. I used to think he wanted me to experience the joy of seeking out knowledge on my own. And maybe that was the case sometimes, but when you get to a certain age... you realize that more often than not, our parents don't have the answers either. They're still seeking too.

So I decided to look up the word "sorry." "Feeling sorrow, sympathy, or regret." I feel all those things right now. Sorrow that I missed so much of watching you grow up, sympathy that you now need to juggle all these big feelings, and regret that I couldn't be forthcoming with you from the get-go. But regret for having had you? You, you, wonderful you? No. No way. Never.

The day I found out I was having you was the happiest, scariest day of my life. The day I had to step away from you was by far the saddest. But knowing Abe and Helen would be taking care of you eased it somewhat. I never wanted to hold the truth from you. But Abe and Helen thought it was better that way, and I wasn't strong enough at the time to object. Being your "aunt" meant I could be in your life, so I took that opportunity and gave it everything I had. Being close to you those first nine years of your life meant the world to me.

I gave them my word that I would stick to what we - or rather they - had decided. But nine years later, I was so much stronger. I was having a really hard time keeping my promise.

I'd met Chloe's dad, we found out she was on her way, and we decided we wanted you to be with us. I made my case to Abe and Helen, but this frightened them tremendously, and they cut us out.

I'm sure it's difficult to see it now, but they really were trying to take care of us both. Give me a chance to finish school, grow up, and make my way in the world. Give you a chance to have all the love and care you deserved from day one. Did they make a ton of mistakes along the way? Yes. Did I? No doubt. But do we all love you? Absolutely and forever.

It's my greatest hope that you know that down to your bones.

As I've gotten older, I've discovered that I really love gardening (yes, I realize that makes me sound all sorts of lame). One of the first things you learn when trying to grow things is that roots are important. They're amazing systems for grounding us and feeding us. But they can also be messy and destructive.. They can tear up the earth around us and choke our growth if we don't learn their patterns and figure out how to partner with them. You're so smart and strong, Mabel. Always have been. I have full faith that you will plant yourself where you need to be now, giving yourself the space and nourishment you need, and—whether that includes me or not—I can't wait to watch you grow.

Love Always,
Tina

Chapter Twenty-Nine

"How was the dinner?" I feel his voice vibrate in his chest as I rest my head close to his heart.

"Oh right, we didn't do much talking when I got back, did we?" I tease.

"No, ma'am, we did not." He chuckles and kisses the top of my head.

I'm lying in Wally's arms, back in our tent, staring up at the sky and waiting for the rescheduled fireworks from last Saturday's rained out Fourth of July.

"It was...nice," I respond, finding it kind of hard to choose a word to describe my evening.

"Nice?"

"Yeah," I say with a smile. "Tina cooked a whole chicken. Chloe and I collaborated on a white cheddar mac-n-cheese, and Chloe's dad, John, baked a chocolate cake that went soupy in the middle, so we all pretended it was a massive soufflé and attacked it with spoons. There were a few awkward moments here and there, but generally lots of laughs and good conversation." I shrug. "It was nice. Oh, and Tina and I took some time to chat just the two of us where she let me ask any questions that I still have. The guy she was dating when she got pregnant with me isn't really in her life anymore, but she knows how to get in touch with him if that's something I want to do."

"That's great news," he says as he strokes the strands of my hair. "Think you're going to do that?"

I sigh and shrug. "We'll see."

"How about your mom and dad? Did they end up joining?"

"They stopped over for coffee afterward. Baby steps. Maybe next time you'll come with me." I peek up at him and give him a sassy look.

He sighs. "Next time, I'd absolutely love to be there. I just felt like this first time, you should go get to know them sans buffer." He says this like he's already expressed this opinion. That's because he has. Several times. I just really wanted him to come with me. When he's with me, I feel the most like myself. And yes, I know that's odd, because I've only known him for... I've only known him for...

"Hey, I just realized something." I prop myself up on an elbow so I can look directly at him.

"What's that?" He stays lying on his back and looks up at me with those dreamy blue eyes that I love so much.

"I don't count the days we've been together!"

"Hmm?"

"That's something I've always done! Count the days I've known someone. A new friend. An acquaintance. A boyfriend. But I don't do that with you."

"Uh-oh," he murmurs. "Should I be worried?"

"No." I shake my head and smile. "I don't think you should." I take a moment to consider how to explain this, even to myself. "I think... I've done that for so long because I never really trust that a new connection with someone will last. It's almost like I'm counting the days until it's inevitably over. But with you... I don't know... it's like from the moment you whooshed past me on that trail, it felt like we were picking up where we left off. Like somehow, I'd always known you. And somehow, I'm confident I always will."

"Damn girl." He wraps his strong arm around my neck to draw me close until our lips are almost brushing. "Look at you, romancing the shit out of me."

"Is that what I'm doing?" I laugh.

"That's what you're doing," he says with a smile. Then he

closes that tiny bit of distance between us and kisses me until I'm breathless. I barely notice that he's expertly rolled us until I'm lying flat on my back and staring up at this big, beautiful man on top of me who has quite the naughty look in his eyes.

"Oh!" I exclaim.

"Geez!" he startles.

"Sorry." I reach my hand up to cup his cheek. "Didn't mean to scare you, big guy."

He laughs and settles next to me on his side, dropping whatever delicious thing he was about to do. "What is it, milady?"

"Oh, man," I sigh. "For the record, I am not trying to resist 'da pleasure'..."

"Mabel, after what you just did in this tent, I'm very confident now that 'resisting da pleasure' is a thing of the distant past."

"Yeah, it is!" I cheer and lift my hand for a high five. He slaps me a good one. Such a good sport, this guy.

"So what did you want to tell me?" he asks.

"I just finally figured out what bug Chloe is!"

"Excuse me?"

"She's a katydid! She's super chirpy, and when she gets excited, she rubs her hands together. Like this." I do an impersonation of my exuberant new half sister. "Phew! I'm so relieved I figured it out. That was going to bother me, big time."

"Hold the phone, woman," Wally says. "Are you telling me you have a bug equivalent for every human in your life?"

"That's what I'm telling you, yes," I answer proudly.

"Yes?" His face is priceless.

"You heard me. Yes! You think I'm joking, Beiber? Go on, quiz me!"

He shoots up to sit cross-legged like this is serious business. I mirror his position and do the same. I watch him ponder the possibilities for a second.

"Your mother," he challenges.

My answer is instantaneous. "Hibiscus Harlequin bug. A shield-shaped jewel-toned insect. Gorgeous. Protects and shields her young."

"Alright," he applauds lightly, looking only mildly impressed.

He gears up for his next one. "Okay... your father."

"Paper wasp," I say without hesitation. "They have a real knack for construction. They can be aggressive but usually won't sting unless you disturb their nest. Oh, and they can recognize faces. How cool is that? 'I never forget a face,' my dad always says. 'But with remembering names? I'm incompetence personified.'"

"Wow, you've really given this some thought!" Wally marvels.

"Not really," I shrug. "In most cases, the comparisons are just so clear."

"I hate to bring him up, but I'm ashamed to admit I'm curious as hell," Wally admits, then asks, "The ex-fiancé?"

"Hm," I hesitate for just a moment on how to respond to this one. "A year or so ago, I would have said golden silk orb-weaver. No question. But now?" I consider and land on the perfect answer. "Cockroach. No offense to cockroaches, of course, but yeah. Cockroach."

Wally looks eager to steer the conversation in a happier direction. "Okay, I'm going to fire a quick three-in-a-row at you," he threatens. "You ready?"

"I was born ready, sir. But I'm telling you, you can't stump me."

"Cyndi!" he shouts.

"Long-tailed skipper. Loves to travel. Hates the cold."

"Calliope!"

"Leaf cutter ant. Hardworking and insanely strong. Can carry fifty times her own body weight." Wait. I should clarify that. "For the record, Calliope can't physically carry that much weight, but metaphorically, heck yeah, she can. She's a tiny, brilliant beast."

"Louise!"

"Cecropia moth. Emits a scent so powerful, it attracts males from miles around." I feel a need to quickly amend that comparison as well. "Not that Louise smells by any means. She's just super desirable to the opposite sex."

"Hmmmm." He takes that opportunity to lean forward and nuzzle my neck. "I can think of someone else who is super desirable to the opposite sex."

"Yeah, yeah," I playfully push him. "Are you quizzing me or not?"

"Yes, yes, yes," He gets back to business. "Ooh." He gets an evil look in his eye. "Oh. I got one. I'll definitely stump you with this one."

"Try me," I say with confidence.

"Naomi Thornton."

"Easy," I boast. "Tear-drinking moth. They literally feed on tears."

"Yikes. You're kidding me! That's a real thing?"

"Of course it's a real thing. If you haven't noticed yet, Wallace, I don't joke around when it comes to bugs."

"Noted." He puts his hands up in the air and gives a little laugh.

"Get this. Tear-drinking moths line up along the rim of an animal's eye and drink its tears. And if there are no tears present? No worries! The tear-drinking moth will scrape her spine-tipped proboscis across the animal's eyeball until there are."

"Brutal!" Wally bellows. "But what's a proboscis?"

"An elongated sucking mouthpart that's typically tubular."

"Mabel." He leans closer to me again. "Are you flirting with me?"

"I might be. But using bug anatomy to flirt isn't exactly sexy, is it?"

"I dunno. I think everything about you is sexy. Especially your anatomy. And your elongated sucking mouthpart."

"Ew!" I smack at him. "But really?" I dip my chin and smile.

"Really." He laughs. "How about me?"

"You? Oh, I find your anatomy incredibly sexy too," I all but purr at him as I start to nibble along his earlobe.

"That is certainly excellent news." I can hear the smile in his voice. "But I actually meant...what is my bug equivalent?"

Call me crazy, but this one I wasn't fully prepared to answer. So I stall.

And I pull back from him.

"I don't know," I respond.

"You don't know?" His voice booms. "You likely have a bug equivalent for the guy who makes your coffee in the mornings..."

He's right. I do. His is the Brazilian treehopper.

"But you don't have one for me?" He looks genuinely hurt.

"Aw, Wally." I croon. "Of course I've considered one for you.

I'm just torn between two."

"Oh," he says, relieved. "Alright, hit me. Who are my two?"

"Well, the water strider, of course. He moves easily across the water just like you do. Also, he loves using his front legs to hold onto the female while mating."

"I do, in fact, enjoy that." He laughs and wraps his arms around me, pulling me close to him so I'm now sitting in his lap, my legs wrapped around his back.

"But if I really have to choose... you're the Sacred Scarab," I say definitively. "Fascinating creature. The name comes from the ancient Egyptians. They likened their god of the sunrise to beetles."

"Oh yeah? And why did they do that?" he manages to get out between the kisses he's suddenly raining down my throat.

I tip my head back and keep talking, a bit breathier now. "They noticed a similarity between how the sun rolls across the sky each day and how the scarab beetle rolls his dung ball."

"His what?" he asks softly, staying in sexy-mode.

"His dung ball," I repeat, still breathy.

"His dung ball, huh?"

"Yup, his dung ball."

He finally stops kissing me and roars with laughter. "And this made you think of *me*?"

"Absolutely!" I say, not entirely seeing what's so funny about this.

"*Why*?" He continues to laugh his proverbial ass off.

"Because you're so industrious and generous, and you care about the environment!" I fire back. "Trust me, it's a compliment!"

"Alright, alright! Simmer down, lady, I see your point!" He tries to hide the fact that he's still laughing.

"Thank you," I huff.

"Shall we lie back?" he suggests gallantly. "Wait for the fireworks?

"We shall," I say.

We settle back, and I nestle myself in that sweet spot between his heart and his shoulder while we stare up at the sky, still devoid of fireworks.

Then he says, "Best. Birthday. Ever," and my stomach immediately bottoms out.

"Birthday? IT'S YOUR BIRTHDAY?!" I prop myself up and practically squeal. "Why didn't you tell me?"

"I thought I did," he says gently. I can tell he's trying not to make me feel bad. But it's too late for that.

A foggy remembrance of him saying he had a birthday "next Saturday" comes to my mind, and I feel... terrible.

"I'm so sorry!" I wince. "Ohmygod, you *did* mention it. I just— It's been such a crazy time and—oh man, I have no excuse, I'm just plain sorry."

"Nothing to be sorry for," he soothes. "I was serious. Best. Birthday. Ever. I'm here with my girl, out in nature, waiting for fireworks. What could be better?"

"You sure?"

"I'm sure." He gives my hip a squeeze, a gentle request for me to drop it.

So I do.

We lie there in comfortable silence.

Until I whisper, "Can I tell you one more thing about the dung ball?"

"About how many times do you anticipate saying dung ball tonight? You know, just out of curiosity."

"As many times as it takes," I say seriously.

"Atta girl." He smiles. "Go on. Tell me."

"The *female* Scarab beetle—get ready to have your mind blown—she lays a single egg inside a specially sculpted dung ball, then hides it in an underground chamber until her larvae are ready to hatch, at which point they will immediately feed off the dung surrounding them so they can grow."

"Wow," he says, completely serious.

"Amazing, Right?"

"Yeah," he agrees. "You know, in that regard, we humans aren't all that different from larvae then. Oftentimes, it's the dung surrounding us that makes us grow."

I squeeze him tighter. "You, sir, are a miracle."

"A miracle, huh?" He caresses my cheek with his thumb.

"Yes." I laugh. "Any man who can deliver life advice wrapped in bug metaphors with full sincerity and no trace of sarcasm is a miracle. I love you."

"I love you too."

The sound of fireworks overhead has us both looking up.

"Finally," I breathe and snuggle closer to him.

"And will you look at that." His voice sounds so light and carefree when he says it. "Fireflies."

"There they are," I say, awe lacing my words. It's never gone away, the wonder and joy that washes over me the first time the fireflies come out. I hope it never does.

"Sometimes, we have to wait a bit till the good stuff shows up in life, yeah?" He gives me a little wink. "Maybe the fireflies were waiting to accompany the fireworks so they could really put on a show for us tonight."

"Yeah, maybe."

"So I guess, you *could* say the fireflies are right on time this year," he whispers in my ear.

"Yeah, you could," I whisper back, then turn my head toward him and smile. "Right on time."

Epilogue

A Year and Several Months Later

I hear the crunch and crackle of ice under our boots as we trudge into a copse of evergreens. He makes big deep footprints in the snow ahead of me and, my smaller feet follow and slip inside the path he's made.

It's cold, and I can't help my shiver despite how bundled up I am in a warm coat, hat, scarf, and gloves.

"Almost there?" I chirp behind him, a little out of breath.

"Yeah. Almost there," he grunts.

He's been acting strange ever since we exited his truck and started the walk out here. Quiet. Grunty. Nervous maybe? An awful lot like "The Wall" I met last year, not Wally, the man I'm head over heels in love with now. I catch a glint of orange light from the setting sun. It bounces off the silver ax swinging by his side. And suddenly I feel nervous too.

There are no other humans as far as the eye can see.

Ohmygod.

"Mabel," he says as he turns and looks me dead in the eyes. My breath hitches. The cold wind whistles past me, suddenly sounding like a freight train in my ears.

And that's the moment he murders me.

Kidding! Wouldn't that be something?

No. That is the moment he kisses me on the nose, and says, "I love you. And I'm so glad we're doing this."

By *this*, he means chopping down a tree to decorate for our first Christmas living together in our new home.

After everything went down with my parents last year, I thought it was best that I finally move out. On my own. Yes, it was incredibly tempting to dive right into living with Wally, but it felt important that I experience solo-living for a while, so I finally got myself one of those small one-bedrooms "right outside of the city." And once summer season at the arboretum was over, I accepted a full-time position at the museum. So between that and setting up an online shop for The Bee's Elbow, my finances are happily back on track. Apparently my parents' finances are too. Dad went back to work about six months ago, and thankfully there have been no more heart "incidents." I can't help but wonder if that was due to all he was hiding and holding onto. That secret must have been an incredibly heavy weight to carry all those years. As for my relationship with my parents? We're taking things slow. I go home for a monthly dinner with the two of them – Wally even joins us sometimes – and it's great to see that my dad really does seem happier and more at ease. Maybe there's hope for us yet. Baby steps.

A year into my solo-living adventures, Wally asked me to move in with him again. This time, I said yes faster than an Australian tiger beetle scuttles across the Outback. He's put in a ton of work over the past few months to make his tiny home just a little less tiny, expanding it so it's perfect for two. Now I get to live surrounded by nature every single day.

Surrounded by him.

I'm excited. I've never cut down a Christmas tree before. My whole life living with my parents, we had artificial ones, but not this year.

This year is all about what's real.

"I love you too," I say, tipping up on my nearly frozen toes so I can kiss him back. "I am kind of surprised you're into this idea, though."

He scoffs, "What do you mean? I love Christmas!"

"I mean the cutting-down-a-tree aspect. I know how much The Giving Tree upsets you."

"Nah, That's totally different. We're engaged in a time-honored tradition to celebrate the winter solstice and the cyclical nature of life. The Celts did it. The ancient Egyptians did it. The royals in Victorian England did it. However, that Giving Tree punk? He is a total asswipe, a self-centered user who cuts down trees just because he *can*. He wouldn't know a time-honored tradition if it leaped up and bit him in the—"

"Alright," I soothe and cup my gloved hands around his bearded cheeks. "Let's not get you all riled up. Also... really? The ancient Egyptians decorated evergreen trees in their homes?"

"No. But they did bust out some green palms to honor the gods. Same difference."

He takes my hand in his and keeps trudging ahead through the snow.

"Wow," I say. "Wikipedia Wally is in full effect today."

"Well, it is my business to know tree talk."

"True."

Is it me, or has he considerably picked up the pace? I try to slow him down as I look back over my shoulder. "Hey. Wait. We're walking past all the evergreens. I thought we were picking out a Christmas tree, fella."

"We are," he assures me. "Don't worry. There's just something I want to show you first."

We trudge farther out until we're standing in front of a sea of tiny trees, each only about a foot and a half tall and evenly spaced out over a large expanse of ground.

"Well. Here we are," Wally exhales proudly, causing a puff of steam to roll through the cold air from the heat of his breath. He wraps his arm around me and stares out over the tiny trees.

"Um. You know I'm all about the positive thinking," I say. "But these scrawny little guys would make terrible Christmas trees."

"Sure." He chuckles. "But in about twenty-five years or so, they'll make excellent Mabel syrup."

"Haha, you mean *maple* syrup."

"No, actually, I mean Mabel syrup." With that, he swings his backpack off his shoulder, unzips it, and produces a plaque of some sort attached to a stake.

He squats down and starts tapping the stake into the ground. While he does this, he explains, "Soon after I took over the arboretum, the tree farm down the road—this tree farm—went up for sale. My gut told me to go for it. Having a tree farm someday was a dream that had been bouncing around in the back of my brain ever since I was a little kid."

"Because of your grandfather..." I say.

"Exactly. So I bought it."

"What?" I make a full three-hundred-sixty degree turn and take it all in. "This is all yours?"

"Well, *ours*. I hope."

"Why have you never told me?" My heart starts to pound. Why would he keep such a big secret from me?

He gives the plaque one more tap, then rises to his full height and takes my gloved hand in his. He looks deep into my eyes. "Easy Mabey Baby, nobody was keeping any secrets from you. Well," he reconsiders, "I was, but I'd like to think it's more of a happy surprise than some sinister secret."

"I'm listening..." I say as my lips stretch into a smile. If I've learned anything over the past year, it's that Wally is full of the best surprises. I never know what he's going to do next.

"I didn't tell you right away because... well, if I'm being honest, because I'd just met you and frankly it was none of your damn business—"

"Hey!" I smack him playfully on his shoulder.

"But *also*, because in the beginning, this was just an investment. I needed to focus on the arboretum and get my footing there. Thankfully, the manager and team from the previous owner wanted to stay onboard and take care of things, so that allowed me to be pretty hands off at first." He wraps his arms around my waist. "And hands *on* with you."

I laugh, and he gives me a quick kiss on the lips. "But then..."

"Then...?"

"Then... as I fell more and more in love with you, an idea started to form. I planted these for you. For us."

"What?" I breathe.

"Come here," he takes me by the hand and walks me over

to the plaque.

I squat down beside him, the back of my jacket scraping the snow. I read the inscription out loud.

"Once upon a time, a girl who loved bugs and a boy who loved trees discovered that they loved each other. They decided to stick together through the good times and the bad, through life's sweetness and its stings. Together, they put down roots close enough that they could always feed each other, but with enough space between them so that they could always grow. If over time this grove of 'Mabel' trees you're standing in front of provides an infinite amount of syrup, it will always pale compared to the sweetness the girl herself has brought to the world and to this boy's heart."

My eyes well with tears. "That's... Wally, that's beautiful. Thank you."

"There's more."

"More?" I breathe. "How can there be more?"

Wally points out to the left where the last bits of the sunset are dipping low on the horizon. "See that stretch of land over there by that stone building?"

"Yeah?

"I was thinking that would make the perfect location for a dozen or so hives. It's time you got to spread your wings beyond our two little hives next to the house, yeah? You ready to really let The Bee's Elbow soar? I figured that building would make a great honey-making sugarshack for us."

"A honey-making sugarshack?" I laugh, a little bit confused.

"Yeah, you harvesting honey on one side, me processing syrup on the other? Sounds like some sort of homemade heaven to me."

"To me too." I smile and shake my head in wonder at how this has all come together.

"Oh!" he startles me with his excitement. "And I finally came up with the name for my syrup business. Wanna see?"

"Of course," I say. He fishes in his parka pocket, pulls out a slim silver rectangle of sorts, and hands it to me. I pull off one of my gloves and crack it open with my cold fingers. "Mabel and

Wally Sitting in a Tree," I read the business card out loud. "Wallace Bieber, Sugarmaking CEO, Mabel McGonigle, Inspiration in Chief."

"You like it?" he asks, his eyes wide and his breathing shallow.

"Nah. I *love* it."

He presses his lips to mine, somehow still so warm and inviting despite the cold all around us. Then he takes my hand, and we start heading back toward the evergreens, my heart feeling full to bursting.

"Come on, Mabel Again," he says. "Let's go cut down our Christmas tree."

I laugh as I walk alongside him. "Level with me. You're never going to give up the Mabel Again nickname, are ya?"

"Not a chance, darlin'." He squeezes my hand. "Because what on earth could be better than 'Mabel Again?' That's all I need to be happy for the rest of my days: Mabel. Again and Again and Again."

The End.

Backstage Pass

This book exists! I need to celebrate that fact, because it feels like a small miracle. I'm sure I speak for everyone when I say 2020 was an insane year, yeah? For the record, I don't really recommend giving birth to your third child during a worldwide pandemic, while homeschooling two kids age five and under, working full-time as an audiobook narrator *and* trying to write your second novel like I did.

That said, I've been fortunate throughout this process in so many ways. My family has stayed healthy and safe. I got to spend lots of time at home cuddling a sweet new baby and getting to know how awesome he is. I got to witness my now six-year-old son learning how to read and my three-year-old daughter becoming a loving, big sister. And Mabel was fantastic company for me during a stressful and scary time. It was comforting working on a book about a woman determined to see the good in everything and everyone, despite what is happening around her. I liked getting to slip into her mindset and worldview while I was writing, and thankfully she was very patient with me as I typed her story literally with one hand most days (the baby was almost always in the other arm), moving much more slowly than I had initially anticipated.

I definitely learned some lessons this time around about what kind of time and space I need to write a novel too, at least at this point (I'm hoping to get faster!). With *Flirtasaurus* – Book One of this series – I got to feel all sorts of sneaky while writing it. It was my fun, naughty little secret that only a handful of people even knew was happening. There were a few reasons for that. One: I wasn't completely sure I could pull it off. Two: For the most part, I believe in the "magic of containment," (i.e. keeping details to yourself while you're trying to create something new). I find that sometimes if I spill details too quickly with too many people, it's often a surefire way for the "magic" (or my author enthusiasm) to dissipate. And Three: It was really fun to announce my first book after it was already written and ready to rock. I kind of felt like Beyonce when she drops a surprise album. Boom, look what I made!

This time was different though. I already had a book under my belt, which was thankfully pretty well received. And now people knew that Book Two was being written. This was awesome in a lot of ways. Readers met Mabel in *Flirtasaurus* and were eager to hear her get her own book. I loved getting to share my excitement with them along the way. It was also tricky though because there were expectations now and a lot of well-meaning questions coming at me about "when is it releasing?" But pressure can definitely be a good thing, and I'm so glad I stayed the course and made it happen despite all the craziness of this year. Major lesson learned? Do not announce a release date until you are 100% sure you can stick to it. Another lesson learned? Ideas come to us for a reason and the books you want to write also want to be written. So your creative plans will usually be patient with you if you are patient with them.

Moving forward, I think I will always do a little post-show wrap up of sorts like this at the end of my books, a little "Backstage Pass" to let you in on some of the things that went on behind the scenes while I was writing.

Here are a few fun facts that went into the creation of *Lovebug*:

- I stole Mabel's last name from one of my very best friends in real life. Thanks Laura!
- The character of Cyndi is a little surprise treat for my pal (and Feisty Fitzies admin) "Cyndi Marie." She mentioned that there are rarely characters named Cyndi in romance books, and if there are, they are always spelled C-I-N-D-Y and they are usually bitchy, home-wrecking, not-nice-women. So I decided that C-Y-N-D-I gets to be the best friend role in this book! It was very hard to keep this a surprise from her. Surprise!

- My first paid job as a performer was working for a company that utilized actors to help train camp counselors. At the beginning of each summer season, we'd travel to sleep away and day camps in the area and do workshops with their staff where they tried out their counselor skills on us. I'd play homesick campers, concerned parents, disgruntled co-counselors... It was fun to think back on those days as I was writing the day camp scenes for this book.
- Like Mabel, I too got involved in multi-level marketing company during my twenties which was not good for me. It felt a bit cathartic to write about one here and watch Wally take it down with sheep sounds!
- Like Calliope, I played Rosie in the Carol King Musical "Really Rosie" when I was a teenager. We toured to perform at daycares and malls throughout the suburban Philadelphia area.
- I decided on the name Wallace (aka Wally) after polling my readers group for their favorite "non sexy guy's names" that we could make sexy again. Becca, Bixby, Kerri and Renée busted out the Wally suggestion and it felt oh so very right paired with Mabel. Thanks for the idea, friends!
- Life keeps imitating art when it comes to my books. After I decided to have a decapitated praying mantis on the cover of this book (risky behavior, no?), my son's interest in praying mantises seemed to keep growing and growing. We recently bought him two baby praying mantises as his first pets. He named them Saxity and Clierophome – I have no idea how he came up with those ("Those are just their names, Mom."). He also declared that for his sixth birthday he wanted to eat an Oreo cupcake while wearing a praying mantis costume. Mission accomplished! If you get my newsletter and saw the picture, I think you'll agree that the costume we got him is pretty darn legit.

So... let's wrap this up! The third and final book in The Natural History Series will be called *Sharkbait*. It's Louise and James' story and it is coming to eyeballs and earbuds... sometime this year. Ha! Like I said, I learned my lesson on setting release dates prematurely, so I'm going to focus on writing the best story I can and I'll let you know when it's ready for ya.

Here are some things you can look forward to in *Sharkbait*:

- Seeing Louise embark on her career as a marine biologist
- Figuring out what's behind all that tension between Louise and James
- The return of Ralph and Calliope from Mexico
- A fully liberated Mabel
- And lots of weird fun with underwater sea creatures... the ocean is a *crazy* place

xoxo,
Erin

About the Author

ERIN MALLON is an author, an award-winning narrator of over 500 audiobooks and an accomplished playwright and producer in New York City. She has written over 40 plays, which have been produced Off-Broadway and all over the country, including *These Walls Can Talk*, *Skin Hungry*, *Come Find Me* and *The Bromantic Comedies*, all now available as audio plays on Audible. com. Erin lives in a little yellow house on the outskirts of NYC with her husband and Three J's.

For updates visit: www.erinmallon.com

And be sure to follow me on Social Media:

Facebook: /ErinMallonWriter | Twitter: @ErinMallon

Instagram: @mallonerin | Goodreads: Erin_Mallon

Bookbub: www.bookbub.com/authors/erin-mallon

Join my Facebook Readers Group: Erin Mallon's Feisty Fitzies!